THE SECRETS OF LATIMER HOUSE

JULES WAKE

One More Chapter
a division of HarperCollins*Publishers* Ltd
1 London Bridge Street
London SE1 9GF
www.harpercollins.co.uk

HarperCollins*Publishers*
1st Floor, Watermarque Building, Ringsend Road
Dublin 4, Ireland

This paperback edition 2021

1

First published in Great Britain in ebook format
by HarperCollins*Publishers* 2021

ISBN: 978-0-00-840898-5

MIX
Paper from
responsible sources
FSC™ C007454

This book is produced from independently certified FSC™ paper
to ensure responsible forest management.

For more information visit: www.harpercollins.co.uk/green

To my dad, for giving me the priceless gift of reading. He taught me to read before I even went to school and I've never looked back.

Chapter One

Evelyn - Falmouth

The bedraggled sailors might have varied in rank but the expressions on their sullen, wary faces were indistinguishable. Huddled into salt-stained, crumpled uniforms, the younger seamen looked little more than boys and while she didn't show it on her own face, Evelyn Brooke-Edwards's heart contracted a little. Had her own brother suffered the indignity of being scrutinised like this when his plane was shot down over France? Now he was held in a prisoner-of-war camp, and she prayed that he was being well looked after, although her mother hadn't had a letter in months.

Aware that her own clean, crisp uniform emphasised their uncertain situation, giving her significant advantage in the small amount of time she had available, she turned to face the most senior officer. *'Leitender Ingenieur. Wie ist Ihr Name?'* Her fluent German and the recognition of his rank of Chief Engineer surprised him and his face blanched in dismay as it

1

dawned on him that she knew exactly how important he was. She'd already earmarked him as a potential important source of information. It was her job to identify those POWs from whom useful intelligence could be gleaned under further strategic interrogation.

Quickly she stated, in German, the standard protocol of the Geneva Convention, to reassure those assembled in front of her that they would be treated humanely despite the gimlet-eyed, grim study from the guards flanking her, all on high alert at being face to face with the enemy.

The Chief Engineer stared at the Lieutenant stripes on her sleeves, frowning. Being confronted by a female Naval Intelligence Officer – a deliberate tactic – surprised and disconcerted prisoners, which meant that they often blurted out more than they planned to, usually under the mistaken belief that this initial contact, if conducted by a woman, clearly wasn't being taken seriously by the English authorities. After all, interrogation was men's work. Serious work.

Evelyn's gentle, kind voice belied significant training as she asked for his name, rank, serial number and the name of his vessel. Despite the mutinous line to his mouth, he complied, reeling off the basic information, which was recorded by a young Wren. As soon as this was done, with a nod to a junior officer, Evelyn instructed the man to be taken to a different holding area. He would be transported for a more detailed interrogation elsewhere. Quickly she worked through the sad collection of survivors, conscious that the majority of their comrades from the U-boat were lost to the lonely, cold depths of the Atlantic.

A tired sense of relief flooded her as nearly all followed their senior officer's lead; it had been a long day and her watch was nearly over. She was ready to return to her billet and the cosy fire in the kitchen that her landlady Mrs Rankin would have stoked on this miserable spring day. These men, still in damp uniforms, would be spending an uncomfortable night here before they were transferred in the morning. But at least if she hurried up they would receive a hot meal sooner rather than later, even though the cook begrudged feeding those 'damned Jerries'.

At last she came to the final group, still in training by the looks of their frightened young faces, and was working her way through them when Lieutenant Commander Williamson strode up.

'Can you wrap this up, Edwards? Some of us have places to be. There's a nice bottle of brandy with my name on it in the Officers' Mess. Get these Fritzes out of here.' He eyed the men with a malevolent glare before saying, 'If I had my way, I'd have left the bastards to drown.'

'Yes, Sir,' she said with a bland expression, while she gritted her teeth at his unwelcome interruption. Even if they didn't speak English, his obvious contempt had made a few of the men straighten up, their wary attitude changing into instant patriotic defiance.

Thanks a lot, Sir, she thought to herself. *Typical of Williamson. His usual odious behaviour.*

Ignoring him, she gave the boys – not one of them could have been more than eighteen – a kind smile and continued her unhurried questioning. One seaman turned bullish, refusing to give her his name and rank, standing with his chin, that still had little need of a razor, lifted.

She mentally cursed her commanding officer. Time to use the fall-back option.

Evelyn wasn't the least bit vain – well, perhaps just a little – but she knew she'd been blessed with good looks: fair skin, blonde hair with its own curl and well-shaped blue eyes as striking as her own mother's, and although she'd been encouraged in training to use her looks to her advantage, she never felt quite comfortable doing so.

However, she was aware that more flies were to be had with honey than vinegar. Ignoring the sailor's juvenile defiance, she turned her gentle smile up a few notches as she reminded him in firm tones that the sooner they finished, the sooner they could be moved inside and receive a hot meal. Thankfully, this approach provided quick results and with five minutes to spare to the end of her watch, she was able to hand over all the official paperwork to one of the other subordinate Wrens and head away from the docks back into the offices in Forte 1 to file her own report, rubbing her hands together as she escaped the chill wind blowing off the sea.

To her dismay Lieutenant Commander Williamson had returned to the office ahead of her and was sitting behind the main desk, his feet up on the surface, lounging back with his head behind his hands.

'Ah, Edwards. All done. You took your sweet time.'

She swallowed and nodded politely. There was something about Frederick Williamson that she couldn't like even though she knew lots of the younger Wrens found him rather dashing with his David Niven moustache and slicked-back hair. Personally, even aside from the way he viewed the prisoners, she thought he had a cruel mouth, more inclined to sneer than smile, and cold, grey eyes that looked down on the rest of the world as if he knew better than them.

She moved to the other smaller desk, even though the files she needed were beneath Williamson's heels on his desk.

'Want a nip to chase away the cold?' He produced a bottle from beneath the desk and she involuntarily looked at her watch.

'Off duty now, Edwards,' he said as he poured himself a generous slug.

'Best not, Sir,' she said, and unable to stop herself added, 'and it's Brooke-Edwards.' She knew it was a stupid thing to say but he irked her so much, and of course he pounced. She really ought to have known better.

'Of course, Brooke-Edwards. Mustn't forget that Uncle is Vice Admiral must we?' Williamson's eyes lit with malicious glee.

Evelyn regarded him steadily, determined to remain pleasant. He was a nasty piece of work that enjoyed toying with the lower ranks like a cat with mice at his disposal – never prepared to let go until he was ready. Unfortunately, as he was her superior officer and the most senior in this small unit within the base on the Cornish coast, it made it difficult to tell him to leave her and the other girls alone.

Swinging his legs off the desk top, he stood up and tossed back the whisky in his glass.

'I think you need reminding who's in charge here. Debs like you have no place in the Navy, playing at being an officer. I notice you're all smiles with those Krauts. You think we don't know what you're saying to them? With your pretty, girlish smiles?'

His moustache framed the snarl twisting his mouth and a tiny frisson of fear crept up her spine as she realised that she had backed herself into a corner behind the desk, one side of which was flush against the wall.

Her fluency in German had always been a source of contention. He didn't like not knowing what she was saying to the prisoners or that she treated them with basic decency. Moreover, he particularly disliked that her record for gaining co-operation from the POWs was higher than that of her predecessor, a particular crony of Williamson's. It wasn't the first time he'd intimated something so unsavoury. Her mother would be appalled and her father would have most certainly punched him.

'Do you like that? Those boys panting after you.'

Evelyn clenched her fists and tried to move out from behind the desk but Williamson moved quickly, his body coming into contact with hers and shoving her up against the wall, breathing whisky fumes over her. She reared back, her head making sharp, painful contact against the bricks. He smiled, a nasty smirk, his hands at his sides, palms vertical in mock surrender as if he wasn't doing anything, while his pelvis and rib cage pushed at her. His face was too close to hers and unpleasant excitement sparked in his eyes as his heavy body settled up against hers, pressing into her. Peter, whose kisses had set light to a stronger yearning, had never pressed himself upon her like this. The musky masculine smell of Williamson, sweaty and wet-doggish mixed with alcohol, filled her nostrils.

'Lieutenant Commander, please stop this,' she said, trying to sound calm and authoritative, knowing that any sign of panic or fear would incite him further. Instinct rather than experience told her this. In truth she had very little understanding of men like Williamson, ruthless in their quest for promotion and power, unlike the male contemporaries she'd known at Oxford or the men at the summer parties of her youth. Her experience of men was limited to the protective respect of her brother and his friends and the gentle, loving courtship of Peter, whom she hadn't heard from since the summer of 1939, and she had no idea when she might ever see him again. If it weren't for this damned war, they would have been married by now.

The thought of Peter and how much she missed him, made her shove Williamson sharply with her hands, pushing him away.

He stumbled back a pace before righting himself, with a cold smile filling his face.

'Lay your hands on a senior officer, would you, Edwards? That's a court martial offence.' He advanced again and this time grabbed her head with both hands in a cruel, tight grip and mashed his moustached mouth against hers and forced his fat slug of a tongue into her mouth. The intrusion almost made her retch and for a moment her knees weakened and panic started to take over. Pressing his advantage, he ground his body against hers and she recoiled, trying to process all the horrible sensations, the awful slobbering tongue, the bullish barrel chest squashing her and the ghastly grinding and rubbing below.

She couldn't breathe until his hands slid along the skin between her stockings and cami-knickers. More shocked than she'd ever been in her life, she twisted her head painfully against the wall to wrench her mouth away from his and sucked in a furious breath.

'No!' she gasped and pushed at him. Bigger and stronger than her, he simply grinned and his sausage fingers touched the edge of her knickers. Desperate now, fearing what would come next, she grabbed a heavy torch from the desk. Raising it, without thinking, she hit him on the side of the neck as hard as she could. The resulting sickening crunch as it connected with his jaw made her freeze in horror for a second.

Williamson staggered a little and fell away from her, his hands clutching his face.

'You bitch,' he said, the words slurred. Before he could say anything more, she dropped to her knees and scooted under the desk, wriggling beneath the vanity board to the other side and, breathing hard, got to her feet again.

Now standing, she stared terrified at him, horrified by what she'd done, shaken by what had occurred. She was for it now. She'd be court martialled, lose her rank.

Williamson, still holding his face, glared at her but there was triumph in his eyes.

Cupping his chin, he ground out, 'You just put an end to your career. Report here at 0900 tomorrow morning. That's a direct order.'

Now tears threatened to fill her eyes but she wouldn't let him see her cry. Instead, she lifted her chin, gave him a cool stare and said with ill-concealed contempt, 'Yes, Sir.'

She turned and yanked open the door, letting the tears come, and raced down the corridor. As she reached the end the double doors opened and she came stuttering to a halt at the sight of the man there. She swallowed, conscious of the tear streaks on her cheeks, but managed to lift her hand in a salute, wondering what on earth he must think.

'Captain Jennings,' she managed to gasp, frantically straightening. He was the area commander and occasionally called in, although usually he was expected and Williamson would have met him at the gate.

'Lieutenant Brooke-Edwards,' he said, a smile lurking in his eyes although it dimmed quickly when he looked at her face. 'Everything all right?'

'Yes, Sir. Just going off watch.' One stray tear trickled down her neck but she kept her ramrod posture.

'At ease, Lieutenant. I hear you had another U-boat crew pass through. All processed?'

'Yes, Sir.'

'Excellent work. Williamson still here?'

She nodded, stiffening again as her stomach rolled and bubbled with nausea.

'I'll let you get off.'

She nodded and, with a sense of dread and shame, lifted her eyes to his face. At sixty he had the weather-beaten grizzled face of a veteran of the Great War and deep lines scored his forehead which was now furrowed into a deep frown.

Without a shadow of doubt, she knew that her days as a Lieutenant were numbered; at the very least she would be demoted and most likely court martialled.

Chapter Two

Judith - London

For the first time in a very long time, Judith's faded spirits stirred a little as she looked up at the famous Nelson's Column and the bright-red buses skirting Trafalgar Square. Being in London made a welcome change after spending several months in a British northern town. Her reprieve, however, was brief. Tonight, she'd be travelling back up to Hull on the train.

She didn't belong there, anymore than she belonged here but at least in London she enjoyed a sense of anonymity, something that had been a bit of a relief when she'd first come to this country before the outbreak of war. But, even after five years, England still seemed alien and she still felt more dead than alive inside. She glanced around at the thin, pinched faces of the people walking by. Although no one deliberately jostled her in the street, called her names or pointed to her, she kept herself to herself, avoided eye contact with anyone and rarely spoke unless she absolutely had to. It was difficult to hide a German accent.

She tucked her hat more firmly onto her head, tugged at the jacket of her uniform and hurried towards the far corner of the square, following the directions she'd been given to Whitehall. It felt strange to her to be in an Auxiliary Territorial Services uniform, officially signed up to fight against her homeland. When she'd first come to England in 1938 she'd been able to get a job through family friends of friends and had worked in a shoe factory in Kensal Green but as soon as war was declared, no one wanted to employ a German, even though Germany had turned its back on her and her kind. Not long after that she'd joined the Pioneer Corps and then transferred to the ATS, and while she knew she ought to be grateful for the work, endless filing was not to her taste. Which, she thought, straightening her shoulders and crossing the road, narrowly avoiding being flattened by a No. 15 bus, was why she was here. A little shiver of anticipation ran through her and she crossed her fingers even though she didn't believe in such things. Neither crossing fingers nor praying had helped thus far in her life but even so, she was hopeful.

Major Wardlow had intimated that her native language could be employed in far more useful ways which she would find more satisfactory, when he'd talked with her just over three weeks ago in the barracks in Hull. He was an earnest and forthright young man, and she had no reason to disbelieve him or think that he was making impossible statements.

Three weeks ago, that was all it was. She'd been nearing the end of her shift when she'd been asked to leave her filing to take Major Wardlow to the Officers' Mess on the other side of the barracks. The place was an absolute rabbit warren and at any time, the ATS could be asked to stop what they were doing and help a guest find their way.

'You seem keen to abandon your work,' he'd observed as she'd led him through the long corridor.

She looked at him guardedly. It didn't do to sound ungrateful.

'Boring? What is it you do? Filing?'

She nodded before cautiously venturing, 'I'm not sure how it helps with the war.'

He replied in German, 'How long have you been here?'

Surprised, she answered in German, 'Since December 1938.'

'And what did you do back home?' He sounded interested, which was more than most people did when they heard her accent. Even when she explained she was Jewish and had fled from Germany, she was still eyed with suspicion. It was the first time anyone had asked her about her working life before she'd come here.

'I worked in a factory that designed and built aircraft.'

His eyebrows rose and he suddenly looked almost excited. 'And what did you do there?'

'All sorts. Originally I was responsible for making sure the blueprints for the designs were looked after. After that I was responsible for ordering parts and stock-taking, making sure that we had sufficient supplies. Then I moved into the *Funkmeßgerät* section.'

He frowned.

'The radio measuring devices – they used radio waves to detect and track.'

Major Wardlow stopped dead, a look of absolute wonderment on his face. 'Range and Detection Finding systems.'

Wanting to quell his sudden enthusiasm, she added, 'I

don't understand how they work but I know how they are made.'

'I think you're wasted here. I'd like to recommend you to another department where I can guarantee the work would be a thousand times more interesting. And you'll be making a real contribution to the war. Do you think you might like that?'

'Yes,' she said. Anything had to be more interesting than the monotony of filing, which left her too much time to think. After all, what more was there to lose? She'd left behind everything she'd ever cared about and lost all the people she loved.

So here she was, standing outside the War Office, ready to report for interview as per the instructions which had been handed to her by her commanding officer several days ago.

Judith was intrigued. If, as Major Wardlow had implied, this work could make a difference, it was her duty to do so. She wanted to bring this awful war to an end, although when that happened she had no idea what would happen to her. The Germany she'd once known had changed too much, had inflicted such terrible damage on her family and friends. Could it ever be home again?

Judith pinched her mouth together and marched up the steps. Thinking about everything she'd lost wasn't going to help now. She was on her own. Life was hard for everyone. She gave her name at the front desk and was ushered up a flight of stairs to a small office where one other woman and a man sat. None of them spoke to each other and she kept quiet from habit. Eventually a young Naval officer came into the office.

'Do I have a Judith Stern, a Susanne Adelsdörfer and Georg Bayerthal?'

It was as if there was a rush of air in the room as the three of them looked at each other, a sudden release of tension, as they glanced shyly at each other, realising that they were all compatriots. Were they also Jewish, she wondered? Like her, no doubt they'd learned to keep their mouths shut in the company of strangers. Having a German accent could single you out for trouble.

'If you'd like to come with me,' he said, opening the door and inviting them to follow him.

Now the three of them exchanged tentative nods, recognising kindred spirits. The woman addressed a few commonplace comments to the man but Judith, more reserved, kept her counsel. As always when she met fellow Germans, she wondered how they'd all made their way to England and whether their journeys had been as terrifying as hers, hidden in the boot of a car with her eyes tightly shut and her heart hammering so hard in her throat, she thought it might choke her, as she crossed the border to Austria with all that she was allowed to take. A trusted friend of her father had had a contact in the British Embassy in Austria who had provided her with the necessary papers to leave. She was one of the lucky ones and owed everything to Mozart. A mutual passion for the composer had been at the heart of the friendship between her father, his friend and his diplomat friend.

And then she shook away those thoughts because they didn't do her any good. Hard as it was, all she could do was look forward. There was nothing left for her in the past.

They filed into one large room, which looked as if it had once been a ballroom, except now there was nothing but a row of three desks which had papers and pencils on them.

'If you'd like to take a seat. You have an hour to translate the papers on the desk in front of you.'

Judith took a seat behind. The three solitary desks were marooned in the huge room. It was like being back at school in her final year and doing her *abitur* all over again and for a moment her stomach knotted in anxiety. She could barely turn the paper over with her shaking hands.

To her relief, the paper was quite simple and involved translating words and phrases from German into English, although none of them were very commonplace.

───────────

'That was difficult,' exclaimed the woman called Susanne when they came out and went back to the small office again. Judith nodded, although some of the vocabulary they'd been asked to translate had been familiar from her work in the factory. She'd completed the task well within the hour allowed and had been able to spend some time looking at the elaborate plaster cornices of the room and wondering what this elegant building had been before it had been commandeered by the War Office. She'd been able to take refuge in daydreams, imagining elegant ladies, dancing to the strains of Strauss, in silks and taffetas, and picturing how it would have looked before war had cast its blighted shadow across the whole of Europe.

'I didn't know some of the words. Do you think they made them up to trick us?' continued the woman.

Judith didn't reply. She'd known all but one and even then had been able to hazard a guess, but lifted her shoulders in an almost-shrug which seemed to satisfy her companion.

'Beautiful plasterwork,' commented Georg on her right, catching her looking up.

'Yes,' said Judith offering him a quick, sad smile.

'Makes you think of a bygone age,' he sighed and for a brief moment the two of them looked at each other, united in melancholy thoughts.

'Of dancing and music,' said Judith.

Georg smiled. 'I used to play for the Berlin State Opera, first violinist, until all the Jews in the ensemble were dismissed.' His eyes took on that resigned, blank look that Judith knew, from experience, hid the depth of pain for all who had been ripped so brutally from their day-to-day lives.

She simply nodded. Normally she didn't have the energy to bring up her father – there were too many tragic tales from Germany – but for a brief moment, she allowed herself to think of him.

'I went to the Opera House many times. My father ran a music shop on Gartenstrasse.'

'Herr Stern?' He looked animated for a moment. 'I knew him. All of the orchestra bought strings and reeds and sheet music from him.' He sobered, the question in his eyes.

Judith shook her head. 'It's gone. The *Sturmabteilung* on the ninth of November.'

Georg knew better than to ask but Judith told him anyway. 'When he saw what they'd done, he had a heart attack. He never recovered.' Until then, she'd never believed people died of broken hearts but her gentle father had seen the damage and destruction of his beloved music shop after the paramilitary forces had ransacked the place, trampling on violins, ripping up sheet music and defiling the premises with swastikas and offensive slogans.

'I'm sorry.' His eyes clouded and together they sat in silence, both lost in thought.

Not long after that, Susanne was called and led away to another door further down the hallway, leaving the atmosphere in the corridor tense and quiet.

She came back, her eyes bright with excitement, clearly itching to say something but prevented by the presence of the tall Naval officer, until he beckoned Georg to follow.

'You'll never guess who interviewed me. Charles Richardson. The actor and broadcaster. I saw him in *Great Expectations* in the West End. He spoke to me in German the whole time.'

Judith didn't like to reveal her ignorance. She'd never heard of the man.

'Did they tell you what sort of job it is?'

'No, but they asked lots of questions. I told him I really like the theatre. So, he knew I knew who he was.' She talked incessantly until Georg's return and then it was Judith's turn. She was relieved to have a bit of peace.

Following the young Naval officer, she found herself seated opposite a man in a smart suit.

She eyed him warily. Why wasn't he in uniform? It made her uneasy. They weren't going to send her back to Germany as a spy or something, were they?

'Thank you for coming, Private Stern. I'm Marcus Goring, although I suspect the garrulous young Susanne has told you I've also frequented the stage and broadcast on the radio as Charles Richardson.' His mouth quirked in amusement. 'I'm now head of the BBC German Unit.'

'Er, yes,' she replied and decided that with him she wouldn't lose by being honest. 'I'm afraid I've not heard of you.'

He smiled. 'And nor should you have. I think you perhaps have a more serious bent. I believe classical music is more to your taste.'

She nodded and he asked a few questions about her favourite musicians before seamlessly moving on to ask her a variety of questions about the words she'd found difficult, those she'd found easy and where she'd gained her technical vocabulary and how she came to be in England.

At last, he asked, 'Do you have any questions?'

Relieved that it was all over, instead of asking about the job for which he was recruiting, Judith leaned forward and said, 'I struggled with one word.'

He gave her a wry smile and looked down at the paper in front of him before saying, 'It's a tiny pin in a firing mechanism.'

'Ah, I did wonder.'

'So, Judith Stern, one last question. Are you good at keeping secrets? Keeping things quiet.'

She eyed him gravely before she responded. 'I was a Jew living in Nazi Germany; we learned to keep our secrets and the secrets of those around us. Our lives depended upon it.'

He nodded and closed the folder in front of him with a sharp snap. 'Thank you for your time. We will be in touch.'

Judith very nearly skipped down the stairs, which was very unlike her, but it was a long time since she'd felt any sense of achievement or hope. She couldn't for the life of her figure out why the English would want translations of such technical language but if, as Major Wardlow had promised, the work was interesting, then she was ready for it.

Chapter Three

Betty - Latimer, Buckinghamshire

'Ma, I like being in London.'

Betty also liked being away from Ma's watchful eye and enjoyed going up to Trafalgar Square to buy cheap forces theatre tickets with her pal, Colette, on their shifts off.

'We went to the Variety Club last week. Only one shilling and threepence. Saw Arthur Askey one time. And they have some wonderful singers.' She clasped her hands together. She loved singing, perhaps more than anything else.

'But them bombing raids. I worry something chronic.' Her ma shook her head, tugging an apron over her faded, patched cotton dress, and began peeling the potatoes that made up so much of everyone's diet these days. Betty was heartily sick of carrot, swede and potato mash, which had become the staple food at home. 'If anything happened to you... Don't you get scared?'

Betty couldn't say she was particularly fond of the regular

bombing raids but like a lot of her generation she had the view that if your number was up, it was up.

'None have come close to us at the huts. Mill Hill isn't central London. That's where they clock the worst of it.'

'It's all very well for you to say that but you know Sheila's daughter very nearly caught it. Poor girl, her face all ripped to shreds.'

Betty winced. Poor Barbara Clarke might as well wish she were dead. She'd been caught in a daytime raid in the East End on her day off. Seeing what remained of Barbara's face had been worse than anything Betty could have imagined. The blast had clean blown off her nose and top lip. It had given her nightmares for weeks.

'How is she?'

'How d'you think? She won't ever get married. Her life's as good as over. You ought to count your blessings you have a man who's got a good living and he's not been sent away to war. I wish you'd come home. Bert misses you like the devil, he does.'

Her mother scraped potato peelings into the chickens' bucket as she spoke, pointing her knife at her daughter to emphasise her words.

Betty wasn't so sure about that – she rather enjoyed not being at home – but thinking of Barbara made her appreciate how precarious life was. So many men had gone off to fight and not come back and there was no sign of the war finishing any time soon. 'Bert's just fine. I'm on duty and my shifts don't always make it that easy to get home.'

'Well, mind you don't give him a chance to go off with someone else. You need to think of the future. He'll only wait so long. He's a good-looking lad and that new barmaid in The Red Lion has been giving him eyes.'

'How do you know that?' asked Betty.

'Told me hisself. Popped round last week. He's such a good lad. Always calls in on a Tuesday.'

'Does he now?' Betty's eyes narrowed suspiciously. 'What for?'

'Just checking up on me and Jane.'

Funny that. The same day that what she could send of her pay packet arrived. And funny that if he were checking up, he hadn't seen fit to mend the chicken coop where the door had got a hole in it. It would be down to her to get it fixed, as usual, and she was going to have to do it before she caught the train back to Baker Street.

'You ought to see if you can get a transfer here.'

'Here?'

'Yes, at the big house. You know the military took it over years ago but there's a new lot there now with lots of young girls working there. See them in the village in their uniforms. Same as yours. Some sort of distribution centre, they say. Lots of lorries thundering up and down Ley Hill Road at all times of the day and night. What his Lordship must think I don't know. He's a good man, giving up his home for the war effort.'

'Distribution centre?' She definitely wouldn't want to work here in the village and it sounded very dull. She'd known his Lordship had moved out and that there'd been a lot of building work going on at the site for many months. 'I wonder if he misses it,' Betty mused. It was a marvellous house and she was rather fond of the fourth baron. Her aunt, Daisy, had been the housekeeper there for many years and when Betty left school she'd got a job as a parlourmaid there.

'I daresay he does. Why don't you pop and see Daisy? She'll know what's going on. She might be able to get his Lordship to put a good word in for you. He was always fond of you. Let you play on that typewriter of his.' He had too. Caught her tapping the keys when she was supposed to be dusting one afternoon and then invited her to teach herself to type using it whenever she finished work. That was until Lady Chesham got wind. She'd not been happy about it at all and Betty had very nearly got her cards. Denied access to the typewriter, she'd continued to practise on an old bit of cardboard that she'd drawn the keys on in the right order.

'Because I've got that chicken coop door to fix and I need to be back on duty this evening. You don't want the foxes getting in.' She looked at the watch on her wrist, inherited from her dad who'd died ten years before, having never really recovered from the wounds he received during the Great War.

'If you got a job here, you wouldn't have to rush back. And your sister wouldn't worry about you all the time. Convinced, she is, that you're going to get blown up.'

Betty wasn't sure that Jane thought of anything much these days but her favourite layer, Baby Face, a very feisty young hen, who took exception to every human except Jane. She didn't relish getting pecked on the legs when she patched that door.

'The ATS doesn't work like that, Mam. I can't just up and transfer.'

Her ma pursed her thin lips and folded her arms. 'Anyone would think you didn't want to be with your family. Too good for us now, are we? I think you spent too much time up at the big house.'

Betty, who'd heard this a hundred times before, whenever she wouldn't do what her ma wanted, ignored the comment. Pushing her cup of tea aside, she stood up. 'I'd best put on my boiler suit.' Although it was a bright spring day, her bare legs weren't ready to spend an hour freezing out in the garden. She hadn't been prepared to waste her one precious pair of nylons on a trip home and she refused to wear those hideous khaki lisle stockings when she was on leave. It was bad enough that she had to put up with the darned hideous things bagging round her knees and ankles when she was on duty. With a grin, she held out her arm to admire the sleeves of the bright-red boiler suit. It wasn't half bad and even better, she hadn't had to use any clothing coupons because it was classed as working clothes. A win–win if ever there was one.

Her dad's old stock of wood and nails hadn't been touched nor his tools, which she kept wrapped in cloths so that they wouldn't rust. She sorted through the yellowing boxes and took a handful of pinhead nails, shoving them into her pockets before grabbing one of the hammers. Carefully she tucked the immaculate toolbox back into the corner of the shed under a large piece of sacking. No knowing what some people might help themselves to if they knew it was there. Her ma certainly didn't venture out here and Jane wouldn't be interested in poking about in a dusty corner.

Half an hour later she was examining the new piece of wood tacked into place to patch the rotten section which had given way. It would do for now until she could replace the whole door on a subsequent visit. Squatting on her haunches, she leant forward to tap in the final tack.

'Well, what do we have 'ere?'

'Bert.' She swung round, bringing an automatic smile to her face. She didn't want to give him any excuse to find fault with her. His moods were so uncertain these days and as Bert's family owned the whole row of cottages and the rent was extremely low, she needed to keep him onside for her ma and Jane's sake so they didn't find themselves slung out of their home.

'Look at you, regular little miss carpenter.' His mocking tone made her tighten her grip on the hammer. 'Don't you think you should leave man's work to the men?'

'I would if I thought it would get done,' she retorted, feeling a little put out that she'd had to do it when he'd been here earlier in the week. 'I thought you were going to do it.'

'Being in the services ain't doing you no good, my girl. When did you start speaking to me like that? Come and give me a kiss.' He held out a hand and none too gently yanked her to her feet.

'Sorry. I'm cross that it's not been done. I'm worried about the foxes.'

'Not been done,' he mimicked. 'You're getting a few too many airs and graces about you. You're not going to turn into one of those nagging women, are you? It might put me right off you.' He raised his dark eyebrows. 'And we wouldn't want that, would we? Now give us a kiss.'

'Sorry, Bert.' She tried to smile, thinking of poor Barbara Clarke, who would probably never have anyone look at her again. Sometimes she didn't like the way he spoke to her but like her mum said, men like Bert expected and deserved respect. He was what her ma called 'a man's man' and also considered quite a catch. His dad owned Home Farm and its one hundred and thirty acres of prime sheep grazing. The family wasn't short of a bob or two thanks to the wool from the flock which garnered high prices each year and, of course, the rents from the cottages. Marriage to him would secure her future and her ma and Jane's.

'What are you wearing?' After claiming his kiss, Bert

stepped back. 'I don't like my women wearing trousers. Next thing we know you'll be thinking you can do stuff like we can.'

It was pointless trying to explain that her boiler suit was more practical when you were lying on the chicken-poop-covered floor. He didn't like her answering him back either. Bert didn't like anyone answering him back. He'd definitely become more irritable in recent months, like a powder keg that could blow at any moment. Or maybe seeing more of the world, away from the village, had opened her eyes? Either way, she knew she ought to keep on the right side of him, as much for her family's sake as anything.

With a flirtatious smile, she stuck out a leg. 'Don't it suit me?'

Betty tried to tell herself that his bad-tempered spats came from the deeply felt frustration that he'd failed an Army medical, not that he would ever admit as much. As far as everyone round here was concerned, Bert was in a reserved occupation and, being over twenty-five, couldn't be conscripted. The truth, however, was he'd been rejected because of flat feet. A fact Betty only knew because his mother had inadvertently let it slip.

'I prefer you in a skirt. You've a cracking pair of legs.' He pulled her to him and kissed her again. 'My Betty Grable. Your hair looks good like that. Fixed it up for me, did you?'

She smiled. 'Do you like it?'

'You're still the best-looking girl in the village even in those bloody things.' He sighed. 'Let's have a look what you've done. I tell you, you should have waited for me to fix it for you.'

She bit back the thought that she might have waited a long time.

As Bert inspected the coop, Betty couldn't help but

remember that there was a time she'd have put up with things the way they were because she didn't know any different, but being in the ATS had shown her that she could do things for herself. That she didn't have to rely on a man.

He bent down and shook his head. 'This is man's work,' he said with a sudden derisory kick at the panel. 'What's the world coming to when a woman thinks she can do man's work? Look at that.' He kicked again, this time putting his weight into it, and the wood beneath the panel, holding it in place, disintegrated. He shook his head again. 'Looks like I'll have to do it. Shame I haven't got time now.'

Betty eyed him steadily. She wasn't going to apologise. The panel would have held. It would have done.

'Want me to walk you back to the station?'

She looked at the hole in the door and thought of the foxes. There was an air of triumph on his face.

'I've got another half hour,' she said.

'That's OK. Time for a cuppa and I reckon your mam's got a bit of cake tucked away.'

Giving the wooden door one last glance, she slipped the hammer into her pocket. She didn't want to leave it out or bring it to his attention. It would be the last she'd see of it.

'Bye, Ma. See you in a couple of weeks' time.' She turned at the bottom of the garden path to give her a last wave.

'Bye, love, and think about seeing about that job. Want me to speak to Daisy about it?'

'No, Ma. I'll go and see her next time I'm home.' Now she heartily wished she had gone to see her aunt Daisy. She could have avoided Bert altogether. She stepped out into the lane and Bert took a possessive hold of her arm.

'What's this about a job?'

'It's nothing.'

'Didn't sound like nothing.' Bert's tone was laced with that touch of menace that always accompanied his voice when he thought he wasn't being told the whole story.

'Ma's got this idea that I can get a transfer to a job at this distribution centre.'

'And what's wrong with that? I'd see more of you.'

'Nothing, but I've no idea if it's possible.'

'I think it's a good idea. You could keep an eye on your mum and sister. You wouldn't want anything to happen to them, especially Jane.'

She looked up at him, startled by a sudden chill that slithered down her spine.

'What do you mean?'

He shrugged, a too-innocent air on his face. 'Well, Jane's growing up. She's got a fine figure. Men have…' He leered for a moment before lifting his shoulders again and then slung an arm around her, anchoring her to his side. 'I miss you. She reminds me of you.'

Nausea surged in her throat. Jane, a gentle soul, was only fifteen and young for her age. Some might say she wasn't all there but Betty preferred to say that she took a while to think things through. She was the sort that was eager to please and scared by loud noises and shouting. All she was interested in was her beloved chickens and the lambs that occasionally had to be hand reared in the Davenports' kitchen. Mrs Davenport was a good sort, hard-working and stern, but she ran a busy farmhouse. Jane was not her responsibility. Bert's words worried Betty, especially as she wasn't sure she could trust him to keep an eye on her little sister.

As she got on the train, she wondered if perhaps she should think about applying for a transfer but it wasn't really what she wanted. She liked having her independence, being able to do her own thing and away from the watchful eyes of the village where she was as good as engaged to Bert. But what about Jane? Her vulnerability was a constant worry and Bert's words had alarmed Betty. He could be a bit of a bully sometimes but surely he wasn't threatening her little sister. Was he?

Chapter Four

Evelyn - Falmouth

'You need to keep your strength up, dearie.' Mrs Rankin shook her head at the half-eaten breakfast as Evelyn pushed the food around her plate the following morning. Knowing that there was a war on, even before her landlady could remind her, she forced herself to eat the unappetising grey slice of national loaf bread with its thin smear of gooseberry jam. 'You're looking peaky this morning. Little 'un didn't wake you up, did he?'

'No, Mrs Rankin. I just didn't sleep very well.'

The kindly landlady settled her thin frame in the chair opposite the tiny table. Everything in the terraced house was small compared to what Evelyn was used to. 'Is everything all right? Have you heard from your brother, your ma?'

Evelyn dredged up her best attempt at a smile. Mrs Rankin wanted to look after everyone, along with her three spindly-legged children, her tiny, elderly mother and the entire ragamuffin street. 'It's a worry. My mother is quite anxious that there's been no word from David for three months now.'

'He'll be right. The post from France is bound to be a bit disrupted with all them U-boats patrolling. Another one sank in the Atlantic, they're saying down the harbour. Someone saw them bringing Jerries in.'

As far as Mrs Rankin was concerned, Evelyn worked in an office, as Evelyn had found to her cost that any discussion of POWs invariably brought forth strong views. She therefore avoided telling people outside the military exactly what she did and even then, there were still people like Williamson that believed prisoners should be ill-treated, if not shot on sight. Having a brother at the mercy of the Germans tempered one's view somewhat, as well as the fact that she had German relatives and had, before the rise of the National Socialists, spent many a happy summer in Heidelberg. For her, Germans were people just like anyone else, but she knew that this view placed her firmly in the minority. After all, so many had lost so much to this war already. Most people viewed foreigners with deep suspicion and not everyone sympathised with the plight of the Jews in Europe either.

Evelyn swallowed down the last bit of bread and let Mrs Rankin pour her more tea, which had now steeped enough to give it a bit of flavour. 'I'd best be off,' she said, rising to her feet, swallowing down the lukewarm tea, tugging at her uniform, glancing at the stripes on her sleeves.

She'd been so proud of those stripes, of being able to make a real contribution to the war. Her uncle was a Vice-Admiral, her grandmother had been a lady-in-waiting to the current Queen and her father a royal equerry, having been awarded a Distinguished Service Order medal during his Army combat years in the Great War. The Brooke-Edwards family had been doing their duty to King and country for generations.

Time to face the music. Williamson would take his revenge to the absolute letter of military law. Striking a superior officer was insubordination. There'd be a court martial. Offering violence to an officer rated prison and removal of rank. She could be detained for up to three months. She closed her eyes. It would bring such shame to her family, particularly her uncle.

With leaden feet she walked down the cobbled street, skirting the harbour and up to Forte 1 where she was stationed. As the Navy had taken over much of Falmouth, now HMS Forte, they'd commandeered a number of large buildings and renamed them Forte 1, Forte 2, Forte 3 and Forte 4, which suggested they were surrounded by barbed wire and gun towers. In fact, Forte 1 was situated in the rather attractive Membley Hall Hotel, although this didn't offer Evelyn any solace this morning as she walked through the grand entrance and mounted the stairs to the offices on the first floor.

Dismay warred with relief at the sight of Captain Jennings sitting behind Williamson's desk. At least she wouldn't have Williamson gloating at her.

She saluted and waited for Jennings to speak as her heart plunged to her feet. Schooling her face, she tried to look penitent although inside fury bubbled that a senior officer could get away with this.

'Good morning, Lieutenant Brooke-Edwards. I have good news and bad.'

Her legs wobbled but she managed to keep her face impassive.

'I'm afraid you're being transferred to a new unit.'

She blinked at him, unsure if this was good news or bad news and then waited for the guillotine to fall.

'And their need is greater than ours. You're to take a week's leave and you'll be sent details of where to report.'

Waiting, she studied his face, while behind her back she gripped her right wrist with an iron fist.

'I'm sorry you have to leave us,' he paused and for a moment she could have sworn he looked a little apologetic before a mask slid back in place, 'but I think it's for the best.'

Not daring to speak and still unable to believe his words, she nodded.

'You should receive your orders in the next few days. In the meantime, enjoy your leave. Where's home? Henley upon Thames, is it?'

She paused for a moment before answering. That was it? No court martial?

'Yes, Sir. Just outside. Binfield Heath.'

'Ah, you must know the Everlys then?'

'Yes, Sir. In the next village. Mummy plays bridge with Lady Everly.'

'Excellent. Well, do give her my regards when you next see her. She's my mother's sister.'

'I will, Sir,' said Evelyn with a rush of relief, still not daring to believe in her reprieve. Perhaps Williamson hadn't told him what had happened, but that was too much to hope.

'Right-ho. That's all. I suggest you get back to your billet and pack your things. Pick up your travel warrant and pass from the registry.'

'Yes, Sir.'

'Good luck, Lieutenant. I hope your next posting is to your liking.'

He eyed her gravely and she knew without a shadow of a doubt that she'd had an extremely lucky escape and that for some reason Captain Jennings had intervened on her behalf.

She had no doubt that her new posting would be a lower rank but she'd been spared the shame of everyone in this unit knowing of her demotion.

'Thank you, Sir.' With that she backed out of the room, still on wobbly legs, and virtually ran out of the building in case he changed his mind or she bumped into Williamson.

The journey northwards gave her far too much time to think and worry about what she was going to tell her mother, and as she neared the station at Twyford she gathered her kitbag, still none the wiser as to what to say.

As soon as she stepped from the train she was swept into the fur-lined embrace and the familiar scent of 'Evening in Paris' filled her nose.

'Darling, what a glorious surprise.'

Evelyn hugged her mother back, grateful that she was so much more demonstrative than many of her friends' parents. Both Mummy and Daddy were still, after twenty-eight years, very much in love and were quite happy to show the world. Her school friend Cynthia had grown up in an austere atmosphere where her parents barely tolerated each other's presence.

'Hello, Mummy. Thank you for coming.'

'Don't be silly, what else would I do? Come on.' She led the way to the car, trotting along in her smart peep-toe heeled pumps with her pale-blue and lilac floral patterned tea dress flapping in the light spring breeze. 'Besides, I needed to pop out to collect a few things. We've been knitting jumpers and socks for the Merchant Navy. I must say Mrs Dawtry is a marvel.' Her mother sighed rather tragically. 'She quite often has to sort me out. I do have a terrible habit of dropping stitches.'

Evelyn laughed at the idea of her mother, who wasn't remotely practical, and the redoubtable Mrs Dawtry, their housekeeper and cook, with heads bent over knitting. Through her mother's letters she'd learned with considerable amusement that in the last six months, with the absence of her son, daughter and husband weighing heavy on her, her delicate, ladylike mother had become a leading light in the Women's Voluntary Services and had co-opted virtually every female in the village into joining.

'To be honest, I'm a terrible knitter. Mrs Dawtry quite despairs. However, one must do one's part and I'm sure if you're cold and in the middle of the Atlantic you're not too fussed about whether the rows on your jumper are straight or have the odd hole.'

Evelyn laughed. It was so lovely to be home for a few days. She would enjoy her mother's company while she awaited her orders.

Her mother drove home in the middle of the road, turning her face towards Evelyn as she told her all about the goings-on in the village. Thankfully they didn't meet anyone coming the other way along the narrow country lanes.

How they missed the pineapple-shaped stone-topped gates as they wheeled suddenly into the long drive, Evelyn wasn't sure.

'Home sweet home, darling.'

Evelyn studied the graceful Queen Anne mansion house with a slight smile, thinking of Mrs Rankin's tiny terrace, as the car crunched over the gravel, swerving around a small stone fountain. The mellow stone walls looked almost golden in the early spring sunshine and a couple of fat wood pigeons cooed from the tall chimneys.

Her mother screeched to a halt a hair's breadth from the grey Bentley already parked outside the drawing-room window.

'Is Uncle Crowthorne home?' asked Evelyn, puzzled to see her other uncle's car there.

'No.' Her mother suddenly gasped and clasped her hands together. 'Didn't I tell you?' She beamed and tucked her arm through her daughter's, leading her up to the yellow stone porch draped with winding branches of wisteria. 'The most splendid news. He's been posted overseas and is on his way to Australia. All hush-hush. At least I think that's what he said. Isn't it wonderful?'

Evelyn frowned, trying to follow her mother's butterfly-brain logic as they stepped into the house and the open hallway with its magnificent sweeping staircase. 'Wonderful, why?' She dropped her kitbag on the carpeted floor.

'Silly me. He's left the car for you. He said, "No point it not being used for the rest of the war. Evelyn might as well drive it." Didn't I tell you?'

'No, Mummy. You didn't tell me,' replied Evelyn, grinning at her mother and kissing her on the cheek. 'But it is rather wonderful. If I could find some official business to go on, I could drive up to London and see the girls.'

'That would be marvellous, I can sort something out. Perhaps you could deliver some blankets to one of the evacuation centres. The Vicar has got the rest of the congregation crocheting squares. In fact, you could help sew them this week while you're here. Do you know when you have to leave?'

'Not yet. I'm awaiting instructions.'

'What? Not going back to Falmouth? How exciting, a new posting. Do tell?'

'I'm not sure yet.' Evelyn widened her eyes, hoping to persuade her mother it was an exciting conundrum and not the loss of rank she was expecting. Thankfully her mother was already full of the Vicar and his ghastly sermons which were a little too holy and not lifting people's spirits in the way that she thought he ought to be doing. 'Haranguing us from the pulpit. I much preferred Mr Weston, the last Vicar, shame he was so young and got called up. We're all doing our bit, after all. And I gave him a pot of Mrs Dawtry's best pickle.'

Evelyn, pleased to be home despite her worries, was quite happy to let her mother's prattle carry on and wash over her. There would be time enough later for difficult conversations.

'Morning, darling. How did you sleep? You're still looking so pale.'

'I'm not used to the quiet,' said Evelyn with a faint laugh as she entered the lovely, sun-filled morning room where her mother had taken to having breakfast now that everyone was away. The walls were covered in a pretty William Morris wallpaper of pale lemon with willow leaves. 'My last billet was next to the railway line and the coal depot and my landlady had three small and very lively boys. It seemed as if one of them was always awake during the night.'

'How dreadful for you, darling. I know there's a war on but you'd have thought they'd house you with … well, you know, something a bit more in keeping with your rank. You are an officer, after all.' Her mother pursed her lips. Evelyn being an officer was small comfort to her. She would still far rather

Evelyn had completed her degree in modern languages at Lady Margaret Hall in Oxford.

Evelyn helped herself to a cup of tea, pouring from the delicate Wedgwood teapot that had been a wedding present to her grandmother from Cecilia Bowes-Lyon, the Countess of Strathmore, now the Queen's mother.

'Do you have any plans today?' asked her mother, which Evelyn knew was a prelude to a request for some kind of aid.

'I promised Hodges I'd help in the garden.' The old gardener, for all his grumbling, was a particular favourite of hers and the walled garden was getting to be too much for him. Beyond the main house a magnificent kitchen garden kept the house and its dwindling staff in fresh fruit and vegetables. Rows of carrots, caulis, spring cabbage, radishes and asparagus lined the garden but there was a lot for one person to do.

Her mother pursed her lips again, once more torn between disapproval and acceptance as she dusted a crumb from the linen tablecloth. She still wasn't happy that she'd lost her rose garden and the croquet lawn, both of which had been turned over to vegetables.

'The garden is far too much for him on his own.'

'I know, dear, but the Vicar comes to help when he can and the blacksmith's boys come up, which I don't mind because they take vegetables to their mother. We send as much to the village as we can spare and Mrs Dawtry is a genius at pickling and preserving. Oh, that reminds me, there's a letter for you. From the War Office.'

Evelyn's heart jumped in her chest. 'Where is it?' she asked a little too quickly.

'It's on the console table in the hall. I meant to bring it

through but then... I can't remember but I was doing something else.'

Evelyn wasn't listening. She rose and left the room with unladylike haste, her pulse racing.

The official brown envelope sat on a silver salver like an unexploded bomb.

She stared at it, dreading its contents, and glanced back towards the morning room. What would Mummy say when she told her? Evelyn bit her lip. And Daddy – currently the commanding officer on the battleship *Warspite* in the Pacific Ocean – he was going to be so disappointed in her. And Hodges? Having served in the Navy in the Great War, he'd been tickled pink that she was a Lieutenant. If only David were here. She could have told her older brother what Williamson had done, although he'd probably have been so angry he'd have told their uncle what had transpired. She caught her lip between her teeth, but David wasn't here. David was in a POW camp hundreds of miles away with far worse things to worry about. Her brother had always been her hero and when she'd heard he'd been captured she'd been desperate to do her part and make him and the family proud of her. Despite being invited to model on occasion, she'd always been a bit of a tomboy, preferring the company of her brother to the girls who were inevitably invited to play with her. The two of them had had the run of the grounds and the guidance of Hodges, who'd helped them build fires, cook illicit sausages smuggled from Cook and build dens in the coppice. They'd had an idyllic childhood. Poor David. She crossed her fingers and said a silent prayer. *Please, please, let him be all right. And Peter too.* She had no idea where he might be or whether he was alive.

She didn't deserve to feel sorry for herself. Both men, along with her other male relatives, were no doubt enduring hardships she would never know. She snatched up the envelope and hurried up the stairs to David's bedroom, knowing that it was unlikely that anyone would chance upon her in there.

Sinking onto his bed, she glared at the envelope and then carefully slipped a finger in one end and lifted beneath the flap, easing open the seal to pull out the flimsy paper.

For a full minute she stared at the words, too surprised and amazed to think straight. It was a summons to a new posting, with her rank of Lieutenant intact, and quite the most extraordinary turnabout. Although Captain Jennings had clearly intervened to prevent a scandal, she'd been sure that he would take the side of her commanding officer and she'd be punished.

Relief made her laugh out loud. Apparently she was still going to be an Intelligence Officer. She wasn't going to be demoted. Instead she was to go to London for her training. Her reputation remained intact and she could carry on in the Navy. She read the letter again, still none the wiser as to where she would be going after that or what she'd be doing. Her curiosity was well and truly piqued. What on earth was her new role to be? Suddenly she couldn't wait to find out.

Chapter Five

Judith - Latimer House

The train rattled along the lines, leaving the dark confines of Baker Street station before bursting out into light and a brilliant, full of life and promise, spring day. Judith turned in surprise, blinking and staring out of the window at the bright-green leaves unfurling on the shrubs beside the track, the golden yellow of buttercups nestling in the undergrowth, the new growth of wisteria clinging to walls and brickwork, and pale-purple lilac blooms weighing down tender branches.

Spring, a season of rebirth. For a moment she allowed herself a tiny hope that life was about to get better. Please let Major Wardlow be right, that this new work was going to be interesting. She desperately needed something to take up the space in her brain that tended to the melancholy. Already this week had been a whirlwind of activity, quite a change from her usual stolid routine. Only two days ago, she'd received a letter with a travel warrant to a railway station on the underground line and

40

instructions to report to her new posting. It was two months after her interview, long after she'd expected to hear anything. She had no idea where Chalfont and Latimer station was but she now realised from the changing scenery that it wasn't even in London.

Thankfully the sight of the other women in ATS uniforms in the same carriage reassured her that she hadn't made a mistake, until they all rose to leave the train at Harrow on the Hill, chattering among themselves like lively canaries. She stared after them, slightly envious that they all knew each other so well, aware of uncertainty twisting in her stomach. She'd deliberately kept her distance from the other women in her dorm; how could they know or understand what she'd been through? And she certainly didn't want to revisit that time by talking about it. She stood up and then froze, not knowing what to do. The blonde girl sitting opposite her smiled and said, cupping her hand across her mouth, 'Where you headed?' The Careless Talk Costs Lives message had been drummed into everyone.

Judith bit her lip and held up her train ticket.

'You're all right. We've got ages to go. Another eight stops. They're all off to Eastcote.'

Judith nodded but didn't speak; she hoped her perfunctory smile would serve as thanks. The other woman smiled at her and picked up her book, one that Judith recognised as one of the popular Mills and Boon books that the other ATS girls had borrowed from the Boots Booklovers Library at the pharmacists in the town. Judith tried not to stare at her bowed head with its shining golden hair curled up in two elaborate rolls. Everything about her was bright and beautiful; she wore a green A-line skirt topped with a saffron-yellow hand-knitted jumper that clung to her curves, accentuating her figure. There was something show-stopping about her, as if she were bubbling with energy.

At the next station, two shambling men boarded the train in woollen caps and crumpled dirty trousers with their shirtsleeves rolled up to their elbows. When they spotted the pretty blonde, one of them promptly sat down in the group of seats behind her.

'Hey, Betty Grable. How's tricks?' he called with unexpected familiarity. Judith stiffened. He seemed to be the worse for drink.

The blonde hid her quick grimace well. 'Donald,' she said acknowledging him. Judith uncurled her fingers and forced herself to relax. They clearly knew each other.

'Hey, shove up, lass,' said the other man, coming to sit down in the seat opposite Judith, next to the blonde woman. As he did so, he kicked her battered valise, sending it skimming across the floor.

'Ooops, sorry, love.'

Judith jumped up quickly and retrieved the case, holding it to her for a second and carefully settled it back by her legs. It had been her father's case and she had memories of him returning home from trips away visiting foreign music publishers, the sheets of music spilling out when he opened it to reveal his new treasures.

The man stared at her and she looked away, her heart thumping a little uncomfortably.

'I said I'm sorry,' he said, belligerent this time.

She nodded, praying it would be sufficient acknowledgement, but she could tell by the dogged brightness in his eyes that he had sensed some kind of weakness and in that bullying way was determined to seek it out.

'Cat got your tongue?'

She shook her head.

'Leave over, Jim. Leave her alone.'

He sneered at the blonde girl. 'You tellin' me what to do, Betty? Don't think Bert would be pleased to hear that. I heard you've been getting a bit uppity of late.' He turned back to Judith. With his short curly hair, cut close to his head, the broad barrelled chest and small round eyes, he reminded her of a bull, ready to charge at the least provocation. Even his nostrils quivered.

'It's polite when someone speaks to you to talk back to 'em. Hold a conversation. I say hello, you say hello back. Hello.'

Judith froze, fear crowding in. She'd met bullies like this before, in black shirts and jackboots, aware that they were untouchable. Pushing and shoving, sometimes even spitting. She'd fled Germany to escape that. And here it was, happening all over again.

'I said, Hello.'

'Hello,' she said in a low voice, trying to sound as English as possible but it was no good, even in one word she couldn't disguise the accent of her native tongue.

'You foreign?' came the sudden belligerent challenge. 'Did you hear that, Donald?'

She shrank into her seat.

'Where you going?'

Scared now, she blurted out, 'Chalfont and Latimer.'

'You're German. Lads,' he yelled, turning to the whole coach, 'we've got a spy on board. Trying to pass herself off in uniform.' He turned back to her and rose clumsily to march along the carriage with nightmarish goosesteps, saying, 'Heil Hitler!'

Now everyone had turned to look and point at her, muttering to each other, staring with suspicion and hostility.

'Give over, Jim, you big lug,' said the blonde woman, standing up, pushing him out of the way and sitting down next to Judith.

'Ignore them. Pig ignorant, the pair of them. The Army wouldn't take 'em. Too bloody stupid by half.'

The man turned an unattractive shade of red.

'You wait, Betty Connors. Your Bert won't like you behavin' like this.'

Betty simply turned her nose up and gave him the sort of look that suggested he was of as much interest as a beetle under her shoe.

Judith hated these confrontations, even though she should be used to them by now, but despite her whole body shaking, she had to bite back a smile. The other girl had nerve, that was for sure.

'I'm Betty, as you probably heard the oaf saying.' She held out her hand before adding in a loud, carrying voice for the benefit of the rest of the carriage, 'And I'm guessing you're Polish.' Out of sight of them all, she kicked Judith quite hard on the ankle.

'Yes,' said Judith, remembering this very piece of advice from another German girl she'd once met. The British liked the Poles. The Poles had flown in the Battle of Britain and had already made a huge contribution to the Allies. 'From Krakow,' she added loudly. Immediately everyone nodded to themselves as if that made everything all right.

'Polish, Donald,' said Betty, hands on hips, a furious scowl on her face. 'They're on the same side as us.'

He grunted and scowled back at her but then with an impotent shake of his head, he and his equally unprepossessing companion got up and ambled off down the carriage, opening the door and disappearing into the next one.

'Always slow, that one,' observed Betty.

'Thank you. I'm Judith.'

'Nice to meet you. So you're going to Chalfont and Latimer too. Are you going to be working at the big house?'

Judith clamped her mouth shut for a minute before answering. 'I'm not actually sure. I was told to get the train to the station and I'd be met.'

'Probably the house. I'm reporting there this afternoon once I've dumped my kitbag at home. My family live in the village. I'll be living back with my ma and sister. I've got a job as a typist. Bloody marvellous. I've been filing for the last few months. Deadly.'

Judith laughed. 'Me too. I hate filing.'

'You going to be a typist too?'

'I don't know. I don't think so.' She allowed herself a small smile. 'I can't type.'

Betty let out a laugh of delight. 'I'm not sure I can.'

Although this girl with her perfect rolled curls, ready smile and bright-red lipstick was louder and brasher than women Judith normally associated with, she also seemed kind and open-hearted. Judith couldn't help warming to her. She'd been so closed off from other people for such a long time, but this girl seemed like a ray of sunshine in an otherwise grey life.

'Where were you posted before?'

'Somewhere in Yorkshire. Filing.' They both snorted with laughter. Judith thought it was probably relief on her part. Her heart rate was only just returning to normal.

'I was in Mill Hill.' She stopped as if struck by something. 'Do you know where that is? I mean, how long have you been in this country?'

'I came in 1938. I lived in Kensal Green. I worked in a shoe factory.'

'Oooh, how lovely. I wouldn't have minded doing that.' Betty's pretty face lit up with enthusiasm that made Judith laugh again.

'We weren't able to take the shoes home with us. Besides they were mainly workmen's boots.'

'Ah, maybe not then. I'm not sure I'd have fancied that. I think if I wasn't in the ATS, I'd like to have worked in a cinema. As an usherette. You get to see all the films for free.' She sighed. 'I love the films. Being in the dark. It's like stepping into another world.'

Judith smiled. 'I like films too.' They shared a quick glance of acknowledgement. She went as often as she could to the cinema. It offered a few hours' escape from real life and she wondered if, perhaps, someone like Betty needed escape as much as she did. With her movie-star looks and confidence, Judith found it difficult to believe.

'*Casablanca*'s my favourite. I cried,' declared Betty.

'I liked it.' Judith couldn't say it made her cry. Her tears had run dry a long time ago.

For the next fifteen minutes, Betty chattered away about the films and shows she'd seen in London. Judith, entranced by the other girl's vivacity, was quite happy to listen and make the odd comment as Betty said 'Don't you think so?', 'Wasn't he lovely?' and 'Isn't she wonderful?'

'Well, this is us coming up,' said Betty, jumping to her feet and pulling a kitbag from the luggage rack. 'Good luck and maybe I'll see you at the house. It's some sort of distribution centre.' She scrunched up her nose. 'Doesn't sound that interesting to me.' She shrugged, 'But needs must, eh?'

Judith nodded, feeling anxious. She had no idea what she had come to but she'd faced worse. Leaving everything she'd known, to start again. Nothing could ever be as bad as that again and she wasn't going to let it. Getting close to other people was too much of a risk. She'd learned to cope with loneliness by keeping herself to herself and not allowing her emotions to get the better of her. It was easy to keep them under lock and key by keeping her distance.

She stared out of the window at the rolling hills and thickets of trees, spreading across the dents and bumps of the landscape. Her spirits lifted. They were in the country. She hadn't even known that the underground came out of the city. In her time off, she could explore the area, she told herself; something that she could do on her own without that awful pervading sense of loneliness and isolation that had dogged her in the confines of the northern town she'd just left. But she knew she probably wouldn't.

'Chalfont and Latimer. Chalfont and Latimer,' called the guard on the platform.

Betty jumped off the train onto the platform and Judith followed, a little like a cautious cat, keen to see where she was.

'Well, this is me,' said Betty. 'See you around.' With that she gave Judith a cheery salute and marched off, her hips swaying and her bag swinging.

'Bye,' said Judith, her voice trailing away as she looked around at the rapidly emptying platform. Picking up her bag, she followed everyone out to the road where there was a corporal in uniform beside a large dark car.

'Hello,' she said hesitantly. 'I'm Judith Stern.'

'Ah, Private Stern. Another German lady?'

She nodded, stiffening a little, but he seemed indifferent to her nationality.

'Good to have you on board.' He gave her a friendly smile. 'Welcome to No. 1 Distribution Centre.' He looked over her shoulder and frowned. 'I'm waiting on one more.'

'Betty?'

He shook his head. 'Who? No. We'll give it a minute. I hope she didn't miss the bloody train. I'll have to come back again. Honest to God, I'm up and down that lane a dozen times a day at the moment.'

They waited for a few minutes and Judith was quite happy to stand there in the warm spring sunshine listening to the birds flitting through the nearby trees. It seemed so peaceful and quiet, it was difficult to believe that the rest of Europe was at war, with such a large portion under German occupation.

Suddenly there was a roar of an engine and a big grey car came speeding up the road and then stopped dead beside them.

'Gawd. Look at that,' said the corporal.

'Hello,' called the young woman in the driving seat in a very carrying voice. She exuded rosy good health, with round cheeks and twinkling eyes as if the world were here to entertain her. Judith couldn't help noticing that she looked rather resplendent in a smart Navy Wren's uniform. 'Am I in the right place. Chalfont and Latimer?'

'Yes. The station.'

'Hallelujah. Made it. I'm Lieutenant Evelyn Edwards-Brooke reporting for duty. Sorry I'm a bit late. Got stuck behind a cart. Isn't it pretty round here?'

The young man gawped and gazed at the car.

'Beauty, isn't she?' Evelyn patted the steering wheel, while Judith stared at her. She'd never seen anyone with so much elegant self-possession.

'It is, ducks. And I was expecting you on the eleven o'clock. You'd best follow us up to the house.'

'Jolly good,' she called.

The corporal nodded to Judith. 'Sling your bag in the back and hop in.'

After a slight hesitation, she put her case on the back seat of the car and joined him in the front.

'Did she say Lieutenant?' she asked, still bemused. She'd not come across many female officers and certainly not a Lieutenant. At the barracks she'd been based at, the officers were all men.

'Got all sorts at this place, you'll see. You'll probably be promoted before you know it,' he said as they drove out of the small town. 'This is Little Chalfont. Trains run regular to London. Nice neck of the woods, if you don't mind it being a bit quiet, but better that than running down the Anderson shelter every night, I figure.'

She nodded, busy taking in the open fields and hedges around them. A few minutes later they turned left onto a smaller lane and a small village came into view. Judith stared out at the terrace of black and white timber-framed cottages with tiny dormer windows set into the red-tiled roof and slightly crooked chimneys grouped together in the centre of the building. It was an England she'd heard of but never seen before. A world away from Berlin, from Hull, from Kensal Green, from everything she'd known before. She let out a breath and hugged the tiny kernel of hope to herself as the Jeep swung left and the corporal gunned the engine up the short sharp incline, past a few more houses and then out onto a straight road.

'Here it is.' The corporal nodded ahead to a pair of red-brick pillars. 'Latimer House.'

As they passed through the gateway and drew closer, Judith's eyes widened. 'House?'

He laughed. 'Grand, isn't it?'

'It's like a palace or a castle.'

'Don't get your hopes up. We don't get to stay in the house. Round the back it don't look so fancy. There's a prefab village. That's where we get billeted.'

Judith didn't care; she couldn't take her eyes from the house and its imposing three-storey facade with decorative brick corners, the grand stone porch, tall intricate chimneys and what she later learned were mullioned windows. To the left, the grounds sloped away, giving the house a commanding view of the valley and the wide expanse of river that curved away into the soft, lush green clouds of trees.

Behind them came the growl of the grey car that had followed them up the drive.

'Well, isn't this rather wonderful,' exclaimed the woman. Judith eyed her tall, slender figure. Even in uniform she managed to look as if she'd stepped off the front page of a magazine.

'It is, isn't it,' she agreed, taking some consolation that the sophisticated woman was as impressed as she was.

'Oh, you're German,' exclaimed Evelyn, with seeming delight which shocked Judith, holding out her hand. '*Wie schön, Sie zu treffen. Ich bin Evelyn. Wie heißen Sie?*'

'I'm Judith. Pleased to meet you too,' she replied, shaking Evelyn's hand with a genuine smile. When was the last time that someone had been pleased to meet her, an enemy alien? She couldn't remember.

'Sorry to interrupt, ladies, but you need to report for duty. My orders are to take you straight up to the Colonel. He's a busy man. Get those stars out of your eyes. You are here to work.' Despite his words, the corporal's face held a smile.

'What do they, we, do here?' asked Judith.

'Yes, I'd like to know that too,' chimed in Evelyn, exchanging a bright-eyed glance with her. 'I have no idea.'

The corporal sobered. 'I'm just the driver. And what I do know, I'm not at liberty to discuss. It's a house of secrets. And we all know careless talk costs lives.' He tapped his nose and led the way as Judith stared up in fascination at the vaulted roof of the stone porch through which they passed, her shoes clicking on the black and white tiled floor. She turned slightly, startled by a shadowy figure in an alcove and then smiled to herself, realising it was a real-life suit of armour, complete with a terrifying-looking mace in one hand. What an amazing place and what on earth did they do here? She couldn't begin to imagine but she was glad that this other woman seemed as in the dark as she was.

Chapter Six

Evelyn

Evelyn was perplexed. It had been a relief to receive the telegram and see that she'd not been demoted but this place was a long way from the sea and the other woman sitting next to her, a German no less, was ATS, a different service altogether. Maybe she was still being punished in some other way even though she'd kept her stripes. They were both sitting outside a closed door in what was now an office with a Wren busy typing at the desk opposite. Clearly, judging from the pretty feminine pale-blue floral carpet and the co-ordinating pastel drapes, it had once been a lady's bedroom.

At last, the door opened. 'Lieutenant Brooke-Edwards?'

'Yes, Sir.'

'Do come in. I'm Colonel Myers.' He stepped back and invited her into what must have once been another bedroom even though it was now lined with books. The enormous desk, with neat piles of folders and papers, which had clearly taken up residence in more recent years, looked rather incongruous against the stylish wallpaper of vines and ferns. There were three other desks lined up in a row at the back of the room, equally piled with papers, which gave the impression the occupants had recently stepped away to run some errand. The room looked out over the long drive leading down to Latimer village and provided a useful view of anyone arriving or departing.

She stood with her arms behind her back, still a little tense.

'Welcome to Latimer House, Lieutenant. Nice to have you with us. I've heard excellent reports of your work with prisoners of war in Falmouth. Captain Jennings was very impressed.'

'Oh,' she squeaked, her head buzzing with questions. Jennings had recommended her. Was this a good or a bad thing? Where on earth had she come to? What was this place?

He smiled. 'Why don't you take a seat and I'll explain a few things. One of the reasons you've been recruited is because of your fluency in German. How did you learn your German?'

'My mother's sister married a German professor at the University in Heidelberg. We spent every summer there.' She smiled at the memories of sunshine-filled garden parties with her cousins and their friends. She, David and her parents had visited every summer for as long as she could remember. Except for the last few years, of course. 'I made some good friends there.' Her smile dimmed as she thought of all those dear people. 'And now I have no idea what has happened to them. The country changed but not all of its people did. Not all Germans are Nazis and not all of them support Hitler.'

'I know that only too well. My sister's husband is German and many of his family are still living there.' His face clouded.

'I'm sorry. It's difficult, isn't it?' Their eyes met in a moment of shared affinity. He understood the uncertainty of not knowing how or where your friends were. Since the suspension of postal services between England and Germany on the third of September 1939, there had been no way of contacting anyone over there.

'I think it is one of our strengths when we know our enemy and understand that in many ways they are like us. Did you visit any other parts of Germany?'

She frowned at the question.

'Sometimes if you can talk about a place with a prisoner, you can develop a relationship with them. It's part of our,' he paused, 'our overall strategy.' She wondered at that pause and what he wasn't saying but he was looking at her expectantly.

'I was also in Bavaria. In 1938, in preparation for going up to Oxford. I spent,' she broke off and bit her lip, 'I was supposed to spend a year there but it was cut short.' He didn't say anything so she pressed on. 'I stayed with a Graf and Gräfin.' Her smile dimmed, thinking of the lovely old couple in their castle who were nobility in Germany. 'They were very kind and although they were discreet about it, they were anti-Nazi.' She paused, wondering whether she should admit the next part. In hindsight it seemed childish and not very disciplined. 'There was a diplomatic incident.'

Myers raised his eyebrows.

'I and another girl who was also staying there… well, we were rather incensed by the attacks on the Jewish people, especially a particularly nasty anti-Jewish newspaper, *Der Stürmer.*' She shuddered in disgust. 'It was awful. They wrote the most hideous, inflammatory things and it was put up in the town centre for everyone to read. It was shocking.' Evelyn could feel her vocal cords tightening as the remembered rage came back. 'I couldn't believe they could treat people like that.' She collected herself. 'And now I realise it was ill-advised and rather immature. I'd like to think that I've grown up since then, but I had to tear one down. I'm afraid I did it rather publicly in the centre of the town.'

She could have sworn she saw the Colonel quirk his lips very quickly.

'Unfortunately someone saw me and reported it and … well, I was an embarrassment to my hosts, and then the Foreign Office got wind and it was decided it would be best if I came home.'

'I see, and then you went to Lady Margaret Hall to read modern languages.'

'That's right,' she said, relieved that he hadn't commented further. She wasn't exactly ashamed of her behaviour but now she realised how ineffectual and silly her actions had been. 'And then I left in 1940, when my brother was taken a prisoner of war. I wanted to do something.' She'd wanted to serve, to make a difference in the way that her brother, her father and uncles were all doing. All her life she'd been constrained by what she could do as a woman; as a girl climbing trees with her brother, insisting he taught her to drive, to shoot and to fish. It had always been a battle to be able to do the same things as him. Even going to university, she was restricted to an all-ladies college. The advent of the war had changed all that. Women were allowed to do things that they'd never been able to do before and she'd been determined to seize that opportunity.

Myers nodded. 'Well, you'll be doing something here, that's for certain. What I must impress upon you is that the work we conduct on this site is of the utmost secrecy. You come highly recommended. You'll sign the Official Secrets Act and you won't be able to talk of our work here, not even with colleagues. Latimer House to outsiders is known as Camp 30 or No. 1 Distribution Centre. It's actually one of three Combined Services Detailed Interrogation Centres and your role here will be with Naval Intelligence.'

Evelyn nodded, still reeling from the shock of the words 'highly recommended'.

'You will be involved in interrogating German prisoners of war.'

She frowned, looking out of the window. 'You have some here? This is a POW camp?'

Colonel Myers smiled rather wryly. 'Officially no. We'd rather keep a low profile. We like to think of it as more of a transition camp. We receive newly arrived prisoners deemed of sufficient rank to harbour useful information and glean as much as we can from them before sending them elsewhere. They're here for a short period only. Hence the official title of Distribution Centre.'

'Ah, I see, Sir.'

'You've already had training in interrogation techniques, so you'll be aware of our strategy. The POWs think it's because we have so few men and are so desperate we have to recruit women to do men's work. As a result, they often relax their guard. Forgive me, but as military men they don't take women, especially women officers, very seriously.'

'I have come across that before, sir.'

He looked back at the folder on his desk. 'Yes, you have an excellent record of success.'

Evelyn nodded again and for the next half hour Myers explained a little more about the work before another officer arrived.

'Ah, Wilkins. Excellent timing.' He stood up and shook her hand. 'Good to have you on board, Lieutenant. I think you're going to fit in here just fine. Once you've been through all the paperwork with Lieutenant Wilkins, here, someone will show you your quarters.' He directed them to one of the desks opposite.

'Thank you, Sir.'

'Although I would appreciate it, if you have any trouble with fellow officers, if you refrain from breaking their jaws.'

Evelyn froze and stared at him, her pulse kicking at his words, but his expression remained perfectly impassive. She could feel the heat racing across her chest and she prayed that it wouldn't reach her face.

'Yes, Sir. I mean, no, Sir. I won't, Sir.'

'That will be all.'

With her face blushing furiously, she avoided Lieutenant Wilkins' eyes as with a shaking hand she signed the Official Secrets Act. She backed out of the room and closed the door behind her before leaning against the wall, her hand across her eyes. 'Oh my God.'

When she straightened she looked into the eyes of the shy German girl, Judith.

'Is everything all right?' she asked, looking nervous.

'Oh, it's fine. It was … something from my last posting.' She allowed herself to shudder properly now. How in heck's name had she got away with it? Now she grinned at Judith. 'Good old Captain Jennings, what a poppet.'

Clearly thinking she was quite mad, the other woman nodded slowly. 'Do you know what you will be doing here?'

'Yes, but it's all hush-hush. He'll tell you.' She cast her eyes to a young woman at the desk beyond them. 'Excuse me. Would you know about our bunks? Where the cabins are?' She picked up her suitcase.

Judith frowned and she laughed. 'Navy terms. They always use 'em even though we're not at sea.'

'Ah. I understand now. It's confusing that the Army and Navy are here.'

'The RAF as well,' piped up the girl. 'That's why it's called the CSDIC, Combined Services Detailed Interrogation Centre.'

Evelyn took pity on Judith's confusion and jerked her thumb to the door. 'The Colonel will tell you all.'

At that moment another uniformed woman arrived. 'Lieutenant Brooke-Edwards?'

'Yes, that's me,' said Evelyn, swinging round to find another officer addressing her.

'Welcome. I'm Lieutenant Wenham. Here to show you your cabin.'

She turned to Judith and mouthed, 'See.'

'I'm afraid there's been a bit of ballyhoo and you're going to be bunking down with a couple others. The quarters in the old dairy have been flooded and so they're putting two extras in your allocated cabin up in the old servants' quarters. Lower ranks, I'm afraid. Not what we're used to but you'll find round here that we don't always stick to the formalities. Especially with combined services. I hope you're not going to kick up a stink.' She gave Evelyn a narrow-eyed stare from cool grey eyes. Her short hair, swept across her head from a low side parting, fanned around her ears in soft curls, but despite the fashionable hair-do, the grim expression made her look much older than her years, which Evelyn put at around twenty-nine.

Evelyn hurriedly shook her head. It was unconventional but hardly the end of the world and she quite liked the idea of sharing with other women. It would be like the camaraderie of the dorms at her boarding school.

The stocky, stern Lieutenant Wenham was still talking. 'But needs must. Make do and all that. I'm sure they'll be decent types.'

'I'm sure they will,' said Evelyn. 'And I can sleep anywhere these days.' She had a quick longing thought of her bed at Quartiles in Henley, and then thought of the box room at Mrs Rankin's, which had been freezing in the winter, boiling in the summer and decorated with the slime trails of slugs across the linoleum for most of the year. How her life had changed since those wonderful summers in Heidelberg.

'You got lucky. You're in the main house. No rats up there.' She shot Evelyn a sudden grin and Evelyn wasn't sure if she were joking or not. She sincerely hoped she was.

Chapter Seven

Judith

After the elegant Evelyn was borne away, Judith sat alone, feeling both curious and terrified. Where had she come to? And why did they want her here? She'd picked up on the words 'Interrogation Centre'. The thought of coming face to face with fellow Germans who were fighting for their country filled her with unease.

Before she could puzzle further, the door opened and she swallowed down her nerves, smoothing her clammy hands over the rough fabric of her skirt, and followed an invitation into the office as the man standing there introduced himself as Colonel Myers.

'Do take a seat, Private Stern.'

'Thank you, Sir.'

'I expect you're wondering why you're here and what this place is and why you've been selected.' There was something immensely … no, likeable wasn't quite the word. He had a pull about him that made you keen to please him. She immediately surmised that he was the sort of man you would trust with your secrets.

'You have a very good understanding of engineering, which will be invaluable. Your test scores were excellent.'

'Thank you.' Why the importance of engineering?

'I imagine life has been somewhat turbulent for you but I hope here you'll find a safe harbour for the time being. There are over fifty German staff here. Many of them Jews who escaped the National Socialist regime.'

She blinked. So many. She'd never been posted with fellow Jews or Germans before.

He took off his glasses and kindness softened his lined face. 'My sister and her family, two small children, had to flee Germany in the middle of the night.' He took out a handkerchief and polished his glasses, shifting his gaze away from hers. 'By all accounts a terrifying experience. I myself had to leave Austria in rather a hurry after an unfortunate, but thankfully brief, episode in Gestapo custody.'

Although he didn't look at her, she could feel his warm empathy. Like her, he understood what it was like to be hunted and to have that sweat-drenching fear of what might happen if the Gestapo got hold of you.

'Here we have created an important operation, which is a vital part of the war effort.'

Some of her frustration must have shown in her eyes because he laughed. 'Sorry, I've been talking in riddles for too long. Why don't I show you something?'

He turned around and grasped the edge of a floor-length green velvet curtain next to the large map of Europe tacked onto the wallpapered wall. With quick hands he beckoned her to follow him through a heavy wood-panelled door as he stepped into a narrow corridor which she imagined had once been a servants' passageway. The floors were bare boards and the walls here were a dull white, contrasting sharply with the opulent wallpapers and thick carpets of the bedrooms. They walked along and then down a few steps before coming to another door, which he opened. Inside was a solitary chair and a single desk pushed up against a wall, and on top of it were a series of black boxes full of dials and switches reminiscent of an aircraft cockpit. Pressing one of the switches below the mesh wires of a small round loudspeaker, Myers held up one finger. 'Listen.'

To her surprise she could hear two German voices talking. She listened intently, wondering if this was another test and he expected her to translate. One of the men was bemoaning the fact that he hadn't seen a newspaper in days and complaining that he was bored, while the other suggested that perhaps they could ask for a chess board to pass some of the time. Before the conversation had finished, Myers cut it off by pressing another switch.

Judith waited, trying to remember word for word what the two men had said.

'Poor chaps. They're going to be bored for a while longer. They're airmen, the Luftwaffe, and we've been interrogating them to try and find out more about the ground-based radar systems the Germans are using to detect our fighter planes. I understand you have some knowledge of radar systems and that you worked for Siemens and Halske.'

She nodded, although she still didn't follow.

'We listen in to all their conversations and sometimes we overhear some very interesting and helpful information. All of the prisoners of war here are officers of high military rank that have useful intelligence. Of course, they're not always prepared to reveal it during interrogation, but they often talk when they return to their cells. Some of them think we're quite stupid and relish telling each other what they wouldn't tell their interrogators. It would be quite amusing if it wasn't so very informative.'

Judith's mouth dropped open. 'How? Here?' She looked around the room, remembering the beautiful house beyond its walls.

'Yes, and no one knows what goes on here.'

'Really, Sir?' She stared at him with disbelief.

'Oh yes, what we do here is of the utmost secrecy.' His face broke into a sudden grin. 'It's ingenious. Each cell is wired with tiny microphones situated in various places so that we can listen in to every word they say. The information we gather is invaluable; from what morale in Germany is like through to where gun emplacements are positioned in Europe, how U-boats protect fleets, the equipment they use on planes and boats, the plans they have for air attacks. From the information we gather we compile in-depth reports which are then disseminated to all sections of the military. This is an intricate and complex operation which has the full backing and support of the Prime Minister.'

Judith's eyes widened as she tried to take in what he was saying. It seemed almost impossible to believe and in some ways ridiculous, but also incredibly clever. Her brain darted this way and that, trying to gather together all the different implications. 'So the prisoners have no idea. Nor do the people in the village. I've never heard of such a thing.'

Myers smiled. 'And I hope you never will. It is vital that what we do here is kept a secret. You will need to sign the Official Secrets Act and not speak of what you do to anyone, even members of the other services and departments here. This is an extremely well-oiled machine with a team that does its utmost at all times to deliver. With increasing numbers of POWs, we are busier than ever. Make no mistake, this is no sinecure.'

'Good,' said Judith, sticking out her chin, fascinated by what she'd heard. 'I want to work. I want to help.'

'Excellent,' said Myers. 'The work we do here is every bit as vital as being on active service. It might feel a long way from battle but I promise you, it is essential. Don't ever believe otherwise.

'You will be part of the listening team. Your technical vocabulary will be very useful when we're listening in to some of the officers from the U-boats and captured airmen. Welcome to the team.' He held out his hand.

'Thank you, Sir.' She shook his hand, feeling a little overawed and just a little thrilled by his words, but already her tidy, ordered brain was trying to understand the mechanics. It had always been the way with her, like breaking down a technically difficult piece of music. Her father and aunt had teased her about her constant curiosity to know how things worked. It was why she'd enjoyed her work in the factory so much, even though it was a long way from playing the piano, which had been her primary passion. She couldn't help herself asking the question, even though it might be considered an impertinence to a senior office. 'But how does it all work?'

Myers beamed as if she'd asked to hold his baby. 'You really want to know?'

'Yes,' she said, suddenly fascinated, the questions suddenly bombarding her brain. 'How far away are the cells and how do you hear here?'

'Come with me, I'll show you.'

After the tour of the house, with her head still reeling, she left Myers on the main stairs and a Wren showed her to another smaller, narrow staircase which led up to the attics. It was like stepping into another world. The M room, as Myers had shown her, was one of the most fascinating and interesting places she'd ever been and lots of people in this house didn't even know it was there. The room in the basement of the house, in what had been the old wine cellars, was where all the listening to the POWs was done. It was accessed from a Nissen hut extension on the outside of the building that was disguised as an ordinary administrative office. However, behind the office, down a long corridor, double locked with doors at either end, there was a room taking up a whole cellar area where teams of listeners were arranged in groups of four around the listening equipment which was positioned in the centre of a table. There were ten tables in all and each team could listen to up to three cells at any one time. She'd been inspired by the intense concentration in the room and the sense of important work being done. Even better was that she would be part of it, a cog in the machine, and that at long last she had a place and meaningful work to do. Inside a small knot unravelled, as if, like a feather blown about on the breeze, she'd finally come to rest. Her excitement wasn't diminished by the sight of the small room that was to be home for the foreseeable future.

'Here you go, your quarters are at the top of the stairs.' With that the Wren hurried off as if she had a dozen other places to be.

'Hello, again. Looks like we're going to be cabinmates.' Evelyn was standing in the room, a case at her feet, sliding a pressed uniform shirt onto a coat hanger.

'Hello.' Judith looked around the cramped quarters. Three beds were crammed in, one along the wall with the head of the bed tucked under the eaves and the other two on the longer wall opposite arranged like the interlocking teeth of a zipper. Between them there was just enough room to weave in and out of them.

'It's going to be snug,' said Evelyn cheerfully, 'but I reckon we've got the best view in the house.' She pointed to the dormer window cutting into the slope right down to the floor. 'And look, we can climb out.' Judith, intrigued by her enthusiasm, crossed the window to look out. From here she could see across the river and a wide stretch of fields to either side. Below the window was a tiny roof area no more than a couple of yards wide, behind the crenellated walls at the top of the house.

'Our own private terrace.' Evelyn grinned. 'Doesn't get better than that. Do you have a preference for which bed?' It looked as if she'd already bagged the bed on the far side of the room as her smart suitcase lay on the pile of sheets and blankets.

'No,' said Judith. 'At my last posting there were twenty of us in one room. This feels like luxury. And I think I'll have this bed.' She put her father's case on the bed under the eaves.

'You sure?'

'Yes,' said Judith firmly. She needed the security of being able to escape through the nearest exit if she ever had cause. At the barracks, she'd swapped places to be by the draughty old window. She would never forget the terrifying journey from Berlin to Austria, always looking over her shoulder from the moment she'd left the family home. Four generations of Sterns had lived in the spacious apartment in the tall four-storied building into which her mother had moved with her in-laws when she married her father. Judith had had to leave taking just what she could carry, without saying goodbye to her neighbours opposite, the Cohens, or the Ackerlands upstairs. She'd only been able to take two photos, one of her mother, who had died when she was three years old, and the other of her father.

Evelyn began to unpack with the blithe, uninhibited ease of one who'd never had to worry about the state of her undergarments. Judith averted her eyes from the sight of the silk underwear that came out of the top of her case, feeling embarrassed. What would the other girl think of her knitted vest tops and the flannel nightgown that had been her grandmother's? Thank goodness for the ATS-issued directoire knickers, shoes and shirts. Her coat, the only one she possessed apart from her uniform greatcoat, was made from an old blanket that had belonged to her great-aunt and, like the few clothes she had, all had been made or altered from her grandparents' wardrobes when they'd died. Things had been difficult in Germany long before the Nazis swept to power. Evelyn's wardrobe didn't look as if it had suffered.

Ducking her head, Judith decided to make her bed instead, focusing on making tight hospital corners.

'Oh Lord. How do you do that?' asked Evelyn, coming to stand beside her and patting the neatly tucked-in blankets.

'Do what?'

'Make everything stay in place. When I do it, I always wake up with everything almost on the floor. Thankfully my last landlady always made the bed for me and at home, our maid.'

'Would you like me to show you?' asked Judith.

'Would you? That would be super. I'm not very good at housewifely things. My mother despairs.'

Judith pursed her lips.

'I can't sew or knit.' Evelyn gave a self-deprecating grin. 'But men aren't expected to, are they?'

'I suppose not,' said Judith, never having thought about it before. Judith shook out Evelyn's sheets and smoothed both over the bed, tucking one end underneath the mattress and pulling out the side and folding it to make the neat hospital corner.

'Now you try.'

Evelyn mimicked her movements.

'No, no,' said Judith. 'You need to pull it tighter.' She took the sheet corner from Evelyn's hand and pulled it taut. 'See.'

Evelyn nodded and immediately moved up to the head of the bed to try herself. This time she made a much better fist of it and smiled with satisfaction.

'Thank you, Judith. I think I've got it.'

'Except you've tucked in both sheets,' said Judith tightly, irritated by her incompetence. 'The top you leave open so that you can get inside.'

Then to her surprise Evelyn began to laugh. 'I'm such a ninny! Honestly. No wonder Mummy and Mrs Dawtry think I'm so useless. It's because I am.' She laughed harder and Judith had to smile. It showed a touch of humility that she hadn't thought Evelyn was capable of and Judith felt a little chastened that she'd rushed to judge her. They'd both been pitched into a situation not of their making and they all had to get on and make the best of it. It wasn't Evelyn's fault that she came from a wealthy family and had never experienced any great tragedy in life.

'Well, hello,' came a voice from the open doorway and Judith recognised the girl from the train.

'Betty!' she said in surprise. 'I didn't expect to see you here.'

'Me neither. Got the surprise of my life when they said I was to be billeted here.' She looked round and her eyes brightened. 'This is all right, isn't it? Lawks, what luxury. My own bed.' With a cheerful grin, she slung her tatty kitbag onto the free bed. 'At home I have to share with my sister and she doesn't half fidget.'

'Betty, this is Evelyn,' said Judith, feeling a rare sense of being in the know. Normally she was the outsider looking in when everyone else knew each other.

In two quick strides, Evelyn crossed to Betty's bed and held out her hand.

'Evelyn Brooke-Edwards, pleased to meet you.'

'Betty Connors.' She took Evelyn's hand and dipped in a funny little curtsy as if Evelyn were royalty or something. Judith shook her head. She'd found it hard to get to grips with the English class system, and here she was, plumb in the middle. Neither one thing nor the other.

'Lawks, you're an officer.' Betty stared at the stripes on Evelyn's sleeves. 'Feel like I've gone up in the world. Never thought I'd be staying in this house.' She looked around the room. 'I remember when Ethel and Doris roomed up here. They were her Ladyship's dresser and parlourmaid.'

'You know the house?' asked Evelyn, sitting down on Betty's bed. 'Do tell.'

'Oh, yes,' said Betty, tossing her golden curls, which next to Evelyn's looked a lot brassier. 'I lived in the village nearly all my life, until I got posted to Mill Hill when I joined the ATS.' Her smile dimmed. 'I'm going to miss London. But I'm glad that I'm staying here and not at home.'

'Why?' asked Evelyn. 'The train to London only takes fifty minutes from Chalfont and Latimer.' Evelyn's eyes shone with mischief. 'And I've got a car.'

'You've got a car. Stone me.' Betty's eyes looked as if they might pop out of her head. 'Are you like a lady or something?'

'A something.' Evelyn's eyes twinkled. 'So tell us about the house.'

'It belonged to Lord Chesham. Lovely man but he moved out in 1940 and some Army corps moved in. They left in '42 and this lot moved in. He lives in another house not far outside the village now but he's hardly ever here. My Aunt Daisy is his housekeeper. That's how I know the place. As a kid when his Lordship was up in London I'd have free run of the place while my ma worked in the dairy, and then I...' She paused, her face tightening. 'Never thought I'd be living here and getting paid for it. It's all very exciting. Fancy having to sign the Official Secrets Act. Do you think we're going to be spies? Like Ilona Massey in *International Lady*. I loved that film. Basil Rathbone and George Brent were both marvellous.'

'Didn't the Colonel brief you?' asked Judith, still reeling from the extraordinary information he'd regaled her with but mindful of the instruction not to reveal what she was to be doing. She knew for a fact that this whirlwind blonde was not going to be translating secret conversations.

'I'm going to be typing. Reports and things. Sounds the same as my last posting, except I wasn't typing then. Just filing.' Her mouth twisted mournfully. 'And that is not going to win the war, is it? At least I've moved up in the world. What about you, Lady Evelyn? No disrespect, but this must be a bit of a comedown for you?'

Evelyn laughed. 'You have to be joking. My last billet was in a box room with three noisy boys next door, in an end-of-terrace railway cottage. And the most obnoxious commanding officer known to man. The Colonel seemed quite charming.'

'Scary,' said Betty. 'He kept saying how important it was not to talk to anyone about what we do here. I'm going to have to make something up for Ma and Jane and...' She dropped her head. 'So what time's dinner? I'm starving.'

Chapter Eight

Betty

Betty stretched, feeling as lazy and cosy as a cat, despite the slightly scratchy cotton sheets. She couldn't remember the last time she'd slept so well. It was heaven to be in a bed of her own and in a dorm of only three. At Mill Hill there'd been twenty-four of them arranged head to toe, with standard-issue horsehair pillows and biscuits, the Army mattresses of straw-packed cushions, which she could never get comfortable on. Sleeping on a real mattress again was a proper luxury.

While the other two women were sleeping she took a minute to peek around the room. Each of them had been given a small set of drawers that just fitted between the beds. The solitary wardrobe had been built into the space at the end of the room on the other side of the door, which meant you couldn't open the door and the wardrobe at the same time. On the opposite end wall, against which abutted the full length of Evelyn's bed, was a geometric-shaped bevel-edged mirror hanging from a chain which all three of them would have to share. It would be jolly difficult to do her hair at this distance; she hoped Evelyn wouldn't mind her stepping right up, next to her bed. She looked enviously at Evelyn's neat drawer top, tidily laid out. It had a beautifully embroidered vanity set, a silver-framed photograph of a young man, a bottle of perfume and what looked like a Stratton special-edition compact.

Betty sighed. Her own dresser would soon be covered in an untidy mess of hairnets, bobby pins, an ancient brush with a cracked back that had been her grandmother's, her one precious Cashmere Bouquet, orchid-red lipstick and a Yardley compact that she'd saved for several weeks to buy. She certainly couldn't afford Stratton, no matter how much she'd longed for one. Mind you, she didn't have a silver photo frame either, which she was quite grateful for. After yesterday she wasn't sure she wanted a picture of Bert by her bed. Who, she wondered, was the man in Evelyn's picture? Boyfriend? Brother?

She turned her attention to Judith's bed. The top of the drawers was barren except for a battered leather envelope handbag. There were no other clues as to Judith's background or identity. Her suitcase was pushed under the bed and she'd unpacked nothing but her uniform, which went in the wardrobe, and underwear, which had all been hurriedly put into the drawers. Compared to Evelyn, Judith seemed to own almost nothing. The only glimpse into her personality had been a large bundle of gorgeous cherry-red wool and a pair of knitting needles.

Bored with her perusal of her neighbours and tempted by the sun streaming in through the dormer window, she crept out of bed to look at the view. Although she'd grown up in the Chess Valley and had longed through her teenage years to escape, she had to admit that the river this morning, with the early mist creeping across the meadows, was rather beautiful. Pulling on an old hand-me-down cardigan of her late grandmother's over her nightie, she took her cigarettes out of her handbag and quietly opened the window, taking a quick peep at Judith, who was sound asleep curled in a ball like a small brown mouse. Betty smiled to herself. What a set-up! Who'd have thought it, here she was with Lady Evelyn, as she already nicknamed her, and Timid Town Mouse.

Climbing out onto the roof, she took a good lungful of clean, crisp air and acknowledged with a rueful nod that it was a relief to not taste cordite and ash in the air. Despite what she'd told her ma, Mill Hill saw plenty of bombs. Just three weeks ago the barracks had had a near miss. Betty gave a little shudder. Lawks, that one had been a bit too close for comfort. She'd been picking glass out of her hair for days and it started up the nightmares again about Barbara Clarke's face. Their vivid images had also helped change her mind and made her ask for a transfer nearer to home. If something like that ever happened to her, she'd die. Imagine not being pretty anymore. She'd have asked a lot earlier if she'd realised that she could live in. This was a proper result. Far enough away to keep her independence and close enough to keep an eye on things at home and put an end to her ma's nagging.

She inched a cigarette out of the packet and lit up, taking a long slow drag and watching the smoke curl up into the morning sky. There was something to be said for being alone with your thoughts on a quiet morning. It was peaceful here. Her mouth twisted with a wry smile. Gave her time to think, although her thoughts weren't comfortable ones. Her ma was keen for her to wed Bert and not so long ago it would have seemed like the best option. After all, there weren't that many choices in the village, but joining the ATS had given her fresh eyes. Meeting lots of other girls and enjoying the company of women had made her start to think differently. She might not be as good as someone like Evelyn but she was worth something. The way Bert treated her, like she was less than him, wasn't right anymore.

'Morning,' drawled the proper BBC announcer voice of Lady Evelyn as she shimmied through the window, her slender form encased in the most gorgeous camiknickers and vest that Betty had ever seen.

'Is that real silk?'

Evelyn grinned. She seemed to do that a lot. 'Yes. Mummy bought it in Paris before the war. It's a few seasons old, of course.'

'Of course,' said Betty gravely, her mouth twitching ever so slightly.

Evelyn looked at her and threw back her head and laughed. 'Listen to me. I don't actually care. That's Mummy's thing. She does like to be up to date… Have you got a spare one of those? Mine are in my trunk, which is still in the car. I couldn't face lugging it up all the stairs yesterday.'

'Sure.' Betty offered her the pack and matches. They smoked in companionable silence.

'Where do you think the prisoners are?' asked Evelyn, peering over the battlements.

'What prisoners?' Betty stared at her.

Evelyn coloured up and bit her lip. 'I imagined this was a castle, with the battlements.'

Betty wasn't stupid but the other woman looked so uncomfortable, she wasn't going to press her. Instead she said, 'I thought this was a distribution centre. That's what everyone in the village says. They're all hoping a few fags or bottles of gin will fall off the back of a lorry on one of the lanes.'

Evelyn recovered, ignored the question and stubbed out her cigarette. 'I think we ought to head to breakfast. I've got my first briefing this morning.'

'My shift starts at eight.' Despite her words, her brain was elsewhere. Why had Evelyn clammed up? What was going on at this place? She'd wondered yesterday when she'd signed the Official Secrets Act. What was so secret about sending boxes all over the country? As far as she was concerned it sounded like there was probably going to be a lot of paperwork involved and she hoped she'd be working with some fun people, otherwise this place was going to get old very soon.

By the time they clambered back through the window, Judith was up and dressed, having used the bathroom down the corridor, which, to their shared delight, seemed to be theirs alone.

'Honest, it's like staying in a hotel,' said Betty, thinking of the cold, damp outhouse at home and washing in the tin bath in front of the fire, having to share the water with Ma and Jane.

Evelyn raised one of her elegant eyebrows. 'Not The Ritz, I promise you.'

'You've stayed at The Ritz? Oh my. How was that? Were the sheets silk? Did you drink champagne?'

'I've only had tea in the Palm Court, but it was rather sumptuous.'

As Betty pestered her for details, she noticed Judith's face darkening. She might be a timid town mouse but she was also a bit of a misery.

'What's that?' asked Evelyn, suddenly as alert as a cat spotting prey, her eyes bright and focused.

They all stilled. Betty's pulse thundered in her veins and

she put her hands up to her face as the drone of plane engines filtered in through the window. Like idiots, all three of them rushed towards the window, doing exactly what they'd been told countless times not to do.

Skirting the top of the hill, two planes, unmistakably German Junkers, flew across the sky, coming in low and fast, casting ominous shadows on the fields below. Betty's ATS handbook had taught her how to identify the different planes, both the enemy's and the RAF's.

'Get down!' shouted Evelyn and they all dropped to the floor, hands over their heads, rolling underneath the nearest beds.

Betty tensed, listening hard, waiting for an explosion; the engine noise was louder now. She held her breath, only gradually easing it out when she absolutely had to. Barbara Clarke's face, or what was left of it, filled her mind. She squashed her own face into the bare board under the bed, her arms cushioning either side as the musty smell of dust filled her nose.

The sound of the planes faded away, their persistent whine dulling until finally it was gone. For a moment none of them spoke, all lost in their own thoughts.

'Phew,' said Evelyn, rising to her feet and dusting down her skirt. 'Does that happen often here?'

Judith lifted her chin, her mouth wrinkling. It must be strange, thought Betty, knowing your countrymen were bombing you. She couldn't begin to imagine how it must feel.

'Annoying visitors,' said Betty, sounding braver than she felt. 'Those were heading north-west, away from London. Done their dirty work. We don't often see planes out this way. They're usually on their way to London or coming back. Sometimes you see the odd dog fight as the RAF boys see them off. But they're not interested in us.' She gave a small laugh. 'The village doesn't even know what we're doing here, so I can't see how the Germans would know.'

'True,' said Evelyn, already regaining her equilibrium. Betty envied her poise. 'I don't know about you chaps but a brush with adventure always makes me hungry. I'm ravenous.'

When they went downstairs to breakfast, they went their separate ways. Evelyn turned right at the bottom of the stairs and headed to what Betty knew had been a large drawing room in Lord Chesham's day, which was now the Officers' Mess. She and Judith turned back on themselves under the stairs to another set of stairs which certainly didn't have a fine red-and-gold carpet held in place with brass rods or elaborate carved and polished banisters. Instead the painted brick steps were framed by iron railings on one side and led to the enlisted mess down in the servants' kitchen. Crossing the familiar red quarry-tiled floor, Betty looked around. 'My Aunt Daisy used to sit at the head of the table just there,' she said, pointing to the end of the long battered wooden table, remembering how all the servants used to gather around it at meal times. 'She was the housekeeper here.'

Judith eyed her sombrely.

'What?' asked Betty a little impatiently. She didn't like the way the other woman made her feel; there was a touch of disapproval in the downward tilt of her mouth. Surely after yesterday on the train, Judith should feel more grateful towards her instead of being so guarded and reserved.

It took a moment for Judith to respond. 'It must be pleasant to know you belong.'

Betty snorted. 'I don't belong here. This is a house for posh folk.'

'Yes, but you know the house. You have memories here. You know the people. It's familiar.'

'Oh, I see what you mean. But it's also a bit boring. Being stuck in one place all your life.' She looked up and surprisingly spotted another familiar face. 'Elsie!'

'Well, hello, young Betty. What are you doing here?' Elsie beamed at her. Likewise, the Vicar's sister was the last person Betty expected to see, although she guessed Elsie had had plenty of experience of cooking for large numbers. She was always in charge of the children's Christmas party in the village hall and the lovely thing about her was that although she did a lot of good, she wasn't a do-gooder type. Despite being the Vicar's sister, she wasn't the least bit holier than thou.

'I thought you were with the ATS up in London? Mill Hill, I heard.'

'I was, but Ma wanted me closer so I managed to get a posting here.'

Elsie eyed her for a second before her face sharpened and she nodded. 'Probably a good idea.'

'And what are you doing here?'

'I fancied doing my bit. I wanted to sign up but I couldn't leave Frank. Poor man wouldn't cope.' She rolled dark eyes in her thin, angular face. *All arms and legs,* thought Betty. When she was younger, she'd likened Elsie to a scarecrow made out of broomsticks. Her sleeves were always too short and showed off a good few inches of skinny wrists, but for all that she was strong in body and character.

'My own fault. I brought it upon myself. But this way I'm

not at his beck and call all the time. It's good for him, even if he is the Vicar.' Her eyes twinkled. 'And who might you be?'

'Sorry, this is Judith. We're both starting today.'

'Well, sit yourselves down, grab a cuppa from the pot and I'll bring you some porridge, and help yourselves to toast. No butter today but there's jam. Everyone's a-twitter this morning with the excitement. Don't see many bombers out this way. I hope those poor buggers in London haven't copped it too much.' She shook her head and bustled off.

They sat down at the end one of the three long trestle tables lining the kitchen, where men and women in a variety of uniforms sat chatting and eating. It looked as if everyone knew each other and they were already in that settled routine of having their own friends and knowing their places. Betty sighed. She hated being the new girl again, having to work out who was friend or foe. At Mill Hill most of the girls had been sound but there were always a couple you had to watch.

Betty shook the thoughts away. It wouldn't be long before she'd worked out the pecking order. She reached for a teacup and the pot, noticing that Judith hung back. 'Want one?'

Judith nodded, her gaze busily darting around the high whitewashed walls of the room and glancing cautiously at the groups of people dotted along the tables. She really was so very reserved, and then Betty realised, with a jolt of awareness that made her feel guilty, the poor girl was a long way from home and in an environment that was probably very different from what she was used to.

'This is probably all a bit strange for you? How long have you lived in England?'

Judith shrugged. 'It's a new experience. I've been here a while, five years, but,' Betty saw her visibly swallow, 'it's always different. You never quite... I've never been in a big house like this before. Or lived in the country.'

'Where did you live?'

Judith gave her one of those guarded looks before she answered. 'Berlin.'

Betty realised that she wasn't so much timid as reserved.

'Gosh. I've never been anywhere except round here and London. I love watching the films set in America. Is it very different here? I can't imagine travelling to another country. I'd love to one day. It must be so romantic.'

'Betty,' said Elsie, appearing with two very small bowls of steaming porridge. 'You do rattle on.' She sounded unusually sharp and when Betty glanced up she was shaking her head slightly and her eyes were narrowed.

'Oh!' said Betty and turned to Judith, putting her hand on her arm. Judith flinched. 'I'm so sorry. What must you think of me? Prattling on about travel. I am an empty head.'

'It's all right,' said Judith stiffly, keeping her head down, focusing on her porridge.

Elsie gave Betty a chiding glance and disappeared back to the big oven. Now Betty felt even more of an idiot. There was only one thing for it; she kept talking.

'So, are you nervous?' she asked.

Judith's head lifted and there was a touch of contempt in her eyes. 'No. I'm looking forward to getting started. To helping with the war effort. To make a difference.'

'Yes.' Betty figured maybe the girl didn't have that great a command of English. Shifting boxes from one place to another didn't seem like it was going to help win the war. There were men out there fighting, losing their lives, and here they were responsible for shipping things, but she'd already put her foot in it once with Judith, so she decided that keeping quiet for once might be the best idea.

They ate in silence for the next ten minutes, Judith steadily ploughing through each mouthful with methodical, neat bites.

'Great jam, Elsie. Hides the taste of this awful bread. What I wouldn't give for a lovely white loaf instead of this wholegrain stuff. Where did you snaffle the jam from?'

Elsie beamed. 'William is still here. The garden's pretty big and he seems to have the fairies working for him. I've no idea where he gets the help but I had a bumper crop of strawberries, raspberries and gooseberries last year. I've got more beetroot than I know what to do with and I'll be shelling peas for the next few days, not to mention the spinach and new potatoes. I'll be pickling beets for the rest of the week. Not that I'm complaining, mind.'

Betty frowned. Labour was in short supply. Most of the men in the village had gone away to fight and William was on the wrong side of seventy to be doing all that work on his own. Who was helping him? The only land girls in the village worked on the Davenports' sheep farm.

'You'd best be off,' said Elsie, starting to clear the table.

'Good luck, Judith,' Betty said to the other woman, who was due to report to someone in the room next to the library, which had once been Lady Chesham's morning room.

'Thank you. And you.' Judith actually smiled.

Betty left, heading for the first floor, where a suite of bedrooms had been turned into offices, still puzzling over who was helping William.

'Welcome to Bedlam,' said a cheery ATS sergeant when Betty peeped round the door to a room filled with bustle. 'I'm Kate, Sergeant Phipps.'

'Betty, Private Connors.'

'Welcome aboard. I'll show you to your desk. You'll get to know everyone in time.'

Betty was pleased to see that her desk was beside one of the big stone-mullioned windows with a view out over the stable yard and the estate offices. There were ten other desks crammed into the room with barely room to move between them, and already uniformed ATS girls were busy typing with steady concentration at the large solid typewriters. Betty swallowed, watching the nearest girl firing her fingers over the keys. They were all very fast and clearly knew what they were doing. She flexed her hands, hoping that she could pick up speed quickly.

'Here you go. It's all very straightforward. The Wrens compile the translations, they're typed up, then they go to Naval Intelligence, who assess them, then they pass through those they want compiled into the reports, which come here. Once we've typed them up they're passed through to the office next door where they do the analysis and prepare the final report.'

'Reports?' asked Betty.

'Yes. They go on to the Admiralty.'

Betty wrinkled her nose. What was that about translations? But she didn't want to look stupid so she kept her mouth shut. She was beginning to think that perhaps Sergeant Phipps was right, she had come to Bedlam.

Just as she was about to sit down at her desk, a door on the opposite wall opened and a peal of laughter rang out as two ATS girls carrying sheaves of papers entered, along with a man in an American USAF uniform. The girls went over to a central desk and immediately began sorting through the papers.

'Well, hello, who have we here?' The American man sauntered, there was no other word for his rolling casual walk, over to her desk.

'Betty. Betty Connors, Sir,' she added hastily, staring up into the bluest eyes she'd ever seen, her heart flipping stupidly over in her chest. For a moment she was completely bowled over by how good-looking he was. He could have stepped straight out of a film. Even his uniform looked smarter than anyone else's in the room.

'Betty. That sure is a nice name. Anyone ever told you, you look a little like Betty Grable?' He gave her such a ridiculously suggestive, theatrical wink that she forgot to be starstruck.

'Lots of times,' she said cheerfully, completely forgetting he was a superior officer. 'It's not terribly original. You'll have try harder than that.'

He grinned. 'Be happy to, ma'am. Where did you spring from?'

'That's for me to know and you to find out,' said Betty, slipping smartly behind the desk and sitting down, looking up at him through her lashes. He laughed.

'I like a gal with a smart mouth,' he said, looking very deliberately at her mouth and making her very glad that she'd used her favourite lipstick this morning as a confidence boost for her first day. There was something about the way he looked at her that made her feel a little tight and fizzy inside.

She couldn't help herself looking right back at his full lips and wondering what it would be like if he kissed her. Which was darned odd. Whenever she could, she avoided kissing Bert like the plague; she didn't like it very much. So, why, now, was her imagination picturing her in the arms of this man, being soundly kissed by that very mouth, when she didn't even know his name?

Suddenly, as if he remembered where he was, he stood up straight. 'Major Carl Wendermeyer, at your service, ma'am. Welcome to the unit.'

'Thank you, Sir,' she said, realising that playtime was over as he walked over to the Sergeant in the corner to confer with him. Feeling a little foolish and determined not to look at him again, which was difficult because her eyes seemed to have a life of their own, she eyed the monster of a typewriter and hesitantly lifted one finger to pick at a key. Around her the noisy room was filled with the clack of typewriter keys. The very speedy clack of typewriter keys. She chewed anxiously at her lip and taking a deep breath, she sat up straight and prepared herself a bit like the organ players she'd seen at the cinema. It was all very well telling people she could type, having practised on that bit of cardboard, but she'd not touched a real typewriter for three years. Ironic really. Not since the last time she'd been in this house. She took a quick peek around; no one seemed to be paying any attention to her, well, apart from Carl whose eyes slid away as soon as she glanced his way.

She eased out a breath and looked out of the window, trying to summon up the courage to get started. As soon as she did they'd know she was a fraud. For a moment she frowned and then sharpened her gaze. Through the trees she could see what looked like a gun or a watchtower that had never been there before. She stared harder. Was that an armed soldier at the top? Puzzled, she looked down at the stable yard. Heavy metal doors had replaced the open-topped wooden stable doors and there were bars at the window. Then as she watched she saw two Army privates march into the yard bearing rifles.

It dawned on her that none of the military personnel she'd seen in the house bore arms. Curious now, she saw them approach one of the old stables. Her eyes very nearly popped out of her head when one of the soldiers emerged escorting another man. A German! In a Luftwaffe uniform. She'd seen enough Pathé newsreels to identify the foreign uniform. What was he doing here? Had a plane come down recently? Surely not, it would have been the talk of the village, and if it was in the last twenty-four hours, wouldn't Elsie have mentioned it at breakfast?

She watched, holding her breath, as the three men crossed the stable yard, the German in the middle – seeming quite happy to walk with them, in fact it looked as if he were chatting to the two guards – and headed towards one of several newly built prefab blocks.

Now she really was mystified. She picked up the paper on her desk and read the neat script, wondering if it might shed any further light on what was going on here.

Interview with A1332.

Conducted by Naval Intelligence, Lieutenant F. R. Wesley.

Airman A1332, a bomber gunner with the Luftwaffe, described the remotely controlled gun-turret system on the Messerschmitt Bf 109. There was also talk of prototypes which utilise four MG 131 for a quadmount system for tail defence.

Betty read on, the furrow between her eyes deepening. She picked up the second and third sheet, skimming their contents quickly.

What on earth was going on at Latimer House?

Chapter Nine

Evelyn

Evelyn slipped into a seat next to a girl she'd met over breakfast, Lieutenant Bradley. There was an expectant hush in the air in the elegant dining room as she studied the faded patches on the dark-red walls where family paintings must have once hung. The long glossy mahogany table and plush velvet chairs looked as if they belonged to the house, unlike the utilitarian filing cabinets lining one of the walls next to the beautiful gothic-style stone fireplace, which were like upstart invaders with their flat grey finish contrasting with the rich, warm wood of the panelled walls. Around the table everyone looked alert and ready for action as if they enjoyed their work. It made a very pleasant change after her tenure in Falmouth beneath Williamson, who had not commanded a happy ship. She sipped at her coffee, listening to the lively conversation around her, which seemed principally to be about whether there would be a dance at RAF Bovingdon later in the summer, now that the American Air Force had taken over the site.

Everyone fell silent when the door opened and Colonel Myers, accompanied by two other senior Army officers, entered the room. They all rose to their feet and saluted.

'At ease,' said Myers in a loud commanding voice and took his cap off, before pulling out a chair. The other two officers sat down on either side.

'This morning's schedule. Andrews and Bradley, you'll take W2335 in interview room 2. He's feeling a bit homesick. Needs a bit of mollycoddling. Bradley, be gentle with him.'

There was a laugh around the room. 'If you can, steer him back to Gafsa, Tunisia. Find out what he knows about any defensive positions there.'

Evelyn listened avidly as the man on the right of Myers then made some suggestions as to how to treat the prisoner and his current mental state, and Andrews and Bradley took copious notes.

'That's Lieutenant Colonel Weston,' muttered Bradley as she scribbled away, 'psychologist with the RAMC. He advises us on the best way to approach each interview.'

Evelyn nodded gratefully. The meeting continued at a rapid-fire pace and Evelyn realised that the workload was significant. She herself was allocated several interviews before lunch, thankfully with a much more experienced officer, and clear guidance and direction from Weston as to how they were to take things.

The meeting drew to a close and everyone looked as eager as a hare in spring to be off.

Myers stood up and then looked at Evelyn. 'And welcome to our latest recruit, Lieutenant Brooke-Edwards. We'll look forward to introducing you properly over gin cocktails in the Officers' Mess this evening. Six o'clock sharp.'

There was a collection of nods her way but everyone seemed more anxious to gather their notes and disappear, apart from an officer with a shock of thick dark hair that looked as if no amount of brilliantine would ever tame it, and warm brown eyes, which crinkled into a happy smile. He looked rather familiar.

'Lieutenant Brooke-Edwards, Lieutenant Frederickson. Your partner in crime for the day. I'll be showing you the ropes.' The broad-shouldered man with a wicked dimple held out his hand, grinning at her. 'Nice to see you, Evelyn.'

She gasped. 'Freddie. I didn't even notice you. Oh, my goodness.' She beamed at him, delighted to see a friendly face. 'Gosh, I haven't seen you since Oxford days. How are you?'

'Excellent and all the better for seeing you. Although I'm sorry to hear about David. Heard from him recently?'

She shook her head, her smile dimming. 'No, not for a while but the post is so bad and we'd get a telegram if it were bad news, I'm sure.' She'd been telling herself this for weeks now but it was starting to wear thin. Why hadn't they heard from him? Pain pinched at her heart. *Please let him be all right.*

He winced. 'Did you hear about Henry?'

'He joined the RAF, didn't he?'

Freddie's face tightened and he didn't need to say anymore. Evelyn laid a hand on his shoulder. 'Oh, I'm so sorry.'

Henry had been Freddie's best friend at Oxford; they'd both been at Balliol. She saw Freddie's Adam's apple dip and she gave him a moment. With a deep breath, he lifted his head and was able to say, shortly, 'Bought it on a mission and shot down over France... Right-ho, we'd best get off. Lots to do today. Some of these buggers like to drag it out. Interrogation gives 'em a change of scene from their cells. Got a couple of tricky sods on the list this afternoon.'

'How long do they stay here?'

'Depends on how good for gen they are, but usually not more than a couple of weeks and then they're shipped out elsewhere. Only as long as they're useful, Myers likes to say.'

They left the main building by a set of doors at the back of the house on the western side, following a path which was very quickly blocked by a tall fence, topped by barbed wire and manned by armed guards. Evelyn was introduced to the guards and had to show the pass which had been issued upon her arrival. For the first time, she realised that security was tight and guards were positioned around the perimeter of the site. Through the trees she could now see a watchtower manned by more armed soldiers. This was a prison. A small shudder ran through her as her stomach knotted at the thought of conducting a face-to-face interrogation.

She started when Freddie, as if reading her mind, asked, 'Done much of this sort of thing before?'

As they walked at a brisk pace along the path Evelyn told him about her work in Falmouth.

'Sounds like you were one step away from fishing the poor buggers out of the sea,' commented Freddie, making her laugh. 'But you've experience of meeting POWs face to face, which is good. Some people are a bit daunted. Not sure what to expect.'

Evelyn chose her words carefully, keen to hide her nerves, and because she wasn't sure what the prevailing attitude to the prisoners was here. 'They're men with families back home that have left a life behind them to fight a common enemy. Some are bitter and resentful or resigned and prepared to make the best of it, others surprisingly keen to co-operate. I've seen all sorts, although admittedly that's when they've been at their lowest ebb. A lot of them were scared and disorientated because they'd been captured by the enemy and had no idea what to expect, which was a huge psychological barrier to overcome. I imagine here they're perhaps a bit more settled and accepting of their situation.'

'Hmm, not always. Sometimes they've had time to regroup and get bolshy. To be honest it's like anything in life, they're all different. You never know what to expect with a new chap. We've got a couple of unknown quantities this morning and this afternoon are all old favourites. This will be a last hurrah for them, throwing you into the interrogation to shake things up. If nothing comes of it, they'll be shipped off to a POW camp proper. Won't be as cushy as here, that's for sure.'

'Is it cushy?'

'Two to a cell. I'd say so. A lot of the personnel here are crammed into Nissen huts.'

As they crossed a courtyard and skirted around some of the blocks at the back of the house, she recognised the signs of a walled garden, a lot bigger than the one at Quartiles, and a stable block. All the while Freddie kept up an entertaining stream of chatter. 'Did you ever know Dilly Fortescue? You did? Well, her sister, Pamela, was the redhead at the briefing. And remember Alasdair Spencer? His cousins are both Naval Intelligence; you'll meet them tonight, along with Katherine Ruddings, who was at Oxford the year before you. She's related to the Buckinghams in Henley.'

'Oh, I saw Gracie Buckingham when I was home last week,' said Evelyn. Compared to her last posting, this all sounded rather jolly. She rather thought she was going to enjoy herself here.

The purpose-built block they entered was split into a number of offices along with one long and separate corridor of six rooms, all of which had a pair of armed guards standing outside the heavy doors. As soon as she stepped inside Evelyn's mood turned sombre, matching the grey-painted cement-block walls and flooring. This was to all intents and purposes a prison and the men they were to question were the enemy. She surreptitiously wiped her hands down her Navy skirt and wished she dared check her notes again. Their instructions were to leave all notes outside the interview room. The aim was to make the interactions as informal as possible, which, according to the strategy, made the prisoners feel more relaxed. Each officer was armed with additional packets of cigarettes which they were encouraged to offer.

Freddie glanced down at her. 'Chocks away. Don't worry. Follow my lead.'

As it was her first interview here, she was quite happy to do just that, but, she thought as she eyed his back, following him down the corridor, she knew her job and knew that she was damned good at it. Part of her skill was building rapport with people and Freddie needn't think she'd be playing apprentice to him for long.

He opened the door to interview room no. 5 which was flanked by two serious-faced Army privates. Inside a German *Hauptman* sat at a table looking ill at ease in his uniform. In her last role Evelyn had had to learn all the different insignia that appeared on uniform sleeves and shoulders, so that she could identify at a glance what rank someone was. This man was the equivalent of a British Captain in the Army and a Flight

Lieutenant in the RAF. Pale and hunched, there were dark-purple shadows under each reddened eye and a large swelling on his forehead. His bloodshot eyes darted anxiously from her to Freddie as they entered and he seemed to shrink in his seat and cradle the arm that was held in a sling. She could almost smell his fear. The Gestapo were renowned for their interrogation and torture techniques, particularly among their own people, something that played well into the hands of the British. German POWs assumed that a similar fate awaited them and lived in dread of this first interrogation. Those she'd come across before had been too relieved that they were still alive to worry about torture at that stage, but this poor man had had time to think about his position. Compassion as much as her job made her give him a reassuring smile.

'*Guten Morgen,*' she said softly before Freddie had a chance to speak. The man looked up startled, wary now.

'I'm Lieutenant Brooke-Edwards, this is Lieutenant Frederickson.' She spoke in German and went on to ask him how he was feeling, what had happened to his arm and whether he needed any further medical attention for the bump on his head.

At first he answered with cautious, suspicious, monosyllabic replies but gradually he began to relax. Evelyn had done as much as she could in making him feel more at ease but now they needed to get down to work. They'd been tasked with trying to find out more about the capability of the aircraft that he'd been shot down with. Her knowledge of aircraft, weaponry and aerial tactics was minimal; she had a much greater understanding of U-boats, having been based in Falmouth.

This airman had had the foresight to burn his plane and its

papers before he was caught. Freddie took over and Evelyn listened intently. Freddie seemed to know an awful lot about the gun mountings on a Messerschmitt, about how many rounds the gun could fire. She was impressed and so it appeared was the airman, who conceded, 'You know everything.'

Freddie nodded and they carried on chatting about the plane's specifications, the issues with flying it and how the guns occasionally jammed if they overheated.

After a while Freddie's questions drew to a close and the airman, Captain Stadtler, accepted a cigarette and let out an audible sigh of relief. Evelyn knew that the interrogation was not over but the general questions about life in his own country were designed to find out about morale there and any useful facts that could be fed back to the teams responsible for sending propaganda back to Germany. He did let slip two potentially useful facts: one, that air defences in Berlin had been strengthened with additional flak towers and two, that non-essential citizens of the city were being evacuated.

Once the airman had finished smoking his cigarette, looking considerably relieved, Freddie started asking him more about the plane, flying formations and aerial tactics, all of which the airman refused to answer, with a genuine smile that accompanied his frequent 'I can't tell you that' responses. He almost sounded regretful. Finally after another half hour of fruitless questioning, Freddie nodded his head and said in German, 'I understand,' and leaned forward to shake the airman's hand, saying, 'We are officers and men of honour.'

Evelyn had to bite back a smile. This was all part of the strategy, building empathy with the prisoner, emphasising that they were equals and starting to create a working partnership.

He'd be questioned many times more while he was here but today they'd made a good start in building those bonds.

As they walked back to the main house for morning coffee, Evelyn took in a deep breath, relishing her freedom. Although the airman was safe and he would be well treated, he was still a prisoner and didn't have his liberty.

'Good job, there, Evelyn. Especially at the start. You read him perfectly.'

She turned quickly to face him to gauge his sincerity. 'You're not offended that I took the initiative?'

'Gracious, no. This job's all about acting on our instincts. You got it spot on.'

'Even though I'm a woman.' She thought about Williamson and his continual harassment of female officers.

Freddie laughed. 'I'm man enough to appreciate feminine skills and anyone who doesn't appreciate a fellow officer's contribution, no matter what their sex, will soon be booted out. Myers would see to that. He thinks women on the team are our greatest asset and I'm inclined to agree. That poor bugger was shit scared. You put him at his ease with that lovely smile of yours.'

She rolled her eyes. 'Freddie!' It bothered her that men automatically assumed she used her looks deliberately. She'd harboured genuine compassion for the man. Not so many years ago she might have brushed shoulders with him in a market in Germany, been to a party with his sister or sat opposite his mother on a train.

'Just joking, but it worked.'

'It must be terrifying, don't you think? To be in a strange country and not know what is going to happen to you.' As she said it, she suddenly thought of Judith and it struck her how brave the other woman was and how much she must have been through to leave her own country. What had happened to her family? She remembered vividly the awful atmosphere of Munich when she'd been there in the summer of 1937, the jackbooted thugs that had marched around the market square demanding that people salute them. It had been bad for Jews then; how much worse must it have got?

'Yes,' said Freddie in response, his cheerful face sobering immediately. 'You hear some tales. Especially about what the Gestapo get up to in occupied Europe. I heard that they strung one poor bastard up by his wrists until his shoulders dislocated. And that's nothing. They're not averse to bringing family members and torturing them in front of a prisoner. That's what they do to the resistance fighters over in France, or go out and shoot a whole village.'

Evelyn shuddered. 'The things men do in the name of war. Did you get much out of him? And how did you know so much about machine-gun mounts in that particular plane?'

Freddie laughed. 'I was primed with it. Information from another interrogation. It all builds up into a picture. You tell them enough to make them assume you know it all and then they let slip something because they think you already know it.'

'Did it work?'

'Not this time but … we'll see him again. The next one should be interesting, he's a telegrapher picked up out of the sea. Only two survivors from his sub. The Admiralty are desperate to know more about how those bloody U-boats communicate. Those wolf packs have been too darn successful. We desperately need to turn the tide.'

Over coffee in the Officers' Mess, which really was a lovely room, Evelyn was introduced to a few more people, many of whom she found she had some connection with. As promised, Freddie introduced her to Katherine Ruddings.

'Kathy, this is Evelyn. She knows Gracie.'

'Hello,' said Evelyn.

'How the devil do you know my cousin Gracie?'

'I live just outside Henley, Binfield Heath. My parents, Lavinia and Geoffrey, are great friends with Gracie's parents.'

'Oh lord, I've met Lavinia a dozen times. I practically lived at their place when I was on summer vac at Oxford.'

'I remember you,' said Evelyn, a memory suddenly clicking into place. 'Gracie, my brother David, you and two of David's friends went out in a rowing boat and we went to Remenham.'

'Gosh yes. And that idiot boy, Francis, nearly capsized us all.'

Evelyn laughed. 'He's still an idiot. How they let him into the RAF I'll never know.' She hoped he was still an idiot and still flying. For a moment both of them went quiet.

'Sorry to hear about your brother,' said Katherine.

Evelyn shrugged. 'At least he's alive.'

'Yes, there is that.'

They began chatting about their time at Oxford, discovering more mutual friends and acquaintances. In some ways, Britain was such a small world and yet it was standing firm against the combined resources of the rest of Europe. Evelyn was grateful when the talk turned towards London and what was on at the theatre and how Katherine planned to spend her off-duty time in the next week.

'I hear you have a car,' she suddenly said. 'That's jolly handy.'

'Only if I can get petrol rations.'

Katherine laughed. 'That's easy, you put yourself at the

Colonel's disposal to do the run to the station when you're not on shift. Your car will impress visiting bigwigs.'

'Do we get many visiting bigwigs?'

'You're kidding. Now we're getting more POWs of interest, the Admiralty are really taking notice. Winnie loves us. Two weeks ago we had a bunch of American bigwigs visiting. Myers was strutting around afterwards like a peacock. Actually that not's true, he's not the sort, but you could tell he was pretty chuffed. Right-ho, look at the time. Better get back to the grindstone.' Katherine knocked back her coffee and said, 'TTFN,' before bounding off like a big overgrown puppy.

Freddie reappeared at her side. 'Lord, she's exhausting, that one. Demon tennis player, though. If you can get her on your doubles team it's marvellous because you can sit back and let her do the work.'

Evelyn laughed. 'Don't give me that. I remember you being a demon tennis player.'

'You were pretty handy yourself. We'll have to get a mixed doubles set going.'

'They've got courts here?'

'Yes, and extremely well maintained. William the gardener often uses willing prisoners to help roll the grass.'

'Is that allowed? I thought officers didn't have to work.'

'They don't but they get bored and fed up with being cooped up, so they volunteer to help in the garden or in the grounds. Why do you think we're so well fed here?'

Evelyn smiled, thinking of Hodges at home. 'That explains it. Our gardener does a great job but he's on his own. He has me digging potatoes when I go home.'

'Tough luck.' He gave her slender form a quick, cursory inspection, like most men underestimating her wiry strength. Typical man, he could appreciate that she could serve and rally in a tennis match but it didn't occur to him that she could wield a garden fork with the best of them.

Evelyn shook her head. 'It's that or knitting and believe me, that really is a recipe for disaster.'

Freddie was still teasing her about her lack of domestic skills as they headed back through the barbed-wire fencing to their next interrogation.

Chapter Ten

Judith

The room was so quiet, it made her want to creep in and hope that no one would notice her, but nearly everyone was wearing headphones and listening with intent expressions on their faces, so she guessed they wouldn't hear the scratch of her shoes on the hard concrete floor.

Sergeant Flesch, a chatty man who'd apparently lived his whole life in Dortmund before escaping with his wife to live with relatives in Rye, wherever that was, had met her and escorted her down to the basement of the house, leading her to one of the tables. As she slid into her seat, one of the other men, listening almost trance-like to something on his headphones, nodded absently to her.

'This will be your regular station,' said Sergeant Flesch and proceeded to explain to her in his friendly, helpful manner, how to operate the complicated-looking switchboard in front of her. He was clearly a man who enjoyed his work and it gave her a sense of confidence. 'Walther is your team leader. A good man. He'll be able to help with anything and he'll brief you on today's operation. Ask him anything you need to know.' With that he turned and left, closing the big heavy door behind him. The room, Judith observed to herself, could have doubled as a prison cell. There were no windows and the low ceiling made it feel slightly claustrophobic. Whitewashed walls along with the slight dampness to the air added to the overall dingy aspect, although someone had tried to alleviate the cold with paraffin heaters in two corners of the room which gave off their own distinct smell. Despite the slightly depressing atmosphere there was an air of intense concentration like a roomful of chess players all working out their next move.

Anxiously she tried to remember everything the sergeant said, but there was so much to remember that when he left she wasn't even sure which socket to plug her headphones into. It was one of two, but which one? She dithered for a moment, her hand shaking slightly as she raised it.

'This one,' said the man who'd nodded to her, who'd put down his earphones and come to stand at her shoulder.

'*Danke schön*,' said Judith, embarrassed now. He must think she was incredibly stupid.

To her relief he replied kindly, in German, 'It takes a little while to understand how everything works.'

'I hope so.' She cast an anxious look around the room; everyone else looked calm and confident.

'Don't worry,' he said, smiling. 'You will soon get used to everything. Ask me if you need to know anything. I'm Walther Spier.'

Giving him a half-hearted smile, she lifted her headphones from the table and he plugged the socket in for her.

'This switch to listen in. If there is nothing of interest or it's general chatter, you can swap to a different network by plugging into a new socket and pressing this switch. You are monitoring three different cells. You'll get to know the voices quite quickly if you have a good ear. Do you like music?'

She frowned, surprised by the question but there was a warmth in his eyes as he regarded her that made her say, 'Very much.'

'Excellent. We musical types are much better at this work.' He winked and she smiled back at him, feeling the stirrings of a sense of kinship. It felt like he was someone she had something in common with. 'You've been assigned Luftwaffe officers. I believe you have some technical knowledge.'

Judith widened her eyes, worried that her expertise had been overstated. 'I worked in a factory. That is all.'

'Don't worry, you'll become an expert very quickly here. If they mention anything that you feel is important, you have to choose whether to make a recording. If they talk about atrocities, you must record it.'

'Atrocities?' Judith lifted her head and stared at him.

'Murder. Executions. Massacres. Anything like that.' His mouth firmed in a grim line and he went back to his seat.

She put on her headphones, praying that she wouldn't have to record anything today. With an unsteady hand she flipped the switch and began to listen to the two men. It felt very odd to eavesdrop on their conversation when she had no idea of what either man looked like or the surroundings they found themselves in.

One of the men had had a letter from his wife whom he missed very much. He hadn't seen her for four months. The other man asked questions about what part of Germany he was from, where his wife was from.

They chatted generally about their backgrounds before the first man began to read out excerpts from the letter, detailing the activities of friends and neighbours and celebrating the birth of a new calf. Both bemoaned the fact that they were so far from home and had no idea when they would see their loved ones again.

Good, thought Judith, a flood of vicious satisfaction streaking through her veins. They deserved to be locked up. These were men fighting for Hitler, supporting a regime which had destroyed her way of life and killed her father. They were still alive. She held not a scrap of sympathy for either of them.

She continued for a little longer but neither had much of interest to say. Feeling a little more confident, she unplugged the earphone and put the socket into the next slot, pressing the switch to open the line.

This time the conversation was a little more interesting; the men were having a heated debate as to whether the Russians were more to worry about than the British and American forces and which they considered more efficient.

'By the rations we've had here, I'd say the British aren't suffering at all,' said one of them. 'When was the last time you had food as good as this? And we're prisoners. Imagine how the British are eating.'

Judith scowled, remembering Elsie and Betty's conversation this morning. She couldn't believe that they were sharing the produce with prisoners. Surely they should be on minimum rations. The point of her pencil snapped off and she sucked in an angry breath at the injustice of it all. She yanked out the socket and moved it to listen to the third and final cell. There was no reward there either. Neither man spoke very much; all she could hear was an odd tapping. She listened for a good ten minutes, hearing the taps and then the much louder sound of small pieces rattling together. Then one of the men said, 'Another game?' and she realised that she'd been listening to the pair of them playing backgammon or draughts.

This didn't feel like punishment to her. By the time they broke for lunch she thought she might explode.

Back in the Mess, she sat on her own, her hands almost shaking with impotent rage. Betty was further down the table with a group of ATS women and had gaily waved as if they were at a tea party. Judith pretended not to see her and found a solitary spot at the second table. Although she was grateful that Betty had helped her on the train, the girl talked of nothing but films and movie stars. Her comments at breakfast had compounded Judith's view of her. She knew nothing of music or art. Judith missed those things with a physical ache and longed for the solace and soul-soaring joy that music had once brought her. The grief at what she'd lost washed over her again. It was wrong to take that grief out on Betty but she needed an outlet for the ache and dissatisfaction that churned in her soul.

She'd got used to life being unfair, to things being tough – the coldness of the barracks in Hull, the thin blankets, the poor food rations and generally miserable conditions – but at least other people were suffering alongside her, the thin, hungry population in the streets, bent like wind-whipped trees, as drawn and downtrodden by war as she was. So it was all the more shocking that the prisoners here had such an easy life. Prisoners should be enduring more deprivation, they should be hurting, not playing board games and eating freshly grown food.

'Hello, how was your first morning?' Walther slid into the empty seat beside her.

'Good,' she said stiffly.

He raised an eyebrow and looked pointedly at her hands clenched around the tea cup as if she might crush it at any second.

She turned and narrowed her eyes. 'Doesn't it bother you?' she asked in a furious whisper, conscious that there were other people around. The last thing she wanted was to draw attention to herself.

He gave her a solemn smile. 'No.'

'Well, it should,' she hissed.

'And how would that help anything?' His voice was gentle and his gaze calm.

Staring back at him, she hunched into her chair, her emotions too churned up to articulate.

'Why don't you come for a walk with me? It's a beautiful day and we have half an hour before we have to go back.'

Judith was about to refuse but she saw something in his face that made her quietly acquiesce and she stood up.

He led the way out of the house through the front door and round to the front façade of the house, skirting the balustraded terrace and guiding her to the flight of steps leading down into the extensive gardens which went as far as the river several hundred yards away.

'This is a beautiful part of the world. I love the British countryside. One day I'd like to visit Scotland. Have you ever been?'

Judith shook her head.

'Where were you before?'

'I was in Hull. By the sea. It wasn't like this.' She waved a hand and had to admit to herself that after the cold grey of the barracks near the dockyard, this was a significant improvement.

Walther didn't say anything, instead he tipped his head slightly to one side, his eyes half-closed, as if he were listening intently, and a faint smile on his face.

She waited for him to move but he seemed quite content to stand perfectly still, so she took the time to look around her. Now as she took in the sights, the smells and the sounds, she realised, it was indeed beautiful and a little peace stole into her heart as she tipped her face up to the warm spring sunshine, aware of the bird song in the trees and the rush of the river.

Walther straightened. 'Come,' he said and began to walk. She fell into step beside him but now her gaze darted about, looking this way and that, with an eagerness that was new to her, spotting the primroses peeping through the grass, the ripples over the river dancing in the sunshine and the flock of starlings wheeling overhead against a backdrop of blue sky and shape-shifting white clouds. From the woods on the other side of the house, she could hear the distant coo of birds in the trees and the baa of plump leggy lambs from the fields on the opposite bank of the river.

They walked in silence, following the path of the river, and the tension in her neck and shoulders started to dissipate. After ten minutes without looking at her, Walther asked, 'Feeling better?'

'Yes,' she said quietly, feeling rather embarrassed. It was unlike her to let her anger and grief spill over. Normally it was kept tightly bound. It was easier that way, tucked out of reach so that she couldn't give in to it. She often thought of it as a physical burden dogging her that had to be strictly controlled, otherwise it would overwhelm her. It was why she shunned the overtures of people like Betty. If she let her guard down and they found a way in, she might feel again. Feel the pain of all that had gone. Could she afford to do that? Was friendship worth the risk?

'I understand. I found it difficult when I first came here.'

She looked at his face and saw he understood the emotions warring inside her. For the first time since she'd come to England, she didn't feel quite so alone.

'You're angry at the injustice of it.'

With relief she nodded. 'It seems so wrong. These prisoners of war, their war is over, they are being fed and looked after. Playing games. Where is the hardship? The suffering?' She wrung her hands.

'They are fellow men. Would you have them suffer?'

She winced and said in a small voice, 'Yes,' and risked a guilty look at Walther's face to gauge his reaction. To her relief his gentle smile was understanding.

'But would you be the one to inflict the suffering?' The question took her by surprise. 'Would you be the one to twist the knife? By your own hand.'

She swallowed, remembering the commandments. Although she was no longer particularly religious, it was hard to forget the principles that had been bred into her from birth. She wasn't a violent person.

'Would you become what our persecutors are?'

Remembering the brutality and violence of the Gestapo and the SS, she flinched. *Do not commit murder.*

'Would you allow what they have done to change you?'

Shame flooded her. This wasn't her way at all. *Honour your mother and father.* Her father had been a gentle, forgiving man who believed in the good of others.

'God will be our judge.' Walther's dark eyes bored into

hers, there were lines around his eyes that spoke of his own suffering. 'He will be their judge too.'

The words held quiet resonance, their meaning seeping into her like balm. It had been a while since she'd been to a synagogue or heard such wise words. Her soul had been left untended since her father had died. She'd allowed bitterness to twist her spirit, grief to dull her senses and loneliness to disconnect her from others.

Tears began to run down her face. There was an ache in her heart, she missed him so much.

Walther took her hand and squeezed it.

'I'm sorry,' she apologised, wiping at her face, trying to stem her tears, but now they'd been released they seemed to be overflowing like an unruly river that had burst its banks.

'Don't be. Grief is a heavy burden to bear. You are not alone here. I know what it is like to be dispossessed, to be stateless, to lose everything.'

'Where did you live?'

'In Munich. My family lost their business. It was taken over.' He clicked his fingers. 'Just like that. My mother was beaten in the street. She died a few weeks later and my father died not long after that. My sisters were able to obtain permits to go to Palestine. I was able to gain a work permit to come here. What about you?'

'I'm sorry for your loss. That's…' It was hard to speak but it was a reminder that others had lost as much, if not more, than her. How did you measure such things? 'My father had a heart attack after his shop in Berlin was ransacked during *Kristallnacht*. They destroyed his life's work. He died a week later. It was always just the two of us. My mother died when I was a baby. My aunt died, thankfully, before Hitler came to power. I'm glad of that, she was a character, a forceful woman who wouldn't have been quiet. Not like me and my father. My father had made plans for me to get away.' She swallowed. 'On my own. He knew he would never leave and then it was too late. And now I have nothing. My family is all gone. Friends vanished in the night. I don't know where they went. I can't even visit their graves.'

He squeezed her hand again. 'I'm sure your father would not want you to lose yourself in bitterness. That allows them to win. Being human, living again, it is the proof that we cannot be defeated.'

'I like that thought,' she said. It sparked a kernel of hope inside her.

'We must look forward now and our work here will help. I truly believe that. Whatever we can do to bring the war to an end must be of value. And I'm afraid we must go back to our little dungeon.'

'Thank you, Walther. You've made me feel much better.'

'It's not so hard to talk to a beautiful girl.' Suddenly his face was transformed and he gave her a cheeky wink.

She laughed, feeling a rare sense of freedom. 'I haven't been a girl for a long time.' And no one had ever called her beautiful, and even though she was sure he'd said it to cheer her up, it had done the trick and her spirits lifted.

They turned and retraced their steps. Judith smiled and looked towards the house up at the battlement roof where her room was. Walther was right, their work here would help and she would try to make sure she did her absolute best. She would work hard and get to know her fellow workers. Like Walther said, many of them had experienced what she'd been through. She might even make some friends here.

Chapter Eleven

MAY 1943

Betty

'Connors.'

Betty lifted her head from her work where she was trying to decipher the crabbed handwriting that crawled across the page like a delinquent spider. It was her third week in the office and she knew this particular sergeant was one to be wary of.

'Yes, Ma'am.'

'Haven't you finished yet?'

'No, Ma'am.' Betty tried to smile and look confident, even though she knew her typing wasn't anywhere near as quick as the other girls in the room.

'Hmm,' said the sergeant, looking at the stack of paper in her hand. 'You need to get a move on. This lot needs to be done before you finish your shift.'

'Yes, Ma'am.' She was proud of her acting skills, managing to sound perky even while her heart sank as the sergeant handed over the stack of paper.

Addressing the typewriter, which had become her mortal enemy, she began to type again, concentrating hard. Not that it made an awful lot of difference. By the time the others left at the end of the shift, she still had a good pile of transcripts to type up. Her wrists ached as she looked longingly at the clock, but the urgency and the rate at which everyone else worked had infected her. She knew this was important work, so she carried on even though it was nearing dinner time in the Mess. She'd asked one of the other ATS privates to ask Elsie to keep something for her.

An hour later she was on her penultimate transcript, her eyes gritty and sore with strain. Grimly she tapped at the keys. Part of the problem was that she ended up reading the reports and thinking about the contents rather than simply copying and letting her fingers do the work. Knowing if she broke the Official Secrets Act she could go to prison, she hadn't dared ask any of the other ATS girls for more information about what went on here. Betty wasn't stupid though. From what she could piece together, the transcripts she was typing up were from conversations between German military personnel who had to be secreted somewhere in or near the house. From the volume of the transcripts, there must be quite a few men here and they had to be prisoners of war, which meant that this was a secret facility. Certainly no one in the village had any idea what was really going on. She watched the activity outside her window like a hawk and had quickly realised there had to be more blocks somewhere in the substantial grounds that led right up to the Cassels Farm boundary. It was known in the village that a lot of building work had been going on here. Had they built a whole prison camp? Did Mr Cassels have any idea what was going on right on his doorstep?

'Still here?' A deep voice interrupted her thoughts and she guiltily snatched up the final transcript.

'Just finishing,' she said and deliberately turned away from Major Carl Wendermeyer, focusing on winding a fresh sheet of paper into the typewriter.

'Don't let me disturb you,' he said as he perched himself with his usual casual ease on the edge of her desk, reaching for one of the sheets she'd already typed. She winced, knowing that it contained plenty of mistakes. She was neither fast nor accurate despite recent constant practice.

With what she knew was her prissiest face, she carried on typing and did her best to ignore him. Major Wendermeyer was too darned good-looking for his own good and he knew it.

Unfortunately, despite her best intentions, she was fascinated by him and found her gaze drawn to him constantly and on quite a few occasions he'd caught her and smiled. Direct, confident smiles, as if he knew what she was thinking. They made her blush. He was the handsomest man she'd ever seen. Tall and broad, he had a lithe energy about him that made her aware of him the minute he walked in the room. Despite his superior status he was friendly to all and treated every member of staff with equal respect. She'd never come across an officer like him. Perhaps it had something to do with him being American.

She sneaked a peep his way and found that he was watching her.

'Don't do that.'

'Do what?'

'Look at me. You're putting me off.'

He laughed and looked down at the piece of paper in his hand. 'Really?'

'I need to concentrate,' she said primly. He raised an insufferable eyebrow.

'Will it make much difference?'

She gasped and then laughed. 'Are you always this rude?'

'It's not rude, Betty, just honest. You're not much of a typist, are you? You can't spend every night in here catching up.'

'Yes, I can,' she said, becoming serious again, regretting her lapse. 'I'll stay for as long as it takes.' While she wasn't a very good typist, she did find the work interesting. The transcripts she typed up were fascinating.

'Why?'

'Because I want to do this. It's interesting work. I mean, it's obvious that these men can tell us a lot about the positions of the wolf packs and the way they operate. And last week I typed up the transcript of a telegrapher from a U-boat; what he said backs up what they said. That's got to be good information, hasn't it?'

He frowned and she realised that she shouldn't be discussing this sort of thing.

'Sorry, Sir.'

'Have you talked to anyone else about this?'

Her eyes widened and her mouth went dry. 'No, Sir. Absolutely not, Sir.'

'Hmm.' He studied her face again, his eyes sharpening. She met his gaze, her heart pounding. Now she was for it. She'd probably get the sack or be moved on to do filing or even... No, they wouldn't. They wouldn't send her to prison. Not for this.

Without warning he swung off the desk, put back the sheet of paper. 'Goodnight, Miss Connors.'

'Goodnight, Sir,' she said, holding her breath until he'd gone.

'Darn it.' She put both hands over her eyes. She'd really gone and done it now. Why couldn't she hold her blessed tongue? Heaving a heavy sigh, she finished the final sheet and bundled up all the paper and pushed open the door to the office next door which was where all the typewritten sheets had to be lodged before anyone left. The sergeant in there took them without comment, checked the numbers on them and then locked them in one of the tall filing cabinets, a bank of which lined one wall on either side of an ornate fireplace.

Feeling very weary, she switched out the light in the office and tramped down the two flights of the wide staircase to find out what Elsie had saved her for dinner, although she wasn't sure she could eat a thing.

Although the Mess was still busy, with people nursing their Ovaltine, Betty wasn't in the mood to talk to any of the new friends she'd made in the last few weeks. Keeping herself to herself, she ate the supper of corned-beef fritters Elsie had kept by. They weren't bad at all although she could have done without the additional cabbage and yet more carrots. At this rate she'd be able to see in the dark. Maybe that was the government's plan so that everyone would be able to cope during blackout. Pondering this, she ate as quickly as she could, desperate for the haven of her own room.

Each step up to the very top floor seemed an effort and when she reached the room, she threw herself on her bed and stared up at the ceiling. At least it was quiet and peaceful up here. She lifted a hand to her temple to try to soothe her headache but she could still hear the constant clatter of typewriter keys. Each night it took ages for her to wind down and then she dreamt of rising piles of paper that she could never get through.

It wouldn't have been quite so bad if the office hadn't been characterised by an air of frantic activity and urgency. It exacerbated the knot of anxiety riding low in her belly. She didn't want to let anyone down but at the same time she didn't like failing. Even at the village school, she'd always been the smart one. Among the other ATS girls in London, she was the bright, clever one that the sergeant relied on. Unfamiliar tears began to collect in the corners of her eyes and she dashed them away angrily. She wasn't up to the job; her typing wasn't as fast or as accurate as any of the other girls'.

Until her dad had died, she had felt invincible. At school she was the clever one, asked to help teach the younger ones. Her dad had been proud of her ability. There was hope she might become a teacher. Her ma had been bright and gay, and theirs had been a happy home. She'd been the apple of her dad's eye. When he died, everything had changed. She'd left school and gone to work at the big house, the extra income vital to supplement her mother's widow's pension. Then life had become more of a struggle and she'd had to grow up fast. Her looks rather than her brains were the useful commodity; she'd caught Bert's eye and her mother had pinned all her hopes on that. Marrying Bert Davenport wouldn't make them rich but it would rescue her mother from perennial poverty.

'Are you all right?' asked a soft voice.

Betty started and sat up, looking straight into Judith's sympathetic eyes. The other girl must have been out on the roof; she hadn't noticed the open window.

She blinked furiously, hoping that it didn't look as if she were crying, but there was something in Judith's lost, slightly defeated expression that made her shake her head and mutter, 'Not really.'

To her surprise Judith came and sat down next to her and they sat side by side for a minute. Her quiet presence was rather soothing. There was something undemanding about her and guilt pricked at Betty for not making more effort to get to know her, although, to be honest, usually the three of them in the room got up early and were gone all day. Their paths crossed only when they were going to bed.

'Sorry. I'm being silly. Compared to you, I have no problems,' said Betty, remembering Elsie's rebuke on the first morning.

Judith shrugged. 'My problems, as you call them' – Betty winced, there was a definite bite to her tone – 'are behind me now. I have a job I like, accommodation, food. The future is impossible to even think about at the moment. I live for each day because I can't change the past.'

Betty's guilt increased. She couldn't begin to imagine what Judith's life was like and she hadn't even bothered to ask her. 'Look, I'm really sorry about that first morning. Over breakfast. You must think I'm an empty-headed idiot after what I said about travelling being romantic. I tend to talk a lot of nonsense when I'm nervous.'

'Nervous.' Judith screwed up her face in disbelief. 'You? But you were – I don't know the English – bold. Like you were on the train. You walk as if you own the world.'

Betty let out a burst of laughter and clutched Judith's arm.

'It's all an act. I'm not bold. Inside it's different. Very different. I don't fit in here. You and Evelyn, you're educated. I went to the village school until I was fourteen. Then I worked…' she swallowed, wondering if her confession would make the other girl look down on her, 'I worked here as a parlourmaid until I joined the ATS.'

'That's how you know the house so well.'

Betty nodded, feeling a touch ashamed. 'Please don't tell Evelyn.'

Judith frowned. 'Of course, but why?'

'Evelyn would probably be horrified if she knew she was sharing her room with a servant.'

Judith's face softened and she reached out a hand and, to Betty's surprise, took hers and squeezed it. 'You're not a servant, you are serving your country.'

'That morning, I was really worried about... about being good enough for the job. I told them I could type and well, I can't really. I'm really sorry.' She paused, still trying to make amends.

Judith stared at her. 'But you...' She waved a hand at Betty's face.

'I pretend like I'm in the movies. Like I'm Betty Grable.'

'You should go into the movies then,' Judith's face creased into an impish smile, 'you're very good. I wish I could be like that.'

'I don't know about that. I like what you said just now, about living for each day because you can't change the past. I know I ought to be grateful that I've got a job and I'm near my family – even if Ma does drive me mad sometimes.' She touched Judith on the arm. 'I bet you'd give anything to have your ma drive you mad.'

Judith smiled. 'My father actually. My mother died when I was a baby. I don't remember her but I was close with my father.'

'Is he...?'

Judith nodded.

'I'm sorry. I remember my dad.' She held up her wrist and showed Judith his watch. 'He was my hero. He could do anything, build fences, pluck chickens, tell stories and he could sing.'

'My father played the piano and the violin,' said Judith. 'And I miss him.'

'Do you have a picture? What did he play?' Betty always felt better talking about her father even though he'd been gone for a long time now; it brought him closer to her in some way and she wanted to do the same for Judith.

'He played a lot of Mozart. His favourite composer.' She stood up and rummaged in the case under her bed and came back with a wooden-framed photo. 'This is him.'

Betty took the picture and studied the man before handing it back with a smile. 'I can see you have his eyes and his smile.'

'Thank you.' Judith heaved out a sigh. 'It's the second time I've talked about him in the last two weeks and it's a surprise, it feels better.' She turned and laughed, and Betty saw that under Judith's veneer of sorrow, there'd once been a happier, brighter character. 'I never thought talking would help, but do you know what, it really did. It's made me think so differently. Before I held onto everything that has happened to me and it was choking me inside. Talking, letting it out, it's quite freeing. It makes me feel lighter. So tell me, what is so bad?'

Betty looked at her warily, not really understanding what she was saying, but she realised that the other woman did look a lot brighter in the face.

'I'm not very good at typing. Everyone else is so fast. I stayed behind to finish tonight but I'm worried that I'll get my cards. I like it here. It feels like I'm part of something. Something important.'

'I know that. I feel it too. But surely if you finished your work, you have done your part.'

'I hope so.' But Betty wasn't reassured. Major Wendermeyer had caught her and she'd talked about secrets and then he'd gone very quiet. No doubt because he knew he was going to have to ask her to leave.

'Hello,' said Evelyn, suddenly appearing in the doorway. 'Are you two having an early night as well? I'm absolutely pooped.'

Betty nodded and gave her a half-hearted smile. This super-confident, elegant woman probably never had a moment's doubt in her life. She was probably good at everything. She'd already been talking about going home on one of her days off to collect her tennis racket.

She shot Judith a conspiratorial smile. She'd enjoyed talking to her. They'd just built a bridge, a very small one but it felt important. They were so different but she experienced a flicker of a friendship even though she wouldn't know Mozart if he yelled in her ear, although she did love the Andrews Sisters. One of the girls in London had brought her brother's His Master's Voice gramophone with her along with a pile of shiny black 78 Decca records. Gosh, they'd had some fun dancing in the dorm around the beds. Not much room for jitterbugging though. She did love to dance.

Evelyn crossed to her bed. 'So how's everyone settling in?'

They all looked warily at each other and she held her hand up. 'Official Secrets and all that. I'm not asking what you do, just how you're finding it.'

It was funny, both Betty and Judith relaxed as soon as Evelyn said that.

'It's a bit strange not knowing what is going on,' said Betty, tentatively, trying to work out if she could test her theory without giving away any secrets. 'But we all know that there are prisoners of war here.' She said it confidently and was relieved when the other two both nodded. 'But we mustn't tell anyone else that. I'm not sure even the kitchen staff know. The people in the village definitely don't.'

'I, for one,' said Evelyn, 'am enjoying it enormously. Interesting work, fun people and the food is wonderful. At my last billet, Mrs Rankin did her best but she couldn't cook if her life depended on it.'

Judith laughed. 'The food is wonderful,' she pulled a face, her eyes twinkling with sudden mischief, 'especially as it's tended to by our guests. I think that makes it taste even better.'

Betty slapped her forehead. 'Ah, of course. That makes sense now. The prisoners of war work in the gardens. They're huge here as well. I did wonder. William's under-gardeners all went off to fight years ago.'

Evelyn laughed. 'I know about that. Our poor gardener, Hodges, is swamped trying to "dig for victory", bless him. I shall tell Mummy she ought to investigate getting some help. There's a prisoner-of-war place at Badgemore, which isn't far.'

Betty glanced at Judith – of course Evelyn had a gardener – and hoped the other woman wouldn't give her away.

'Who fancies a quick snifter?' asked Evelyn. 'We've been here two weeks, I think we ought to celebrate, don't you? I've got a bottle in the boot of the car. Only thing is, I don't want anyone to see me.'

'Celebrate what?' asked Judith uncertainly.

Evelyn shrugged her elegant shoulders and wrinkled her delicate nose for a moment as if giving the question serious consideration. 'Being roommates? And I do think we've got the best room in the house, our own balcony, fabulous views and none of us snore. And I feel like celebrating.'

Her gaiety was infectious and Betty managed a giggle. Evelyn looked at Judith who lifted her shoulders and said, 'Why not?'

'And I know how you can get downstairs without anyone seeing you,' said Betty.

'You do?'

'Grab your torch and come with me.'

Both Evelyn and Judith followed her to the top of the stairs and she led them down the first flight of stairs to the corridor leading to the main stairs, but instead of turning right she turned left and led them to a blank wall between two faded squares where portraits of the third and fourth Barons had once hung. She giggled at their puzzled faces.

'Look, you twist the rail here.' As she did so the outline of a door appeared.

'How exciting,' said Evelyn, thankfully not questioning how she'd come by her knowledge. Judith gave her an admiring look.

'If you go down there, there's a short corridor and then two flights of stairs which lead you down to another corridor. At the very end of that, it opens at the back of the alcove in the front hall behind the suit of armour. You'll have walked past it lots of times and never suspected it was there.'

Evelyn's eyes widened. 'What an adventure.'

'Do you want us to come with you?' asked Betty, enjoying her roommate's enthusiasm.

With a shake of her golden head, her eyes gleaming, Evelyn said, 'Absolutely not. I shall navigate myself. What a lark!' She switched on her torch and shone it into the dark passageway. 'Excuse me. Won't be a mo.' And with that she disappeared from view into the dark corridor.

'Rather her than me,' said Judith, shaking her head. 'I don't like dark, enclosed spaces. They remind me too much of having to hide.' She shuddered and Betty wondered what she'd been through to escape from Germany.

She squeezed her arm. 'Thank you, Judith, for talking to me and making me feel better. You've been very kind.'

Judith smiled back at her. 'No, I've not been as kind as I could have been. There was so much unkindness and unpleasantness that I lost myself. I forgot how to be human for a long time. Now I feel as if I'm starting to wake up.' To Betty's surprise, she hooked her arm through hers and together they walked back up the stairs to their room, which, to Betty's even greater surprise, was starting to feel like home.

Evelyn returned, aglow with excitement and triumph, laying a small wicker picnic hamper on Betty's bed, opening it with a squeak of leather against the woven willow. She pulled out a bottle of champagne and then solemnly handed out three beautiful, shallow, crystal glasses.

She handed two to Betty.

'Champagne!' gasped Betty before she could stop herself. She was glad her hands were full because she wanted to trace the pretty decoration around the glasses with her fingers. They were simply beautiful. Of course, she'd seen the like before when she'd helped her Aunt Daisy polish the glasses before one of Lord Chesham's grand parties, but she'd never drunk from one and certainly had never tasted champagne.

'Seems a shame to waste it. Daddy bought a couple of cases for my twenty-first but then I gave up my place at Oxford and joined up, so there's never been the opportunity to share with anyone.' She was already expertly untwisting the wire and then twisting the cork. Judith, meanwhile, was holding up the glass to the light. 'Are these Baccarat?' she asked.

'Yes, I believe they are,' said Evelyn. 'Pretty aren't they?'

Judith nodded and turned to Betty wide-eyed and mouthed, 'Baccarat,' while Evelyn, oblivious to her amazement, pulled out the cork with an exciting pop.

A rush of warmth filled Betty. Come what may tomorrow, this evening was one that she would remember all her life. Sitting at the very top of Latimer House, drinking champagne from expensive glasses. She'd never heard of Baclerat or whatever it was, but she knew from Judith's stunned reaction that it was very posh.

Evelyn poured the golden fizzing liquid into each glass and put the bottle down, reaching for the second glass in Betty's hand.

'What shall we make a toast to? I feel like we're the three musketeers.'

Betty glanced at Judith and said, 'To tomorrow, because today is done.'

'What a jolly good idea,' said Evelyn. 'Excellent.' She raised her glass and the other two raised their glasses so they just touched. 'To tomorrow, because today is done,' she repeated and they all took a sip.

'Oooh,' said Betty blinking, wishing for once she could have been a bit more sophisticated. 'It went up my nose.'

'Then you must make a wish,' said Evelyn. 'Close your eyes tight, take another sip and wish.'

Betty did as she was told.

'What did you wish for?' asked Evelyn, with a wide smile.

'It's a secret,' said Judith. 'Or it won't come true.'

'Oh pish, that's superstitious nonsense.' And they all burst out laughing at the irony of her words.

Betty, personally, didn't think a wish was going to save her but she was going to enjoy every last drop of her champagne. Who knew when she'd ever get the chance to drink it again? This time tomorrow she could well be drinking weak tea in her ma's kitchen and sharing a bed with her and Jane again.

Chapter Twelve

Evelyn

The Officers' Mess, situated in what was once a rather grand drawing room, with pale-lemon wainscoting covering the lower walls and colourful co-ordinating wallpaper above, was a lively place after work. Already the leather chesterfield sofas and armchairs were full and the bar was several people deep.

Evelyn was greeted by Freddie with a loud yell.

'Brooke-Edwards, get yourself over here.' Greeting a few people that she now knew as she went, she crossed over to the small group gathered near the mullioned bay window. 'Pink gin, darling?' asked Ian Spencer.

'Lovely, thanks,' she said, taking the offered cocktail glass. 'Chin, chin.'

'Chin, bloody chin indeed,' said Alexander Spencer, Ian's brother. She'd known their cousin Alasdair at Oxford which immediately cemented an introduction; like many of the people here, there was always some common connection. 'I bloody well deserve this. What do they think we are, super-human or something? Never known anything like it.'

'Lots of U-boats been sunk last month. I heard it was forty-three,' said Ian. 'The tide in the Atlantic is turning.'

'I heard that's twenty-five per cent of their operational fleet.'

'Whatever it is, it's bringing us a lot more trade. And the Axis surrender in North Africa is sure to bring us some high-ups. Both German and Italian. Might bag ourselves a general or two. That'll excite the bigwigs.'

Evelyn nodded but didn't join in the conversation, instead letting it wash over her. She'd completed several interrogations today and felt exhausted. The responsibility and the intensity of the interrogations were quite draining. It was difficult staying alert the whole time and not missing a single clue but also trying to remember all the details. Her hand felt cramped after frantically scribbling notes and doing a debrief with Lieutenant Colonel Weston, who wanted to know how N1431 was doing. He'd been quite a recalcitrant prisoner to date and had been swapped to her. She'd found him cocky and condescending throughout this afternoon's interview and quite frankly she'd had enough of arrogant, full-of-themselves young men for one day. She sipped at her cocktail wondering if she could find a tray and sneak another two up to her room.

'You all right there, Evelyn?' bayed one of the young officers.

'Fine, thank you, George.' She gave him a cool smile.

'When are you going to make a foursome with me and Freddie for tennis?' he demanded.

'When I've collected my tennis racket and clothes from home,' she said patiently. He'd asked the same question every day for the last week, ever since Freddie had let on that she played a mean game. He was harmless enough; she was feeling a bit jaded and forced herself to give him a dazzling smile. She did enjoy a good game and would look forward to expending some energy. She wasn't used to spending this much time indoors.

Sipping at her drink, she drifted over to the window and looked out at the view. With a pang she thought of holidays in Germany, walking in Bavaria and a memorable trip to Switzerland where a group of them had gone walking in the mountains. The memory made her smile even as it brought back the aching muscles and the physical demands of the strenuous climb up to the top of one peak in order to get the best view of the Matterhorn. Peter had kissed her at the top. Held her hand. Asked her to marry him. She threw back her gin cocktail and swallowed down the lump in her throat, staring fixedly out of the window. Where was he now? She had absolutely no idea. She didn't even know if he were in the Army, the Navy or the Air Force or where he might have been posted.

She still wore his ring around her neck. It had broken her heart to break off their engagement but he, like her father, had agreed that it was the sensible thing to do as the threat of war had become ever more likely.

When they'd announced their engagement to both families it had been the happiest day of her life. Peter's parents lived next door to her Aunt Gertrude in Heidelberg and the two families had grown close over the ten years since Gertrude and Leonard had moved in. For two summers she and Peter had seen each other daily with love blooming and bursting between them, to the delight of both families. They'd taken many an excursion out in the nearby countryside and then that final trip to Switzerland in the May of 1939 when he'd proposed. For a few scant months they'd enjoyed being an engaged couple with Peter spending early June at the house in Henley before she'd gone back to Heidelberg on her own in August, despite her parents' misgivings after her escapade in Bavaria. Germany had turned into a dangerous place.

That was the last time she'd seen him.

The declaration of war had struck like an axe separating them.

Some days she forced herself to accept the truth; it was unlikely that she would ever see Peter again. Other times she daydreamed that they might find each other at some distant point when the war was over. But it had already gone on for nearly four years. Was his family still in Heidelberg? Her aunt and uncle had moved to the United States. Their house was standing empty. Who knew what would happen to it. She had no way of knowing or contacting any of his family. The stark, awful truth that haunted her nights was that he could be dead and she would never know. She fought back the sob that threatened to rise in her throat, lifted her chin and fixed her gaze on the river, counting under her breath. It took until she reached twenty-seven before her equilibrium returned, but even so she didn't feel like socialising with the other officers.

Skirting the group, she moved towards the bar and asked for three cocktails and before anyone could stop her or wonder where she was going, she glided out of the room with a small tray and down the hall to the secret passage that Betty had revealed the day before. Her usual mischievous attitude asserted itself and she smiled, clutching the knowledge of the secret passage to herself like a naughty child. Glancing cautiously about, making sure no one was in sight, she slipped behind the suit of armour and with her elbow managed to turn the piece of wood forming the latch. She crept forward into the gloom and waited for a moment while her eyes adjusted. When she'd come down here last night she'd discovered that there was some ambient light and, on the staircases, light switches.

Hurrying along, careful not to spill the drinks, she climbed the two flights of stairs and then paused at the wooden door that opened out onto the final hallway, mentally crossing her fingers that no one was about when she emerged. Peeping out, she hissed out a small sigh of relief. The coast was clear and she scurried to the servants' stairs at the end of the corridor.

'Home and dry,' she said to herself as she mounted the stairs. From this point on, the little room tucked under the eaves was their own private eyrie, especially with the rooftop access and their own personal terrace with a view. No one but the three of them had any reason to come up here and she rather liked the fact that her two roommates were so different from her. It was a welcome change because the people downstairs, like so many she'd mixed with all her life, were all the same. They came from the same sort of families, had the same expectations and the same narrow views. She liked Betty's wide-eyed, open honesty. The fact that she blurted things out without thinking was refreshing. Judith she found fascinating, although she was harder to read, but since Evelyn had lived in Germany too, they had some common ground. Evelyn had loved rural Germany before the Nazis got their stranglehold on the place. Over the years, she'd made some good friends there. It seemed impossible to believe that those people were now supposed to be her enemies.

She entered the room with the sort of flourish people expected of Evelyn Brooke-Edwards, her self-indulgent moping over. 'Ladies, I've brought some refreshments because if, like me, you've had a killer day, then we deserve them.'

Betty sprang to her feet. 'I think I might have fallen in love with you. Cocktails! You're spoiling us.'

'No Baccarat glasses?' teased Judith.

'No, but the finest pink gin cocktails known to the Navy.' She held out the tray.

'What shall we drink to tonight?' asked Judith.

'To me keeping my job,' said Betty with a huge grin. 'And getting promoted.'

'Really? That's wonderful.' Judith took a drink and lifted it. 'To Betty.'

'To Betty,' repeated Evelyn.

'To me,' said Betty, beaming from ear to ear.

'So tell us what happened?'

'Let's go out on the balcony.' Betty was already on her way to the window. Evelyn smiled; 'balcony' was rather grand for the small area that could just accommodate the three of them sitting down.

It was however an excellent suggestion. The early summer sunshine had heated the tiles on the roof and they held the latent warmth of the day as the sun dipped lower in the sky.

Once settled Betty lifted her glass in another toast. 'To our private balcony. And no planes today.' There'd been quite a few overhead in the last couple of weeks but nothing to cause alarm.

'So you are still a typist?' Judith leaned back against the sloping roof.

'No! I'm not. I am now…' she paused for effect, her big blue eyes almost as wide as Grandmama's best tea plates, 'an analyst. Honestly, it was such a surprise. Major Wendermeyer… Do you know him?' She sighed and looked dreamily up at the sky. Evelyn exchanged a quick look with Judith, who rolled her eyes but in a motherly sort of way rather than with out-and-out disapproval. 'He's quite a dish. He looks like a young Gary Cooper. And he's with the USAF. Anyway, I had to go see him and I swear to God, I thought he was going to have me transferred or court martialled or sent to jail.' She clutched at her heart in the most dramatic fashion but Evelyn remembered exactly how she'd felt when she thought the same not so long ago. 'I didn't get a wink of sleep last night.'

Evelyn had heard the other girl tossing and turning when she'd lain awake for several hours but she'd been taught not to interfere, not to ask questions, to make the best of things. Now she regretted it.

'I'm sorry, Betty. I know what that feels like. I thought before I came here, I was going to be court martialled.'

'You?' said both Judith and Betty in unison.

She grinned at them, able to find it funny now that she was well and truly on the other side of the affair. 'I'll tell you all about it, when Betty has finished telling us her news.'

Betty was only too eager to step back into the spotlight. 'Well, my heart damn near exploded out of my chest when he started asking me what I thought about what I'd read and asked if I could elaborate on my views. It took me a minute to figure out what he was talking about. So I figured by that stage I'd got nothing to lose and any idiot could see what was what. I told him straight.' She let out a delighted giggle. 'And now I'm going to be reading all the ... the things and making reports on my observations about what's been said by who and how they all link up. He said I had a good eye and sharp instincts.' Evelyn bit back a smile; she could tell that Betty was bursting with pride. 'And I don't have to type anything up anymore. I have to read everything and write up what I think.

How's that? Me, Betty Connors, he thinks I've got opinions worth listening to.' She looked quite incredulous. 'Me!'

Evelyn shook her head. 'You should have more confidence in yourself. You're a smart girl. The powers that be have recognised it.'

Betty snorted disbelievingly. 'It's just common sense.' Then she giggled. 'But I'm so made up and I got promoted.' She tapped the single stripe on her arm. 'You'll never believe this, but to sergeant!'

'That is wonderful,' said Judith. Evelyn glanced at her. Was she the only one that had noticed that Judith had been promoted to sergeant as soon as she'd arrived?

'My ma might even be impressed. I'll be seeing her the day after tomorrow. I'm going onto the night shift for a week.'

'Same here,' said Evelyn. 'What about you, Judith?'

'I don't know. I forgot to look at the rota.'

'When you find out, perhaps we should do something together. I've got my car and if I don't use the petrol ration for this month, I'll lose it.'

'Sorry,' said Betty, with a disappointed grimace. 'That sounds a lot more fun, but I promised Ma I'd go visit.'

'Not to worry, maybe next week.'

When Colonel Myers walked into the briefing the following morning everyone fell silent. Before his arrival the room had buzzed with rumours that a large contingent of soldiers from North Africa were on their way.

'Ladies and gentlemen, the first convoy of German soldiers from Tunisia will be arriving tomorrow. I'm afraid it's going to be an extremely busy few days. We'll be working extra hours to process everyone.'

Evelyn, like the others in the room, stiffened, not with disappointment – there wasn't a single groan from around the room – but with that alert, we-have-a-job-to-do attitude that characterised the unit. As she exchanged glances with a couple of others, she felt that shared sense of pride in the work they were doing.

'I'd like to divide you into two teams. We have one group of POWs who fought under General Von Arnim, and morale among them is strong, while the second group served under General Hager. They are disillusioned and disaffected.' For the rest of the briefing, he explained what the tactics would be in questioning the new arrivals and who would be in which team.

When she went out to her first interview she saw that security had already been increased and when she crossed the checkpoint at the fence she saw that there were a lot more soldiers on patrol than she'd seen before. She hurried across the damp grass towards the interview block, clutching her notes from the briefing. After nearly four weeks, she felt like an old hand and quite confident in herself.

As soon as she entered, a Captain at the door motioned to her.

'Ah, Lieutenant Brooke-Edwards. Do you have a moment?'

She could hardly say no, but they were all aware of the pressure each member of the section was under to get through as many interrogations as they could. Top brass wanted to ship out a number of prisoners to make room for the North Africa men.

'Colonel Myers has sent down a message. He'd like to see you at lunchtime.'

'Oh, right-ho.' Why hadn't he said anything in the briefing?

She put it to the back of her mind; she had a job to do. She made her way to interview room 4 and, as always when she approached the door, wondered what she'd find on the other side. This work certainly gave you an insight into the thoughts of one's fellow man.

Today the prisoner was angry and defiant. He didn't want to answer any of her questions, and instead demanded to know where he was and what had happened to his fellow officers. He made it quite plain that he wouldn't go down without a fight.

'I will die a man of honour,' he said for the third time, at which point Evelyn realised that he thought he was going to be executed.

'This isn't a death camp,' she snapped sharply. 'The British have honour. We don't murder fellow soldiers. This is a prisoner-of-war camp where you will be treated with dignity and respect. Are you able to say that the Tunisian people were accorded the same treatment?'

He sneered.

'I thought not. I have nothing more to say to you.' She curled her lip in disgust and he stared at her in amazement.

Sometimes harsh words worked better. She rose and walked out. 'Take him back to his cell.'

'Wait,' the man called.

She eyed him with utter disdain.

'What will happen to me?'

'That depends on how you co-operate. If you've got nothing worth telling us, you'll be shipped out to a camp that is much less pleasant than this one.' She said this knowing that he was about to be placed in a cell with another prisoner who'd been here a while. She'd also deliberately given him an easy ride, knowing that it was likely that he'd say plenty to his new cellmate about how ineffective his first interrogation had been. No doubt he would also boast about what he did know and wasn't going to reveal. She smiled to herself as she walked out of the room. This early part of the interrogation process often paid dividends and she had a good feeling about this one. She went back to the general office where she sat down and wrote a very quick note about the meeting and a note to the M Section to listen in to M1636. After only a couple of weeks she'd developed good instincts about the prisoners and to date, she'd been pretty accurate in her early assessments of those who'd deliver good intelligence. Even Lieutenant Colonel Weston was impressed with her psychological understanding of the prisoners. Funny how everything about the war was rather beastly but her job brought her great satisfaction and interest. What would her life have been like if it hadn't been for the war? She had an unpleasant feeling that she might have found herself rather bored. And now she had to go and see Myers. What on earth was that about?

Chapter Thirteen

Judith

Judith came into the Mess on her own this morning. Betty and Evelyn had swapped shifts and were both still in bed when Judith left their room. Elsie greeted her with a smile and said the next lot of porridge would be out very soon. She nodded her thanks to the ever cheerful woman and her stomach rumbled in anticipation, which made her laugh to herself. Just one of the things she'd grown to like in this country, the hot coarse oatmeal porridge that was very different from that at home.

Across the room someone waved and she recognised Frida, one of the other listeners from her shift. Over the last few weeks she'd gradually got to know more of them and although they rarely talked about what they'd left behind, she would guess most had similar tales to tell. Nearly all of them had come to England from Germany since 1937. On the whole, they were a friendly but often serious bunch. It was hard going listening all day. It took a huge amount of concentration, so when they broke for tea or lunch, there might be a lot of light-hearted, silly chatter but it never did more than scratch the surface and Judith knew better than to ask.

As she sat down, she realised that Walther was also sitting there.

'Morning,' he said, raising his mug of tea.

'Morning,' she replied, suddenly shy.

'Where is your friend? The film-star girl.'

'Betty? Is that what you call her?' Judith smiled thinly, thinking that Betty would like the description. 'She's on nights this week.'

'Not me, some of the other men. I prefer brunettes.' One corner of his mouth quirked as he said it.

'Oh,' said Judith, not knowing how to respond. 'That's nice.'

He nodded. 'There's a shift swap coming up, do you know what yours will be?'

'I don't know.'

'You haven't looked? Don't you want to have some free time during the day?'

She shrugged. 'It makes no difference to me. I wouldn't have anything to do or anywhere to go.'

'But we are so close to London, the train is less than an hour. Or there is the beautiful countryside. Amersham is a pretty place.'

Judith rubbed at her thumb. The thought of going to London with no real reason didn't appeal. What would she do there on her own all day?

'You should enjoy a day out. Go out and smell the flowers, get some sunshine on your skin. It is good for you to take some time away from here.'

She gave him a perfunctory smile. 'Perhaps I'll go for a walk in the village.'

'That won't take you very long. There's really not a lot there. You have to walk to Little Chalfont to find a shop or a pub. There's a lot more in Amersham but that's about three miles away.'

Judith nodded politely. What did he expect her to do? Go wandering about and get lost? And what about the animals? There were lots of sheep in the nearby fields – were they safe? Did they bite?

He shook his head. 'I can see I'm going to have to take you in hand. Let's find out from Ralph when you're on nights. He's the warrant officer. Can you use a bicycle?'

'Er, yes. I haven't ridden one for a while.'

'There is an English saying that you don't forget how. I will find one for you.'

She wished he'd leave her alone. He was being kind and she was grateful for that, but she really wasn't used to being in the countryside. What if she did lose her way and then had to ask someone, and they thought she was a German spy or the enemy or something?

Elsie brought over a steaming bowl of porridge and Judith gratefully gave it her attention, hoping that Walther would talk to someone else. Thankfully he obliged and began chatting away to the man opposite which allowed her to give him a covert study. A little older than her, he reminded her of an inquisitive bird with those dark, deep-set eyes that seemed to miss nothing. Although he had a ready smile and a wide mouth, there was a reticence about him.

Just as she was finishing her breakfast, he rose and caught her watching him. He smiled and gave her a wave as he walked off.

'I think he likes you,' said Frida.

'I don't think so, he was just being friendly.'

Frida rolled her eyes. 'No, Judith, he wanted to know when you were off. And he was trying to find out what you might like to do. I think he wants to take you on a bicycle ride or to London.'

Judith shook her head in denial.

'Want to make a bet?' asked Frida with a cheeky grin.

'No,' said Judith firmly. 'I need to start work.' She scooped up her cap and hurried off. Frida could be a tease. She liked to make jokes and find the funny side of things. Sometimes Judith found it irritating, especially today. Walther was nice to her because she was on his team. They were colleagues and they were here to work and to help bring down the National Socialist regime that had destroyed their country. This was no time to be going for bicycle rides or trips to London. There was a war on.

———

The warrant officer approached her that afternoon after tea in the Sergeants' Mess. 'Sergeant Stern. I understand you aren't aware of the change in the off-duty rota.' His face softened. 'You are on nights for a few nights from Thursday.'

She gave him a perfunctory nod of thanks and left the noisy dining room, wondering whether to go into the other part of the Sergeants' Mess where everyone congregated in the evenings, playing cards or listening to the radio. Neither appealed and she found herself walking down a parquet-floored corridor just for the sake of walking. It looked as if it were a dead end but then she realised there was a door on the far right that was almost hidden from view. Keen to be by herself, she crept forward and carefully pushed open the large, heavy wooden door. It closed behind her with a soft thud, reinforcing the sensation of being sealed off from the rest of the house.

The half-furnished room held a sad, melancholy air as if all the fine pieces had been removed, leaving the shell of a previous grandeur, the feeling akin to how she felt, as if she'd lost all the best pieces of herself. In her eyes, however, there was only one piece of furniture in the room – two, if you counted the stool. Her gaze was drawn to the wonderful grand piano bathed in sunlight streaming in from diamond-paned glass. It was framed by the heavy, plum velvet curtains draped elegantly on either side of the panelled dark-wood wainscoting of the deep bay window.

She held her breath and crept over to the piano, running a hand over the patina of the glossy walnut-burr lid. She breathed out a tiny sigh of awe as she moved in front of it to read the gilt letters on the fall board. A Bechstein. Tears filled her eyes. It was so like the one her father had owned. Although she was almost too scared to touch it, her hands crept towards the ivory keys, longing consuming her. The silence of the room hung heavily as if it were waiting for something. Holding her breath, she lifted one finger and pressed the nearest key. The low C note vibrated loud and clear, filling the room with a delightful hum that made her heart bloom with sudden warmth. For a moment she let the delicious feeling of anticipation fill her, the expectation of the music already swirling in her head.

Giving in to the yearning that tugged at her heart, her soul and every fibre of her being, she pulled the stool underneath her bottom and sat down. Her hands held aloft, shaking slightly with reverence and fear. What if she couldn't do this magnificent instrument justice? But she couldn't have walked away, not now. With a deep breath, she placed her fingers onto the keys and tentatively began to play. It wasn't long before her touch became confident and sure, although she played pianissimo, a personal and private contract between her and the piano. She played for herself, ignoring mistakes and falters, for the sheer joy of the music and wondered how she could have lived without this for so long. Tears bubbled up and rolled down her face, as her spirits soared like a ship's sails escaping their tethers, losing herself in the music.

It was only when she came to the end of the piece, her heart fluttering with sheer pleasure, her fingers gradually and reluctantly drawing to a halt, that she realised there was someone standing by the door. They must have come in while she'd abandoned herself to the music. Sudden embarrassment seared her cheeks but she forced herself to look over. When she saw Walther, wiping his own tears from his eyes, she sighed, relief easing from her like air from a punctured bicycle tyre.

'Sorry, I didn't mean to interrupt,' he said.

She nodded and put her hands primly in her lap, feeling exposed and laid bare, the tears still drying on her cheeks, wet drips between her collar and neck. He walked across the soft carpet through the beams of late sunshine cast through the big windows and came to stand next to her, his hands brushing the surface of the piano exactly as hers had done.

'It has the most beautiful tone,' he said almost reverently.

'It does.'

'And you play extraordinarily well. Were you a concert pianist?'

'No. I wanted to be.' Her mouth crumpled. 'There was no place for a Jew playing music.'

His face softened and he took one of her hands and squeezed it as if he knew the pain she'd suffered.

'I'm sorry. That is a tragedy.'

'No,' she said, shaking her head. 'A tragedy is the loss of a loved one; it's being persecuted and taken away to certain death.'

'I think you are too hard on yourself. Being denied a gift like this is a terrible tragedy and you deserve to grieve.'

'Grieving doesn't help,' said Judith tersely, embarrassment pricking her.

'No, it doesn't. Finding a way forward does. Will you play something else?'

She shook her head.

'For me?'

How was it that he understood?

'I can play something for *you*.' But not for herself. She looked at him for a moment and began to play *Für Elise*.

Once again, despite being very rusty, her fingers unerringly found their way across the keys. This time she watched him as she played. Leaning on the piano, his eyes never left her face the whole time and it was the most intimate thing she'd ever experienced in her life, as if he were there with her for every note, for every breath she took, for every musical refrain, every cadence.

When she finished he smiled and said, *'Danke Schön,'* the words holding a wealth of meaning beyond simple thanks.

A laugh outside from further down the hallway brought them both back to earth and she smiled ruefully at him. 'I'm not sure I'm meant to be in here.'

'I think you are,' he said, stroking the piano. 'It would be a great shame to deny this instrument. I'm sure no one would begrudge you playing here.'

She rose and smoothed down her skirts, awkward now and not sure what to say to him. She'd exposed a part of herself to him that had been hidden for so long, it didn't feel as if it were her anymore.

'I checked with Sergeant Jones. You swap to night shifts on Thursday.'

'Yes, he told me.'

'I wonder if you would care to accompany me on a bicycle ride. I'd very much enjoy showing you some of the beautiful countryside and we could perhaps have lunch in Amersham.'

Frida's words came back to her and she blushed, which was silly because he was a very kind man, but it would be more pleasant to have company for the day than spend it on her own.

'That would be very nice. Thank you, you're very kind.'

His eyes suddenly twinkled. 'There might be a price to pay.'

She looked at him warily.

'I might ask you to play for me again.'

'Oh.' She gave a nervous laugh. 'That's not a high price. I can afford that.'

'Excellent. Now all I need to do is procure two bicycles by Thursday.' His smile was pure mischief and Judith realised she really wanted to go for that bicycle ride.

'I might be able to help there. My roommate is a local girl, she might know someone in the village that might lend us a bicycle.'

'*Das ist wunderbar.*'

'I'll talk to her right away,' she said, already in her head halfway up the stairs.

'Excellent. I'll see you tomorrow. At breakfast?'

'Yes,' said Judith, surprised by the little flutter in her heart. 'At breakfast.'

Betty was out on the roof smoking and she went straight out to see her.

'Betty, do you know where I might be able to borrow a bicycle – no, two bicycles – in the village? Walther, one of the lis… one of the men in my section, has invited me to go for a bike ride.'

'Has he now?' Betty fluttered her lashes.

Judith blushed. 'It's not like that. He's a nice man. We have some things in common. He likes music. He's German. He's Jewish.'

'Well, if he's just a nice man, that's fine then,' said Betty with a teasing glint in her eye as she followed Judith back into their bedroom.

'He's a nice man. That is all,' said Judith shortly and went and sat down on her bed. 'We're only going out to see the countryside.' That was all. Like her, he would understand that it was wrong for them to be enjoying themselves. A ride in the country wasn't frivolous. And lunch would be a necessity if they were going to be out for a while.

'Right-ho,' said Betty, still with that air of disbelief. It irritated Judith but she didn't want to say anything else. Judith pulled out her needles and wool and began knitting furiously.

'Hey, I didn't mean to upset you,' said Betty. 'I can see if there's a spare bicycle at the farm and Elsie has one she might lend you. She could use the Vicar's for a day, I'm sure.'

'Thank you,' said Judith, feeling a little guilty for her stiffness.

'You should go down to the weir on the River Chess, that's very pretty. Or there's Chenies Manor, or you could see the steam engines at Amersham Common. Or you could cycle to the station and go to London. There's a cinema in Chesham.' Betty clapped her hands. 'If I could I'd go up West. See a show or something, but Ma would play merry hell. Bert too. They don't like me going up to London.'

'I suppose they're worried about the bombs.'

'Suppose so,' Betty sighed, 'but I always make sure I know where all the shelters are before I go. What are you knitting? Lovely colour.'

Judith allowed herself a small smile. It was indeed a gorgeous colour, a rich cherry red. 'A jumper. The wool came from an old cardigan that belonged to one of my aunts. There might be enough wool left to make a scarf, if you'd like.' Her aunt had been an interesting character, bohemian, forthright and outspoken. How she would have hated the war and everything Hitler and his cronies stood for. She'd probably have been shot for opposing the regime. Thankfully she'd died in 1932 before things had really started to deteriorate.

'Are you sure? That's very generous.'

Judith nodded. 'I think the colour will suit you.'

'I think it will suit you too. What are you going to wear for your trip?'

Judith narrowed her eyes at Betty. 'You never give up, do you?'

'I like looking nice for me. It makes me feel better and if the men look twice...' she paused before adding with an insouciant grin, 'why not?'

Judith carried on knitting but she smiled to herself. Walther probably wouldn't even notice. Her father had rarely noticed what she wore. Men looked at Betty for something other than her clothes; she had that innate womanly appeal that had bypassed Judith. It hadn't mattered when she was growing up that she was plain and understated because she'd been taught that music and art were more important. But that life was gone now and she had already accepted that it was unlikely that her future held a husband or the things that she'd once held so dear.

Chapter Fourteen

Betty

Freed from the wrist-pounding typing and the anxiety over her slow pace, Betty was enjoying her new job immensely, and the office in which she was now situated had once been Lord Chesham's bedroom, which tickled her no end. Although now, instead of the big four-poster bed and heavy wooden furniture that had been in his family for generations, the room was full of functional desks and filing cabinets, jammed into every bit of space. The rich burgundy carpet was still in situ as were the plump lined damask golden-yellow curtains with their pattern of roses picked out in the same burgundy colour as the floor. She enjoyed staring at the heavy wallpaper with its huge floral repeat as she reflected on the latest reports. It was so different from the bedroom she'd shared at home. Who could have imagined she'd end up working in this lovely light room with its big stone mullioned window and the wonderful view from the west side of the house looking down towards the river and the fields? As working spaces went, it was a definite improvement on the drab green walls of the offices in Mill Hill.

She leaned back in her chair, going back over the reports she'd just read, her brain busy comparing the information contained with an earlier transcript, with the notes in front of her.

It was another frantic morning, with a whole pile of urgent reports that had to be gone through. Intel was coming through on a number of potential battle plans and more talk of Hitler's secret weapons. Every day there was more and more to do, although Betty was in her element. It seemed she thrived on being challenged, as did her roommates. All three of them fell into bed after their shifts, and the dark circles under Judith's eyes were so bad, it almost looked as if she'd been thumped. Despite this, they each agreed that they were glad that they were doing meaningful work. Although they couldn't discuss exactly what they did, they knew enough to realise that each of them was an interlocking piece in the overall jigsaw puzzle.

Gazing thoughtfully out of the window, trying to piece things together, her attention was caught by a dark, fast-moving shape on the horizon. Then another. Before she could register that the three planes moving low and fast were coming this way, there was a loud whoomping bang and the house shook for a brief moment. Over the hill a plume of smoke began to rise.

'Bloody hell.' One of the girls came racing over to the window.

'Amersham way,' said Betty through tight vocal cords, praying that no one had been hurt. 'Poor sods.' She crossed her fingers and Major Wendermeyer came to stand behind her, putting a sympathetic hand on her shoulder as they stared at the billowing dark clouds rising into the sky.

Suddenly a fourth plane swooped out of the sky, slower than the others, a Heinkel, one of the German long-range bombers. It flew parallel with the river, so close that Betty could make out the pilot in his cockpit. To her horror, at the same moment, she saw the torpedo-shaped bomb drop from the plane.

'Down, everyone down!' she yelled at the same time as the Major, who grabbed her and pulled her to the floor next to him, tugging her under the desk, his arm over her shoulders. There was silence for a moment apart from the sound of the plane flying away. They waited. And waited. And waited.

The seconds ticked by, the quiet heavy with fear and anticipation, punctuated by the nervous rustle and fidget of people trying not to breathe too deeply or loudly.

Betty was aware of the Major next to her, his arm heavy across her back, his head next to hers. His shallow careful breaths were in tandem with hers and as she inhaled with trepidation as if each breath might be her last, she could smell his Lifebuoy soap. She dared open her eyes, which had been tightly shut, and focused on the smooth chin and golden tan of his skin, within touching distance. For a man, he was beautiful. She'd never thought of men as beautiful. She studied his face as if her life depended upon it, trying not to think about the moment the bomb might blow. His head turned slightly and he stared back at her. Their gaze held for seconds, not a flicker of emotion between them, just a candid, searing look at each other. In that moment, Betty felt a deep soul connection and her heart stuttered in her chest.

Someone across the room emerged from a desk. Betty lifted

her head, fear paralysing her muscles, and she hated the feeling. Hated that it had taken control of her body. She fought back, and moved her legs, drawing them up beneath so she could get onto her knees.

The whole house had gone silent, there wasn't a sound anywhere.

'What do you think happened?' she whispered.

'Not sure. You stay right there.' He wriggled out from under the desk and crawled to the windowsill, to peer over the top. Betty crossed her fingers and held her breath.

He lowered himself to the ground.

'OK everyone. We've got ourselves an unexploded bomb right out back. I want you all to crawl to the door, one by one, those closest to the door first, as quiet as you can, and head towards the front of the building to the muster point.'

At last, it was Betty's turn. She looked at the Major. 'How close is it to the house?'

'Close enough. We'll have to call in the Royal Engineers, try and defuse it. If it goes off, it'll take most of this side of the house with it, not to mention the prisoners' cells. We're going to have to evacuate.'

Betty cast an anxious glance at the piles of paper on her desk. 'But there's so much to do.'

'I know. Bloody Jerries, don't they know there's a war on?'

She let out a small inappropriate giggle; his using English slang sounded funny. 'So inconsiderate.'

'That they are. Come on, let's get out of here. You go first.'

As she crawled out, she was horribly conscious of him following her. Fear still coursed through her but she was desperate not to give in to it. She looked over her shoulder. 'And keep your eyes off my behind.'

'Yes, ma'am.'

As soon as they reached the door, Betty stood up and quickly looked back out of the window. A tail fin protruded from the green lawn only a few yards from the house, a menacing threat with vicious capacity. The bomb had buried itself nose first at a forty-five degree angle deep into grass. Less than a quarter was visible.

She shuddered as memories of the carcases of buildings in London came flooding back, a bed balanced precariously on the edge of what was once the middle of a bedroom, a kitchen sliced in two, a sofa upended in the street, and hollow-eyed, shocked, dust-caked people raking through rubble.

'Betty.' The soft voice brought her back. 'Off you go. I've got to report to Colonel Myers. Get our contingency plans in action. I expect you'll be evacuated to the church, that's the emergency plan.'

'Right,' said Betty, shaking her head as if it might dislodge the all-too-clear images. 'Do you think you should stay in the building?'

'Don't worry, the Colonel's office is the other side of the house.'

'Yes, but if that bomb went off, it might bring the whole place down.' She caught her lip between her teeth.

'Off you go.'

Leaving him, part grateful to be escaping and part guilty that he was staying put, she ran down the stairs towards the front of the house, where everyone was being evacuated to the churchyard on the opposite side of the estate.

'Be the biggest congregation Frank's ever had,' said Elsie as Betty caught up with her. 'Do you know what's going on?'

'Apart from a ruddy great bomb has landed on the front lawn, no idea,' said Betty, sounding a lot more nonchalant than she felt. 'Thought I was safe from all that back here. I might as well be back in Mill Hill.'

Everyone was crammed into the pews of Mary Magdalene Church awaiting Colonel Myers, who was due to address them. Betty looked round to see if she could spot Evelyn or Judith. Evelyn waved from a spot near the back surrounded by her fellow officers but there was no sign of Judith. Betty frowned and scanned the church again before hurrying over to Evelyn.

'Have you seen Judith anywhere?'

'No.' Evelyn frowned. 'She must be here somewhere. Everyone's been evacuated.'

'I'm going to take a look.'

'I'll come with you. You go down that aisle, I'll do the other.'

When Betty met Evelyn in front of the altar, the other woman shook her head. 'No sign of her. Or Walther.'

'Or that girl Frida she works with.'

'I wouldn't know her.'

'I'm wondering where the prisoners are?'

'They were all shipped back to their cells smartish,' said Evelyn, 'although if that bomb blows, who knows what will happen. Those prefab cells aren't the strongest and the stable block will be right in the blow-out zone. That will really set the cat among the pigeons if we have a dozen Germans escaping into the village. It'll put paid to what we've been doing.'

'Oh no.'

'Let's hear what Colonel Myers has to say. Here he comes.'

The Colonel, flanked by Lieutenant Colonel Weston and all

the different section heads, Navy, Army and RAF, strode to the front of the church and without a moment's hesitation climbed straight into the pulpit. Everyone fell silent immediately, eyes swivelling towards him.

'Well, this is a turn-up, I'm afraid. Officially our orders are that we have to stay out of the building until the Royal Engineers get here. There's a team coming out from London pronto. If you could all report to your section leaders, we'll give further instructions. The key thing is that we keep the integrity of this site, maintain what we can and at the same time protect the village. We don't want the local fire wardens coming up here.'

Betty realised that his vague observations were to cover every member of personnel, as not everyone knew what went on here. Elsie and her assistants standing a few rows along had no idea that there were German prisoners of war just a few hundred yards from her kitchen.

'I've stationed a couple of men at the gate in case anyone has raised the alarm. I'll go down there to brief the team when they arrive and explain where the bomb is. Likely thing is that they'll have to dig it out to get to the fuse. It could take some time, if they manage to defuse it.'

There was a ripple through the assembled crowd. No one was in any doubt of the dangers faced by the men that had to disarm a bomb. Betty, like many of the ATS girls who'd served in London, knew that during the Blitz the life expectancy of a bomb disposal officer had been ten weeks.

As Myers descended from the pulpit, everyone began to move, searching out their units and their senior officers for further instructions. Betty saw Evelyn go into a huddle with the other Navy uniformed officers as she went towards the chapel where Major Wendermeyer and his British Army opposite number, Major Smith, were corralling the team together.

Betty crowded around the two men with the rest of the team and listened as they gave a quick briefing.

'Obviously we'll have to wait until the bomb disposal boys get here, so you'd best make yourselves comfortable for the time being,' said Major Wendermeyer. 'It's not safe for anyone to return to their quarters. In the meantime, the Major and I will take a small team back to the office to retrieve what we can before the Royal Engineers get here. They'll stop anyone going back in, but if that bomb blows we'll lose valuable intel, and we can't afford to allow that. No one is under any obligation to come with us but if anyone feels like volunteering, we could do with a few hands.'

Betty stared at him. All that work. They couldn't let it go up in smoke. There was so much there that might help, especially the recent information they were picking up about the radar systems, the secret weapons and the coastal defences in the Low Countries.

As Major Wendermeyer moved among them, talking to a few of the men on the team, she stepped forward. 'I volunteer.'

His face underwent a series of expressions. 'That's all right, Sergeant Connors, you don't need to do that. But thank you for the offer.'

'But I want to, Sir.' She couldn't bear the thought that all the work that she'd been doing would be in vain. The work that any of them were doing. She, Evelyn and Judith, like everyone here, had been working so hard recently. She was proud of what she was achieving. For the first time in the war, she genuinely believed, she, Betty Connors, was making a difference.

'You really don't need to, Connors,' he said, more sharply this time.

She gave him a level look, lifting her chin, meeting his eyes. 'But I want to.' This time there was a steely determination in her words, challenging him.

His mouth tightened and he held her gaze but she wasn't budging. She lifted her chin higher.

He huffed out an exasperated sigh. 'Very well, Connors. Meet me in the church porch in two minutes. I need to speak to Colonel Myers.'

Betty turned on her heel and made her way to the back of the church, passing Evelyn, who was being handed a rifle. She gave her a surprised glance and Evelyn gave her a rueful smile across the heads of the other officers. Betty gave her a quick nod. They each had to do what they had to do. She wished she knew where Judith was. Knowing the other girl's dedication, she assumed she was probably still at work. Betty had no idea in which part of the building either of her roommates worked, it wasn't something they'd ever discussed. She prayed that Judith was somewhere safe.

As they approached the building, one of the officers handed out tin hats – no one was reprimanded for the fact that they all had them but they were still in their quarters. No one had ever thought there'd be any danger here. Betty's hands trembled as she fumbled the strap under her chin. *Please don't let anyone see,* she prayed. Now that she was here, her earlier spine had deserted her. It was all very well to be brave when you were safe. What had she been thinking? Trying to impress the Major? Prove something? She swallowed. What if the bomb went off while they were in the office? They'd be right in the bomb blast. Her hand strayed to her nose thinking of poor Barbara Clarke.

'Everyone ready?' Major Smith looked at them one by one.

The words stuck in her throat. No, she wasn't ready. Not at all. She clenched her hands to stop them shaking. They moved quietly up the wide staircase with the speed and determination of a battle-hungry unit. There were ten of them, all men bar Betty and a battle-axe of a woman, Sergeant Major Baxter, who didn't seem to like any of those under her. As Betty's hand touched the rich mahogany of the sweeping banister, she wondered what the house must make of its new occupants. It had gone from the world of Lady Chesham in her silk Chanel evening gowns, drifting through its rooms, genteel and delicate, to sturdy women in uniform thundering along corridors with purpose and dedication. Was this the future? Or would things ever go back to how they'd been before?

Once they reached their room, Major Smith drew down the blackout blinds and the heavy yellow damask curtains at the diamond-leaded windows, as if that might protect them, and they worked as fast as they could in the dim light with torches, filling boxes with papers under Baxter's direction. Battle-axe or not, she knew exactly what was where. With direct, concise decisions she prioritised which of the filing cabinets needed to be emptied, which desks cleared and what could be left behind. Betty was given the job of tying bundles of paper with string to keep the reports, relevant statements, and transcripts together before putting them into the few boxes they'd been able to gather. The rest were going into shopping baskets, empty desk drawers and anything suitable for carrying files that they could find.

With their first load ready to go, it was agreed that they'd take it down to the front hall where it could be stored in the big stone porch before coming back for more. Major Smith was anxious that no one should be left behind, so they all gathered up what they could and moved quickly down the stairs to the hallway by the front door. Betty was at the rear with Major Wendermeyer when a lorry roared up to the front of the house, spitting gravel as it came.

'Hell's teeth,' said Major Smith. 'We'll have to take what we've got. That's a blow.'

There was still another stack of paperwork upstairs.

Uniformed soldiers bundled out of the lorry, unloading wheelbarrows, shovels and large planks of wood, and beyond them Betty saw Colonel Myers coming up the drive on foot.

'Hey you! What are you all doing here?' a stern voice bellowed. 'You need to evacuate the building immediately. Is there anyone else in there?'

The man in front of Betty who'd stepped out from the porch looked back. Wendermeyer shook his head, putting his fingers over his lips.

'No, Sir,' said the man, as Wendermeyer slipped back into the shadows. Betty stepped back.

'No, you go,' he said urgently.

'No, they haven't seen me. There's still too much to leave. Even if we only get it down to the porch, it's still safer than in the offices. That bomb could bring down the whole of that wing.'

'Yes, which is why you should go.'

She shook her head, even though the thought of going back up those stairs terrified her. She could never live with herself if she left and he was the only one here. No one should die alone.

'I'm staying.' Her resolute look had him sighing as he watched the other eight members of the team scoop up their loads from the porch and begin to carry them down the path to the church.

For the hundredth time in the last hour, her fingers strayed to her nose, stroking the bridge, and she said a silent prayer before following the Major back up the stairs.

Chapter Fifteen

Evelyn

I t had been a while since she'd held a shotgun but a rifle wasn't so very different. At least she hoped not. Thank goodness she'd pestered her brother to teach her to shoot and that Daddy had allowed her to join in the grouse shooting every August rather than be left behind with the other ladies.

'Ready?' asked Freddie.

'As I'll ever be.' She shot him a quick nervous grin as they filed out of the packed church towards the back entrance of the house where the prisoners were kept.

'I'm glad you are. So much for this being a cushy number. My mother would have kittens if she knew, and yours.' Freddie winced. 'Not what she'd want for her little girl.'

'She's been destined for disappointment on that front for a long time.' Ever since Evelyn had given up her place at Oxford, to be precise. Her mother had finally accepted that Evelyn wasn't going to settle into the role of debutante, although it had been plain for years to her father, who'd written to her congratulating her on her decision to join the Navy and told her how proud of her he was and how delighted to hear that she was following the family tradition of doing one's duty.

'Let's hope this bally bomb doesn't blow.'

'Fingers crossed.' Evelyn hefted her rifle onto her shoulder as they walked through the tree-lined path to the prefabricated H-block of cells. It felt good to be doing something and she was glad she hadn't been left in the church. In her head, she thanked her brother for always letting her tag along. It would have been unbearable to sit idle.

Until they knew the size of the bomb, there was no way of knowing how far its blast might impact, but Myers couldn't afford to take any risks. They'd each been allocated a partner and the two of them were responsible for escorting two prisoners from their cells to an underground holding facility beneath the house. Time was now of the essence, to escort the prisoners before the Royal Engineers arrived. Myers was worried that if the bomb did go off, the prisoners could escape, which would not only cause mayhem but give rise to an awful lot of inconvenient questions.

The usual prison guards had been stationed around the perimeter as an extra safeguard but Myers wanted those fluent in German to deal with the prisoners, so as not to alarm them but also so as not to give them any ideas about mass flight. Escorting them all at the same was a considered risk, hence arms being provided. They were probably breaking a ton of military regulations but that was Myers all over. Needs must was his eternal motto.

They approached the cell and the guard unlocked the door. Evelyn handed him her rifle as she mentally rehearsed the script they'd been given. Freddie would be armed as she blindfolded the men. She wanted to make sure she sounded authoritative and in charge, not that they were winging it. The instruction was to get the prisoners into a tunnel under the house. Myers had decided it would be the safest place and the easiest to guard. Apparently the tunnel was built with the house in the 1860s, although Evelyn couldn't imagine why. What purpose would it have served? It seemed an expensive extravagance for ensuring the family didn't get wet on the way to matins. According to one of her early briefings in that first week after she'd arrived, since CSDIC moved into the building the tunnel was designated the main escape route in the unfortunate event that the country was invaded.

Today the plan was to use part of the tunnel as a holding area. The only problem was, because of where the bomb was situated on the path between the house and the cells, the only way of accessing the tunnel was through the M room, which was incredibly risky, especially as none of the officers had ever seen it and it had been agreed that the usual soldiers responsible for guarding the prisoners shouldn't be made aware of it, which was why Evelyn and her fellow officers would be escorting the German prisoners. It was imperative to keep the knowledge of the room and its purpose between as few people as possible. The current shift of listeners were still in situ as it had been decided that they were comparatively safe in the cellar.

Evelyn spoke in German: 'We're here to escort you to a new holding cell. We need to put these on.' It came out clumsily, she'd meant to be more authoritative, but now it came to it, she was acutely uncomfortable about blindfolding them. It seemed easy enough, talking about it in the packed church surrounded by friends and colleagues. Normally when interrogating a fellow officer, she treated them as equals, as human beings. Blindfolding someone seemed inhumane, an unpleasant demonstration of power, and it didn't sit well with her. People were blindfolded before they were executed. Freddie looked equally ill at ease.

The Luftwaffe pilot in the bottom bunk rose, frowning in suspicion. 'Why? Where are we going?'

Words failed her for a second. With his blond hair, steel-grey blue eyes and sharp cheekbones, in the dim light he looked just like Peter.

'Stand up and turn around,' she said briskly, hoping her voice didn't betray her. She glanced at Freddie who seemed as disconcerted as she was and narrowed her eyes at his gun. He got the message. 'Put your hands above your head and do as you're told.'

The pilot ignored them as the second man, a U-boat engineer, looked down from the upper bunk with wide blue eyes. *Damn*, thought Evelyn. Of the two of them he clearly would have been more compliant. She hoped he wouldn't follow his cellmate's lead.

'Where are you taking us?' The pilot thrust his chin forward, bullish and demanding. *He isn't Peter*, she told herself, wanting to reassure him. She was desperate to tell him it was for his own safety but they'd been expressly forbidden to talk about the bomb. 'It will be easier not to answer any questions,' they'd been told. 'You are in charge.'

'Hands on your head. Turn round,' she repeated, her heart thudding. She gripped the cotton fabric in her clammy hands.

He stood defiantly, his feet set apart as if anchoring him to the floor, his arm muscles bunching.

Evelyn couldn't afford to give an inch. She jutted her chin out and met his belligerent stare, taking a step forward, pretending to be far braver than she felt. Inside she wanted to back away.

'I said, turn around.' There was a flicker in his eyes and she thought she'd lost but then he sneered at her and insultingly slowly turned around.

She eased out a tiny sigh of relief and gripped her hands into fists to steady them before she lifted them to thread the blindfold through the crook of one of the man's raised arms. Determined not to show any weakness, she took her time, carefully knotting the fabric and making sure the broad strip of material covered his eyes and that there was no way he could see anything.

Freddie stood at attention, the rifle focused on the man as Evelyn turned with regal disdain and looked up at the other man on the top bunk.

'Now you,' she said.

He nodded. She kept her face blank, not showing her immediate relief at his simple acquiescence. Once down the ladder he turned without being asked, raised his hands and she tied the blindfold.

The guard was to accompany them to the entrance of the M room and from there they were on their own.

'Keep your hands on your head.'

She retrieved her rifle, grateful that Freddie and not she had had to point it at someone. If it came to it, could she shoot someone? It wasn't a question she'd ever asked herself before and yet the men in her family would have to do it without hesitation. The men on the front had to shoot without reservation.

They ushered the prisoners out of the cell and down the path towards the house and Evelyn held her rifle tightly, every nerve ending on alert. Her cheery gung-ho attitude had dissolved in shame and irritation with herself. It wasn't a game. Never had been and yet she'd been sucked into the easy life. Yes, they worked hard here at Latimer House and there was a lot at stake but they didn't have to make life-or-death decisions or do battle daily. They were removed from the action and the do-or-die of war. The thought of her brother plunged her into guilt. She would never have to make the sort of decisions that a soldier on the field of battle had to make. Was she fooling herself, that she was making a difference? There was an awful realisation that she wasn't as brave as she'd imagined. She'd almost quailed under the scorn of the German officer. If he'd pushed harder, what would she have done? Disappointment filled her, tinged with a strong sense of failure. Had she been playing at being an officer all this time?

They came to the entrance to the Nissan hut which led into the M room. Evelyn had never been past this point. The guard nodded and retreated as the door was opened.

'Put your hand on the shoulder of the man in front of you,' said Evelyn as Freddie went to stand at the front to guide the first man. Of course, it was the recalcitrant Luftwaffe pilot who stubbornly stood his ground. 'Where are you taking us?'

She raised her rifle and prodded him in the back.

Perhaps if she hadn't been so frightened herself, she might have realised how frightened he must have been but she was focused on getting the job done and didn't have time or room for any other thought.

The man immediately put his hand on the shoulder of his cellmate and they set off through the first door, then to the second, entering the top-secret M room. Evelyn wanted to take her time to look around but she didn't dare; all she registered was the silent, wary faces of the men and two women in the room, one of whom was Judith. She glanced over at her and nodded and gained some small comfort from the encouraging smile she received. It reinforced her defences and reminded her of what people like Judith had suffered and thousands more would, if Hitler wasn't stopped.

As they moved through the room, Evelyn registered the chill in the air as their feet echoed on the concrete floor. Every step through the room with its unfamiliar equipment seemed to take for ever. If one of the men ripped off their blindfolds and saw the room, the game would be up. Evelyn watched the blue-grey fabric of the uniform of the man in front of her with unwavering attention, ready for any deviation of movement. She didn't trust him. There'd been challenge in his eyes in the cell and she wasn't foolish enough to believe she'd won.

One of his hands twitched and she gritted her teeth as he lowered his arm and then just in time she realised it was a distraction technique as with the other hand he began to tug at his blindfold.

'*Nein!*' she shouted.

Raising her rifle she stabbed sharply at his elbow, surprising herself with her own vehemence.

He grunted and stopped but she was ready for him. She prodded him again. Freddie stopped and looked over his shoulder, worry lines creasing his forehead.

'*Rausgehen!*' she snapped.

With a surly swagger he began to walk again. She closed her eyes, trying to rally herself, her pulse tripping with a burst of adrenaline. She gripped the rifle. There was too much to lose. Latimer House was vital in the war effort, and this room housed the biggest secret of all. It would not be revealed on her watch. In a voice she didn't recognise she spat, 'One more move and I will shoot you.'

She watched as the wool-clad shoulders tensed, both pleased and horrified that her threat had registered.

They filed through the last half of the M room without

incident and through to the corridor on the other side, passing the now empty wine cellars under a vaulted ceiling. As they walked she shivered in the dank air, the sounds of their footsteps ricocheting off the brick walls of the approaching tunnel. The mouth yawned. Ahead there were torchlights bobbing. Other prisoners were already being told to sit down against the walls and to keep quiet.

Suddenly a voice yelled in German, '*Sie werden uns erschießen!*' ('They're going to shoot us!')

The pilot reacted instantly. Ripping down his blindfold and turning to face Evelyn, he pushed her out of the way and bolted towards the door leading to the M room.

It happened so fast, the only thought in her head was that she had to stop him. There was too much at stake. With steely determination she hadn't known she possessed, she raised the rifle and fired.

The noise roared around the tunnel and Evelyn's ears sang as her arms reverberated with the power of the gun blast.

A shower of brick rained down as the man fell to the floor.

'Bloody hell,' breathed Freddie. 'You shot him.'

'No, I didn't,' snapped Evelyn. 'I fired over his head. He threw himself to the floor.' She drew in a breath and strode over, still holding the gun in both hands. Standing over him, she said, 'Move again and I will shoot you this time.' Her grim voice belied the nausea in her stomach and her fervent gratitude for all those lessons from her brother.

She'd deliberately shot above his head at the roof, hoping that it would stop him. If it hadn't, she would have had to shoot him in the back, and that would have been unconscionable, to shoot a defenceless man. She couldn't have lived with herself.

Behind there was shouting, crisp orders: 'Nobody move. Nobody will get hurt.'

Lieutenant Colonel Weston appeared at her side, along with Ian Spencer.

Spencer dragged the man to his feet. His blindfold was pushed down to his neck. He shot Evelyn a surprised look and muttered in German, 'I didn't think you'd shoot.'

She gave him a grim smile. 'For King and country, I shoot.' And realised she meant it.

Chapter Sixteen

Judith

When the gunshot rang out from beyond the door, every head jerked upwards and they all turned to stare at the door through which the last lot of German prisoners of war had been taken scant minutes previously. Walther and Sergeant Flesch jumped to their feet and ran towards the door, Flesch drawing a pistol.

Everyone in the room froze, with that awkward see-sawing balance as if unsure whether to leap to their feet any moment, like gazelles ready for flight. The tension everyone had been keeping under wraps since they'd heard about the bomb was now leaking out, almost palpable in the air. Judith held her breath, wondering why the two men were running towards the danger. Where did they find the courage?

What had happened? Was someone dead? What about Evelyn? So steady and stern with that rifle, concentrating hard on the job in hand. Judith felt oddly proud of her, even though she didn't really know her that well.

They all waited in silence, Flesch's gun trained on the door, wavering only slightly when it opened and Lieutenant Colonel Weston came through. He closed the door carefully behind him, putting his finger to his lips.

'Stand down, Sergeant,' he said in a low voice. 'False alarm. Everything is fine.' Despite his reassuring words, his mouth twisted with grim resolve. 'Everyone all right?'

They all nodded. He gave them a silent thumbs-up and disappeared back through the door again, leaving them as much in the dark as they had been all afternoon. There was a collective sigh, not quite of relief, as there was still the bomb above to think of, but at least there was one fewer thing to worry about.

It had been an eerie, oppressive few hours since they'd heard from a Naval Intelligence Officer, via a microphone in one of the cells. She'd filled them in and given the order that they were to stay put until further instructions. It was clear that they were marooned until the bomb was defused or... The alternative was too worrying to consider. Then came the news that the prisoners of war were going to be taken to a tunnel beneath the house and had to come through the M room. One by one the microphones in the cells had gone silent and then pairs of prisoners in their blindfolds had filed through the room. As they shuffled through, Judith had studied them impassively, faceless and anonymous – the blindfolds rendered them featureless. It was impossible to relate any of them to the voices she'd become accustomed to. They were the opposite to ghosts, just empty bodies rather than spirits.

It had been impressed upon them how vital it was to maintain absolute silence. The Germans were to believe that they were being led through empty cellars; not one clue should be revealed that there was more going on in these close confines. Every listener knew the importance of guarding the secrets of Latimer House.

Judith had looked up at the ceiling countless times in the last few hours, wondering if it would hold under the blast. Would a bomb rip out the heart of the M room? Would it be as destructive as the *Sturmabteilung* had been in her father's shop? Closing her eyes, she recalled the pages of sheet music strewn across the floor, fluttering in the wind through the smashed windows, and the bones of violins, crunched underfoot. Would a bomb toss everything in this room upwards in chaos before coming back down to rest in similar mangled disarray? Would it hurt as much to die this way? Her poor father had seen his life's work destroyed and died in an agony of emotion. She caught sight of Frida's pinched face on the other side of the table and another listener with his head in his hands. They all needed to be brave, to have faith. This time she wasn't alone.

The gunshot had startled her, startled them all, and now the unanswered questions as to what had gone on had rattled everyone in the room. They still had to keep quiet. What was happening above them? Not knowing strained the nerves, made everyone edgy. Frida tapped a pencil on the table, unaware of the tap, tap against the surface. Sergeant Flesch kept patting the pocket holding his gun. Walther had put his feet up on the table and had closed his eyes as if catching up on some sleep. *Calm as ever*, she thought, watching his sleeping face.

'He's got the right idea,' murmured the Sergeant next to her, leaning back in his chair, folding his arms and following suit. A couple of others copied and for a moment Judith was tempted to lay her head down on the table and try. It was already two hours after their shift should have finished but the thought of sleeping in a room of other people made her feel vulnerable. The not knowing what was going on chafed at her nerves. She flexed her fingers and thought of the piano she'd found. Closing her eyes, she imagined the keys in front of her and *Für Elise* in her head again. Imagined herself playing again. For the first time in a long time, she was able to lose herself in the music and the pinching fingers of tension gripping her shoulders eased their grip. She let the melody in, swirling around her head, enjoying the notes' rise and soar. Time passed. The music caught her up and tossed her like the waves in the sea, through Chopin, Beethoven, Mozart and Liszt. When she finally opened her eyes, blinking with that back-to-earth, dropped-out-of-the-sky feeling in the bright lights of the M room, she made herself a silent promise: she would let music back into her life. She'd cut it out because it reminded her of her father, her life in Berlin and all that she'd lost, but what she'd really done was cut out the very heart of who she was.

'Judith, Judith.' A hand shook her on the shoulder and she jerked awake, conscious of the dribble running down her chin.

Walther smiled gently down at her. 'Time to go.'

'Is it all over?' she whispered in response to his soft voice, watching as the other listeners were filing out in silence.

'Yes. We can leave and then they'll take the prisoners of war back to their cells.'

'Did they make the bomb safe?' She stood up and stretched, glancing at the clock on the wall. She'd been asleep for half an hour but it had been a very long day.

He laughed. 'Unless you slept through an explosion. I don't

know about you, but I'm ready for a cup of tea. Do you think they'll let us have extra biscuit rations?'

'I hope so,' she replied with feeling, conscious of her grumbling stomach. They'd been down here for eleven hours and she hadn't eaten since lunchtime. It was now seven o'clock but she was anxious to find out what had been going on with everyone else.

After plenty of toast, extra biscuits and unexpected sausage rations, Judith slid out from her place at the table, awkwardly clambering over the wooden bench seat and putting down her teacup, anxious to reach the quiet calm of her quarters. There wasn't a seat to spare in the Sergeants' Mess and the noise banged against her already aching head. Everyone seemed to be talking non-stop about the events of the day, snatches of this and that, enough to fill a kaleidoscope and certainly as dizzying. Judith had had quite enough of the drama. As she inched her way out of the room, she caught sight of Betty's wan face, her hand propped up under her chin as if she could barely manage the weight of her own head. The poor thing looked washed out.

Before Judith had even reached the bottom step of the staircase, Betty appeared at her side.

'What a day,' she said, rubbing at her temples.

'Yes,' said Judith. 'Were you in the church all afternoon?'

Betty's eyes lit up and she looked around with a sudden mischievous grin. 'I'll tell you all about it when we get upstairs.'

'Wait up.' They turned to find Evelyn behind them. When the three of them reached the door to their room, she flapped open her coat to reveal a bottle of brandy. 'Think we need a bit of a reviver. I've been keeping it in my car for an emergency, I think today qualifies, don't you?' Despite her upbeat tone, Judith could see the strain around her eyes and the droop of her mouth. Clearly she'd had a difficult day.

'Lawks, yes,' said Betty, crossing to Evelyn's dressing table where she kept the three Baccarat glasses.

'It's been interesting,' said Judith, sinking onto her bed and unlacing her shoes, her bones sagging with relief. Every sinew seemed to have been stretched taut all day. 'And you can tell me what happened when that gun was fired. Everyone in the M room jumped out of their skins.'

'What gun? How come I missed all the excitement?' asked Betty, handing a glass to Evelyn.

'Drinks first and I'll tell all,' said Evelyn, opening up the brandy.

By the time three tots of brandy were poured, Evelyn sat on the end of Judith's bed and Betty sprawled across hers on her stomach, propped up on her elbows facing them both.

'It was pretty hairy,' said Evelyn, taking a hefty swig of her drink after she told the full story.

'And I thought I had a nerve-racking afternoon,' said Betty, lifting her glass to toast them. 'I'd have probably dropped the blinking gun and shot him in the foot or something.'

'It was one of those split-second decisions. I really didn't want to shoot him. All I could think was of my father and my brother and how cowardly it would be to shoot someone in the back.' Evelyn shuddered. 'Those poor men, I think some of them honestly thought they were about to be executed. They must have been terrified.'

Judith pursed her lips. The German prisoners deserved everything they got. What they'd been through wasn't nearly as bad as the suffering so many others had experienced at the hands of the Nazis. Luckily Betty had begun to talk so it stopped her voicing her thoughts but there was a tiny voice in the back of her mind wondering if she could have pulled the trigger. What had Walther said? 'God will be our judge. He will be their judge too.'

Chapter Seventeen

JUNE 1943

Betty

'Betty, Betty, Betty!' her little sister trilled happily, running up the lane to greet her, throwing her stick-thin arms around Betty's waist.

'Jane, Jane, Jane,' she sang back to her sister's delight.

'There was a bomb. Did you know? We saw the men take it away in a lorry. They stopped by the green so we could all see. It was huge.'

Betty had seen the bomb. She'd seen the men digging so carefully around it while she and Major Wendermeyer cleared the last few boxes from the offices. Every punch down of their shovels in the ground around it had brought with it a heart-clenching wave of fear. The thought of what could have gone wrong that day had brought back familiar nightmares last night.

'Are you staying for tea? We have a cake. Bert's coming. And Dennis, Minnie and Baby Face all laid eggs this week.'

Typical. It annoyed her that Ma made cake for Bert using all her butter ration for him. She could bet he wasn't suffering from starvation up at the farm. The Davenports weren't short of a bob or two whereas without Betty's wages, Ma would struggle to pay the rent. Her war widow's pension didn't go very far.

Betty pasted on her best smile as Jane chattered on about the chickens, observing that her sister was almost bursting out of her dress. Her bosom seemed to have sprouted overnight and all of a sudden she looked like a young woman.

'Come see the chickens. Come see.'

They rounded the cottage and Jane led her over the small enclosure where five chickens scratched and pecked at the bare earth. Her sister immediately scooped up the smallest hen and stroked it. 'This is Baby Face, she's my favourite but Ma won't let her in the house.'

'I don't think chickens like being in houses,' said Betty gently, imagining her ma's reaction. She kept the cottage spotless. They might not have much money but her ma was a proud woman and no one would ever accuse her of being slatternly. In her youth, before Dad had died, she'd been a gay, carefree woman, someone Betty had had a lot more in common with. Worry had made her anxious and snappy.

Betty was about to turn away when she noticed the door to the coop had been fixed, with what looked like exactly the same piece of wood that she'd used to patch the hole. She bent to study the work which wasn't as neat as hers had been, not by a long chalk. The tiny pin tacks were shiny and she frowned.

'Who fixed the door?'

'Bert. He…'

Without listening to what Jane said, she raced over to the shed and stepped over the boxes and old hessian sacks to the corner where she'd hidden the toolbox. It was still there but not as well covered as when she'd left it. When she opened it, she knew that Bert had been in there. Pin tacks were scattered all over the inside layer and when she lifted it out, she saw that Dad's hammer was missing. Feeling her anger start to boil, she carefully put the metal tray back and closed the lid. She carried the toolbox to the door and left it just inside. Bert would not be helping himself to anymore of her dad's tools if she had anything to do with it. Her dad had been the centre of this family. His word was law but it was law that was dispensed in a fair and just way. He wasn't one for losing his rag, he weighed things up, but if you were in the wrong he made sure you knew about it. Betty had inherited his strong sense of right and wrong.

Marching inside, she found her ma making a pot of tea and Bert sprawled in one of the kitchen chairs.

'Have you taken Dad's hammer?' she demanded, too angry to curb her tongue.

The lazy smile left Bert's face and he lunged to his feet and slapped her. Her ma gasped and Jane whimpered.

'Don't you go talking to me like that,' he snarled.

'Betty! Show some respect,' said her ma, in horrified tones.

Betty stood, fists curled at her sides. 'You have no right.'

'I have no right. What are you talking about? They're men's tools. There's a war on. I needed a good hammer. And I'll mind you watch your mouth.'

Her ma glared at her. 'Betty Connors, you sit down. Bert, pay no heed to her. I don't know what's got into her.'

'I know what she needs,' Bert growled. 'A good thrashing. Beat some sense back into you. Since you joined up you've got ideas above your station. That'll stop when we're married, I can tell you.' There was a vicious look in his dark eyes and she managed to hide the shiver of fear that gripped her, but she couldn't bring herself to apologise.

'I need your help, Betty. With the laundry.' Without ceremony, her ma dragged her by the arm out of the room. 'What's got into you?' she hissed. 'And what use have you got for your dad's hammer? Bert's right. You have got a bit big for your britches, young lady. He's not going to want you if you keep on behaving like this. And then what will you do? There's lots of men who won't be coming back to this village. Want to end up a spinster?'

Betty, too angry to listen, exhaled heavily. 'That's Dad's toolbox. He has no right.'

Her ma grabbed her by the arms and shook her. 'You listen to me. What will happen to us if we're thrown out of this cottage? Me and your sister? We have nowhere to go.' Her eyes widened, filled with a mix of worry and terror. Remorse pricked at Betty. This wasn't just about her.

'Betty, you have to stop this nonsense, right now. Go apologise to the man. That toolbox is as good as his. When you're married, what you going to do, hide it under the ruddy bed?'

Betty stared at her mutinously but her dad would have wanted her to do right by the family. While every part of her rebelled at the idea of apologising to Bert, there was a desperation to her ma's gimlet stare that she couldn't ignore. Being a single woman with two daughters, she knew how hard it was to make ends meet and she wanted to avoid that struggle for Betty.

Betty nodded. 'Sorry, Ma.'

Her apology stuck in her craw but she made it even as Bert

smirked at her.

'That's more like it, Betty. Now come give us a kiss.' He yanked her onto his lap and ground his mouth into hers, giving her a sharp nip on the lower lip and pinching her on her thigh with vicious, mean fingers. 'They working you hard up there?' His eyes bored into her and she knew she'd got off lightly for the time being but there was promise of retribution in the furrow of his brow. 'Been busy of late up at the house. Lots of deliveries going up the lane. Must have a lot of stock at the moment.'

She nodded and sat placidly in his lap, praying that he wouldn't ask any more questions, knowing he wouldn't take kindly to being told she couldn't tell him. Luckily Ma changed the subject by asking after Mrs Davenport and the new land girls that had arrived.

Bert grinned and shot Betty a sly look. 'Nice girls, all of them. A bit of a laugh and ripe for a bit of fun in the country.' Under the table he slid his hand up her skirt and she jumped up, horrified. He laughed. 'Bit skittish, aren't you?'

'Let me help with those potatoes, Ma,' said Betty hurriedly. 'Do you want all of them peeling?'

'Ta, love. That would be— Oh Jane, look at that mess. I told you not to bring that chicken in here!'

While they'd been talking Jane had crept in clutching Baby Face who had managed to leave a nasty stain down her dress and the floor.

'It's all right, I'll tidy it up,' said Betty, grateful for something to do to keep out of Bert's reach. He'd not been so bold before and it had unnerved her. Normally she was able to keep his hands at bay but it was obvious that he thought that with Ma eating out of his hand, he could do what he liked. Well, he could think again.

Pulling Jane over to the sink, she grabbed a cloth and began sponging her sister's dress, lifting the skirt to clean the soiled fabric. The chicken was now pecking around the floor and her ma scooped it up and went outside scolding as she went, 'For the love of god, how many times do I have to tell that girl.'

Jane sniffed. 'But Baby Face wanted to come in. He wanted to say hello.'

'I'm sure he'd rather stay with his friends, Jane. They'll get lonely without him.'

'I'm lonely without you, Betty. When are you coming home?'

'I'm home now, aren't I, silly.'

'It's not the same.' She lowered her voice and whispered. 'I don't like him.'

With her head bent over her sister's skirt, Betty glanced at Bert from under her lashes. Thankfully he hadn't heard but she felt a ghost step on her shadow as she saw the lascivious look he cast Jane, his eyes running over her body. There was no mistaking that leer. Her heart clenched in sudden fear for her sister. _____ protect her when Betty wasn't around? Ma needed _____ over her _____ to keep it.

In a loud voice she said, 'There you go, Jane. All done.'

Ma came back in the kitchen as Jane dashed past her back to her beloved chickens.

'That girl is going to be the death of me. She'd sleep out there with those ruddy birds, if she could. She's daft on them.'

'Hen witted,' said Bert with a loud guffaw, laughing at his own joke.

Betty held her tongue and bristled. No point in telling him what she thought.

A little while later, with great ceremony, Ma brought out the cake, which brought a smile to Jane's serious little face. The four of them sat around the old table which bore the scars and stains of many family meals. Betty could still remember her dad sitting at the head where Bert now lounged as if he owned the place. She wondered what her dad would have thought of him. He certainly wouldn't have allowed slouching like that at the table.

'Mmm,' said Jane with a blissful expression on her face and a mouthful of cake. It was a rare treat even though the chickens laid plenty of eggs. Ma tended to sell or barter as many as she could to help make ends meet. Which reminded Betty that she'd slip her most of her pay packet when Bert wasn't looking. Now she wasn't in London she wasn't spending so much and could give Ma a little bit more, and she was trying to put a little bit by herself.

'Why don't you and Bert go into the front room, while I clear up here,' said Ma.

'No, it's all right. I'll give you a hand.'

Ma gave her a sharp look and Betty sighed. 'Why don't I take the peelings out for the chickens?' and before Ma could say anything she grabbed the bowl and went outside, anything to escape the stuffy atmosphere inside.

She stood watching the chickens scratching about, lifting her face to the sunshine, wishing that she was back at the house, out on the balcony on her own, with no one knowing where she was. She'd lie, she decided, say she had to get back for a late shift.

As she turned to go back inside, Bert came up behind, putting both arms around her waist and nuzzling at her neck. 'Still the best-looking woman I know,' he said, pulling her back against his body. She couldn't help stiffening.

'What's wrong with you?'

'Nothing, it's just Jane could be...'

'Jane? Probably about time she learned what's what. Time she grew up. Don't you worry, I'll keep an eye on her.' His hands slid up beneath her breasts. She held her breath, knowing that if she tried to move he could turn nasty. 'So why don't you tell me more about what's going on up at the house?'

'Nothing. It's a distribution centre. We ... distribute things.'

'Exactly. And I know what.' His eyes gleamed.

'You do?' she faltered.

'No big secret, although I know why they want to keep it all secret.'

Betty swallowed. How did he know?

'They don't want every Tom, Dick and Harry knowing there's a fortune in fags and booze up there.'

'What?' The word was startled from her.

'Ha! You thought I didn't know,' he crowed, with sudden delight. 'You should appreciate that Bert Davenport knows everything going on in his patch. One of the lorries always coming and going broke down on Flaunden Hill. Donald stopped and says it were full of cigarettes, Players, Capstans and half a dozen cases of gin and, he thought, whisky.'

Betty heaved an internal sigh of relief, grateful that Bert had no idea what was going on.

'I don't know about that. I just do the typing.'

'Come on, Betty. I weren't born yesterday. And you ain't stupid. You must know where it's all stored. Where they keep everything. There was a lot of building work up there, Nissen huts and the like, probably storage places if it's a distribution centre.'

Betty shrugged. 'I have no idea.'

He tightened his hold. 'I reckon you could find out. You being on the inside and all that.'

'I can't, Bert. I don't go out of the offices.'

'Come on, bright girl like you.' He lifted one of his arms and hooked his elbow around her neck. 'Ask a few questions, find out the lay of the land. Don't seem to be any proper soldiers up there.'

Betty swallowed, feeling his arm pressing against her windpipe. There was no way she was giving away the secrets of Latimer House. 'I think that most of the stuff is equipment for soldiers, uniforms, supplies and such like.'

'Well, you can find out, can't you? After all, you wouldn't want anything to happen to you ma or sister, would you? Or your ma to have to find new accommodation?' He tightened his hold and a flicker of genuine fear burned like neat lemon juice in her stomach.

'Bert,' she huffed, gasping in a breath. 'I don't have the access. I'm a typist in the office.' It galled her to have to say that when she was so chuffed about being promoted to sergeant. He hadn't even noticed the new stripes on her arm.

He breathed heavily in her ear. 'You find out where they keep the cigarettes or when the next lorry is going out.'

'I can't.'

'If you know what's good for you, you will.' He tightened his grip again and for a moment she thought she was going to pass out.

'Bert,' she managed to gasp.

'I can't protect your ma and your sister all the time, you know. What with you being away and no one to look after them.' She wanted to spit. He'd never looked out for them in his life. He was more often down the pub. 'You go back there and you find out everything you can, right?'

She nodded because what else could she do, and he loosened the hold on her neck. Sucking in a much-needed

breath, she tried to plant her feet firmly on the ground, fighting a disorientating, light-headed sensation. She was determined not to show any weakness in front of him.

Just as she straightened, he lunged and punched her hard in the chest. Taken by surprise, she fell backwards to the floor, the pain and shock reverberating through her. As she tried to scramble to her feet he put one booted foot on her hand and she fell back with a pathetic whimper of which she was heartily ashamed. Before she could say anything he dealt her two swift kicks in the ribs that left her gasping for air.

'Get up, you little cow. Now you listen. There'll be more of that if you don't do as you're told. I want to know where everything is kept. I want a map and what sort of guard, if any, is kept. You understand?' He trod harder on her hand, putting all his weight on his foot as he raised the other one to nudge at her ribs again.

She nodded, feeling traitorous tears of pain trickling down her face.

'Right. I've got to go. Some of us have got real jobs to do. None of this mucking about.'

He released her hand and leaned down to pull her unceremoniously to her feet. Her bruised ribs protested and she cried out as a sharp jab of pain sliced into her, making her double over, clutching her sides.

'Stand up and face me.' He grabbed her hair and forced her head up. Furious and ashamed, she gave him a look of utter contempt, her lip curling and her eyes narrowing with hatred. She would never cower to him.

He scowled. 'You'll learn,' he snarled with a crude laugh and gave her a sharp slap across her left cheek which left her ears ringing and her eyes smarting.

'Next time you're home you'll have the information I want.'

Resisting the urge to rub her face, she lifted her chin.

'Do you understand?' His voice throbbed with violence.

This time she nodded, making sure her face was wiped of all expression.

With a wicked turn of mood, he suddenly grinned. 'Don't take on so, Betty.' His hand stroked down the front of her skirt and he grabbed her between her legs. 'You're still getting the better end of this bargain. There are other women out there who would give it up. I like that you're saving yourself for me. But when we're married, I expect you to be a little more, shall we say, respectful.'

Over her dead body, she decided. She wouldn't marry him. Not now. Not ever. But she needed to make things safe for her ma and Jane and she didn't know how she was going to do that.

Feeling resigned, angry, humiliated and horribly impotent, she trudged up the driveway to Latimer House, wishing she could swap the heavy toolbox to her other hand. It had been an act of pure stubbornness bringing it with her but there was no way that she was leaving it at the cottage for Bert to help himself. Even though she was now paying for the stupidity of letting emotion win over common sense, it felt like a small victory.

'Excuse me, ma'am. Could I help you with that?' Before she could answer the toolbox was smoothly taken from her hand.

'Major Wendermeyer. Er, thank you.' She wanted to close her eyes and let the ground swallow her up. She hadn't seen much of him since that afternoon when they'd been thrown together and had refused to think of those moments under the desk when her whole body had been so aware of him.

What must she look like? Covered in mud and chicken shit with her hair loose and a pocketful of bobby pins. There'd been no way of rectifying the damage done to her curls from her ungainly sprawl on the floor, and after Bert had left with that boorish swagger, she hadn't wanted to stay in case he decided to come back for the toolbox.

'My pleasure, ma'am. It looked mighty heavy and it wouldn't be very gentlemanly of me to leave a pretty girl like you to carry it all the way up the driveway.'

They might have shared that afternoon of camaraderie when they were equals working to rescue the reports – all of which then had to be put back – but now she really didn't want to talk to him. All she wanted was to get up to her room and burrow under the bedclothes and cry while there was no one there to see her. Not only was her body battered and bruised but worse still, she felt raw and exposed. No one had ever hit her before and she hated being so vulnerable. Hated that a man could make her feel like this.

'That's very kind of you, thank you,' she said stiffly, suddenly horribly aware of what he, like Bert, could do if she displeased him.

'Can I ask why you're carrying a toolbox? I'd expect flowers, candy from an admirer or something, but a toolbox?' He raised one of those well-sculpted blond eyebrows that fascinated her so much and there was a decided teasing twinkle in his periwinkle blue eyes. Well he could tease away, she was not interested, although her faithless heart decided to find its own wayward rhythm, which was annoying to say the least. After Bert's sardonic gaze and rough treatment, this charming attention should have been balm to her soul but instead she felt bitter cynicism and was determined not to be charmed.

'It was my father's,' she replied coolly. And when had she ever called her dad her father? Was she trying to impress him? She hated herself for a moment but she didn't want him to know about the cottage she'd just left or the life she was expected to live when the war was over. Suddenly the bleakness that she'd always managed to keep at bay descended like a suffocating blanket. 'My dad, he was injured badly in the last war. He died. This was his toolbox. His pride and joy.'

'And what are you doing with it? Out here?' He sounded genuinely perplexed as if the toolbox had fallen out of the sky or something.

She sighed. 'I live in the village. Someone was taking things from it. I didn't want them to have my dad's things.'

'You mean stealing, right?'

She turned to face him, grateful that he understood immediately. He stopped dead, put the toolbox down with a thud and with one hand cupped her face.

'Who did this to you?'

She turned scarlet and stammered. 'No one.'

'No one,' he drawled, his smooth American accent suddenly dangerous. 'That's very strange because I can see a handprint.' Now he studied her more carefully, taking in her muddy clothes. 'Are you all right, ma'am?' He frowned and stared down at the hand she hadn't realised she'd cradled defensively against her waist. 'Can I see that?'

She swallowed back tears of shame. What must he think of her? That she asked for it? That she deserved it?

'It's nothing.'

He raised an eyebrow and in a second she saw his face change, the charming façade disappearing to absolute fury. 'Did a man do this to you?'

She nodded miserably.

'Oh, sweetheart, are you OK?' He reached for her hand and she instinctively recoiled.

'Hey, it's all right, I won't hurt you.' With reluctance, she let him look at her hand, studiously looking up at the sky, aware of the proximity of that handsome face. He must surely be revising his opinions of her. She'd been secretly so proud when he'd recognised her talent for analysis. Since she'd started her new job, she'd found a new sense of purpose and she loved the work. Loved finding the jigsaw pieces to make the whole. Now he'd know that she was the nothing that Bert knew she was.

'That needs medical attention. A cold compress.'

She nodded as if she knew what he was talking about and withdrew her hand.

'I'll be fine.'

'Do you want me to report this?'

'No,' she blurted out. 'It's a family matter.' If she put it like that he might drop the subject.

He studied her face with candid blue eyes and that sense of shame washed all over her again. She wanted to shrink into herself.

'Ma'am, where I come from, any decent man treats a lady like a lady. He would not raise a hand to her.'

She sighed, feeling defeated. What could she do against Bert? 'Maybe I'm not a lady.'

Carl Wendermeyer looked fierce. 'You are a lady and don't you ever forget it. Can you tell me who did this to you?'

She shook her head. 'No. Please. It's fine. It was a misunderstanding.'

He frowned and looked at the toolbox. 'And the tools?'

'I want to make sure they're looked after.'

'OK,' he said and he picked the toolbox up. They walked

side by side, his face still grim. When they reached the house, he turned to her. 'If there's anything I can do to help, you will ask me?'

Her eyes filled with unwelcome tears. It was hard to believe his kindness, it wasn't something that she was used to.

'Thank you,' she said, deliberately avoiding saying yes because there was nothing that he could do.

He insisted on carrying the toolbox as far as the bottom of the servants' stairs to her room, which left her feeling uncomfortable. Thankfully, at this time of the day, most people were hard at work so no one saw him escorting her up the main stairs.

'Along here? I've never seen you and my room is just down the hall.'

She managed a laugh. 'No, it's up another two flights. We're up in the servants' quarters.'

'My mistake.'

They reached the bottom of the final set of stairs.

'I can carry it from here,' she said, suddenly anxious that he might insist on coming up and that might place her in a potentially comprising situation if anyone saw them.

'You sure?'

'Yes. It's only a few stairs.'

'OK, ma'am. Well, you take care of yourself, Betty.' His voice softened as he said her name and suddenly she couldn't bring herself to look at him. Inside her stomach turned to jelly and her legs were in danger of following suit. Since when had she ever been shy?

He swept his cap off and bowed to her as he backed away down the corridor.

It took her nearly a full minute to gather her scattered wits and push her legs into action to climb the stairs. Dropping the toolbox by the bed, she sank onto the mattress and began to cry. Proper heartrending sobs, covering her face with her hands.

It was only when she heard footsteps clambering through the window, she realised she wasn't alone and she looked up to find Evelyn's perturbed face.

'Oh, darling. Whatever is the matter?' The other woman put her arm around her and pulled her into a wonderfully soft embrace that made Betty cry even harder. If she'd been embarrassed before, it was now increased tenfold but it was so comforting to be held and to have someone stroke her hair and tell her, 'Shh, darling. It will be all right. There. There.'

Eventually Betty came to a gulping, soggy stop, wiping at her face with the fine lawn handkerchief that Evelyn had pressed into her hands.

'Sorry. I – er – I'm—' Then they both turned towards the door, hearing footsteps on the stairs outside. 'Oh no.' Betty's face crumpled, thinking it might be the Major again. She really didn't want him to see her like this. It had been bad enough downstairs and out on the drive.

'I'll see to it,' said Evelyn, crisply going to the door.

Betty buried her face in her lap, listening to the murmured conversation outside but she couldn't make out the words. Then Evelyn returned carrying a bowl and cloths.

'That was Elsie. She was asked to bring up some iced water for you.' There was a question in Evelyn's voice and Betty held up her now swollen hand; two of the fingers looked like fat little sausages.

'What happened?'

Betty's eyes began to fill with tears and she realised that she was suffering from shock. Bert's punches were the first time that she'd ever experienced physical violence and she realised it wasn't the pain that upset her so much – although her ribs and hand were sore, as was her cheek – but the awful sense of powerlessness she'd felt. What as a woman could she do? And how was she going to tell him that the information he wanted didn't exist, without giving away the secrets of the house?

Evelyn took over, soaking her hand in the bowl of ice-cold water, talking in calm, no-nonsense tones.

'So what has happened? You look like you've been beaten.'

Betty winced and she reluctantly told her what had happened, although not the real reason for Bert's determination to show her who was boss.

'You poor darling, that sounds absolutely beastly. Did you tell your mother?'

'No. She thinks Bert's wonderful and I'm worried what he'll do to my sister when I'm not there to look after her.'

'That's dreadful. But I think you should tell her. And avoid going home for a while. At least if you're not there he can't hurt you again.'

'I can't tell her.' It would place an intolerable and unfair burden on Ma. She already had enough to worry about. 'But I can avoid going home for a while.'

'Tell you what. I've got to go on a driving mission for Myers, so I'll have extra petrol rations. I'm planning to go to Mummy's. Come with me and maybe we'll borrow one of my father's old service revolvers. You could threaten to shoot this Bert.'

Betty burst out laughing at Evelyn's serious, determined expression. 'I'd like to see his face if I pointed a gun at him.'

'Well, as long as it wasn't loaded. I think you might get into trouble if you actually shot the blighter. But sometimes we have to fight back.'

'Thank you, Evelyn.'

'For what?'

'For being so nice.'

'Why ever would I not be?'

'Because it shows what sort of girl I am.'

A furious expression crossed the other girl's face. 'Don't you dare say that. It doesn't matter what sort you are, no one should have put up with that sort of behaviour.' She paused. 'You're embarrassed.'

Betty nodded.

'Well, you have nothing to be embarrassed about.' Sudden humour touched her mouth. 'You have no idea how I came to be here, have you? I broke my commanding officer's jaw when he tried to molest me on duty one night.'

'You did what!' Betty stared at her with a mix of horror and admiration.

Evelyn grinned. 'Come and have a cigarette, and bring that bowl with you, we can balance it on the ledge and I'll tell you all about it. And I'll tell you what Myers said.' She lifted her eyebrows in comical exaggeration that had Betty laughing again, although she suddenly said:

'You won't tell Judith about this, will you? I already think she disapproves of me. Thinks I'm a bit fast or something.'

'Nonsense, Judith is too lost in grief to disapprove of anything. She's adrift, that one. Needs to find her place in life. But she's ever so brave at the same time. I admire her, starting again in a new country, having to live in a strange place. It must be jolly tough but she never complains. I don't think she has time or the capacity to judge you, darling. Now come on, let's get some fresh air and I'll tell you all about my misdemeanours and we'll try to think of a way to make sure that Bert and his filthy mitts keep their distance.'

Chapter Eighteen

Evelyn

A t nine o'clock, a few days after what was now being called UXB (unexploded bomb) day, Evelyn found herself standing to attention beside the driver's door of the Bentley at the back entrance of the house by the checkpoint underneath the guard tower. She was still trying to make sure she'd memorised the route correctly following her extremely unusual meeting with Myers a few days before when he'd summoned her to his office.

Latimer to Chenies, to Sarratt, then onto the A500 Watford bypass which would take her through to Edgware and then Marble Arch and finally to Mayfair before circling up to Trafalgar Square. Nerves sizzled in the pit of her stomach as she waited in the bright spring sunshine for the arrival of Myers.

At some point, very early this morning, someone had cleaned and polished the Bentley. They'd done a rather good job, she thought, admiring the sheen of the grey paintwork and the gleam of the silver trim. She couldn't have been prouder of her uncle's car or the mission she'd been asked to undertake. Myers wanted her to act as driver as he hosted – his word – two newly arrived prisoners on a trip around London, taking in the sights.

'The aim,' he'd explained, 'is to show them that far from London being beaten and levelled to rubble, as the Germans have been constantly told, we are continuing as normal and that the "alleged" bombing raids are having no effect. Our planned route will show very little, if any, damage and will take in the south and west side of the Houses of Parliament, Westminster Abbey and Whitehall. At some point I will also point out the undamaged dome of St Paul's.' Unreserved glee glinted in his eye as he contemplated the ploy. 'We'll be taking two senior officers from the Wehrmacht on a scenic tour, both of whom will return to their cells, their beliefs shaken to the core, which they will then share with their more obdurate cellmates.'

Evelyn's instructions were to be silent and pretend not to understand German. She was not to make eye contact with either officer but to appear as insignificant and unobtrusive as possible. For the purpose of the trip she'd had to don a Wren's uniform to hide the fact that she was a Naval Intelligence Officer. She was used to wearing an officer's cap rather than this curved brimmed hat.

As she stood by the car a frisson of excitement doused her nerves. She bristled with the thrill of doing something important. Myers would be sitting in the front passenger seat next to her so that he could lean over the back and address the two prisoners. He planned to make friendly small talk, at which he was notoriously good. At some point he would address a remark to her in German and then have to rephrase it in English to ensure that the pair in the back weren't aware that she was fluent in their native tongue.

With the crunch of feet on gravel, she pulled the unfamiliar hat down further over her eyes, standing rigid. Without looking at either man's face, she waited while a batman opened the rear doors and ushered the two German soldiers into the rich red leather seats in the back of the car.

She heard one of them say, '*Ein schönes Auto*' – 'a beautiful car' – but schooled herself not to react as Myers slid into the passenger seat.

Switching on the engine, Evelyn guided the beautiful car out of the drive and set off through the Buckinghamshire countryside. Myers had devised a route that took them through the most prosperous towns and villages. Thankfully she enjoyed driving which was just as well, as this convoluted route would take well over an hour to get to central London.

She moved in her seat, grateful for the comfort and luxury of the big car, which had definitely impressed the two men in the back. Myers chatted away to them, talking about his own time in Germany and places he'd visited and how much he'd liked them, all the while her face impassive as she heard them gradually start to engage in the conversation. The man directly behind her had said nothing to date, leaving the other man to do all the talking.

'Where do you come from in Germany?' asked Myers. 'I spent a lot of time in Frankfurt and Mainz, both beautiful cities.'

'I am from Bonn.'

'Ah, not so far from Cologne. Only half an hour by train,' said Myers, demonstrating his considerable knowledge of Germany.

'That is so,' said the German officer.

'How about you, Lieutenant Colonel? Where do you come from?'

'Heidelberg,' said the other man. 'Do you know that also?' A slight trace of sarcasm tinged his words and Evelyn had to focus all her attention on the road ahead, gripping the steering wheel hard so as not to swerve across the road. It couldn't be. She was imagining things, possibly because he'd been in her thoughts so much recently. All the hairs on her arms rose. She knew that voice, she was sure of it.

Now as she drove, willing him to talk again, her ears almost twitched in anticipation and she found it hard to stare dead ahead and resist the awful temptation to look in the mirror mounted on the dashboard.

'I believe Heidelberg University is the oldest in Germany and one of the world's oldest universities,' said Myers. 'It has a reputation for academic excellence, does it not?' Although she was impressed with his knowledge – she knew Heidelberg equally well – she waited with a thumping heart to hear what the German officer would say, desperate to hear his voice again.

'Yes, it is a beautiful city. My family lived in the Neuenheim district. In Wederplatz.' This was said with pride and she knew exactly why. It was one of the most attractive parts of Heidelberg. Her lungs contracted in her chest as if every last piece of oxygen had been squeezed out of them. Peter Van Hoensbroeck.

She'd last seen him in the summer of 1939.

Her mind whirled in turmoil but at the same time she had to concentrate on the route. How could she drive and not turn to look at him? It was the hardest thing she'd ever done, having to navigate her way while being aware of the man who'd once been her fiancé. The man she thought she'd never see again, mere feet away from her, and she couldn't say or do a thing. There was no way she could give herself away to Myers or to Peter. Despite that, elation filled her. Peter was alive. The realisation brought the sun bursting out in her heart. And now he was here, safe. As a prisoner of war, he'd been delivered from battle and would stay safe for the rest of the war. A smile played on her lips and she hoped no one would notice. Peter was alive!

The surge of happiness barely dimmed as other thoughts pressed upon her.

How would he feel if he saw her? Her father had been the one to insist they call off the engagement. How could you be engaged to someone you were at war with, he'd said and Peter, damn him – it had been hard to forgive him for that – had agreed, although he had asked her to keep his ring. In a long letter he'd explained that Germany was well prepared for war and that he would have to fight. Coming from a noble military background, there was no question of him not doing his duty. Something that she understood only too well. Those shared values had been part of what had drawn them together. Like hers, his family were well connected, part of the ruling classes. His parents had been good friends with hers. The two families had been intertwined by the bonds of friendship and similarities; Peter's mother had met hers in Paris for shopping trips, their fathers joined hunting parties seeking out boar in the Black Forest and their younger brothers had rowed together on the River Neckar. While he and his family had not supported the Nazis, they had felt the shame of losing the Great War and had resented the reparations that had brought the German economy to its knees. He might not have supported Hitler's ideas but he had national pride and would fight for his nation. That was the last letter she'd ever had from him.

Myers spoke to her in German and she calmly ignored him, exactly as she'd been told to do. Every bit of her was rigid with tension. He repeated the question in English.

'How much longer do you expect the journey to be?'

'About twenty minutes until we reach the centre of London, Sir,' she said in a quiet, gruff undertone which Myers repeated to the two prisoners. Would Peter recognise her voice?

It took all her concentration to make the right turn into Trafalgar Square and head down to Whitehall. She hoped that neither man had noticed the tortuous route she'd taken, doubling back on herself several times to avoid some of the damage from the Blitz. With an inward shudder, she recalled the awful night when the Café de Paris had been bombed. The very night before, she'd been there with a couple of old schoolfriends from Roedean. They'd thought the cellar bar one of the safest places in London. It had been terribly bad luck that not one but two bombs hit the building and went down a ventilation shaft right into the café.

At last, they were driving along Whitehall with Myers pointing out the War Office and Downing Street.

'Slow down, Edwards,' said Myers. 'Just in case there's a chance we see Winston.'

His casual use of Churchill's name almost brought a smile to her face, although it shouldn't have surprised her. He'd had frequent meetings and telephone calls with the Prime Minister, who was a big supporter of CSDIC's work.

She obliged and slowed the car before they continued along the street.

'And here's Big Ben, the Houses of Parliament,' said Myers nonchalantly and while she couldn't see them, Evelyn could hear the rustle of their clothes on the leather seats and their palpable interest.

The car swung left onto Westminster Bridge, crossing the river in order to give the visitors a better view of the Houses of Parliament from the south side, away from the damaged side of the House of Commons, which had been hit several times by bombs during the Blitz. She then drove back over Lambeth Bridge, circling back to take in the undamaged façade of Westminster Abbey. On Birdcage Walk, as instructed by Myers, the car stopped, as he had to deliver some papers to an office there. That, apparently, was the whole purpose of the trip, although she wasn't sure if it was the truth or not. Sometimes it was hard to know what was real and what wasn't when you were working in intelligence.

Myers turned to look at the men and said in German, 'I shall be a few moments. As you're both in German uniform, an escape in this part of London, which is on high alert, would be pointless. You'd be shot on sight. However, my driver will have my gun.'

With careful, choreographed drama he handed a pistol to Evelyn which she calmly put into her lap, retaining her stoic expression, her eyes hidden below the peak of her hat, resisting the sudden temptation to straighten up, tighten her tie and smooth down the collar of her shirt.

As soon as Myers stepped out of the car, the two men began talking. She sat as still as she could, focusing on one of the fat grey pigeons strutting along the pavement.

'This is incredible,' said the other man. 'I can hardly believe my eyes.'

'Nor me,' said Peter. 'Where is all the bomb damage? Hitler said he has brought London to its knees. It certainly doesn't look like it.'

Two men in smart suits and bowler hats walked by, swinging black umbrellas, the epitome of Englishness and everyday activity. They were followed by three attractive young women, chattering happily, each of them wearing pretty, patterned dresses with nipped-in jackets and smart peep-toe shoes. They looked like a gorgeous bouquet of flowers and could easily have been styled by *Harper's Bazaar.* Evelyn wondered for a moment if Myers had staged-managed things and laid them on as extra scene setting. Her mouth curved wryly. She wouldn't have put it past him.

'And where are the people starving in the streets because of the Atlantic blockade?'

If only you knew, thought Evelyn, not moving a muscle, thinking of the paucity of rations that people like her landlady in Falmouth had to eke out each month.

'What else isn't the Führer telling us?' said Peter, almost angrily.

'He has been misinformed. There are too many yes men around him. That fool Von Ribbentrop, for one.'

Peter laughed. 'He is a complete idiot. How he convinced Hitler that he had the ear of Chamberlain, I do not know. The man surrounded himself with even bigger British idiots. One only needed to know the smallest amount about British politics before the war to realise that he had no understanding of how things here worked.'

'You sound knowledgeable about such things, Oberst.'

'I have been to England many times, General,' said Peter mildly in response to the Lieutenant General's suspicious tone. Was the more senior man trying to probe as to whether Peter had been a spy? 'I visited a place called Henley on Thames, several times.'

Evelyn had to pinch her lips tight and pray that he

wouldn't mention her name or her parents. Thank goodness Myers wasn't in the car.

'So you have sympathies with the British?' asked Schmidt.

'I know many British people but I am loyal to Germany. I might not agree with our leading party but they have brought us national pride. We can hold our heads high again.'

'We certainly can, although I am not so convinced that Britain is going to be as easy to invade as has been suggested. There is nothing here to suggest a country that will capitulate easily.'

'I agree. We have been misled over the amount of damage that has been done by the Luftwaffe.'

Evelyn deserved an Oscar for her performance that afternoon. Betty would be inordinately proud of her. Not so much as a twitch crossed her face as the two men talked quite openly, oblivious to the fact that she understood every word.

'I'm quite confused,' said Schmidt. 'I would have expected to have been interrogated by the British but they seem to be disinterested. Apart from being asked my name, rank and personal information, they don't seem to be very worried.'

'No, that is strange. It is not the approach we use to deal with prisoners of war.'

'But perhaps this is the calm before the storm. So that we lower our guard, thinking that this is how we'll be treated and then the torture will begin.'

'If that happens we need to remind them of the Geneva Convention protocols.'

Schmidt snorted. 'The way that we adhere to them! Have you been to a camp?'

She might not be able to see Peter stiffen but she knew from his frigid tone that he had. 'I have had the misfortune to visit one of the camps. I would hope that men of the *Wehrmacht* behave with honour to their fellow soldiers.'

'Van Hoensbroeck, are you so naive?'

'I don't like what is happening in the camps. But the SS are barbarians. They are not soldiers.'

Evelyn blinked, listening avidly, but suddenly, as if aware of her, both men shut up and Schmidt changed the subject. It didn't matter, she'd heard enough to brief Myers on both men's frame of mind. And now she was going to have to report back on the man she'd once promised to marry.

When they pulled back into the rear entrance of the house after a long morning, there were two armed soldiers at the checkpoint ready to escort the Germans back to their cells. Evelyn got out of the car, her hands shaking as she tugged her hat as low down over her eyes as she could. She was desperate to look at Peter but she knew if he recognised her, he'd know that she could speak German and it would ruin, in part, Myers' tactics.

Slowly she stepped out of the car, all her senses attuned to Peter, mere inches away. She had to close her eyes for a moment to fight the wave of longing to reach out and touch him. It had been so long since she'd seen him.

Unable to resist, she turned, keeping her head low, and sneaked a peep. Her heart stalled in her chest and for a strange moment, she thought she might faint. She gripped the car door and straightened herself up, giving herself a stern talking to. Her fingers itched to trace the contours of his face, the strong firm chin which spoke so much of his strength of character, and that aquiline nose that had once nuzzled at her neck, inhaling the scent he'd bought her. She swallowed, noting his grim expression. The lines on his face had deepened and there was a small scar to the right of his mouth. Had he changed as much inside? Was he still the man she'd fallen in love with? That man had been strong, forthright and kind. He'd been a good man. Now she wasn't so sure.

It sounded as if he supported Hitler even if he didn't approve of some of his policies. The promises to restore German interests had been widely welcomed and a blind eye turned to his more fanatical policies. People had believed, perhaps because they wanted to believe it, that his worst excesses could be kept in check by the vast majority of decent Germans. Evelyn had seen at first hand how that hold on decency had been chipped away, how people like the Graf and Gräfin she'd stayed with in Bavaria had lived in fear of speaking out against the Nazis and how their own son had been brainwashed by the Hitler Youth movement.

In his uniform, Peter looked so different – a man now. The last four years had worn away the softer lines of his face, hardening his features, and his shoulders seemed to have broadened. Her pulse quickened and she had to quash the sudden, desperate longing to feel his arms around her and the fierce ache to feel his lips on hers. This could be the last time she'd ever see him, and he didn't even know it was her. There was a strong chance he might only be here a matter of days before being sent on to a permanent prisoner-of-war camp. Panic rose, her throat tightening. She'd never thought she'd see him again and now he was here, within touching distance, but as out of reach as ever.

The guardsmen stepped up to escort him and Peter turned away from her, already walking towards the house. She sucked in a gasp of air and watched him.

'P—'

'Edwards. My office,' said Myers, a sharp snap in his voice.

A blush burned up her cheeks as she turned to her commanding officer. 'Sir.' Did he suspect? Did he know? It wouldn't surprise her. He seemed to know everything.

But Myers climbed back into the car and didn't even give her a second glance.

She straightened and gave Peter's figure one last regretful look as he and the Lieutenant General were escorted away to the checkpoint in the perimeter fence. Then she got back in the car to drive slowly round to the front entrance of the house. It was important the prisoners didn't see the house and they couldn't from their cell blocks. There was a terrible irony in that General Von Ribbentrop had actually stayed numerous times at the house when he was German Ambassador to London, and it was always a worry that a prisoner might recognise the house, which would increase the risk of an escape attempt.

From the car they went straight up to Myers' office where she repeated almost word for word what the two men had said in the car.

'Excellent work, Lieutenant. That gives us a view into their mindsets. The Lieutenant General is clearly very shocked and that gives us a good way of prying him open. We can feed on the fear that Hitler has not been honest with them. The younger man, Van Hoensbroeck, seems to have a sharper grasp on reality, however.' Myers smiled. 'It would appear that you and he have a connection.'

Evelyn gripped her knees tightly together. All she could do was nod. How much trouble was she in?

'Didn't you tell me that you knew Heidelberg?'

She glanced up at his face, realising that he hadn't meant what she thought he'd meant.

'Er, yes, Sir.'

'I think that will give you common ground. I'd like you to take the lead on interviewing him over the next few days.'

'Me, Sir?' Her heart skittered out of control in her chest, sure he must be able to see her consternation.

'Yes.'

She stared at him. The thought of coming face to face with Peter both horrified and excited her.

What on earth would she say to him? Could she even do her job properly? Where did her loyalty lie? To the man she loved or to her country?

'I think appealing to his values of decency and honour will have considerable traction. If we can share some of our intelligence on the atrocities that are being committed in the name of Germany, we might get him to co-operate quite fully. Also having demonstrated that Britain isn't suffering so badly, it will convince him that the war is far from being won by Germany, especially after the collapse of the North Africa campaign. What do you think?'

Her mind was in such a whirl, it was difficult to think about anything but she managed to keep her composure and nod, and was grateful when he stopped there. 'I think we'll reconvene in the morning and discuss strategy in more depth, but what do you think?'

'Yes, Sir.'

'Excellent work, both on the driving and the listening in. You really are shaping up to be an excellent operative. I'm delighted you were able to join us. Reports of your treatment of commanding officers were greatly exaggerated.' His eyes twinkled as he looked at her, reminding her that she didn't have an entirely unblemished service record. She ought to confess here and now that she knew Peter. That would have been the right thing to do, but then they might stop her seeing him, and she wanted to see him more than anything else in the world.

Chapter Nineteen

Judith

'Here, you should wear this.' Betty thrust a plaid skirt with a single pleat at the front towards her. 'It's Norman Hartnell.'

Judith looked at her blankly.

'The Queen's designer. He's designed it for the utility range.' She pointed to a curious two-pieces-of-cheese design on the label which Judith now recognised as being the logo from the Board of Trade that showed an item met the government's austerity regulations. 'It will look marvellous with that jumper.'

Judith was about to refuse but Betty was right, the cherry-red checks of the skirt would be perfect with her newly completed jumper. She had stayed up an extra hour to finish it last night, while Betty had insisted on painstakingly pin-curling her hair. The jumper, knitted from a pattern she'd seen in *Good Taste* magazine, was a little snugger than she would normally have chosen for herself but she didn't have the time to unpick it and both Evelyn and Betty assured her that it was the latest fashion and that she'd look like the cat's pyjamas. A phrase she'd not heard before. She tried to imagine a cat wearing pyjamas and couldn't. It was too ridiculous.

'Let me brush your hair out. You need a roll-in at the front, give you a bit of height. I could put a filler in for you, if you'd like.'

'I'm going out on a bicycle for the day,' she protested, pushing a hand through the loose waves Betty had created for her with the overnight pin curls. They felt rather marvellous and she was secretly quite pleased with how they'd come out. Betty and Evelyn both always looked so well put together. Betty with that touch of glamour and Evelyn ever elegant. It was wrong to be envious of them but there'd been so many times she'd wished she had an ounce of their style.

'I'm very good with a bobby pin. Just you see.'

Under normal circumstances Judith would have declined but it was the first time in a couple of days that she'd seen Betty so animated. The other girl had been rather subdued since she'd visited her mother and it didn't take a detective to see that she was favouring her right hand and was extra careful when she moved, particularly when she stood up or sat down. It reminded her of a time when her father had been knocked to the ground outside his shop one evening. He'd been stiff and sore for a few days, while she'd been boiling mad at the injustice of an old man being taunted by fascist thugs. Even though she hadn't said anything, Judith had been shocked by the bruises she'd seen when Betty had changed into her nightgown the previous night.

As she had another hour before she was due to meet Walther, and Betty seemed to have found her spirit again, she acquiesced although she did draw the line at borrowing Betty's very red lipstick. 'It's just a bicycle ride with a friend,' she said severely. Betty's lips twitched.

'Course it is, darlin',' she said in an American accent. 'Now hold still while I finish your hair.'

By the time Betty's nimble fingers had finished rolling and pinning, Judith almost didn't recognise herself. The smart hairstyle, with the rolls of hair pinned on either side of her head, enhanced the shape of her face, giving her sharper cheekbones, and even – though it was vain to admit it – made her look pretty. What would her father have said? Would he have been proud of her? She'd only been seventeen when she'd left Germany, barely a young woman. She pushed back the threatening sadness that he'd never seen her grow up to become who she was now.

'You look beautiful, Judith,' said Betty with a heartfelt smile, reaching up to touch her cheek. 'Really lovely. I hope you have a nice day. Walther is a nice man.' Her face sobered. 'And they are worth diamonds.' Judith caught her hand, worried by the shadows in Betty's eyes.

She wanted to say something, to offer ... support? Comfort? She wasn't sure what but she didn't feel brave enough to raise it with Betty. Perhaps she'd have a quiet word with Evelyn.

'Go and have a super time,' said Betty.

Judith left her and despite her misgivings about her roommate, skipped down the stairs, feeling quite chipper, one of her favourite English words. It was a lovely sunny day and she had no expectation of the day. She'd enjoy giving her brain some time off.

Walther was waiting for her outside the kitchen with Elsie.

'Oh, look at you, don't you look fine,' said Elsie. 'I do love seeing you girls in mufti. It makes you into real people, if that doesn't sound too strange.'

With surprise, Judith realised that she knew exactly what Elsie meant. It was one of the many nice things about life at Latimer House. The rules were more relaxed and much less strict, especially about having to wear uniform when you weren't on duty. Today she felt like a real person instead of the automaton she'd become, putting one foot in front of the other day after day, plodding through life. She was actually looking forward to the day, even though she hadn't been on a bicycle for years.

'Thank you for lending your bicycle.'

'It's not a problem at all,' said Elsie. 'Once upon a time I'd have made you a nice picnic to take with you. Now off you go and enjoy yourself.' She shooed them with the skirt of her apron as if they were a pair of naughty children, for which Judith was extremely grateful. It took any awkwardness away from the moment when she had to finally confront Walther.

'*Guten Morgen*,' he said. 'You do look very nice. That is a good colour.'

She was delighted that instead of blushing she was able to accept the compliment.

'I made it from the wool of a cardigan that belonged to my aunt. I think you would have found her interesting. She was very Bohemian and interested in architecture and art and music. She lived in Berlin and performed in a very risqué bar.' Judith couldn't seem to stop talking. 'She was, as the British would say, very naughty. She performed burlesque.' And for some reason wearing the jumper made from her aunt's cardigan made her feel brave. Neither Evelyn nor Betty seemed afraid of living or enjoying life; maybe it was time for her to do the same.

'She sounds very interesting. My aunt was a schoolteacher. She went to America.'

'My aunt died in 1932. She would have hated the Nazis and I think would have been arrested many times.'

'Shall we go?'

'It's a while since I've been on a bicycle, so you may have to be patient with me.'

'We have all day and it is so nice to be outside in the fresh air. Sometimes I feel like a rabbit in a hutch all week. I'm glad the summer is here and we have the evenings to enjoy.'

Judith found a pedal with her foot and pushed off, wobbling slightly but pleased that she'd managed to keep her balance and move forward in a reasonably straight line. At least she hadn't knocked Walther off his bike, she thought as they rode side by side up to the main road by the church.

'Do you know, I haven't seen the village since I arrived, but it looked very charming from the car on my first day.' There, she'd opened the conversation, feeling rather proud of herself, especially when Walther responded easily.

'It is very pretty. If you go the other way you reach Flaunden, another pretty village. They have a pub there. The Green Dragon, and would you believe it, but Von Ribbentrop was a regular visitor there when he was based in England.'

Judith shuddered at the thought of a high-ranking German official being here, being so close.

'They say it's a small world,' said Walther thoughtfully. 'I wonder sometimes if I might hear a prisoner that I once knew.'

'I suppose it is possible,' said Judith. 'What would you do? Would you tell anyone?'

'I think so. As long as I was honest about them and how they had behaved when I knew them, then that is the most important thing.'

They rode into the village, the sun bright on the white-and-black timber-framed buildings with their diamond-paned windows that she remembered from the first day she arrived. Walther drew to a stop at the village green, leaning on his handlebars, to point out the memorials built there.

'One is the cenotaph for the Boer war. The other is dedicated to Lord Chesham's horse.' He shook his head in disbelief. 'That is very British. They are very attached to their dogs and horses.'

'Are they? I didn't know that. Most of the time I've spent here has been in the cities. I thought I was being sent to somewhere in London when I came here because it was on the underground. I had no idea I would be in the countryside.'

'I believe that this location was chosen because although it is a reasonable distance from London, this area is as far from the sea in any direction as is possible in Britain. I would imagine it would limit escape attempts.'

'Are there many?'

'Some of the prisoners occasionally talk about it. I've heard them but,' he shrugged his shoulders, gripping the handlebars of his borrowed bicycle, 'it is difficult when they don't know where they are. Most never see the house as they only stay for a little while. We only keep the interesting prisoners for a little longer. Come on, let me show you the English countryside.'

He led the way and she followed, grateful for his thoughtful slow pace, which allowed her to look around. Everything seemed so green, from the lush fronds of grass bordering the sides of the lane through to the different-shaped leaves on the trees through which dappled sunlight danced on the road. Around them endless fields curved and undulated along the valley. The only sound was the chattering of the birds in the copse to their right and the light breeze rustling among the branches. Occasionally a rabbit, its white tail bobbing in alarm, would dart out of the hedgerow and scurry along the road ahead of them before racing away out of sight again.

She lifted her face up to the sun, wobbling slightly on her bicycle, breathing in the slightly sweet air, perfumed by the damp undergrowth of the hedgerows running alongside the road. Every now and then Walther would glance back over his shoulder to make sure she was still with him, but she was enjoying the steady pace and smiled back at him. Was it cowardly to be glad that they couldn't talk so much like this? She had no idea what to say to him. Apart from her father, she hadn't known many men. The only ones she'd met in England were either commanding officers or had treated her with suspicion the minute they realised she was German. One of the things she really liked about being at Latimer House was that it didn't matter that she was German. She suddenly grinned to herself, unaccountably content. She fitted in there.

Up ahead Walther slowed and pointed across the fields. As she came to a halt she could see Latimer House across the valley on the other side of the river. Squinting, she tried to make out the rooftop spot that had become her, Evelyn's and Betty's personal balcony. It warmed her to think that only the three of them knew of their little lookout. *The three of them*, she liked the way that sounded.

Ahead there was a left turn and then a bit of a climb which had her pedalling hard, rising up to stand on her pedals, feeling unused muscles in her thighs complaining, but she was determined not to say a word. At the top Walther stopped and turned to wait for her, watching her huffing and puffing as she made her slow progress to the crest of the hill. So much for Betty being determined that she should look her best, she probably looked like a tomato and sounded like a locomotive train.

'Well done,' said Walther. 'Most people would have given up and walked. I'm very impressed by your determination.' He grinned at her. 'You are a very surprising woman, Judith.'

A small glow of happiness set up camp in her chest. These compliments meant far more to her than being told she looked nice. It showed that Walther valued her for who she was.

'And you look beautiful,' he added shyly, ducking his head and turning back to his bicycle.

Judith clasped a hand to her blushing cheek. Perhaps she wasn't as immune to comments about her personal appearance as she'd thought.

Amersham was a handsome little town spread out along a wide, cobbled high street and Judith was fascinated by how varied the houses were, some small, some large, and how different they were from the ones she'd known in Germany. When she exclaimed over them, Walther proved particularly knowledgeable.

'This is from the Regency period,' he said, pointing to one whitewashed, grand double-fronted house with tall, straight windows. 'When the kings of England were Hanoverians and a German ruled Britain.' He laughed. 'Although the current royal family only changed their name from Saxe-Coburg in 1917. Prince Albert was German. That's not so long ago. It seems madness that our two countries are at war when our royal families are so close.'

'But it's not the country, is it?' Judith hadn't talked of such things since she'd left Germany. 'It's the regime, the politics.

We lived peaceably in Germany before Hitler and his stormtroopers rose to prominence.'

Their conversation about politics and history took them all the way to the end of the street.

'Would you mind if we called in on some friends of mine?'

'Friends?' She immediately recoiled, shy at the prospect.

'Yes, they are friends of friends of my parents and they live here. At the top of the hill, so this time we'll walk.'

When Judith saw the hill, she was extremely grateful. Her legs ached just walking up there. However, the reward was not only the view but also the very grand house that Walther led her towards. It stood apart from its neighbours with garden on every side and a wide, gravelled drive to the left. She looked up at the tall, triangular-gabled front and guessed that the house wasn't terribly old as Walther led her to the big wooden front door tucked into an arched porchway.

He rapped firmly with the brass knocker and she was strangely touched to see the *mezuzah* fixed to the doorpost. She never thought of herself as particularly religious but it brought back memories of visiting friends with her father.

'Walther, how lovely to see you, and you've brought a lady friend.' The woman who opened the door was tall, angular and full of smiles, her eyes dancing with delight. 'Come in. Come in. You will stay for lunch, won't you?'

Walter looked at Judith. 'Would that be all right?'

She nodded, a little dazed by the exuberant friendliness as they were ushered inside the house. Stopping in the doorway, she kissed her finger and touched the *mezuzah* in grateful prayer for the warm welcome.

'Ah, another refugee. From Germany? I'm Mary Kirchener.' She held out a hand and gave Judith a surprisingly strong handshake from such skinny wrists. Judith smiled, finding her tongue had lost its way, and was grateful when Walther introduced her. 'This is my friend, Judith Stern.'

Luckily Mary didn't seem to mind or notice.

'You are most welcome. I'm glad Walther has a friend at work because we don't see him so often. They make him work so hard there.' She tsked and was already holding open a door into a big kitchen dominated by a large table in the middle.

'Then it's a good job I enjoy my work, Mary.'

She turned to Judith. 'How long have you been in Britain?'

Swallowing some of the dryness of her mouth away, this time she managed to respond. 'Since December 1938.'

'Ah, *Kristallnacht*.' Mary shook her head and patted Judith's arm in understanding before turning to Walther. 'Come see the garden, Walther. You'll be impressed.'

She led them out of the back door into an enormous garden, which was organised into neat plots of vegetables and fruit trees. One corner fenced off from the rest of the area was filled with several chickens. Their enthusiastic host turned to Judith. 'We're digging for victory. That's my daughter-in-law, her two sons and my brother and his wife.' She pointed to the various people hard at work in the garden. 'My husband works in London. He's a scientist. I'm not allowed to know what he's doing but I know it's important war work.' With a gay laugh, she led them down one of the paths and gave them a knowledgeable tour of the garden, pointing out cauliflowers and cabbages, beans and peas, apple and pear trees, raspberry canes and blackcurrant bushes, along the way introducing them to her extended family at various vegetable beds, who all greeted them with friendly warmth and paused from their weeding, hoeing and planting to chat. It almost seemed like normal life and Judith's natural shyness began to dissipate under the warmth of Mary's benign charm.

see you again. Don't be shy.' She patted Judith on the cheek just like her aunt used to do.

They left to a chorus of goodbyes from the family and rode out onto the street.

'Downhill all the way,' said Walther, sighing happily, cycling alongside her. 'Just as well, after all that food.'

'They were so lovely,' said Judith, glancing back at the house, which made her wobble a bit. 'Thank you very much for taking me to see your friends. It was a very special afternoon.'

'I took you to meet my family,' he said, his eyes rich with meaning, meeting hers.

Judith's rabbits exploded out of their bag, hopping about with spring abandon in her stomach. She stared at him, unable to say a word. With a sudden grin, he pedalled into the lead and sped off down the hill.

It really was downhill all the way and the journey home was much quicker, as she followed in his wake the whole trip back to Latimer. Her nerves began to hum as they approached the back entrance of the house by the kitchens, where they were to return the bicycles to Elsie.

Walther dismounted first and propped his bike by the wall, reaching out to take hers as she hopped down. Without the barrier of the bicycle, she felt a little exposed, awkward. Betty would know exactly what to do in this sort of situation, Evelyn too. Her shoes were dusty, she realised. They needed a clean. She couldn't bring herself to look up. Her hands were shaking and she tucked one behind her back and clamped the other to her side.

'Thank you, Judith, for a lovely day,' said Walther, his voice a little husky as he took a few steps to stand in front of her. She studied the two pairs of shoes, the toes mere inches apart, and somehow managed to find the courage to look up.

There was a gentle quirk to his mouth and a tender expression in his face. 'Dear Judith.' He reached up and touched her face, 'Would you come out with me again?'

His fingers were warm on her cheek, his eyes locked onto hers and she couldn't have moved if her life had depended on it. It was wonderful, terrifying and exhilarating all at the same time.

'Y-yes,' she stammered, the breath trapped in her chest.

'May I kiss you?'

Her mouth dropped open but she nodded, too stunned to speak.

His arms slid around her waist and he smiled as he lowered his mouth to hers, and it was simply heaven. The softness of his lips on hers was silk, feathers and satin, every gorgeous thing she could think of, and she likened being in his arms to finally arriving home after a never-ending journey.

Although it was the merest whisper of a kiss, she had to clutch his arms to stay upright.

'I've never been kissed before,' she blurted out.

Walther laughed. 'And how was it?'

She gazed up at him. 'Wonderful.'

His hands tightened at her waist. 'That's good, because I'd like to do it again very soon. With your permission, of course.'

His hand slid to her face again and he smiled down at her, which made her heart, already struggling to beat normally, flutter in her chest. 'Would you like to come for a walk with me tomorrow after our shift has finished?'

'Yes,' she said, realising that her tongue was completely tied in knots and she hadn't spoken to him with more than one word since they'd arrived back at Latimer, but all she could do was gaze back at him, still not able to believe the unfamiliar tumble of happiness cartwheeling through her system.

'Ah, you're back and the bicycles are all in one piece. The Vicar will be pleased.'

Walther's hand dropped away and they both turned, stiffening at the sound of Elsie's ever-cheerful voice.

'Nice day?' she asked, stepping out onto the top step, looking up at them.

'Very nice,' said Walther, regaining his equilibrium far quicker than Judith, although to be honest, hers had been shattered ever since they'd left Mary's house. 'Thank you so much for the loan of the bicycles. I wonder if we might borrow them again in a couple of weeks' time? We'll probably catch the train to London for the day.'

'Not a problem, as long as I have some notice. Now, I've got a nice pot of tea on the go in the Sergeants' Mess, if you fancy it. I bet after all that cycling, you could do with wetting your whistle.'

'A cup of tea would be excellent,' said Walther, with a wink at Judith, who had no idea what whistles had to do with anything, but was relieved that everything seemed normal again and she could stand without her knees threatening to give way.

Chapter Twenty

Betty

'**M**orning, Betty.'

She jumped out of her skin. 'Sir!' She'd been absorbed in her reading, frowning over a particular passage, trying to remember another transcript where a prisoner confirmed the same details about a U-boat gun emplacement.

Major Carl Wendermeyer grinned down at her from his lofty six-foot-plus height and even though she'd been feeling fragile of late she couldn't help smiling back. He was still the most handsome man she'd ever seen and he smelled good – clean, and of fir trees or something like that.

'How's that hand of yours?'

'Much better, thank you. And thank you for the iced water. That was ... er ... very thoughtful.' She hadn't known that a man could be thoughtful and as she stared up at him, she was a little disconcerted by the sudden softness in his blue eyes when he sat down on the edge of her desk.

'Mighty glad to be of assistance. And if there's anything

else I can do, I'd only be too happy to oblige.' He crossed his legs as if he were preparing to make himself comfortable.

'I don't think you or anyone else can help,' she said with a brittle smile. 'But thank you for offering.' She was pinning all her hopes on Evelyn's brother's service revolver, but that would only keep her safe for so long.

'Are you sure? A problem shared is a problem halved, so they say.'

'I've never heard anyone say that before,' she said honestly.

'I think it's a Stateside thing, but I also happen to think it's true. Sure you can't unburden yourself to me?'

When he lowered his voice in that confiding way, it was so tempting, but what could she possibly say that didn't show her up for what she was? A nobody from the village. So instead she firmed her lips in a prim line, smiled prettily at him and shook her head, not willing to trust her voice.

And God forgive her, but she couldn't help being a touch gratified to see that he looked a little disappointed.

'OK then, so we'd better get down to work. There's a meeting I'd like you to attend with me. They're discussing recent intelligence reports and I think you might find it interesting.'

'If you're sure, Sir,' she said doubtfully. While she found her work fascinating and compelling, she wasn't very experienced yet and all these people working here seemed very smart and well-to-do. The Major glowed with health and had that sheen of rich people. She wasn't easily intimidated but he was something else, like a comet or a star, hundreds of miles out of reach.

'Yes, I'm certain. Major Smith and I have been mighty impressed with the quality of your work. You have a great eye for detail and an extraordinary memory. We were just saying that you piece things together like no one else.'

'But it's easy,' she said with a quick shrug. 'When I've seen something, I can remember the page that it was on. Like a picture in my head. So, if I've read something, I can remember what the whole page looks like and then I can go back and find what I need.'

'Really?' The Major stared at her and for a moment, she wished she hadn't volunteered the information. She'd never ever talked about it before, partly because when she was at school, learning came so easily to her, she spent more time helping the younger and slower-to-learn children and had never had anyone to talk to about it.

'That's incredible.' He sounded as if he meant it.

'Is it?'

'I've heard of people with what they call photographic memories, but I've never met one before.'

Now it was her turn to say, 'Really?' A sudden punch of pride warmed her to the very tips of her ears. Incredible. He was calling her incredible.

'Yeah, that's really special.'

'Oh, right-ho,' she said, preening a little because after all, it was rather nice to be told that she could do something special.

'No wonder you're one of our best analysts. Brains as well as beauty.'

Now she really did smile. 'Why thank you, Sir.' Compliments about her looks she could swallow quite easily. Even her dad had said she was the prettiest girl he'd ever seen and he didn't approve of unnecessary vanity. He was far more likely to say, 'Handsome is as handsome does.'

'Are you going to the dance next month?'

'Er, I'm not sure yet,' she said. What dance? And why

didn't she know about it? Under his twinkling gaze she finally admitted, 'Which dance is this?'

He laughed. 'At RAF Bovingdon. The USAF have moved in and they're looking for a little entertainment.'

'Well, I'll certainly think about it.' She gave him a sudden impish smile. 'I do love to dance.'

'Know how to jitterbug?'

'I might do,' she said, realising that he was flirting with her. Already her eyes had lit up at the thought of it. Music. Dancing. That would be so much fun.

'Perhaps you could save me a dance.'

'Perhaps I could.' Her spirits lifted at the thought of going out for a change. She enjoyed her work but hadn't felt carefree and joyous for months. When she'd been in London, there'd been a gang of them that had gone up West dancing or to the theatre. She missed all that.

'Ah, Major Wendermeyer,' a voice interrupted and a flash of disappointment darted through Betty when his attention moved to the RAF Flight-Lieutenant who walked in. 'The meeting starts at oh-nine-thirty hours in the library.'

'Excellent. I've invited Sergeant Connors here to attend.'

The Flight-Lieutenant looked at her. 'Connors. Oh yes. We've seen some excellent work from you.' He frowned as he looked at her, as if what he knew didn't match up with her appearance. She shot him a curt smile. 'Brains and beauty,' she said smartly, clearly feeling a dart of satisfaction when the gibe hit home.

'Yes. Yes, of course.' He looked a little discomfited but then he nodded with a rueful smile of apology. 'Indeed ma'am. Brains and beauty. My apologies. I look forward to you joining us in the meeting.' He saluted the Major and hurried out.

'Nicely played, Sergeant,' said the Major, winking at her. 'Sharp as a tack too. I like a woman who stands up for herself.'

'Thank you, Sir.' She didn't dare wink back at him – that was probably pushing it with a senior officer – but she gave him a cheeky grin.

The meeting was a little over her head at first, as they spoke in acronyms and about people whom she'd never heard of before, however she quickly gathered that they were about to have a visit from some VIPs from the Admiralty.

They were talking about intelligence they'd gathered about the communications methods that the U-boats had been using.

'No one believes that they're using underwater smoke signals to communicate, but we still don't know how they are managing to liaise with command. There's a view that there's a powerful radio transmitter which is able to communicate, depending on the depth of the U-boat.'

'That's not been corroborated,' said another officer.

Betty frowned. That wasn't right. She was sure she'd seen something in a transcript from a telegrapher who'd been on one of the recently captured U-boats. She raised a hand, not sure of the protocol. 'Excuse me.'

All eyes turned her way and she froze. Maybe she should have waited until after the meeting.

'There w-was a... er... um... a transcript.' She stopped but they were all listening with intent expressions. 'A telegrapher, N3241, in his cell talking to N2531 about being able to send radio transmissions on frequencies between 15 to 25 kHz.' She had absolutely no idea what 'kHz' meant but she knew exactly what she'd read. 'It was an extract from an SR report, number 4145.'

Major Wendermeyer smiled at her across the table as one of the Wrens at the top of the table began shuffling through files. There was a silence as everyone waited.

'Here you go, Sir,' said the Wren, handing a sheet of typewritten paper over to the Flight-Lieutenant. 'SR report 4145.'

She watched him as his eyes scanned the paper and then lifted to look sharply across the table. 'Thank you, Sergeant Connors. You are indeed correct. Excellent work.'

Although she didn't contribute for the rest of the meeting she knew that she'd deserved her place at the table and when they filed out of the room, Major Wendermeyer followed her. 'Well done, Connors.'

'Thank you, Sir.' She grinned at him, feeling ten feet tall.

It was funny, everyone suddenly seemed to be able to see her in the office that afternoon. People she'd never spoken to before stopped and exchanged a word or two with her. She learned the names of people that she'd been nervous of approaching before. At the end of the day when she trooped off to the Sergeants' Mess for dinner, she felt she'd moved forward somehow. People respected her and thought her opinions were worth something. She grinned to herself. Her dad would have been so proud of her.

When she stepped out onto the balcony later that evening into the warm, almost balmy air, she found Evelyn deep in thought, smoking.

'Hello, how was your day?' she asked. 'And where's Judith?'

'Judith,' Evelyn raised one elegant eyebrow, 'has gone for a walk with Walther.'

'Has she now?' Betty beamed at her, still buoyed up with good humour.

'Mm, with shining eyes and big smiles.'

'Ahh, that's nice. I don't think she's had an easy life.'

'I'm sure of it. If what I saw in Germany was anything to go by.'

Betty frowned. 'What was it like?'

'Oppressive. Like there was a big bonfire built, all ready to go, and at any second a match could be tossed in. When I was there, everyone was on edge, always watching what they said, and the way they treated the Jews was shocking. The Nazi party strutted about and they would pick fights deliberately with anyone they knew was Jewish. It didn't matter if they were old or young, but it was particularly distressing when they knocked over the older ladies. Then they would kick anyone that dared to go to their aid. I can't imagine what Judith has been through. So I'm glad that she's finding happiness. And what about you?'

'I'm fine,' said Betty, unconsciously lifting her chin with new-found pride. 'I had a great day. Major Wendermeyer invited me to an important meeting. And I did all right. I even spoke. He said my memory is incredible.' She smiled to herself, recalling their conversation and the husky timbre of his voice giving her a little shiver. 'I'm really enjoying the work I do here. How about you?'

Evelyn took a drag of her cigarette and exhaled with a long stream of smoke. 'It was an interesting day.' Her mouth tightened and she looked out across the valley.

Betty winced. 'And you can't tell me, can you?'

Uncharacteristic tears glistened in Evelyn's eyes as she said, 'No.' Betty saw the tendons in her neck tighten and knew it cost the other girl to hang onto her emotions.

'I know it's all hush-hush, but if there's anything I can do...' She didn't dare give Evelyn a hug, she was scared it might break the brittle fragility of Evelyn's tight control.

'Tell me about the dishy Major Wendermeyer.' Evelyn's attempt at a smile was quite pitiful but Betty knew a request for a change of subject when she heard it.

'Who said he was dishy?' she asked, deliberately coy, to entertain her roommate.

'You did.'

'I did not.' Evelyn's superior smile, with a hint of amusement, made Betty laugh, realising that she'd given herself away. 'All right, I admit, he is a dish. But I can look, can't I?'

'You certainly can, darling.' She turned away, tossing her cigarette onto the floor and muttered under her breath, 'Sometimes a look is all you get.

'Now while I remember, do you know what your shift pattern is this week?'

'I'm on a late on Wednesday, if that's any good.'

'Excellent. Do you want to come to Henley with me?'

'I'd love to,' said Betty. It would give her a good reason not to go to her mother's and to avoid Bert for a bit longer.

'Let's see if we can peel Judith away from the *wunderbar* Walther and get her to come too,' she said as the two of them climbed back through the window into their room.

Chapter Twenty-One

Evelyn

Evelyn rose extra early that morning and scurried to the bathroom before the other two woke up, like a thief sneaking out before the dawn. She'd washed her shoulder-length hair yesterday evening and set it in soft rollers overnight wrapped in a silk headscarf. Grateful that Lord Chesham had seen fit to look after his servants well, she ran an inch of water into the bath, astonished to find the temperature lukewarm and for once quite bearable. Daddy had spent a fortune on a boiler system at Quartiles and she'd become rather used to bathing in hot water. She mocked herself. *You're too used to the good things in life, my girl,* but even so she wasn't going to give up all her luxuries. From her toilet bag, she took out the carefully hoarded bar of Roger et Gallet, Violette de Parme soap that these days only came out for special occasions. Another treat from her mother's final Parisian trip.

Taking a moment, she sniffed the bar, inhaling the sweet scent, which brought back a flood of memories cascading through her brain, memories that she neither had the time nor the inclination to sift through. Today, she had a job to do. With an impatient huff, she washed herself as quickly and efficiently as she could. Already her hands held a slight tremor at the thought of the day ahead as she brushed her teeth with the Pepsodent toothpaste which promised whiter teeth.

When she returned to the bedroom, Betty and Judith were both up and the three of them undertook the usual chaotic and apologetic weave in and out and around each other to retrieve their uniforms from the wardrobe, button on their collars, pull on their hideous passion-killers (as the regulation stockings were known), and do their hair. She noted that Judith had taken to styling her hair in rolls on either side of her head under Betty's bossy supervision. It was the usual haphazard choreography of arms, elbows, legs and knees which they accomplished with good-natured smiles and yawns each morning. Evelyn was surprised to realise that she enjoyed sharing the space with them.

Shaking out her Navy uniform, she gave it a thorough brush to remove every last speck of lint and dust, glad that she'd polished the brass buttons recently, and then dabbed a tiny bit of perfume on her pulse points. Was it a little vain to be grateful that she joined the Navy and had the benefit of the smart dark blue rather than the drab brown-green of the ATS, which wouldn't have done her complexion any good at all?

'Going somewhere special?' teased Betty, as she pulled on a fresh white shirt, fastened a new, stiff collar and knotted her tie. To Evelyn's horror, she blushed furiously.

'You got your eye on someone, have you?'

'No, not at all,' she said crisply and busied herself fussing with her hair while over her shoulder, in the reflection, Betty shot her a knowing grin.

Judith pursed her lips. 'Betty, that's not kind. Leave her alone. It is nothing to do with you.'

'I know,' said Betty gaily, not taking the least offence. She was a regular sunshine girl and seemed to have recovered from her contretemps the previous week, although every now and then Evelyn saw the shadows in her eyes.

'But,' continued Betty, 'isn't it nice to make a bit of effort every now and then? Makes you feel better.'

Evelyn saw Judith visibly relax and smiled to herself when the other woman, relenting, replied, 'Yes, you are right. Thank you for helping me the other day. It was wonderful to feel like a normal woman again.'

As if there'd been a change in the air, like low pressure before a storm, they paused and looked at each other, a shared moment of sudden recognition that they no longer knew what normal was anymore. The stray bomb had been a salutary reminder that in wartime, nowhere was safe. Now whenever a plane flew overheard, people would stiffen, pause and only relax when the sound of its engine died away. Amongst all personnel, a new wariness had replaced the previous sanguine attitude.

'This war seems to have gone on for ever,' said Evelyn, giving in to unusual pessimism. There was no end in sight and today's interrogation put the seal on how topsy-turvy life had become.

'But if it wasn't for the war, we three wouldn't be here and I, for one, am glad to have met you both,' said Betty, slicking on her favourite red lipstick and patting her perfect curls. She always looked like the cat's meow and Evelyn envied her happy-go-lucky nature, which seemed to have reasserted itself even though she clearly had her problems at home.

And now she had to face her own. Giving her skirt one last

skim with the clothes brush, she turned. 'See you later, ladies. Have a good day.' She gave them a jaunty mock salute, hiding the jitters in her stomach, and headed down the stairs to the Officers' Mess for breakfast before finally acknowledging that she really wasn't hungry. She'd grab herself a coffee and take it out on the terrace. The last thing she wanted this morning was the company of others.

The bright sun in an almost clear blue sky heralded the most glorious day and as she balanced on the balustrade drinking her coffee, her mind wandered, thinking of the prisoners in their cells. It must be awful to be cooped up when the weather was like this. She remembered glorious summer walks along the Neckar River, hand in hand with Peter, laughing at the ridiculous antics of the ducks in the water, the daredevil squirrels with perky tails racing along tree branches, and the sunshine on his tanned skin and blond hair. One of Hitler's perfect Aryan specimens. What was she going to find today, the enemy or her former fiancé?

'Coming to briefing?' called Freddie through the open window.

She nodded and checked the time. There were still a few more minutes for her to enjoy the peace and keep her nerves to herself.

Finishing her coffee, she straightened, pushed her shoulders back and took a deep breath. She had a job to do. She had to push personal feelings aside when she saw Peter. He was a potential source of information, which might just help finish this blasted war. No matter how many times she repeated it to herself, she still felt uncomfortable about having to interrogate him and guilty that she hadn't told Colonel Myers that she knew him.

For a moment she stopped and wondered if Naval

Intelligence were already aware. Were they playing a game of double bluff? Her head started to hurt, wondering about who knew what. She just had to do what she thought was the right thing, and with that in mind, she hurried into the library to take her place at the long table.

As they were leaving the meeting, she had a sudden idea and she ran after Myers, who was heading up the stairs to his private office.

'Excuse me, Sir.'

'Yes, Lieutenant Brooke-Edwards?'

'Er … I wonder, what is the protocol for taking prisoners outside for a walk?' She knew that it had been done a number of times with a couple of the Generals that had arrived after being captured recently in North Africa.

Myers smiled. 'Perfect day to introduce the English countryside. Excellent idea. Be all right on your own?'

'I think so, Sir.'

'Of course, if the prisoner isn't keen then bring him straight back, but most of them respond well. Think that we trust them and almost feel beholden to give something back. Human psychology really is most fascinating.'

She could see that he was about to launch into considerable rumination about intelligence tactics and, now that she had his go-ahead, she wanted to be off as quickly as possible.

'Can you hold fire for a moment, Sergeant Lewis? I've got permission from Myers to take my prisoner for a walk this morning.'

Lewis scowled. An Army stickler for the rules, he was one of those soldiers that had no idea what really went on here at Latimer House. Like many of the non-commissioned men, he was responsible for guarding the prisoners and managing their day-to-day imprisonment. Being allowed to go for walks, he believed, was treating the Huns far too kindly.

The wait exacerbated her jumpiness but at last the paperwork arrived. Lewis scanned it with an even deeper scowl and despatched two guards to collect M1392 from his cell.

'Hope he doesn't try to escape, *ma'am*.' His mouth turned even further down in his lugubrious face that reminded her of a doleful basset hound. *Not helpful, Lewis,* she thought and she hadn't missed subtle insolence in his emphasis of the word 'ma'am'.

Narrowing her eyes, she replied, 'I'm sure he's not going to run off into the English countryside in a German army uniform without a clue where he is or anything on him. It would be rather foolhardy – don't you think? – to expect to get very far.' Her voice rapped, staccato and sharp. 'No money. No map. A strong German accent,' she checked herself, 'if he even speaks English.' Which she wasn't supposed to know. There she went, almost slipping up before she'd started. She'd have been a hopeless double agent.

'Hmph,' he replied and returned to the paperwork on his desk, disapproval radiating from his hunched shoulders.

Suddenly it occurred to her that Peter might blurt out her name when he saw her and Lewis would seize on that for certain. The man didn't like female officers and he wouldn't have a moment's hesitation if there was an opportunity to cause trouble.

'I'll wait in interview room two. You can bring the prisoner there.'

'Right you are, *ma'am*.' She pursed her lips but ignored him and walked briskly away. Once inside she couldn't decide whether to sit or stand. Her hands really were shaking now and it wouldn't do for Peter to see that; she had the element of surprise on her side and she needed to maximise it to her advantage. *Concentrate on the job*, Evelyn.

The door opened and her heart dropped with a sudden rush.

'The prisoner, Lieutenant,' said one of the guards, ushering Peter into the room.

She watched his face closely, even though she'd promised herself she'd be professional, but it was hopeless. She couldn't help quickly inventorying every familiar detail. Grey-blue eyes, the colour of a stormy sea, thickly fringed with those surprisingly dark lashes. Sandy blonde hair swept back from the forehead, which he frequently pushed his fingers through when he was exasperated by something. That square-cut chin that spoke of his strong character and his determination to get a job completed. They were so alike in that respect. Then there was the wide, generous mouth that she knew to be soft to the touch and quick to smile. She might not have seen him for four years but all the feelings she had for him rushed in to refill the Peter-shaped space she'd kept open for him, as if he'd never been away.

'*Guten Morgen*, Oberstleutnant Van Hoensbroeck.'

He gave her an idle glance as if determined to be uninterested. It took a few seconds for the stoic, resigned expression on his face to register her. If it wasn't so heart-breaking, the mix of emotions might have been amusing: consternation, surprise, alarm, horror, longing and finally disbelief.

'Evelyn?' He looked around behind him as if wondering what was going on.

'Hello, Peter.'

'What are you doing here?' He reached a hand out as if to touch her and then quickly dropped his arm by his side before saying, 'Is this a trick?'

'No.' She drew in a shaky breath, hoping he couldn't hear the nerves in her voice. 'I'm a Naval Intelligence Officer. It's my job to interrogate you.' The words sounded utterly ridiculous. She wanted to snatch them back. This job should have been given to someone else. She couldn't stop herself drinking in the sight of him. Her hand, buried in the fold of her skirt, trembled as she fought the longing to touch him.

'This is a joke? Why would you be here?'

She'd hoped he'd be pleased to see her. Composing herself, she replied in a flat monotone voice, 'I speak fluent German. It's a highly valued skill these days.'

She watched as he absorbed the information, the suspicious frown lines gradually relaxing as he took in her appearance. 'I'm sure it must be.'

This meeting held none of the joyous homecoming she'd hoped for and she had to swallow down the sadness that threatened to choke her.

'Would you like to come for a walk?' The words sounded hopelessly inadequate. It appeared she had surprised him but then he stiffened and gave the room a careful inspection as if suspecting the place was bugged.

She shook her head, warily watching him. 'I promise you no one is listening. No one knows that we've met before.'

There was a long pause as the words fell between them like pebbles trickling away into a chasm.

'Met before?' He raised a stern eyebrow and gave her a piercing look, his eyes insolently scanning her lips as if to remind her of the intimacy of those previous meetings.

She coloured with a sudden rush of illicit warmth. No one had ever kissed her like Peter. Those heated kisses had trespassed on the boundaries of propriety but she'd excused herself with the knowledge that they were engaged to be married. She still wore his ring on a chain around her neck.

'No one is aware that we know each other.' How she managed to say it without stuttering, she wasn't sure, although behind her back her hands were interlocked, squeezing the circulation from her fingers.

This time he shot her a teasing smirk, as if to say, 'That's better!'

'A walk would be good,' he said. He looked at her and his face softened very slightly and he smiled, as if remembering the many miles they'd spent side by side. It had been their way of spending time together, hours tramping and hiking mountain, river and lakeside trails.

Her heart lifted. Perhaps outside he might relax and this awful atmosphere might dissipate.

'Follow me.' She led him out of the room, down the corridor and past Lewis's brooding glare.

'Pay no attention to him,' she said in German. 'He's miserable with everyone.'

'It's not me I'm worried about. You don't seem very popular with him.'

'He doesn't hold with female officers.'

'I didn't think I did, but you do look rather fetching in

uniform.' There was no hint of a compliment in his words, more of an accompanying smirk that spoke of disapproval.

She ignored that comment and marched up to the guards at the gate, presenting her pass and the paperwork Myers had sent down. After careful scrutiny they were allowed through the gate.

'Is this how you treat all your prisoners?' asked Peter with yet another one of his superior smirks. 'Sending them out for walks with attractive British girls?'

'No,' she replied tersely, annoyed by his attitude. It wasn't a side of him she'd seen before and she found it unnerving. 'Only our most special guests. You're a senior officer of the Wehrmacht and as such privy to information we would be interested in.' From here on in, she resolved to be nothing but professional. Whatever had been between them was clearly now one sided.

'We?' asked Peter with a slow smile.

Irked, she did her best not to show it and for a moment pondered her strategy: outright honesty or play along with his view that she was dressed up in uniform for larks?

Had he always been this arrogant? It wasn't the Peter she remembered.

'I *am* a Naval Intelligence Officer,' she reiterated. 'It's my job to interrogate you.'

'And are you going to?'

'I'll certainly ask questions. You're under no obligation to answer them but life is easier if you cooperate.'

'Or what? Will you be the one to torture me? That will be interesting.'

Exasperated, she stopped and turned to him. 'Or you can go back to your cell and someone else can talk to you.'

He let out a mock gasp. 'You mean you don't want to take a

walk with me? Whatever happened to you promising that you would wear my ring for ever and wait for the end of the war?'

She could hardly bear the disappointment. Peter was not the man she'd thought he was. While she'd continued to love and pine for him, he clearly no longer had any feelings for her. Bitterly, she wrenched the necklace out from under her shirt and dangled the chain from finger and thumb. She'd embarrassed herself. Let her emotions get the better of her. Even worse, she'd given him the upper hand. Sick and angry with herself, she began to tuck the necklace back under her collar, but Peter's hand stopped her.

When she looked up into his face, the expression in his eyes stopped her in her tracks.

'*Liebling*,' he whispered, his forefinger running across hers. The soft touch set light to her skin and she froze. Motionless, they stood staring at each other and she saw a mix of emotions cross his face before finally he frowned.

'Forgive me. I'm so sorry.' He stepped back and pushed both his hands through his hair.

For a moment they faced each other, studying each other's features as if only now were they seeing each other properly. At last, Peter gave her a sad smile.

'This war.' He shook his head. 'I never thought I'd see you again. I've tried to put you out of my mind. And then here you are and I'm...' He shook his head. 'The war has hardened me. Made me forget. Seeing you today, it's humiliating. I'm the defeated prisoner, not the man you knew.'

The smile she shared with him was wary, like an animal that wasn't sure if it might yet be kicked.

'I apologise. I didn't want to be like that in front of you and you seem so confident, so sure of yourself. I thought the woman I loved had gone. I thought it was a trick and that you were toying with me.'

'No trick. I'm not a believer in fate, or God, or anything like that. You being here is an accident, a coincidence. I never thought I'd see you again either. I didn't know what had happened to you. The nights I've stayed awake imagining where you might be. Whether you were in the army, the navy or the air force. Whether you might have been shot down, sunk or died in a trench somewhere.'

'Yet you wore my ring.'

She shrugged, not wanting to appear weak in front of him. 'One always has to have hope.'

'In a sane world, yes, but war takes us into madness.'

'Only if you are led by a madman.'

He gave her a sharp look. 'You mean the Führer?'

She lifted her shoulders again.

'Is this part of your interrogation?'

'Partly, yes,' she said because she couldn't deny it, 'but also to know you. Do you think he is leading your country in the right way? Do you support him? Do you think Germany will win the war?'

'So many questions.' Peter sighed and they began walking again. 'And once I was so sure of all the answers. Now I'm not so certain. Your Colonel took us into London.'

Evelyn bit back a smile. 'I was there.'

Peter closed his eyes. 'Of course you were. The silent, oh-so-correct, lady driver. Do you know,' he let out a bitter laugh, 'I remember thinking that your uncle had a Bentley just like that one.'

She shot him a grimace of apology.

'So you heard every word we said?'

'I'm afraid so.'

'Well then, you know some of my views.'

'I'd be interested to hear more. Partly for my superiors, but I think personally to find out if we are truly enemies.'

Peter pursed his lips and stared ahead for a long moment.

'I have no love for Hitler, but I do for my country. When he began, taking the Sudetenland, it appeared decisive and strong. Like many, I believed he made our country one we could be proud of again, but now there are a lot of us that will seek to depose him as soon as the war is over, if not before. Being completely honest with you, and I have to trust you—'

'Don't trust me, Peter.' She laid a hand on his arm as she blurted the words out. She gave him a stricken look and he held her gaze, his mouth firming a little.

'If I can't trust you, who can I trust?'

She swallowed. 'You can't trust me. Not with the truth. We're on the opposite side of the fence. It's my duty to report anything I learn that could be useful to the Allies winning the war.'

'And what about love?' he asked with a cynical twist to his mouth.

She closed her eyes, hating herself. Hating herself for being so honest, for not being able to lie to him. For not being able to tell him what he wanted to hear.

Did duty come before love?

'I don't know,' she whispered, feeling broken inside. 'I don't know.'

He walked ahead a few paces and with a sigh she followed him, trying to swallow back tears.

They fell into step again in silence for a few moments and she had no idea what to say to him. She'd blown the first rule of interrogation: win the prisoner's trust.

To her surprise, Peter threaded his fingers through hers and began to talk in a low, vehement voice. The unspoken intimacy made her feel light-headed for a moment. She'd never dreamed that she'd see him, let alone might touch him again.

'There is so much that is wrong. I love my country, the people, the places we have built. When I think of those summers in Heidelberg untainted by hate or violence, I can see that Germany has taken a misstep. There was a path in the road and we took the wrong fork. I hate the way that we can't talk freely of opinions and beliefs anymore. I hate the way that so many people live in fear. Hitler's SS have become notorious, without any sense of honour or morality. There have been things done in Germany's name that have no legal basis and that I am not proud of. In fact, I am sickened by. There is too much power in the hands of one man.'

Evelyn tightened her fingers on his. Grateful for his trust and relieved that his basic decency still existed.

'Thank you,' she said softly.

'Don't thank me. It's a relief in some ways to talk to someone I trust. And yes, I do still trust you. Someone who knows the man I once was. Sometimes I fear we've all become monsters. I never in my life wanted to kill another man and then it became part of every day. At least now I'm free of that. In some ways I feel damaged, in another so inured to having to follow orders that I've become indifferent. I've sent my own men to their deaths. I've given orders to kill the enemy.' He stopped and turned to face her. 'Sometimes when I wake in the night I'm afraid my soul will never be my own again.'

For as long as she would live, she would never forget the tortured pain in his eyes, and her voice cracked as she said, 'Oh Peter.'

The harsh *chack, chack* of a magpie startled both of them as it flew down to peck at something in the scrubby grassland between the trees, and in silence they continued their walk.

'You do know that I have to report back on whatever you tell me,' said Evelyn eventually.

'I do. Don't worry. My conscience will be clear.' Peter smiled, the arrogance gone now. 'And you do know that I will only tell you what I think you already know. We've been warned about the British interrogation. Did that room have a microphone?'

'Actually, no, it didn't.' Not that particular one. 'I thought you would appreciate a walk. We could have talked there quite freely.' She tried not to feel guilty for the truth that covered up the bigger lie. She couldn't reveal that his cell was a different matter entirely, nor could she ask him not to talk to his cellmate about her.

'I could almost forget I'm a prisoner. I could almost forget that I haven't seen you for four years. I could almost imagine that one day we could marry.'

'You're going to be a prisoner of war until the end of the war.'

'Or until Germany invades Britain.'

'Do you think that likely, still?'

'Not anymore. I don't think I have for a while and certainly not now. Not having seen London, like that, barely touched by bombs. Yet Dortmund, Duisberg and Wuppertal all suffered terribly last month. A firestorm destroyed much of Wuppertal. While here... This countryside. It looks undisturbed. You look so well and the food here is good. It feels as if Britain, the little island, is remote from the war, not suffering the way Germany is. Hitler tells us that you are ready to beg for mercy and that the next secret weapon will finish you off.'

Evelyn knew she had to be cautious. There'd been much

talk about secret weapons and it was a hot topic at the moment. She hesitated before she spoke, her conscience flickering between love and duty. There was so much at stake. So very much. She had to do her job. The lives of thousands of her countrymen depended upon it. Was it betraying him to console herself with the thought that at least Peter was safe now and would be for the rest of the war?

'Ah, those would be the weapons that have been developed at Peenemünde. Not so secret.' There, she'd said it. The interrogating officer following her script. Sickness churned in her stomach.

'*Mein Gott!*' He whirled around, horror-struck. 'You know about them?'

She nodded. 'Yes.'

'Is there anything you don't know? I can't believe it. You should know that German High Command have high hopes that they can launch these weapons, although not from Germany, of course. I suppose you also know that the range is not as great as was initially promised.'

'I understand there will be launch sites on the Dutch coast.' Even as she said the words, she knew she was leading him into a trap, pretending to know more than she did, but it was for the greater good. It was vital to gather every piece of information available about these terrifying weapons. If the RAF could destroy them, it would save lives.

He stared at her. 'Those, and more along the Pas de Calais.'

Another piece in the jigsaw. She nodded without blinking, storing the information away. He was giving it freely and she couldn't afford, or allow herself, to feel guilty. This was her job. Her country. She wasn't forcing him to speak. Was this wrong? Was she betraying his trust?

'You are well informed. I think Hitler has underestimated British Intelligence.'

Feeling a little sick at her duplicity, she changed the subject, asking after his family. She was sad to hear that his brother and father were fighting on the brutal Russian front and his mother had moved in with her sister to a rural area of Bavaria. Their lives had been turned upside down too.

As they walked and talked, his hand occasionally brushed hers and they would look at each other. Evelyn had never felt so confused in her life. They were on opposite sides of the war. Her loyalties were divided and she had no idea how they could ever overcome that. She ought to have told Myers she knew Peter. What on earth was she going to do now?

Chapter Twenty-Two

Judith

As the three of them climbed into Evelyn's big fancy car, their excitement reminded Judith of the childhood treat of going to her aunt's house during Rosh Hashanah when all their friends and neighbours would get together.

'I've never been in a car before,' squealed Betty. 'These seats! Look! They're leather. Gosh, this is ever so posh.'

'Are you all right to sit in the back, Betty?' asked Evelyn, turning round to look at her before they set off.

'Oh lawks, yes. I can wave to people and pretend I'm the Queen or one of the Princesses.'

Judith slid into the front seat next to Evelyn and they exchanged a quick private smile as Betty continued to enthuse from the back, even though Judith herself was just as excited, if more reserved about it.

She watched as Evelyn settled into the driving seat, nestling her bottom into place like a broody hen, and checked the mirror at the front before starting the engine, the sound of which vibrated through the car in a growly big-cat sort of purr.

'It's fast, isn't it?' Judith volunteered to Evelyn, watching the countryside speed past, the hedgerows blurring already.

Evelyn laughed. 'You've not seen anything yet. I daren't go too fast on these little country lanes but when we get to the main road, I'll give her her head. You'll see. It's not called horsepower for nothing.'

'How far are we going?' Judith knew that Evelyn lived in a small village outside Henley on Thames, which had meant nothing to her until her roommate had fetched a map from the Officers' Mess and given her a quick geography lesson about Britain.

'It's about twenty miles. So not too far, although if I hadn't got the Colonel's permission, we wouldn't have been allowed to come.' They were delivering some papers to an office in High Wycombe which was on the way, and therefore ensured that the trip constituted official business enabling them to make use of the car.

'How long will it take?'

'About an hour, so we'll be back in plenty of time to go on duty, I promise.'

Although Judith spent much of her off-duty with Walther (last week they'd been to the cinema in Chesham and had a very precarious journey back in the dark – they couldn't use lights on their borrowed bicycles because of the blackout), she'd been looking forward to this day out with the other two girls and had swapped her off-duty to make sure that she could come with them. Much as she enjoyed exploring the surrounding area, she was ready to spread her wings a little and enjoy a complete change of scene. She was getting quite adventurous. Next week, she and Walther were working late

shifts and planned to go to London early one morning to queue for one of the lunch-time concerts at the National Gallery, which she was very excited about. Wouldn't it be wonderful if they saw Dame Myra Hess?

'You look happy,' observed Evelyn.

'Sorry.'

'You don't have to apologise for being happy.'

There were so many people in such desperate situations but she couldn't deny that happiness had started to feature in her life again, like a butterfly emerging from a chrysalis, although without the bright, gaudy wings. Her life had brightened beyond belief in the last three months, gone from being a dull shade of brown to clear blue with splashes of colour. She had friends, good colleagues and Walther. She still couldn't believe that she deserved his quiet, devoted attention or that being with him made her heart beat faster.

As if reading her mind, Evelyn said, 'So how are things with Walther? You two seem to spend a lot of time together.'

'He's a very nice man.'

'A very nice man,' hooted Betty from the back, leaning forward to put her head between the two front seats like a friendly dog. 'He adores you. I've seen his whole face change when you walk into the Sergeants' Mess. Elsie reckons there'll be wedding bells before long.'

Judith blushed scarlet. 'I-I don't know about that.'

'Well, he seems pretty keen,' observed Evelyn.

'We get on well. We have lots to talk about. We have a lot in common, that's all.'

Betty rolled her eyes. 'Seriously, Judith, what about him whispering sweet nothings in your ear?'

'I don't know what you mean,' she said, not quite understanding the English phrase, or rather pretending not to.

'Yes, you do,' crowed Betty from the back. 'Has he kissed you?'

'Betty,' reproved Evelyn before turning, taking her eyes off the road, arching her eyebrows at Judith with the same question.

Judith's brain flopped forwards and backwards, trying to decide what to answer. Part of her desperately wanted their advice and the other part was terrified that they might judge her. She'd never really had girlfriends before. She'd always kept herself to herself and in a dormitory with twenty-four other women, it had been easy to fade into the background. Here she didn't seem to have a choice. Taking a breath, she glanced at both of them.

'Should I let him?' she asked in a small voice, as if that would excuse her when they both said no in shocked horror.

'Yes,' said Evelyn. 'If you like him.'

To Evelyn's and Judith's surprise, Betty spoke with unexpected vehemence. 'No! Only if you want him to. Don't let him if you don't want to. I hate it when Bert kisses me. It's horrible. I don't know why anyone really likes kissing. It's all right in the movies but in real life, I don't think so.'

'But it can be wonderful with the right man,' said Evelyn, her beautiful face turning a little pink. 'Although perfectly beastly with a brute.' She looked in the mirror on the dashboard and Judith saw her exchange a look with Betty. 'How does it make you feel, Judith? How does being with Walther make you feel?'

Judith paused to give it some serious thought, conscious of Betty concentrating on her with almost ferocious interest, almost as if she would leap in front of her to save her if she needed it. She didn't. Just the thought of Walther brought a smile to her face and set off the effervescent champagne

bubbles of happiness popping in her stomach. 'He makes me feel special. That I'm really important and that he'll do anything to make me happy. It's a lovely feeling.' She wasn't sure Betty would be so interested if she also confided that they could talk for hours about art and music, especially music.

Betty sighed. 'Then that is like in the movies. I always wondered. So Evelyn, do you have a boyfriend? What happened to the picture by your bed?'

Judith, in the front, saw Evelyn stiffen and her hands tighten on the steering wheel.

'Oh no, I'm sorry,' Betty's apology tumbled out. 'I shouldn't have asked. I'm sorry, he's not dead, is he?'

'Yes,' said Evelyn. 'No. I don't know. We... It's complicated.'

'You mean he's MIA.'

Judith watched Evelyn's lips frame one answer and then change her mind. It was as if she couldn't bring herself to lie even though she wanted or needed to.

'He's a prisoner of war,' she said eventually and sat up straighter as if she were relieved to have been able to tell the truth, although something told Judith there was more to it than that. It wasn't like Evelyn to equivocate. Judith had learned she was the sort of person who always told the truth, she was fearless and forthright and even on such a short acquaintance, Judith knew that she had a strict code of honour and a strong desire to do the right thing. Living in such close proximity the way that they did, you quickly came to know people. She smiled to herself. And they came to know you too.

An hour later, they pulled up outside a golden stone mansion house, with dozens of small-paned windows and well-trained creepers climbing up the wall around the big porch. Although a grand, handsome house, it also had a squat solidity about it as if it had taken root in the landscape and would not be budged. Leaving Judith with Betty trailing behind, both avidly drinking in the grandeur of the place, Evelyn sailed in through the big front door, decorated with jewel-bright stained-glass panels, calling, 'Toodle-ooh, Mummy. We're here.'

A small, wisp-like version of Evelyn came through a door at the end of the big, light, airy hallway, wiping her hands on an apron tied around her waist which protected a beautiful flower-print dress that fitted her perfectly and showed off the tiniest, well-corseted waist. She made Judith feel lumpish and bovine next to her.

'Darling, you're here. And these must be your friends.'

'This is Betty.'

Betty stepped forward and did a quick bob, almost a curtsy, which Evelyn's mother ignored. Instead, with the most charming smile, she held out her hand. 'How lovely to meet you and who does your hair? It's simply divine.' And in one sentence she'd put Betty at ease immediately, before turning to Judith. 'And you must be Judith. Evelyn's told me such a lot about both of you in her letters.' In fluent German she added that she was most welcome and it was super that she could come today.

'Now, girls, I bet you're starving. Mrs Dawtry has been looking forward to feeding you all week, she gets so little chance to show off her skills, these days. She's been baking all morning.'

'Sorry.' Evelyn grinned at them both. 'Mummy still thinks of me and my brother as teenagers that need constant feeding.'

'Darling, don't tell me you're well fed at your posting. That will be a first.'

'Actually, Mrs Brooke-Edwards, we are,' said Betty earnestly.

'Oh, call me Vivienne, darling,' she said, tucking her arm through Betty's and giving her a dazzling smile. 'I don't think we need to stand on ceremony.' Judith could see exactly where Evelyn got her easy manners from. Her mother was definitely what you'd call a lady.

Evelyn raised an amused eyebrow at Judith, a twinkle in her eye, and the two of them followed her mother and Betty through to a glasshouse at the back of the house. Judith stopped to stare up at the high-arched walls of windows and the ornate finials on top of the roof. She'd never been inside such a beautiful place and immediately thought that Walther, who appreciated every sort of architecture, would absolutely love it. She tried to store up the details of the elegant rattan and bent-cane furniture, the pointed arches of the wrought-iron structure and the proliferations of glossy leaved plants in huge stoneware containers, so that she could tell him all about it later. She was too shy to ask what this room was called in English but she didn't need to worry, Betty had no such inhibitions.

'Oh Vivienne, this is lovely. Is that a real lemon? I've never been in a glasshouse before.'

'It's an orangery. It stays lovely and warm so that we can grow these lovely exotics. Hodges, our gardener, isn't keen. He says, "It ent natural."' Vivienne mimicked a country voice. 'He'd far rather be out with his smelly compost heaps and root vegetables but we can grow cucumbers, tomatoes and oranges in here. Of course, I have to rely on Mrs Dawtry to remind me to water everything now that Evelyn's not here. She's the one

who loves grubbing about with plants and things. She's very good at arranging flowers.'

Evelyn rolled her eyes behind her mother's back and Betty had to turn away to hide her laugh.

'Thank you, Mummy.'

'Well, you aren't terribly good at anything else domestic. I don't suppose either of you knit?'

'Don't answer that,' said Evelyn with a grin. 'Mummy will have you knitting for the merchant seamen.' But it was too late. Betty, with her usual enthusiasm, said:

'Judith can. She made that jumper and I can crochet. I made this,' and to everyone's surprise she lifted her jumper to reveal a pale-blue crochet bra.

'You made that?' said Evelyn, moving close to inspect it, whereas Judith averted her eyes.

'Yes. I don't want to wear out my Army-issue corset.'

'I get mine renovated at a place on Baker Street in town. It only costs twelve shillings and sixpence.'

Betty beamed. 'This only cost me a shilling to make. And I embroidered my cami-knickers to match.'

'It's lovely,' said Vivienne, not even batting an eyelid at Betty's impromptu reveal.

'I think I might have to ask you to make me one,' said Evelyn, reaching out and fingering the strap. 'That is very pretty.'

'Easy. You can get two bras from three balls of Coats Mercer crochet cotton.'

'Make three, we can all have matching bras,' said Evelyn gaily.

'Or I can teach you how to make one,' said Betty.

'Good luck with that,' said Vivienne, laughing. 'Oh, Mrs

animated than usual, and Judith didn't like to admit that she didn't know any of those tunes. She'd led quite a sheltered life in Berlin and her father hadn't really approved of anything other than classical music even though her aunt had worked in the clubs. Judith wondered whether, had her bohemian aunt not died, she herself might have had a different outlook on life; perhaps been a little more adventurous in her music tastes and a bit less dull. Next to the other two women she was quite the dowd in her regulation ATS shoes and underwear, although thanks to Betty she was wearing her hair in a much more flattering style, even if it did take a bit of work. If the warm appreciation in Walther's eyes was anything to go by, it was worth it.

'Anyone want to dance?' asked Betty, already winding up the gramophone with one hand and holding the record in her other.

'Why not?' said Evelyn, kicking off her shoes and pushing one of the sofas back to the wall.

The record crackled and Betty scrambled out of her own shoes and then the music began. It was a popular tune and although she hadn't known the name or the artist, it was familiar to Judith. It was one of those that was often on the radio in the background, or other girls had played it on their portable gramophones. She'd heard it a dozen times before but this was the first time she sat and listened to it properly, and her feet began to twitch at the catchy music. Although it was so different to the music she'd always played, she was quickly entranced by the rhythmic beat, the sparkiness of the brass notes diving in and driving home, and the underlying melody all the way through. Her fingers itched to track the notes on a piano. She was astounded by the dexterity that would be needed to play something like this and longed to give it a try.

She was also impressed and slightly awed by Evelyn and Betty's dancing; the two of them seemed to be in perfect syncopation, swinging each other around, turning and twisting. Betty in particular was extremely athletic, her face alight with sheer joy as her hips wiggled and she sashayed around, her arms up in the air, moving in perfect timing to the oh-so-fast beat. Judith wouldn't have been able to keep up if her life had depended on it.

When the music finished, Betty threw herself backwards onto the plump damson velvet cushions of the sofa. 'That was so much fun,' she gasped, her chest heaving. 'I can't remember the last time I danced.' Suddenly she sat up straight, even though she was still catching her breath. 'Hey, do you girls know there's a dance coming up? At Bovingdon.'

Evelyn, also breathing heavily, crossed to the squat gramophone with its brass horn to select another record before saying, 'Yes, I think Freddie mentioned it.'

'We should go. All three of us. I bet Walther would take you,' said Betty. 'And we could pick up a couple of GIs.'

'That would be fun,' said Evelyn, although her smile didn't quite reach her eyes. 'What would you like next? Some Andrews Sisters?'

'Ooh, yes. I love them.' Betty was already standing up in anticipation. 'Come on, Judith, you have to dance this time.'

'No, it's all right.' She shrank back into her seat, shyness freezing her limbs. They'd made it look effortless and fun but she didn't know the steps and her limbs would likely be tied in knots if she even tried. Her idea of dancing was the ballet or the polka.

'Come on,' wheedled Betty.

It was hard to resist her when her eyes were so bright and shiny with elation and exertion, and it had looked a lot of fun.

'We'll teach you,' said Evelyn, realising in that intuitive way of hers that Judith didn't actually know how to dance those sorts of steps.

Once the record was on, the two of them stood on either side of Judith.

'Right, copy Betty. Betty, go slowly so that Judith can see the moves. And keep it simple. None of the fancy stuff, just yet.'

Although Betty's hips were clearly itching to wriggle at double the speed, she obliged. 'It's three steps to the two main beats. So quick, quick, slow.' She demonstrated twisting her hips in a jaunty manner that Judith wasn't sure she could emulate in any way, shape or form.

'Relax,' advised Evelyn. 'Close your eyes, pretend no one else is here. Listen to the music.'

That turned out to be excellent advice. If she couldn't see anyone, then no one could see her. Closing her eyes, she did as she was told and the more she listened to the cheery, upbeat music and the women singing about the bugle boy of company B, the more her inhibitions melted away. When she opened her eyes, she realised that apart from a cursory check-in, Betty and Evelyn were far too busy having a good time to watch her steps.

To her surprise and delight, perhaps because she had the advantage of a musical ear, she managed to pick up the steps quite quickly and when Betty put on a third 78 record, she taught her some twists and turns, going slowly again at first before she gradually speeded up.

'I'm dancing!' Judith cried, breathless and flushed as the three of them careered around the room.

'You certainly are,' said Evelyn.

'Isn't this so much fun?' called Betty, coming in to take her hand to give her another spin.

When the music finished, the three of them flopped like air-deprived fish on the sofa side by side and Judith, with a stitch in her side, thought she might never catch her breath.

'You're a fast learner,' said Betty. 'For someone who didn't know how to dance.'

Judith grinned. There'd been a fluidity to her body she'd not experienced before. 'I think because I played the piano for most of my life.'

'You play the piano!' Evelyn sat up. 'How wonderful. You must play ours. My brother was a keen jazz pianist. It needs using. It's probably horribly out of tune because no one has touched it since he joined up.'

'Give her a moment,' said Betty with a laugh. 'We've worn her out.'

Judith sat up, the dancing having given her some sort of unexpected burst of confidence, and pushed her shoulders back. 'I'm never too tired to play piano.'

The other two girls laughed. 'That's the spirit,' said Evelyn. 'Help yourself. Do you need some music?'

The piano wasn't anywhere near as grand and mellow as the one at Latimer House and after the music they'd just been listening to, Judith worried that Bach or Mozart might dampen the moment. There was some sheet music sitting on the stand and although she'd not played it before she'd seen the film *The Wizard of Oz* and knew the song enough to play it from sight. As she began to pick out the first few notes, Betty came to stand beside her and put a hand on her shoulder. She needed to concentrate on the notes so didn't look round but a few bars in, Betty began to murmur the opening notes of the song 'Somewhere Over the Rainbow'.

Her voice gathered strength, then she sang the opening words of the song, her voice ringing out so sweet and pure that Judith almost faltered. Betty's voice had the sweetest tone she'd ever heard and simply soared through the notes so effortlessly that it made her own heart sing.

By the time they'd finished, Vivienne and Mrs Dawtry were both at the door open-mouthed and Evelyn was clapping. 'Bravo. Bravo. That was amazing. Betty, you are divine and Judith, I've never heard that piano played so well. My goodness, I think I'm going to be your manager.'

Mrs Dawtry wiped a tear from her eye. 'That was marvellous, girls.'

'It certainly was. We couldn't believe it was coming from this house,' exclaimed Vivienne.

Judith realised Betty's hand was still gripping her shoulder and she glanced up. There were tears on Betty's face.

'I've never sung in front of anyone before,' said Betty. 'And not with proper music. You're so clever, Judith.'

'And you're so talented, Betty. You have one of the most beautiful voices I've ever heard.'

Betty's hand relaxed and she waved her other. 'Don't talk rot. It's nothing special.'

But Judith could tell it was important to her and she placed her hand on top of Betty's and squeezed. 'I promise you, it *is* special, and I know a lot about music. Before I came to England I played piano all my life. My father ran a music shop. Most of our friends were musicians and my aunt was…' Perhaps now wasn't the moment to say that her aunt had been a burlesque performer. It had been quite risqué in Berlin but probably quite outrageous in Britain.

There was a child-like eagerness in Betty's eyes when she said, 'Honestly?'

Judith nodded. 'Do you want to sing something else? Do you know any of these tunes?'

They sifted through the pile of Evelyn's brother's music and chose another song, 'I Thought About You', which Judith picked her way through carefully, reading by sight, while Betty sang in a completely different octave.

'Your range is incredible,' said Judith at the end.

'I just sing the notes like the real singer sang them. And I have no idea what you're talking about.'

Evelyn put her hands up. 'Me neither.'

Judith rolled her eyes and shook her head. 'Philistines.'

'Could you teach me?' asked Betty, suddenly looking plaintive. 'I hate being so stupid all the time.'

Judith and Evelyn stared at her. 'The two of you are so … clever, smart. You know things. Judith, you're educated, you know about music and art, and Evelyn, you know about life, you've got taste and style. Me, I don't know anything. I'm good at pretending but half the time I'm scared to death I'm going to be found out. I mean, they promoted me in the section and I keep worrying that they'll realise they made a mistake. I just remember things. That's all.'

Evelyn stood up and led Betty over to the sofa and sat her down and beckoned Judith to come sit on the other side of her.

'Betty, you are a smart, intelligent, talented girl,' said Evelyn firmly. 'Inside it doesn't matter where you come from, it matters where you go to. And right now, we girls have the best opportunity to prove to the world that we can go places. I've never worked in a place before that values us for what we can do, even though we're women. While this war is on, we have to seize every chance to show what we're made of. That way, when the war is over, we don't have go back to being nobodies or nothings.'

'But you're not a nobody,' said Betty. 'Look at this house. You're a someone.'

'Who's expected to go to parties, look pretty and not do much.' Evelyn pulled a face. 'I know I shouldn't complain, I'm one of the fortunate ones, but have you any idea how boring that sort of life is?'

Judith raised an eyebrow. She might have enjoyed finding out, but then, as she looked at the beautiful room, she wondered what she would have done all day here, apart from play music, and that wasn't fulfilling without an audience or anyone to share it.

'I love working at Latimer House,' continued Evelyn, real passion stirring her voice, 'feeling like what I do is making a difference and that it's important. Even my mother, although she wouldn't admit it, is enjoying herself, feeling useful for a change with all her knitting and Women's Voluntary Service activities. I've never seen her so busy and happy.'

Betty frowned, clearly not inclined to believe Evelyn. 'I wouldn't mind living in a place like this, being warm in the winter, not having to do anything.'

'Not being *allowed* to do anything. Anyway, that's all by the by. What I'm trying to tell you is that you are amazing, and the only person telling yourself you aren't is you. They wouldn't have promoted you if you weren't doing a good job. And Judith wouldn't tell you you could sing if you couldn't.' She suddenly grinned at Judith. 'I don't think Judith knows how to tell a lie, do you?'

Judith shrugged her shoulders. 'I try not to tell lies.'

'Do you think you could you teach me about music and singing?' asked Betty, turning to Judith.

'Yes.' Judith sat up straighter, realising that she would enjoy it. 'There's a piano at Latimer House as well. We could practise in there.'

Betty clapped her hands together. 'And you would teach me? You really think you can?'

'You can already sing. You have a real gift but if you could read music and knew about the notes and things, it would help you be even better. And I could learn to play all these songs.'

'I would really like that.'

So too would she, Judith realised. She'd enjoy teaching and sharing her knowledge. With Betty it would be fun, not something that she'd had a lot of in recent years.

'Lunch will be served in the dining room in twenty minutes. Would you like to come through?' Vivienne announced, putting her head around the door.

'Oh, I must pop out and see Hodges in the garden,' said Evelyn, standing up quickly. 'See how things are going.'

As she rose, Betty suddenly tugged her arm and whispered something in her ear.

'I'd forgotten,' said Evelyn. 'Are you sure you want it?' Betty nodded and Judith noticed the fixed determination in her eye. She wondered what they were talking about, but it was nothing to do with her. Betty was probably borrowing clothes or make-up or something.

While Evelyn dashed out into the garden, Vivienne led Judith and Betty into a very grand dining room dominated by a long tablecloth-covered table. 'Oh, what beautiful china,' exclaimed Judith.

'It's Meissen. We bought it in Heidelberg one year.'

'My aunt had something very similar.' She sighed,

remembering bygone family celebrations in her aunt's apartment with friends gathered from all over the city. 'I wonder what happened to it.' And what had happened to all those people, most of them Jews? So many people had disappeared. Supposedly to labour camps but Judith had heard rumours that there were other camps, that no one ever left.

Vivienne smiled uncertainly. 'Would you like to sit here, Betty, and you there, Judith?'

Betty had drifted to the sideboard by the window which was full of silver-framed photographs.

'I love looking at old wedding photos,' she said. 'Is this you? What a beautiful bride.'

Vivienne went to lift the photo. 'Yes, that was me. With Evelyn's father. He was such a handsome man. He still is. Although it's been so long since I've seen him, I sometimes almost forget what he looks like. My son David looks just like him. And it's even longer since I've seen him.' Her face drooped before she stoically rallied.

'I'm sorry, Mrs Brooke-Edwards. Evelyn told us he's in a POW camp. I do hope you hear from him soon.'

'So do I.' Her mouth firmed primly.

Betty seized another photo. 'And is this Evelyn? Doesn't she look pretty? Was this taken long ago?'

'Ah, that was at her engagement party. So sad. We've known the Van Hoensbroeck family for years, we were so pleased when Peter proposed, but then this beastly war started and it was the right thing for them to break the engagement off. I know she was heartbroken, but what could she do? It would have been impossible for her to marry the enemy. Can you imagine how difficult it would have been if they were married before the war started?'

Betty frowned. 'Evelyn's fiancé is German!'

'Ex-fiancé,' corrected Vivienne.

'Gosh. We didn't know that.' Betty glanced in surprise at Judith, who sighed. Now she understood Evelyn's confused speech in the car on the way here. Poor thing, she obviously had no idea where her fiancé was. Presumably she had no way of finding out either. Her heart went out to the other woman. How on earth did Evelyn manage, working with German POWs every day while wondering where her ex-fiancé might be? Did she still have feelings for him?

Chapter Twenty-Three

Betty

'Ah, Betty, someone was looking for you earlier,' said one of the sergeants as she crossed the Mess to help herself to a cup of tea from Elsie's ever-present teapot tucked into its knitted cosy on the counter on the side. Everyone else was tucking into Elsie's Woolton Pie for tea, but Betty was still full from the delicious spread that Mrs Dawtry had laid on, of stuffed onions, potato pastry turnovers and beans au gratin. There'd been no meat but it had all tasted wonderful.

She'd walked up from the village, having had Evelyn drop her in the lane. When you'd just come from somewhere like Evelyn's grand house, you really didn't want anyone seeing the little terrace cottage you'd grown up in. It was all very well for Evelyn to say it didn't matter where you came from, but Betty knew better.

'Who was that?' Betty was puzzled, wondering what on earth they wanted, but she wasn't in the dark for long as one of the typists from her section came scurrying up with self-important bluster.

'Betty, the very person.'

'Hello, Lucy. Did you want me?'

'It's your mum! Someone came with a message while you were out. Apparently there's been an emergency and you need to go home right away.'

Betty frowned, suspicion darting into her head straight away. That was a load of tommy rot, if she'd ever heard it, because she'd just seen her ma and Jane, who'd been thrilled to bits with her orange.

'Do you know who brought the message?' It was a stupid question because she almost certainly knew who it had been. She squeezed the bag under her arm, thinking about Evelyn's father's old service gun that she had hidden in there. There might not be any ammunition in it but Bert wouldn't know that.

'Yes, a man at the back door. I said I'd pass the message on as soon as I saw you, but that was ages ago.' Concern radiated from her face and she was almost shooing Betty towards the door.

'When?'

'About three hours ago.'

'Right-ho.' Betty nodded and reached for the teapot to pour herself a cuppa. Lucy, fluttering around her, asked, 'Aren't you worried?'

Betty shook her head. 'No, someone's having you on. I've just come from my mum's. She was as right as a trivet.'

'But why would anyone do that? Do you think they got the wrong person? But he asked for you, Betty Connors.'

'What did this chap look like?' Betty had to ask, even though she knew exactly who it was.

'He was dark-haired, labourer's clothes, but a big strong chap.' She giggled a little. 'He was a bit of a looker, if I'm honest. A bit of a brooding Heathcliff type, like Laurence Olivier in the film.'

'Bert. Bert Davenport. He must have got it wrong. Worries over my mum, he does,' lied Betty smoothly, thinking that she'd ruddy kill him one of these days. No doubt his way of trying to bring her to heel because she'd deliberately avoided going home this last couple of weeks. Ma had been quite happy to believe that they'd had a rush on and she was working double shifts. It was worrying that Bert was bold enough to come waltzing up here.

Picking up her tea, she looked around but there were too many people she knew sitting at the table and she didn't fancy talking to anyone. Instead she took herself outside to the grassy bank beneath the windows of the Officers' Mess. There were a few Naval types on the terrace but she doubted any of them would take any notice of her. Putting her cup beside her, she drew her knees up and sank her chin into her hands, her elbows propped on her knees. What the heck was she going to do about blinking Bert? He was so dead set that there were cigarettes and booze here that there was no telling what he'd do. What if he took matters into his own hands? What if he came up here one night, tried to break in and got caught, and told someone she'd given him the information?

'You look like you lost a shilling and found a penny,' drawled a voice above her.

Startled, she turned around and found the handsome face of Major Wendermeyer looking down.

'Just thinking,' she said.

'Mind if I join you?'

Surprised, she found it hard to find the right words for a

moment, and even then they were incoherent at best. 'Er … um … yes … sure … um, if you want to.'

'Why would I not want to sit beside the prettiest girl around?' he teased.

'Shouldn't you be with the other officers?' she asked, ignoring the compliment, trying not to squirm at the foolish flutter in the base of her belly.

'Why would I want to do that? Have you seen those guys? Old and grizzled.' He leaned forward conspiratorially. 'I don't think any of them know the meaning of the word "fun".'

'And I do?' She couldn't help flirting back at him. There was something so appealing about that open, easy charm, even though he probably said the same sort of thing to every blue-eyed blonde that crossed his path.

'You have a glint in your eye.'

'I do, do I?'

'Yes, ma'am.' He paused. 'And one of the sharpest brains to match, which I find kind of appealing.'

'Oh,' said Betty, taken aback. Those blue eyes that she found so blinking mesmerising twinkled at her. Honest to God, she'd never seen anything like them and when he looked at her like that, everything inside her wanted to get up and dance.

'That's taken the wind out of your sails, hasn't it, honey?'

'No,' she said primly, although her pleased smile gave her away.

'So, tell me, what do you do for entertainment when you're not slaving over reports?'

'Not that much. It's quiet around here. Although London's not so far away. You can get there and back before a shift or after a shift. There are some good shows in the West End.'

'Well, that sounds swell, except I wouldn't know where to go. Perhaps you could show me sometime?'

'I... I...' She was about to tell him that she was already taken but something stopped her. She didn't owe Bert anything. Not anymore, and she knew she didn't want to marry him. It wasn't as if he'd ever asked her. Somehow it had been assumed by everyone, him as well, that they would wed one day. She clenched a hand on the grass beside her; she wouldn't be assumed into a marriage with someone she realised she didn't even like. With sudden resolve, she faced the American officer. 'I'd love to show you London, Major.'

'I think if you're going to be my personal tour guide, you could think about calling me Carl, don't you?'

'Yes, Carl,' she said with an impish grin.

Her tea went cold as she talked to him about the places he might like to see in London and it was nearly an hour later when she realised she was cutting it fine to change into her uniform for her shift.

'I've got to go. Gosh, sorry. I have prattled on.'

'Not at all. I could listen to your English accent all day.' Those blue eyes held hers steadily and she almost forgot to breathe. 'I forgot the time.' He rose and held out a hand. 'May I?'

Thinking the gesture courtly and romantic – he made her feel like a proper lady – she extended her hand and allowed him to pull her to her feet. Then she spoilt it by ducking back down, bottom in the air, to pick up her cup.

'I'd have done that for you.'

She laughed and said without thinking, 'Instead of me sticking my bottom in your face.' As soon as the words left her mouth, she flushed scarlet. What had she been thinking? She hadn't, that was the problem. It had been so easy talking to him, she'd completely forgotten who he was. Her commanding officer and a man who wasn't part of her family.

'It's a pretty nice bottom.'

Her eyes widened. No man had ever said anything like that before. Of course, she knew Americans were much more forward, but even so, she hoped he didn't think she was fast or something.

'I must go,' she said and dashed off, the cup rattling in its saucer as she ran towards the house, rather too much like Cinderella for her liking, her heart thundering because she'd made such a twit of herself.

———

'Sergeant Connors, would you mind coming to attend a meeting?' There was an air of suppressed excitement in the Lieutenant's words as if he were hoarding a great secret and his face had that exceptional blandness that was clearly hiding something. 'Now.'

'Yes, Sir,' she replied, instantly rising from her desk and grabbing her hat, a little puzzled but definitely feeling a lot more confident about attending. At the last one she hadn't made a complete fool of herself and they were inviting her back. Gathering up the most recent reports she'd been analysing, she followed the officer and another sergeant downstairs to the library. A couple of people were loitering outside the door trying to look busy with folders of paper and there was a hush among them as if they were listening hard for something. It reminded Betty of the annual occasions when Lord Chesham had come to the village school and all the pupils were wheeled out to stand in front of the building to have their photograph taken.

Wrinkling her nose at the strong smell of cigar smoke, she walked into what used to be the dining room, keeping her head down as she made for the far end of the grand, highly polished table which had been extended to its full size. She remembered it being laid with glistening crystal, polished silver, candle-laden epergnes and dish upon dish of food when the Cheshams had people for dinner. Today there were nearly as many people around the—

Oh giddy aunt. It was Winnie!

Winston Churchill, clear as day, sat at the other end of the table flanked by Colonel Myers, Commander Todd and two men she didn't recognise. Just to the left sat Major Wendermeyer, for once looking serious and stern.

Betty tried not to stare. It was that or pinch herself. She was in the same room as Winston Churchill and she couldn't even tell her ma. Or anyone, ever. There was a shuffling of chairs and Colonel Myers called the meeting to order. Betty prayed that no one asked her any questions. She'd die of fright. The Prime Minister looked exactly like he did in the photographs she'd seen, except he seemed very short and his hands were tiny. But the familiar gruff voice more than made up for it as it boomed down the table.

'Thank you for all your hard work, ladies and gentlemen. The work you are doing here is vital to the war effort. I and my cabinet are indebted to the information that has been forthcoming. This intelligence is the very linchpin on which we base our strategic plans and it directs and informs much of our strategy. Unfortunately, I cannot share them with you but we have great plans afoot based on the intelligence that has been so timely delivered by CSDIC. I must congratulate you on the intelligence work that has helped us to piece together the existence of yet more of the odious apparatus of the Nazis, those secret flying weapons. They may be congratulating themselves on their plans to destroy our way of life, our Christian civilisation, but thanks to your efforts, we will strike at the heart of their plans. Without your work here, we would be in the dark. You have given us light. Your work *will* deliver Victory.'

The stirring speech left the room utterly silent. Betty could almost feel her heart pounding in her chest and she didn't dare move for a moment in case it disturbed the weighty hush that had fallen.

Then Colonel Myers rose and said he was proud of his team but she wasn't listening, her ears were still ringing from the Prime Minister's words. She pushed her shoulders back, bolstered by a definite sense of pride. She'd been involved in analysing the transcripts that helped piece together a detailed report about what they'd discovered regarding the secret weapons and could remember, clear as day, the rudimentary picture of a ramp and a rocket. It had looked like something H. G. Wells might have dreamed up and she didn't believe that such things were possible, but the German prisoner whose conversation was included in the transcript sounded excited and confident about the flying bomb.

Betty was glad that her family weren't in London. If Hitler really did have these things, it would be terrifying. There would be no plane formations crossing the Channel that enabled the Observer Corps to send warning to Air Wardens. The idea filled her with dread, as it did nearly all the people around the table.

For the rest of the meeting discussion focused on the numbers of prisoners coming through, the current fronts of battle and strategic defence plans. Betty listened hard and across the table spotted Evelyn listening equally intently. It was fascinating to see the Prime Minister in action when she'd only ever heard his words on the radio before.

When the meeting drew to a close, he shook each of their hands and thanked them for their work and Betty found herself out in the hall at the bottom of the staircase standing beside Evelyn, her hand gripping the polished banister as if trying to ground herself back in reality.

'Can you believe that?' asked Evelyn, seeming as awestruck as she was.

'No. Did it really just happen?

'It did. And I can't even tell Mummy.'

Betty laughed. 'That's exactly what I thought.'

Evelyn linked her arm through Betty's. 'Do you think one day we might be able to tell our grandchildren that we met the Prime Minister during the war?'

'I hope so. I don't think my ma would believe me even if I was allowed to tell her.'

'Ladies.' Major Wendermeyer stopped them. 'An interesting meeting.'

'Was it ever?' said Evelyn.

'Oh, this is my…' Betty ground to a halt.

'… friend,' interrupted Evelyn with a nudge, pulling a teasing, chiding face at Betty.

'This is my friend, Lieutenant Evelyn Brooke-Edwards,' said Betty.

'Nice to meet you, Lieutenant. Major Wendermeyer, United States Air Force. And what did you think of the Prime Minister?' He turned his attention to Betty after giving Evelyn the briefest of nods.

Betty stared at him, expecting him to want to speak to Evelyn; after all, she was the more senior officer. Evelyn nudged her again and she found her tongue.

'I thought he was … very small.'

The Major laughed. 'Ah, Betty! You always nail it. Sure was a privilege to meet him, though.'

'It was nice of him to thank us. Especially when we're just doing our jobs. That's never happened to me before.'

'I think perhaps because we're doing extraordinary work here,' he replied.

'I'll agree with that,' said Evelyn, but the Major barely looked at her, which was most odd. Couldn't he see that she was the swan next to Betty's paddling duck? But he seemed far more interested in smiling at Betty.

Then another officer walked past. 'Carl, you ready for a drink?'

'Be right there.'

'I think I'll go and search out a pink gin,' said Evelyn. 'Nice to meet you, Sir.' She moved away and behind him she mouthed, 'Nice,' to Betty and put both thumbs up and winked before she disappeared into the Officers' Mess.

'Shame I can't invite you for a drink,' said the Major with a shake of his head as if he were genuinely disappointed. 'But we'll make up for it when we go into London. How do you fancy one day next week? I believe we have the same shift pattern.'

'We have?' she asked with a coy lift of her eyebrow, although inside she wasn't half as collected.

'I might have used my influence to fix it.'

She laughed and pointed out, 'We're always on the same shift pattern.'

'Hell, you caught me. I was trying to impress you.'

Betty swallowed and admitted in a small voice, 'You don't need to do that. I'm already impressed.' While on the outside it might look as if she liked to play games, inside honesty counted all the way. She might have grown up poor but her dad had instilled good values and telling the truth was one of them. 'I must go back to work.' She pulled a face. 'Sergeant Major Baxter will be watching the clock again.'

'Tell her the Major delayed you,' he said.

She gave him a reproving look. 'I'm not sure that would appease her. I don't think she approves of you either.'

'Hell no. I'm a foreigner and a Yank at that. Lucky for me she has no jurisdiction over the USAF, otherwise I might be in a whole heap of trouble.'

Another one of those unbidden giggles sneaked out. For an officer his levity was most misplaced but he had looked very serious in the meeting, so maybe when he was with other officers, he didn't play the fool the way he did with her.

Chapter Twenty-Four

Evelyn

E velyn watched Betty fussing with her hair and sighed as she gave hers a cursory pat. She didn't have the energy to fuss and primp this morning. It had been a long night, most of it spent staring up at the ceiling listening to the soft snuffles of her roommates while her mind turned things over and over and over.

'Are you all right?' asked Judith's soft voice. 'I heard you tossing and turning in the night.'

Evelyn gave her a weak smile. 'Just tired. I didn't sleep well at all.'

'You're worrying about something. I can tell.'

Evelyn considered her for a moment, tempted to confide in the two girls, but it would place intolerable burdens on them. They'd have to keep her secrets too and that wouldn't be fair.

'Just a work thing.' She gave herself a quick look in the mirror, alarmed by the dark shadows under her eyes. 'Think I'll pop out for a smoke.' She climbed onto the roof and stood studying the pink-stained sky and the dark trees silhouetted against it on the hillside on the far side of the valley. She took a long drag of the cigarette and watched the smoke curl upwards. She was due to have another meeting with Peter today. She'd had two now, the last one being fairly disastrous. For the thousandth time she wondered whether she should have told her commanding officer that she knew him. Of course, she bally well should have done. There was no doubt about it and now it was too late. She could kick herself for being such an idiot but then if she had done, she'd probably never have seen him again.

'You coming down for breakfast?' called Betty.

'No, I'm not hungry. I'll stay here a bit longer.' Through the window she saw the other two exchange worried looks.

She stubbed out her cigarette and as soon as she heard them leave, lit up another one. Her biggest fear now was that Peter might inadvertently talk about her in his cell. He had a new cellmate this week, the last one having been transferred to a camp in Northampton. What if he confided in him? She couldn't warn him. That would be a far worse crime than keeping her relationship with him a secret. She sucked in another drag on her cigarette, hating that she didn't know what to do. One thing she did know was that she had to go downstairs very soon and face the day.

Unable to bear the thought of being stuck in an interview room with Peter, which last time had been awkward, their conversation strained, she decided to take him out for a walk again. On the previous occasion she'd met him, he'd not wanted to talk at all, still convinced that there were microphones in the room and it had turned into an interrogation with her putting questions to him that he refused to answer. She'd hated that feeling of being in a position of power over him; it made her deeply uncomfortable. Despite his recalcitrance, she'd lied on her post-interrogation report, saying that the conversation had gone well and that she'd found some commonality and that she was building a relationship that would dispose him to reveal more. Thankfully he'd given her enough small crumbs at that very first meeting for her to recommend that he stay at Latimer House for further questioning, but that couldn't go on, if he refused to co-operate.

They walked in silence until they passed through the gate and moved away from the guards.

'I still can't believe that you can bring me out here, like this,' he said.

'It seemed better, although I'm not sure that the weather is on our side.' There was a very dark cloud on the horizon which could be headed their way.

He reached for her hand and although she tried to pull away, it was half-hearted. 'I'm not sure we should be doing that.'

'Why not? What difference does it make?'

'To me, if someone saw us, a huge amount.'

He gave a twisted smile. 'You could tell them that you were seducing me for my secrets.'

'I would never prostitute myself for my country.' She tried to snatch away her hand, insulted that he could say that.

'I'm sorry. That was unkind. I'm frustrated. You're so close and yet you're so far and I see no end in sight.'

'There will be an end. You'll be sent to another camp eventually.'

'When?'

She lifted her shoulders. 'When you are no longer useful to us.'

'Ah, so that is how it works. And you would like me to be useful. That is convenient.' His mouth twisted in that ugly smile again.

She sighed, possibly her hundredth sigh of the day. 'The final decision will be out of my hands. It will be made on the strength of my reports.'

'So you would have me prostitute myself?'

'No,' she said in a level voice. 'Would you like to go back?' She rubbed at her temple, trying to ease the headache building there. This was hopeless. Perhaps it was time for her to tell the truth to her superiors, explain that he wasn't prepared to talk, and to have him sent on his way.

She jumped when he touched her face, his fingers swiping the purple shadows under her eyes. 'I'm sorry. You are trying to do the right thing and I am being a difficult fool.'

'It's an impossible situation.'

'No, it isn't. What are a few secrets, to spend more time with you? Ask me what you want to know.'

'You don't have to—'

'I want to. I owe it to you.'

'Why do you say that?'

'Because you are doing the job for your country. Because you are a woman of honour.'

'But you're a man of honour.' She hated to take that away from him.

'I've been thinking about that. A man of honour would do everything he could to end this war, to stop further bloodshed, to stop the madness. As would a woman of honour, and that is your purpose. To bring the war to an end. If I stay quiet I am doing the opposite, helping keep the war going. That is not the honourable thing to do.'

She tilted her face to his and studied his serious blue eyes.

'What do you want to know?'

'Are you certain?'

He took her face in both his hands. 'As certain as the fact that I still love you.' His fingers brushed her lips. 'I love you.' He leaned down and gently kissed her forehead, her nose and then her lips before pulling back, tenderness in his eyes. 'I'm so proud of you. You are a woman of principle. I know that this is a difficult situation for you. It's far easier for me. It would have been easy for you to hand me over to someone else, I think.'

She shook her head, tears blurring her eyes. 'I couldn't do it. I should have done.'

He put an arm around her shoulder and pulled her close as they picked their way across the tree roots, wandering along under the canopy of leaves. They came to a stile which led into a field and as they crossed, the first drops of rain began to fall. By mutual consent they continued, it was only a light shower, but by the time they reached the middle of the field, the heavens had opened and the rain came pounding down in a sudden rush.

'Let's run for it. To the cover of those trees on the other side.' Running together they made for the thick wooded area with a number of big oaks which looked as if they might offer shelter. Despite the mad dash, Peter pulling her along, their feet tripping over the ploughed furrows of the field, they were soaked through by the time they reached the treeline.

'Oh my goodness,' said Evelyn, wiping her dripping hair from her face and taking her hat off. 'It reminds me of that time we were in Switzerland.'

'And we had to take refuge in that shepherd's stone hut. And your cousin almost set fire to the place.'

She smiled up at him. 'At least we had a fire to warm us up.'

He put his arm around her. 'I'll do my best. Undo your jacket. We can share body heat.'

Without questioning it she undid the buttons on her double-breasted wet jacket. He did the same and pushed his aside, pulling her to his chest. Through her thin shirt she felt the warmth of his skin and it seemed totally natural to fit her body to his, her arms around his waist.

He groaned. 'You feel so wonderful. I've missed you. This. It's been so long.'

'It has,' she murmured, brushing her lips across his slightly bristled chin, all the pent-up longing inside threatening to burst free. They'd never anticipated their vows, although temptation had driven them close a few times. If it hadn't been for the war they would have been married by now.

He dropped kisses across her throat, loosening her tie knot and undoing the top buttons of her shirt to give him access to her collar bone. She closed her eyes, savouring the feel of his skin and the graze of his chin. How long had it been since she fizzed with this – this intensely alive sensation? It was as if she'd been going through the motions for the last four years, locked in a state of grieving, putting on a brave face to the world.

'Peter,' she sighed, her body softening against him.

His mouth returned to hers and their kisses deepened as her hands roved up his back, stroking through his shirt the muscles that had firmed considerably since she'd last held him. She heard him groan and his tongue touched hers in a familiar dance that she gave herself up to.

He pressed her closer, nimble fingers opening more buttons on her shirt and his fingers skimming tantalisingly across the swell of her chest. Her mother would be horrified but she wanted more, she wanted him to touch her. When his fingers dipped lower she gasped out loud but then moaned at the electric touch which was heaven and hell. Shocking and thrilling. She wasn't sure what to do with herself but she ached for more. Ached so much that it was almost painful. She kissed him more fiercely, holding him tighter as if that might help the terrible need that drove her hips to grind against him. She could feel the hardness against her and instinct drove her to rub her hand over his groin, revelling in the guttural groan that he let out before he rasped in her ear, 'Oh, Evelyn.'

Their harsh breaths punctuated the woodland sounds of the spatter of raindrops on leaves and the accompaniment of cooing wood pigeons. Then his hand swooped down over hers.

'Evelyn, *liebling*, we have to stop.'

'I don't think I can,' she said, trying to wriggle her hand out of his grasp. 'I don't want to.'

He dropped his forehead on hers. 'You will surely kill me. We must stop.'

'Why?' She knew it was foolhardy and against all the teaching she'd been brought up with but how could this be wrong? Two people who loved each other, who could be parted at any moment.

'This is a line you can't ever cross. I'm the enemy. And I don't want to be a father when I'm still a prisoner.'

'We might not have a baby,' she said desperately.

'We might. And how would that be for you? What would you tell people?'

'I'd tell people you were my fiancé and that this hateful war is all that stopped us being married.' Tears pooled in her eyes. It was all so unfair. 'I love you.'

'And I love you, but this isn't possible.' He put a hand under her chin and lifted it so that she had to look at him. 'One day, I promise, we will be together.'

She pulled away, scared that she was going to burst into tears. 'God, I hate this bloody awful war.'

'So let's help finish it.' Peter stroked her face and carefully did up her buttons one by one, kissing her on the mouth once each was safely closed. 'I will tell you everything I can.'

'You don't have to do that.'

'I do, my love. I do. It's my promise to you. The sooner the war is over, the sooner we can be together again.'

'It will be difficult.' Her mouth twisted. 'In the eyes of others, one of us will always be the enemy.'

'I'm prepared to take that risk. And not everyone thinks like that.' He took her hand and they began to walk again.

The rain had slowed to a damp mizzle and as they walked back he began to tell her about the tank capabilities of the Panzer divisions in North Africa.

By the time they reached the camp entrance, she had enough material to write a substantial report but it did nothing to balance the considerable weight of her heart, heavy in her chest.

'Thank you, Peter,' she said softly.

He smiled and gave her a jaunty salute, saying for the benefit of the two guards who had come to collect him, 'Until next time.'

Evelyn prayed that there would be a next time. While she

had some influence over the decision as to whether a prisoner should continue to be interrogated, there were always other priorities and new prisoners arriving all the time. It might be the very last time she saw him until heaven knew when. She wanted to call him back. Wanted to kiss him once more. Wanted to tell him that she'd wait for him, no matter what. But she didn't.

She was due to go straight into her next and last interrogation of the day, one that she wasn't looking forward to. A small mean-spirited Nazi through and through, who had a malicious tongue and a seriously bad attitude. With no one around and with every excuse of needing to change out of her wet clothes, she hurried back to the house, hoping she wouldn't meet anyone. Any minute her composure could crack and crumble.

Once in her room, with tears falling, she undid her skirt, letting it drop to the floor, and sank onto the bed, peeling off her sopping jacket, but before she could remove her damp shirt, she gave in to emotion, and burst into full-blown heart-wrenching sobs, letting her grief and worry come tumbling out. Burrowing her face in her pillow, she cried so hard it hurt her ribs, but now she'd started she couldn't seem to stop. She'd never felt so alone and lost in all her life.

'Hey, hey.' Someone sat on the bed beside her and began to rub her back. Gulping back a sob which gave way to a hiccough, she lifted her head to find Betty looking down at her, her pretty face full of worry, and Judith standing behind her wringing her hands. Embarrassed, she swiped at her tears and sniffed, knowing she must look an absolute sight. She sat up but didn't have the energy or the spirit to say anything. Betty swept her into a hug and pulled her tight and Evelyn let herself sink into the warm perfumed body, grateful beyond measure for the human comfort, even more so when Judith sat down next to her on the other side.

Eventually she calmed and wiped her eyes with the linen handkerchief that Judith had pressed into her hand, realising it was one of the fine lawn ones given to her by her grandmother, who most definitely wouldn't approve of this type of sensibility. She'd have told her to pull herself together, while her mother would have flapped about like an indecisive fairy.

Judith patted her arm. 'It's good to cry,' she said with one of her gentle smiles. 'It cleanses the spirit. That's what my aunt always told me. Tears wash away the sadness.' She pulled a face and added in a dry voice, 'Although sometimes it takes a lot of tears.'

Evelyn couldn't help smiling at that.

'Want to tell us about it? Someone told me a problem shared is a problem...' Betty wrinkled her nose and then with a good-natured smile said, 'Do you know what? I can't remember what it was but it made sense at the time.'

Evelyn sputtered out a laugh. Having company, not being alone, not being told to buck up, was already making her feel better. Funny, she couldn't imagine any of her other friends being this kind or calm. 'Thank you. Things got away from me.' She dried her eyes. 'I've got myself into a bit of a fix and there's nothing anyone can do. I was just feeling a bit sorry for myself.'

'Are you sure?' Betty eyed her with a troubled expression. 'Because I'm in a fix and I don't know what to do.'

'Do you want to talk about it?'

'I think I do. I was scared before because I thought you'd think badly of me.'

'Have you done something wrong?' Evelyn asked, thinking

that if she had, it wouldn't have been done deliberately. Betty wasn't that type and Judith took the words out of her mouth.

'If you have, I'm sure you didn't do it on purpose.'

'Me! No. *I* haven't done anything wrong.'

'Well then, why would we think badly of you?' Evelyn included Judith in the question and the other woman nodded.

Betty gave them both an embarrassed smile. 'When we were at your house, Evelyn, you said it doesn't matter where you come from, but where you're going. I've thought about that a lot. When this war is finished I don't want to stay in this village, I want to carry on doing things that matter. Judith, you've been forced to make so many changes in your life. I admire you for getting on with things. You never complain or moan. You take it all in your stride.'

Judith shrugged and said in her usual stoic way, 'There was no choice.' Evelyn squeezed her hand. Of all of them, Judith had lost the most but she never complained or seemed to feel sorry for herself.

Betty smiled at her. 'And I do have choices and I want to make them. I don't want to get married to the first man I've ever met. I want… I don't really know what I want, I just know I want my life to be different from how it was and how everyone expected it should be.'

'I understand that, exactly,' said Evelyn, thinking about how much her life had changed since she'd decided to leave university. The irony was that the war had given her an insight into a life she'd never considered before. 'This war is grim but it has given us the chance to make those changes.'

'It has, but some people won't let us.'

Betty's tone was filled with bitterness and Evelyn raised a brow, sensing there was more to it. 'Some people?'

'Like I said, I'm in a fix. No one can help, and I don't know what to do, but I'm going to tell you anyway. My … well, everyone in the village thinks we are as good as wed, but I don't want to.'

'Is he the one who hit you?' asked Evelyn.

'Yes. He hit me because I wouldn't tell him what he wants to know. He thinks this place is a distribution centre.'

'And why wouldn't he?' Evelyn frowned. 'That's what everyone has been told.'

'Oh, he believes it all right and he's convinced that there are huge stores of cigarettes and alcohol here.'

'But that's good, isn't it?' asked Judith.

'Not when he wants me to give him the location of where they're stored and how to get past the security.'

'Ah,' said Judith.

'Hell,' said Evelyn.

'Exactly. I've been avoiding him, telling him I couldn't get the information, but he's threatening my mum and sister now. He's a bully and a thug.'

'Can't you speak to your commanding officer? The nice American Major,' suggested Evelyn.

'I can't. I'm scared I'll lose my promotion and they'll … they'll realise they made a mistake.'

'They haven't made a mistake. They promoted you because you're smart and capable.'

'Yeah, they don't know I'm just a girl from the village.'

Evelyn gave her a fierce hug. 'You're not *just* a girl from the village. You're Sergeant Betty Connors, a brilliant analyst. You wouldn't have been in that meeting with Winnie—' She glanced at Judith, realising she'd revealed a secret.

'It's all right.' Judith flashed her a rare grin. 'He came to see us too. Those cigars he smokes are horrible things. The M room stank for days.' She slapped her hand over her mouth. 'I mean the room.'

Evelyn looked from Judith to Betty. 'You don't need to worry, Judith. I know we signed the Official Secrets Act but I think we probably know what goes on here.'

'I know about the M Room,' said Betty. 'I analyse the transcripts and compile reports.'

'And I read the reports,' said Evelyn. 'So you're fine. Not revealing any secrets.'

'Thank you,' said Judith, blushing.

'But that doesn't help us with Betty's problem. They wouldn't have included you in the meeting if they didn't think you were important enough.'

'So even more reason for me not to let them know where I'm really from,' said Betty. 'I can't tell them, I just can't.' Her mouth took on a mutinous cast. 'And I can't avoid Bert for ever. The gun's only going to hold him off for so long.'

'What gun?' Judith looked horrified.

'Don't worry, it's not loaded,' said Betty, although she seemed quite regretful about that.

'I loaned her my father's old service gun. Don't worry, she's not going to shoot anyone.' Although Evelyn was pretty sure that, like her, Betty would fire the gun if she had to.

'I would if I could. If he lays one finger on my sister, I will kill him.'

'Betty, don't say things like that. Even if you do mean them. It's wrong,' Judith begged.

'Oh, bless you, Judith.' Betty clasped her hands. 'I'm being dramatic. Although if I were a bloke I'd have blacked his eyes for him.'

'Maybe you should take up boxing. I remember Freddie used to be a dab hand at Oxford.'

'Do you think he'd teach me?' asked Betty hopefully.

'I can ask him. But I think you're going to need more than a few lessons before you turn into Sugar Ray Robinson.'

'Thank you. Both of you. I know I have to sort it out but you've helped.'

Evelyn wondered for a moment if she dared share her secret with them but inside she was still too confused about her own emotions to know what to say. 'Thank you, too. You've helped me. And I really ought to get back to work. They'll be wondering what happened to me. I popped up to change my clothes.'

'My shift finished early today. They have some new people training so they needed my sta… my desk,' explained Judith.

'And I was owed some time and they said I had to take it this afternoon or lose it,' said Betty.

Giving her hair a quick tidy and putting on some powder to hide her blotchy face, Evelyn put on dry clothes, hung up her wet ones and hurried back downstairs, hoping that no one would notice how long she'd been gone for.

Funny, she'd had girlfriends at boarding school and in her social set but she'd never had a particular friend who was looking out for her or really cared what happened. Both Judith and Betty had offered their unfailing support even when she hadn't been able to confide in them. That loyalty was rare.

Chapter Twenty-Five

Judith

After an early dinner, as she was on the late shift, Judith swallowed down her tea and rose to head towards the door, saying goodbye to the other ATS girls who were sitting with her. She'd got to know quite a few of her fellow German speakers, most of whom worked in the translation department upstairs on the first floor, and she might even tentatively say that some of them were on the way to becoming friends. Since being at Latimer House, she'd found far more people that she had things in common with, even if it was only their nationality. One girl in particular, Lotte, had also come from Berlin and had played the violin and had known her father. They'd talked about music venues in the city and worked out that they might even have played at the same time together.

Her heart quickened as she saw the familiar figure leaning against the wall by the door, waiting for her as he usually did, ready to escort her the short distance to the main house.

'Good evening,' he said. 'How was your day?'

'It was very good. I went for a bike ride with a friend.'

'I hope this friend looked after you.' Walther's eyes danced with amusement and she couldn't help smiling back.

'He was extremely attentive and lifted my bicycle over the fence for me when we got a little too close to some very curious cows.'

Walther laughed. 'I've never been chased by a cow before.'

'Nor me, and I don't wish to repeat the experience.'

'I promise I'll take more care of you, next time.' He took her arm and they set off down the path to the specially built prefab hut that housed the entrance to the M room.

She squeezed his arm. 'You always take care of me, Walther.'

He was the perfect gentleman and not only made her feel safe but also treasured. There was no other feeling like it and she hugged it to herself, feeling grateful that she had met such a wonderful man and not someone like Betty's awful Bert. She wished she could confide in Walther about Betty's problems with Bert. She was sure that, in his quiet, thoughtful way, he would come up with a suggestion or a solution, but Betty had sworn them to secrecy and Judith was nothing if not a woman of her word.

'Would you like to come with me to the dance at RAF Bovingdon? They've arranged transport for the evening and it might be fun.'

'Can you dance?' she asked with a sudden teasing smile, thinking of the steps she'd learned with Evelyn and Betty and how much fun they'd had.

'A little, and I might have a surprise for you, there,' said Walther with that quiet caution she loved so much about him. There it was again, that word. Loved. She loved lots of things about him but did that mean she was in love with him? She had nothing to gauge against apart from what she'd seen in operas, and that picture of love never looked terribly satisfying.

'A surprise? Tell me.' She shocked herself by being almost flirtatious as her eyes gleamed at him.

'It wouldn't be a surprise then, would it?'

'I suppose not.' She gave a mock sigh and the barest hint of a pout. 'Well then, I shall have to go with you. Only because you can dance a little.'

He laughed at her unexpected playfulness and she liked the way it sounded. 'That's very kind of you.'

'I thought so.' Judith gave him a prim, sweet smile and he laughed again and put his arm around her.

'And if I'm not very good, what will you do then?' he teased back.

Betty probably would have told him with a flirtatious smile that she'd find a new partner, but Judith couldn't quite bring herself to do that. Instead she said, 'I'll have to teach you.'

'I can't imagine anything more delightful than being taught by you, my dear Judith. I'll do my best not to stand on your toes.'

———

'How long have you been here?' asked the German prisoner. Judith adjusted the heavy, uncomfortable earphones, her nose wrinkling at the familiar damp smell of the M room, perfumed with paraffin fumes, and held her pencil poised, all of her focus on the conversation to which she was listening. She'd been on shift for over three hours and had listened in to several unhelpful, dull conversations. This sounded promising. When a new cellmate was introduced into a cell with an existing prisoner, in that initial get-to-know chat, they usually divulged new information.

'A week and a half,' replied the second man. 'I'm Oberstleutnant Van Hoensbroeck, Peter.'

'Oberstleutnant Fischer, Wilhelm.'

Judith could imagine the two men shaking hands and summing each other up in their cramped cells. From what she'd gathered over the weeks, there were two bunks in each cell as well as a small table, two chairs and a wardrobe. As her mind wandered, it went back and picked over that name. Van Hoensbroeck. Peter Van Hoensbroeck. She'd heard that name before and recently. Now it rubbed at her. Where? Had another prisoner mentioned him? Had he been talked about as someone to listen out for in one of their briefings?

'You look well.' There was suspicion in the first man's voice.

'I am well.'

'But… You haven't been mistreated. Tortured?'

There was a short bark of a laugh in response. 'No. Contrary to all the rumours. The British, it appears, do not believe in torture. Not directly anyway.' With this addendum he snorted and Judith sensed a tone of derision in his voice. 'Besides, there are far worse things than torture.'

'Really?' The first man sounded alarmed. Judith had grown used to picking up on emotion in people's voices. It was amazing when you listened, how much you heard. Like the despair in poor Evelyn's voice at the moment.

'Don't worry, the torture I'm talking about is personal. They don't hurt or humiliate people here, that's left to the SS and the Gestapo.' Lieutenant Colonel Van Hoensbroeck sounded bitter.

Why did she know that name? Van Hoensbroeck? It was unusual.

'Is it safe to say such things here?' asked Fischer, with a touch of wonderment.

'Who are the British going to report us to?'

'But if word got out.'

'When?' Scorn filled the word from end to end.

'Well, soon. You know. When we go back to Germany. As soon as we win the war, we'll be repatriated.'

Peter laughed bitterly. 'You think we're going to win this war?'

'Don't you?'

'Not anymore. We're beleaguered on all fronts and we're being fed a stream of untruths. I saw London with my own eyes. It's not the bombed-out ruin that Hitler, Himmler, Göring and Goebbels would have us believe. Which makes you wonder what else they've been telling us. The defeat at Stalingrad was a catastrophe that could have been avoided if Hitler hadn't been so determined to hold the city at all costs, ignoring the Generals. It became an unattainable objective. We lost the entire 6th Army through sheer stubbornness and overconfidence.'

'You think he should be replaced?' There was well-advised caution in the question, thought Judith. Just saying such things, she knew, could give grounds for arrest for treason in Germany.

'Once the war is over, I believe the old-school Generals, the original members of the Wehrmacht, have plans to create a new government.' Judith curled her lip at this and listened with interest. Like many, he was hedging his bets, neither denying nor confirming his personal view, but it wasn't the first time she'd heard such views expressed.

'Well, let's hope the war is over soon, otherwise we'll be prisoners for a long time. What's it like here?'

'Good. Comfortable.'

Judith glanced over at Walther, grateful that he'd taken her under his wing so early on and given her a good dose of common sense. She realised now she would have been eaten up with bitterness if she'd allowed herself to hate these men. She noted a few points rising from their comments and added an addendum with her view that Van Hoensbroeck sounded as if he might be amenable to co-operation. Sometimes it was possible to persuade certain prisoners to become stool pigeons, where they pretended to be prisoners of war with German sympathies to elicit specific information but reported everything back to their captors. As the English Sergeant Major was wont to say, this one sound ripe for plucking.

'Oh.' The man sounded pleased until Peter added:

'But don't get too comfortable. It's a holding station. We'll be moved on before long.'

'You seem to know a lot.'

'I have a good relationship with my interrogator.' Judith frowned and listened intently. Hearing voices every day, without the accompaniment of facial expressions, had made her sensitive to the slightest rise or fall in pitch or tone. 'Lieutenant Brooke-Edwards.'

The point on her pencil snapped, the tip firing across the table, and Walther looked up.

With a quick, bland smile she managed to hide her sudden confusion and had to hold back a gasp. Peter Van Hoensbroeck. Evelyn's former fiancé! That's where she'd heard the name before. When Betty had singled out the photograph over lunch at Evelyn's house.

And Evelyn was the one interrogating him. Judith turned cold and then hot immediately after, the shock running through her. It would certainly explain why Evelyn was so quiet and anxious at the moment. If it was the case, Judith couldn't begin to guess what sort of turmoil she must be going through.

Listening carefully, Judith gripped her pencil even more tightly, the rough lead tip scuffing the paper, hoping that her quick tremor didn't give her away and that he wouldn't say anything more about Evelyn. If he did, what would she do? Would she faithfully record his words? Could she do that to Evelyn?

Judith's stomach churned with nerves as she prayed that Peter wouldn't say anything incriminating. That was the key thing.

'Good relationship. What does he do?'

'He's a she.' Her fingers tensed around the pencil. She bit her lip, listening with dread.

'Female. Interrogator?'

'Yes.' Judith caught Walther's eye and realised she was in danger of giving herself away with the taut, nervous faces she was pulling. She'd have to make something up and she was terrible at thinking on her feet like that. Lying did not come easily to her.

'They use women? Because they have run out of men, I daresay.'

'They use women because they're very good at getting under your skin.' Judith wondered if she were reading more into Peter's quick laugh. 'They make you want to talk to them. There are men too. Everyone is very reasonable. They make it seem worthwhile to co-operate. It certainly makes for an easier life. I go for walks with my interrogator.'

'Shouldn't you be trying to escape?'

'Where to? As far as I can see, we're in the middle of nowhere.'

'But it's our duty to try.'

'You can do your best but I think you'll find life is simpler if you accept your fate. We're given cigarettes, whisky, comfort, you can work in the gardens if you like to be outside.'

'Slave labour.'

'No, you idiot. We volunteer. It's better than being stuck inside your cell all day.'

'It is our right to receive Red Cross parcels.'

'You can wait for them, but I promise you there are plentiful supplies here.'

'Bribery.'

'Not bribery. But don't you want the war to end? What if we help to do that?'

Judith relaxed, relieved that the conversation had moved away from the danger zone and that she wasn't *officially* going to be put in an awkward position.

'I am loyal to the motherland. I will not co-operate.'

'I have my reasons.'

'Doesn't that make you a traitor?'

'Not to my heart,' he said cryptically but Judith knew exactly what he meant. *Don't say anymore. Don't say anymore.* She wondered if she dared to switch to listening to another cell.

'I shan't tell them anything about the secret weapons we have. They will turn things around in our favour.'

'You fool. They already know about them.'

'How?' The man sounded shocked.

'I don't know, but they talked to me about them. They know where they're being developed. That there are launch sites in Holland and France.'

'You mean the V1s? They can't.'

'That's exactly what I mean.'

The other man lapsed into silence and Judith made some quick notes for whoever would be interrogating Oberstleutnant Fischer. They'd caught many out by intimating that they knew more than they did.

Someone tapped Judith on the shoulder and she jumped and removed her earphones.

'Tea time. I've come to relieve you.'

'Er...' She gripped the phones tightly in her hand. 'It's all right. I don't need a break.'

'Come on, Judith,' said Walther. 'It's not good to go without a break.'

Her stomach bubbled with sudden acid and she looked anxiously at the switch, wondering if she could transfer the line to a different cell before she left.

What if Peter talked about Evelyn being his fiancée while she wasn't there? The other person would be duty bound to report it.

'I think I'll stay,' she said, putting her earphones back on.

'Nonsense. You need tea and biscuits.'

She really didn't. Her stomach was turning over and over so much she didn't think she could manage either, but Walther and her replacement were insistent and it would have raised suspicion if she'd continued to resist.

With a reluctant backward glance at her station, she followed Walther out down to the canteen.

Thankfully they joined a group of other listeners and translators who were talking about the imprisonment of Mussolini, which had been announced on the radio earlier that afternoon. She kept her head down and sipped at her tea, barely able to get it down, every now and then glancing up at the clock on the wall above the serving hatch, which seemed to tick impossibly slowly. Walther cast her a few worried looks and she had to force herself to listen to the conversation. If he pressed her she couldn't lie to him but neither could she give Evelyn's secret away.

When the clock hand reached eleven minutes past, she rose, deciding that eleven out of fifteen was ample time for a break.

'Just going to the toilet,' she murmured to the girl next to her, who acknowledged her words with a vague wave, and she forced herself to walk slowly out of the room. The minute the doors closed behind her she scurried back to the M room, fumbling with the keys as she unlocked the two doors which led into the room. Such was the secrecy surrounding the operation that the keys had to be handed back to the Warrant Officer at the end of every shift.

Gerda, who had taken over from her, took off the headphones. 'That was quick.'

Judith gave her an absent-minded smile. 'Did I miss anything?'

'No. They've been talking about what units they served with, where they come from and sharing details of their families. I've noted it all down.' She rose and tapped the paper and pencil on the desk.

'Super. Thank you. That's good.' All the time her mind was on Evelyn. Judith remembered her radiant face in the photograph and the picture beside her bed. Now she understood why it had disappeared. She was probably concerned about anyone seeing it, not that anyone ever came up to their room but the three of them.

She hastily plugged in her earphones but there was nothing but silence. Had they gone to sleep? It was early, only nine o'clock. She ought to check on the other cells she listened to, but was reluctant to leave this transmission channel. The indecision weighed on her and she forced herself to flip the switch to listen to some other prisoners. To her relief she heard the two men in this cell talking about switching out the lights for the night, and she relaxed. She waited a few minutes in case they carried on talking but there was no sound, so she flipped back to her original channel and heard Fischer talking again.

'Have you been to England before?' he asked.

'Yes. Many times.'

'I never came before. I would have liked to see London. Did you go there?'

'Yes, a few times.'

'Where did you stay?'

There was a lengthy pause. 'I had an English girl... My fiancée was ... is English.'

Judith's heart sank as quickly and steadily as a stone tossed in the water. She swallowed and kept her eyes focused on the paper in front of her.

'English!'

'Yes, from a place near Henley on Thames.'

'When was the last time you saw her?'

Judith wanted to rip off her earphones and not listen to the answer but dread and duty kept her ears pinned. She closed her eyes, praying hard as Peter clearly considered his response.

'A while ago.'

She released the breath she was hardly aware of holding.

'Does she know you're in England?'

'Yes.'

'When do you think you will see her again?'

Any moment now, Peter might confide in his cellmate. A trickle of sweat ran down her cleavage.

'I'd rather not talk about her,' he replied quickly. 'Do you mind if we switch out the lights for the night?'

'No,' said Fischer, suddenly contrite. 'Sorry. It must be difficult for you.'

'You have no idea,' said Peter and Judith understood only too well the dryness in his voice.

Her heart rate slowed and she listened patiently for another half hour until she heard soft snores. Relieved, she switched channels. It appeared that all her charges had turned in for the day and her shift was almost over. For now she was in the clear but she needed to talk to Evelyn as soon as possible. She checked the clock on the wall; another half hour until the end of her shift at eleven o'clock. Both Betty and Evelyn were on the daytime shift this week. Would they still be awake when she went back? And what was she going to say to Evelyn?

Chapter Twenty-Six

Betty

'Betty, someone wants you.'

She looked around the Mess and down the table before putting down her cup of cocoa and rolling her neck. She wasn't really in the mood for talking now, she'd been thinking about heading upstairs to bed.

'No, outside,' said the Sergeant Major, whom she often chatted to on her tea break in the mornings, shaking his head and indicating the front of the house with his thumb. 'Out on the slope. Chap asking for you. Most insistent he spoke to you.'

Betty sighed and sagged in her seat. It had only been a matter of time. Bert was nothing if not tenacious.

'You all right, love?'

'Yes.' She gave him her best dazzling smile. The last thing she wanted was anyone from the section taking a close interest in her and Bert.

Smoothing down her skirt, she pushed away her cocoa, feeling sickly and heavy in her roiling stomach. For a moment she considered running upstairs and grabbing Evelyn's father's service revolver but if she were seen with that in the grounds it would certainly raise questions.

If anyone saw her with Bert she could claim that her mum was ill and he'd come up with a message, as he'd done last time. She should have known he wouldn't give up.

Making sure no one was taking any notice of her, she left the house through the front door and crossed the gravelled drive, walking over to the lawn now scarred by the deep bomb-burial site, which had been haphazardly filled in, leaving a mound of earth as a permanent reminder of the narrow miss. As usual the thought had her raising her hand to her face as if to reassure herself that all her features were still in place. There was no sign of Bert, so she walked a little further towards the bottom of the steps that curved down from the terrace, keeping an eye above on the doors of the Officers' Mess. Luckily, in the dying throes of the day, they seemed to be content to watch the sunset from inside, although she thought she saw someone at one of the windows looking down curiously at her. She ignored them, hoping that as soon as she was out of sight they'd forget her. Once she was immediately beneath the terrace she breathed out a relieved sigh. No one could see her here, and right on cue Bert emerged from the shrubbery surrounding the doorway of the gardener's room built into the wall underneath the terrace.

'Where the bloody hell have you been, you little tart?' he growled and lunged for her, grabbing her hair. As the pain bit she wished heartily that she'd gone and retrieved that gun.

'Ow, Bert. Stop it.'

'What do you think you're playing at?'

'I've been busy. On duty a lot.'

'Don't talk to me like I'm stupid. You're a bleedin' typist, how busy can you be? Don't think you can get away with playing me blind. Now, you going to tell me where the booze and the fags are, or do I have to beat it out of you? I've cased the place and I reckon they keep them up at the back of the house in those prefabs. I need a map.'

'Bert, you've got it all wrong. They don't keep those sorts of supplies here.'

'Don saw them.'

'He just saw the Officers' Mess supplies. That's all.'

'Don't answer me back. You think I'm stupid.' He backhanded her sharply, his knuckles catching her cheekbone. 'What are you keeping from me?'

'Nothing,' she said it too quickly and he knew it as well as she did.

'Ah, so what secrets do you have?'

She sucked in a breath, conscious of the throbbing of her face.

'Nothing.'

'If there aren't cigarettes and booze, what do they have? What aren't you telling me?'

She wasn't going to tell him anything, no matter what he did to her. Her eyes slid away from his. A mistake, because it gave her away.

'I knew it. Something bigger.' With a sudden movement, he pushed her up against the wall and she glanced upwards, aware that the balustrade of the terrace was only several feet above their heads, but she was probably still hidden by the shrubbery that grew up over the doorway. Her breath came out in a panicked pant as he pressed his body against hers and grabbed at her breast with a hard cruel hand squeezing painfully.

'Stop it, Bert. Stop it.'

'I could take you right here, you little bitch.' His other hand wrenched up her skirt and grabbed at her between her legs with a vicious grip that frightened her more than anything else. She could take a beating but not that. She tried to pull away, her heart thudding furiously but he had her up against the wall, branches digging into her back and scratching at her neck. 'Now you tell me what I want to know.' Her head was pressed against the wall as she tried to back away from him, his hand cupped, painfully grinding against her pubic bone.

'Don't.' Her words came out as a half sob as she tried to twist away from him.

'You don't mean that,' he mocked. His mouth coming down onto hers, he bit her lip hard and she let out a muffled squeal of pain. *Fight, Betty. You have to fight him. Don't let him do this.*

It was hard, though, when her muscles had gone into some kind of panicked spasm and she could hardly breathe. None of her body parts seemed to be able to obey her but she forced herself to push at his hand between her legs. But it was an impossible battle: the harder she pushed, the stronger he seemed.

Then, just as she felt as if she were drowning and that the water was closing over her head, there was light and air and blessed relief. She dragged in breath as the weight and pressure of Bert's body was wrenched off her and she saw him literally hauled backwards. As she took a second unsteady breath, she saw him spin round and heard the hard thwack of a punch and the crunch of bone. He went down on the floor and his nose began to spurt with blood.

Betty looked up and she saw Carl towering over Bert, menace in his eyes, looking as if he were ready to kill. Every muscle, taut and lean, every sense alert and dangerous, and he looked ready to pounce and rip the guts out of the prey.

Bert staggered to his feet, leaking bluster and stupidity in his sideways, clumsy lurch. 'Get lost. This has nowt to do with you.' Next to Carl's suave, panther-like grace, he looked as ridiculous as a pantomime cow.

'I beg to differ,' Carl drawled with contemptuous ease. 'I won't do you the honour of calling you sir. A maggot like you doesn't deserve it.'

Betty wanted to cheer. No one had ever spoken to Bert like that. He'd always ruled the roost round here.

'From what I could see the young lady was not welcoming your attentions.'

'Well, you shouldn't have been looking, should yer? And it's nowt to do wi' you.' Bert rallied and Betty saw his muscles bunch, ready to lash out at the Major, but before she could warn him, Carl had already anticipated the blow, ducked neatly and got his own upper cut in, right on Bert's jaw, followed by a second sharp blow to the stomach.

Bert doubled over and fell to his knees and although he got to his feet, she could see that he wasn't quite as cocky as he had been. Instead he backed away nervously. She realised that aside from herself, who clearly didn't count because she was a woman, no one had ever stood up to Bert. Even his own dad had let Bert take charge on the farm.

'Now you listen to me, fella,' Carl's voice thrummed with menace that had the hairs on her arms standing to attention. 'If I ever catch you within ten feet of this lady, I will kill you.' He stared down at Bert, whose eyes had widened so much they were white pools in his dark, swarthy face. 'Do you understand?' Bert nodded but Carl wasn't finished.

'If you threaten her,' he paused, his eyes boring into Bert, who couldn't seem to look away, 'or her family in any way, I will come and find you and I will...' He leaned down and whispered something in Bert's ear. Bert paled and fell backwards, shuffling back on his bottom before finally scrambling to his feet. Carl smiled but it was a ferocious, malevolent smile that put the fear of God into Betty, let alone Bert.

'And being American, I'm immune to prosecution in this country, so no one will worry. *If* they find the body. Do you understand me?'

Bert nodded, eyes still wide, mouth open, never taking his gaze from Carl. Betty almost felt sorry for him – almost.

'I don't want to see you around here ever again and if I so much as hear that you have been bothering Sergeant Connors, you know what will happen. Now scram before I forget that I'm a gentleman and I rip your balls off.'

Betty blanched, her own eyes widening. She couldn't decide if she was in awe or terrified of Carl. She'd never seen this side of him before.

Bert scrambled to his feet so quickly, he almost tripped over them and he limped away, hunched over, clutching his stomach, without even looking at her.

As she watched him leave, tears began to roll down her face and she realised she was shaking, properly shaking, and her teeth were chattering. Carl looked at her and she wanted to die of shame and embarrassment at him finding her like this. Disgust gripped her. What must he have thought? Bert's hands on her, down there. And now look at her, lipstick smeared, her skirt around her waist and her curls adrift. Her tears ran faster and she wanted to curl up in a ball and hide from him, but there was nowhere to go. And look at him, she thought. So fine and handsome. As he straightened his cuffs and dusted off his smart cap that had gone flying off with the force of his first punch, he looked as if he'd been for a stroll in the park.

Carl came over and she closed her eyes as if that might hide her from his sight. She was so ashamed. When he gently tugged her skirt down back into place, she tried to stifle a sob but it was impossible; it burst out, followed by several more, and then she was crying – full-on, ugly, blotchy crying.

'Oh Betty, sweetheart. My dear girl.' And rather wonderfully he scooped her into his arms, just like in the movies, and carried her into the gardener's shed where he sat down with her on his knee on an old wooden bench.

He cradled her in his arms and she sobbed into his neck, her body still shaking.

'Hey, sweetheart. It's OK, you're safe now. I won't let him touch you again.' She kept her eyes tightly shut, not daring to look at him and see the disgust in his eyes when he looked at her. She couldn't get over the gentleness in his voice when bare minutes ago he'd looked so terrifying.

Finally she hiccoughed to a stop and drew in a heavy breath. Time to face the music. She tried to pull away from him, but his hold tightened, and when she did open her eyes, he was looking down at her with the oddest expression on his face.

'Oh honey.' To her astonishment and uncertain delight, he dropped a kiss on her forehead and used a thumb to swipe away her tears. 'You're safe.'

She stared up at him, so many emotions swirling inside, she didn't know where she was at or where to start.

'You were…' She reached up and touched his chin and her heart did some kind of funny flip in her chest. 'Thank you.'

'Is that the fella that's been bothering you? Did he hit you before?'

She nodded, swallowing.

'Dang, I wish I'd hit him harder.'

'Sir!' She half hiccoughed and half giggled.

'Think you might call me Carl?'

She nodded, suddenly feeling shy.

'Are you OK? Did he hurt you?'

'Not really, frightened me more. What he was going to do...' she said, shuddering as she realised what a fortunate escape she'd had. Carl's arms tightened around her.

'I promise you, he's never going to touch you again. I saw him skulking about and then I saw you and well, you didn't look too happy, and knowing what had happened to you before... I heard him threatening you. What did he want?'

Betty sighed but she desperately wanted this off her chest.

'He's convinced that this really is a distribution centre. A while back his mate saw a lorry full of cigarettes and whisky arrive. He thought he could steal them to sell them on the black market and he kept badgering me to tell him where they were stored. Except I couldn't tell him anything. I tried avoiding him but he caught up with me.'

'Well, he won't be bothering you anymore.' The fierce glow in his eyes made her tear up again but at the same time gave her the confidence to finally unburden herself.

'It's my family I'm worried about. He threatened my ma and my little sister, and his family own the cottage we live in.' She winced. 'Jane is... She's growing up but isn't up here, if you know what I mean.' Betty tapped the side of her head.

Carl's mouth twisted. 'Unforgivable. But if you have any more problems, you come straight to me. He won't dare now.'

'What did you say to him?

'Ah, that's not for a lady's ears.'

Betty lowered her eyes and whispered, 'I don't think I'm a lady.' He put a hand under her chin and gently encouraged her to look at him. 'I'm so embarrassed. Thank you for helping.'

'Embarrassed. You shouldn't be. I've seen that sort before. Bullies, picking on women. He deserved what he got. And you are every inch a lady and you deserve to be treated like one. I don't want to hear you saying that again. Don't you ever doubt yourself. Now, we need to get you cleaned up.'

She screwed up her eyes. 'Oh no. I don't want anyone to see me like this.'

'I'll go and get some things. You stay here. Will you be OK?'

Betty didn't want to be left on her own and she shook her head.

'If you can go in front of me and I can get as far as the hallway, there's a secret passageway up the stairs.'

'There is?'

She nodded. 'It takes you up to the second floor, and then if the coast is clear, I can run along to my room.'

'I've got a better idea. I'll take you to my room. I can get some ice from the Mess and I've got a shaving bowl and mirror.' He cupped her chin very gently and kissed her softly on the mouth. 'I want to look after you, Betty.'

'Me? But I'm...'

'Somethin' special,' he drawled. 'From the first moment I laid eyes on you, I couldn't take them off you. You're the prettiest girl I've ever seen, as well as being just about the damn smartest girl I've ever met. I tell you, sweetheart, it's a heady combination.'

'I'm—'

He stopped her with a gentle finger over her lips. 'Shh. Let's sit here awhile until you feel yourself again.'

As the sun dipped beneath the horizon and darkness fell, he held her in his arms, tucking her head under his chin, his arms wrapped around her, and she'd never felt so safe or cossetted in her life.

After a while they ventured out of the shed, Carl holding her hand, and they walked across the lawn towards the lights of the house. Through the diamond-paned windows of the Officers' Mess, Betty could see the officers clutching their drinks, talking and chatting as if they were at some smart cocktail party. When they neared the front door, Carl left her in the porch and peeped through the door to check the coast was clear.

'Where do we need to go?' he whispered.

'The alcove behind the suit of armour.'

Quickly they tiptoed across the black and white tiled floor and slipped into the alcove.

'This is kinda exciting. I had no idea there were secret passages.'

Despite feeling like she'd been through her ma's mangle, Betty managed to laugh at his little-boy enthusiasm. 'They weren't so secret to the servants. Rich people don't like seeing the staff.'

'Is that so?' His voice echoed with disappointment as she found the latch, but before she could open the door they heard voices coming along the hallway and they both stiffened. Then Carl turned her round but stood in front of her, his arms enveloping her, ducking his head to kiss her so that even if anyone had seen them, no one would know who it was. His mouth was warm and soft and oh-so-gentle and with a little sigh she opened up to him. It was like a fairytale kiss, floaty and magical and she softened in his arms. She could have stayed there for ever but luckily he had a little more self-possession and as the footsteps died away, he lifted his head. 'Plenty of time for kissing later. We need to get you sorted.'

They slipped through the door and into the dark corridor, waiting for a minute while their eyes adjusted. 'There's a light at the end on the wall before the stairs,' she whispered and started forward to lead the way, but he grabbed her hand and insisted on holding it as she moved ahead.

Once they reached the top corridor, Carl stepped in front of her and peeped out of the door onto the empty corridor. 'Wait here.' He slipped out and walked to the very end of the corridor and opened the door to a room at the end. Then he came back and walked to the opposite end where he stood guard and gave her the all-clear and said, 'I'll be right along.' Feeling a secret thrill, knowing that perhaps she shouldn't be doing this (she'd never been in a man's bedroom before; well, not with him in there), she darted down to his room.

She smiled when she entered. She *had* been in this room many times before, although then it was to dust it. The double bed was still the same with its barley-twist posts on each corner, along with the matching burnished chestnut dressing table, boot cupboard and wardrobe. When Lord Chesham had lived here, this had been one of the many guest bedrooms.

She sat down on the damask-covered stool in front of the dressing table and buried her head in her hands, sitting for a while, going back over what had happened. Was that really the end of things with Bert? After all her anxiety, had it been that simple? Her ma wasn't going to be pleased when she realised that things were over with Bert. She'd seen him as a ticket to better things, but knowing his meanness of character, that was never going to happen. Betty prayed that Ma and Jane would be safe from now on.

Feeling more steady, she lifted her head and peered at her face, wondering where Carl had gone. A lipstick smear stained her chin and her hair was an unruly mess of curls. Wearily she sighed and then caught sight of the reflection of Carl standing in the doorway smiling at her. Wiping at her cheek, she turned around. 'I look terrible.'

He shook his head and closed the door. In his hands he held two tumblers of golden liquid and a third full of ice. 'Not to me. You always look beautiful.'

She raised her eyebrows and gave him a stern look, some of her spirit creeping back.

'OK, maybe you could do with a little tidy-up, but you always look perfect to me.'

'That's better,' she managed a prim smile, although her eyes danced a little, and turned back to the mirror, lifting a hand to start removing the bobby pins.

'Here, let me.' Carl stood behind her, his fingers probing and seeking out the pins, gently sliding each one out and rubbing her curls between finger and thumb. It sent goosebumps racing over her skin and she watched him in the mirror as he took his time, absorbed in his task. The air felt thick and heavy and Betty's limbs strangely achy and lethargic, as if she were waiting and longing for something to happen.

'Your hair was the first thing I noticed about you. That and your perky attitude.' A wry smile crossed his face. 'You were never going to let on that you couldn't really type.'

'I thought I could,' she said with an indignant huff.

'Someone lied to you, sweetheart.'

'I taught myself. I'd never seen anyone else type properly. I just thought I could do it.' She wrinkled her nose as she thought about the professional competence of some of the other ATS women who knew what they were doing with a typewriter.

'Priceless. You're just a gem.'

'You don't really know me. Bert, that man, he's the world I

come from.'

'And you think I care about that. Hell, my grandfather was born and raised on a pig farm in Iowa. He was dirt poor but my dad had the smarts and he became a salesman, married my mom and they moved to a nice house in the city.'

'It's not where you're from, it's where you're going to,' murmured Betty.

'Exactly!' He rested his hands on her shoulder. 'And you have those smarts. You're the best analyst we have. Would you do me the honour of coming to the dance with me?'

She paused for a brief moment, hardly daring to believe that he really wanted to go with her, before saying, 'I'd love to go with you. Better make sure you put your dancing shoes on.'

'You like to dance?'

'I love to dance.'

'Well, how about that? Me too. Now, drink this. It's good for shock and I'll get a towel to wrap that ice in so you can put it on your cheek.' His mouth tightened as he looked at her bruised face. 'You're a brave one, that's for sure.'

'I don't think so.'

'I know so. You weren't going to tell him the truth about this place, were you? No matter how hard he beat you.'

'No. I wasn't,' she replied. 'And it wasn't because of going to prison, it was because we're doing important work here. The reports we write, they're being read by people who decide the strategy of the war. It makes me feel so proud inside to know that I'm helping in the war effort. I'd never give what we do away to anyone outside the house.'

'I think we all think like that, it gives us a camaraderie, no matter what rank or class. I've never worked in a place like it.'

Betty thought of Evelyn and Judith and their friendship, three unlikely women. 'Me neither.'

Chapter Twenty-Seven

Evelyn

It should have been Freddie's ball but Evelyn launched herself towards it, determined she could make the point. She swiped wildly with her racket at the same moment as Freddie lunged, and the two of them ended up in a tangle of limbs on the floor, with the ball whizzing past them and hitting the court with a soft thud just inside the line.

Freddie stood up and angrily held out a hand to heave her to her feet. 'My ball, I think.'

'Yes, it probably was,' she said, churlishly refusing to admit fault and ignoring his hand as she heaved herself to her feet and brushed down her tennis dress. It was the fourth or fifth or maybe the sixth time she'd done it in this set and he had yet to admonish her. Even now, ever the gentleman, he didn't say anything.

She eyed him balefully as he threw the ball up and with an elegant arc served it beautifully at the opposition. If they lost this point they would lose the match.

From across the net, Katherine returned the ball with a smart spin shot that should have had Evelyn racing towards the net, but she found herself watching the ball half-heartedly and by the time she stirred her lethargic limbs into action, it was far too late. She missed. Damn! An easy point which she should have got. And now they'd lost the match. She threw her racket down on the floor.

'Yes!' shouted Katherine and Alexander on the other side of the court. 'Game.'

Next to her, Evelyn heard Freddie grumbling under his breath; she didn't blame him. She'd played shockingly. Tennis seemed so ridiculously frivolous when she had other things on her mind, but the others had insisted she joined them and she hadn't had the energy to decline.

Freddie strode forward to shake the other two's hands over the net. She trailed after him, giving Katherine and Alexander a lukewarm smile. They walked off chatting away in buoyant, triumphant spirits, swinging their rackets.

Freddie walked over to her racket and picked it up, handing it to her with a frown. 'I say, Eve? Are you all right? Off your game today.'

'I'm absolutely fine,' she snapped, snatching the racket from him. 'You?'

Poor Freddie looked bewildered at her ill-tempered display and she felt thoroughly ashamed of herself. Any moment she was going to burst into tears.

He opened his mouth and then thought better of what he was about to say, and she knew she ought to apologise but the lump in her throat was nearly as big as the bloody tennis ball in his hand.

'I've got to go,' she said and ran off back to the house, tears already blurring her vision. Head down, she hurried through the French doors, crossing the Officers' Mess and out to the main staircase where she took the stairs two at a time.

When she reached the bedroom, she threw herself on the bed and gave in to the storm of tears which had been building for most of the afternoon. She was rotten company at the moment and she shouldn't have taken it out on poor Freddie. He was kind, if clumsy, and she knew he was keen to take her to the dance, but he wasn't Peter. That was the crux of the matter.

Her heart ached so much, it was like carrying around an unbearable weight, all the time. First thing in the morning, she woke to thoughts of Peter and after that they never strayed far from him. It was torture of the worst kind. Knowing he was so close and yet so far from her. Seeing him, not always being able to touch him, knowing that he could be taken away from her at any moment, was almost worse than not seeing him or knowing where he was.

The greatest irony was that now he was here, she missed him more. Lord, and she was crying again. Whatever happened to stiff upper lip and all that?

If only she sewed or knitted or did something to occupy her. She got up and paced around the tiny room, before climbing out onto the roof to take up her usual position. Some days she imagined she were a figurehead on the front of her ship, buffeted by the slight breeze as she smoked cigarette after cigarette. At this rate she'd turn into a chimney.

She sighed and stared out at the river, a slow-moving, sinuous streak lit by the pink and gold of the sunset. It was so peaceful here and contrasted strongly with the battlefield of emotions that churned inside her. All her life, everything had made sense and there'd been a plan. Now it was as if she'd been knocked out of kilter and couldn't see a way to get the balance back. She should have told Myers about Peter. It would be so much worse if someone found out now.

After smoking yet another cigarette that she really didn't want, she retreated back into the room, checking the blackout blind was in place before switching on the light. From under her pillow, she pulled out the silver photo frame and sat down, tracing Peter's face in the black-and-white picture. She couldn't imagine her life without him but neither could she imagine it with him. After the war, would he still be the enemy? Could they go to Germany, where she would be the enemy? Did people stop being the enemy when a war finished? Could people forgive and forget? What would happen to the two of them?

As she scowled down at the picture, she heard the soft tread of footsteps and couldn't decide whether she welcomed the company or not.

Both Judith and Betty appeared and Evelyn's attention was immediately drawn to the state of Betty's face.

'Betty, what happened?' She jumped to her feet at the sight of the other girl. Her hair was down and there was yet another livid mark on her face, but despite this there was a rather dreamy expression in her eyes. For a moment, Evelyn wondered if she was concussed. Her brother had looked like that once after a particularly bruising rugger match.

'She said she wouldn't tell me,' grumbled Judith, toeing off her shoes and giving Evelyn a sudden considering look.

Evelyn immediately wanted to hide. It was an automatic reaction to any scrutiny at the moment. Every time another officer spoke to her, she was convinced she was about to be hauled up before Colonel Myers. Her guilty conscience was working overtime. She would be out on her ear, especially as he knew why she'd lost her last post. There'd be no second chance.

'That's because I wanted to tell you both together.' Betty beamed at her, which Evelyn found most disconcerting, and it forced her to stop feeling sorry for herself and focus on Betty's problems. At least she thought they were problems, except Betty was positively fizzing.

'You look remarkably happy considering that you've got a bruise coming up on that cheekbone. Did someone backhand you?'

'Yes. Bert,' she said and grinned.

Both Judith and Evelyn stared at her, confused and horrified.

'I don't understand,' said Evelyn. 'Are you all right? What happened?' Was Betty punch-drunk or something?

'It's all right. When he hit me Carl came to my rescue.'

'Major Wendermeyer,' said Evelyn, remembering the tall, rangy, good-looking American.

'That's right. He punched Bert. Honestly, he was like a proper boxer or something. He just went pow!' Betty demonstrated with gusto. 'I tell you, he hurt Bert something wicked and then he told him… Well, he threatened to kill him.' Her mouth opened as if she still couldn't quite believe it herself. 'That's what he said. I never saw anything like it. He was so angry.' She frowned and patted her loose hair. 'I'm sure he wouldn't really kill him, but he told Bert that if he came near me again, he'd … he'd do something terrible which I can't repeat, and then he leaned down and said something else which I didn't hear but I don't think it was terribly nice.

'Then afterwards when he'd sent Bert packing, he … he looked after me.' Betty's smile was angelic now. 'He was lovely and kind, after he'd been so scary with Bert. To be honest, I was in such a state, I couldn't help it, it all came spilling out, about Bert wanting to steal cigarettes and whisky and how he wouldn't listen to me. Carl said I was brave for not telling him anything.' She sighed and clasped her hands together on her lap. 'He was so wonderful.'

Evelyn looked at the dreamy-eyed expression on Betty's face, which, even with the swelling on her cheek, looked prettier than ever. There was a glow about her. Funny how someone else's problems, when you really cared about that person, could transcend your own.

'He's invited me to the dance.' Her eyes sparkled. 'And ... he kissed me, but like a proper gentleman.' She sighed and sank onto her bed.

'Looks like someone's got it bad.' Evelyn winked at Judith and found to her slight unease that the other girl was studying her with quiet, watchful eyes.

'Yes,' said Judith. 'Is he a nice man, this Carl?'

'The best,' sighed Betty. 'Very nice. Very handsome. Very...' Her eyes shone. 'I feel like I'm in a film and he's swept me off my feet. As if it's not real.' She sat for a moment, a silly smile on her face, before she turned to the other two. 'Do you think I'm being an idiot? Feeling like this, so soon after Bert? Am I being too gullible, falling for the fast American? He's so different. Am I going to make a fool of myself?'

'Does he say or do anything that makes you feel uncomfortable?' asked Evelyn, coming to sit down next to her, putting her hand to her lips, remembering Peter's kisses yesterday. In the past she'd always been safe and comfortable with him but those kisses had been urgent and thrilling, filling her with a sense of desperate need and desire. If Peter hadn't called a halt, she wouldn't have stopped him, she'd have stayed on course for the whole exhilarating ride, even though it went against every notion a well-bred young lady had been taught.

'No. He's so kind and gentle but in an exciting way. I'm not even sure that makes sense.' Betty shook her head in wonderment. 'But you mustn't say anything to anyone. He's an officer and I'm just a sergeant.'

'That shouldn't matter,' said Evelyn, her eyes suddenly and unaccountably filling with tears. 'No one should have the right to part two people.' Her lips trembled and then she couldn't hold back the wave of emotion that drenched her.

'Oh, Evelyn, whatever is the matter?' Betty immediately put her arms around her and Evelyn, so grateful for that human touch, leaned into the soft embrace.

'I-I'm just being s-silly,' she said, although that tennis-ball lump was back, wedged in her throat. She buried her face in her hands. 'It's so hopeless.'

As if she hadn't cried enough already, she found that her earlier crying bout had left her as fragile as her grandmother's prized china and now she cracked and broke, the tears streaming down her face as she wept into her hands, the hopelessness of her situation turning tighter inside like a corkscrew.

She was dimly aware of Judith coming to sit on her other side and putting an arm around her.

'You can tell us, you know,' she urged in her low, deep voice.

'I w-wish I could.'

'What if,' Judith squeezed her on her shoulder, 'I already knew.'

Evelyn raised her head and peeped through her fingers, staring at her in horror. 'You can't.'

'Peter Van Hoensbroeck,' said Judith softly.

Evelyn gasped. 'How? Oh no! Who knows?'

'Don't worry. Only me.'

'What do you know?' asked Betty, puzzled. 'Isn't that your fiancé?' She picked up the silver photo frame and put it into Evelyn's lap.

'You know as well?' Evelyn touched the frame, realising that the endless churning in her stomach had slowed to a stop. There was a sense of release at being able to acknowledge Peter and talk about him.

'Only that he's German and was your fiancé before the war. Your mother told us,' explained Betty.

'I know that he's a prisoner here,' said Judith in her quiet, understated way.

'No!' said Betty, all eyes and scandalised disbelief. 'Really! I didn't know that. Gosh, you could see him. I think. Would they let you? I mean, they let people in prison have visitors.'

Evelyn almost laughed at her wonderful naivety but she looked at Judith, whose sombre face told her that the Jewish girl knew a lot more.

'She has seen him,' said Judith.

'Really?' Betty stared at her and Evelyn nodded and suddenly it was a relief to be able to tell them.

'Would you believe I was rostered to interrogate him? Talk about small world. I thought at first the powers that be had done it on purpose but no one said anything to me and by the time I'd done the second interrogation, I couldn't say anything because I knew they'd stop me seeing him again and I couldn't bear that. So I didn't say a word and now I'm so worried that they'll find out. And when they do they'll make me leave here after what happened in Falmouth.' She turned to Judith. 'How did you find out? And do they know?'

'I was listening. I heard his name and I remembered it from lunch. Then he said that you were his interrogator.'

'Have you told anyone? I wouldn't blame you. It is your duty.'

Judith patted her on the arm. 'No, because I only knew because your mother mentioned his name. I listened carefully but he didn't give you away.'

'I couldn't tell him to be careful or that the cells are bugged.'

'The cells are bugged!'

'Betty!' said Judith and Evelyn in unison.

'Where do you think the transcripts come from?' asked Evelyn.

'I never really thought about it. I was focusing on what they were saying and trying to find links and connections to other conversations.'

Both Judith and Evelyn rolled their eyes, while Betty shook her head, shrugged and grinned. 'Well I never. There are so many darned secrets in this place. Including you. So what are you going to do?'

'What can I do? I've been so worried that someone will find out or that Peter would say something.'

'I think you're all right there,' observed Judith. 'He had every opportunity to tell his cellmate and he didn't.'

'But he might.'

'Then we worry about that when it happens,' said Judith. 'But if I hear anything I won't report it.'

'You can't do that.'

'Watch me,' said Judith. 'Are you doing anything wrong?'

'Morally no, but I think ethically I might be, although I'm still doing my job and he's telling me so much.'

'So it's helping your job.'

'Yes, but it can only go on for so much longer. You know they don't stay here for ever. He'll be sent on very soon and then I don't know when I'll ever see him again.' Silent tears ran down her face.

Judith rubbed her back and Betty took her hand and squeezed.

'S-sorry.'

'Don't be sorry. I wish we could help,' said Judith.

'There must be something we can do,' said Betty. Evelyn's mouth twisted in wry amusement. Betty was so full of her own happiness, she refused to give up on someone else's misery. The three of them lapsed into silence as if pondering an impossible crossword clue.

Betty got up to pace, walking backwards and forwards with a focused look on her face. Judith and Evelyn stared at her as she muttered to herself and fluttered her fingers as if she were turning pages in a book or something.

Suddenly she wheeled about and stopped dead.

'I've got it. In lots of reports, I've read about all sorts of unorthodox things that go on here in the name of interrogation and soliciting the prisoner's trust. You need to go to Colonel Myers and tell him everything.'

'I can't do that.'

'Yes, you can. You tell him that you've been working on Peter becoming a stool pigeon,' said Betty.

'A stool pigeon?' asked Judith.

'It's someone on our side that they put in with the prisoners, except the prisoners think they're a prisoner like them. The stool pigeon engineers the conversations so that the prisoner talks about things we want to know about. It's been done quite a few times. It works well, it's just a problem finding the right people to do it. I reckon if you sold it to

Colonel Myers that you were trying to get Peter onside to be a stool pigeon, he'd overlook that you hadn't told anyone. He likes people working on their own initiative.'

Both Evelyn and Judith stared at her. 'How do you know all this?' asked Evelyn, a little stunned. Betty sounded so competent and sure of herself.

'I'm an analyst. I read all sorts of stuff. The means justifies the ends. That's the Colonel's motto. Did you know they took four of the Generals to Simpsons on the Strand for lunch last month? That Katherine girl and a couple of officers took three prisoners on a pub crawl the other week.'

'They did what?'

'True as I'm sitting here. How many times have you seen Peter?' asked Betty, who seemed to have taken charge of the problem. Just watching her was giving Evelyn a surge of hope.

'Three.'

'And that's given you enough opportunity to assess the situation and come to the conclusion that he might be persuaded to be a stool pigeon.'

Betty said it with such authority and conviction, Evelyn lifted her head and considered it for a moment before saying with a sudden smile, 'Betty, that's a brilliant idea. I think you might have saved my bacon. It's a neat strategy and it would allow me to come clean now before I get caught out.'

'I think so too,' said Judith, nodding. 'If Peter mentions he knows you when I'm not on duty, someone else would report it straightaway.'

'Oh Judith, I hope I haven't put you in a difficult position.'

'Of course not. If I hadn't been to your house, I'd never have known. None but us three knows that.'

Evelyn reached out and closed her hand over theirs. 'You're

both absolute troopers. I don't know what I'd have done without you.'

Betty shrugged. 'That's what friends do. Help each other.'

'Thank you.' She took a deep breath, already feeling so much calmer. 'I'll request an interview with Myers first thing in the morning. Phew. Suddenly it seems so obvious. I probably should have done it after the first time I saw him.'

'You were too shocked and surprised,' Betty interjected. 'Then after the second, you needed time to assess the situation and now after the third, you've come to the logical conclusion.'

'She's right,' said Judith with a nod. 'Betty the strategist.'

'Thank you. Thank you for listening.'

'What was that saying?' Betty frowned. 'A problem shared is a problem halved.'

Evelyn squeezed her hand. 'It certainly is.'

Chapter Twenty-Eight

Judith

'Right,' said Evelyn, 'let's do this.' She squared her shoulders. 'Wish me luck.' With her fine blonde hair lit by the stream of sunshine coming in through the open window, she reminded Judith of a Nordic princess ready to go into battle.

'Good luck,' said Judith with an encouraging smile which hid her trepidation. 'I'll be in the music room until I go on shift.' She planned to hide out there because she knew if she saw Walther, with that ready intuition of his, he would know that she was worrying about something, and she didn't feel it was right to reveal Evelyn's secret before they knew the outcome.

'Thank you, I might need a shoulder to cry on, if they don't frogmarch me out of the front door.'

'They won't,' promised Betty.

Judith thought the other girl overly optimistic but, aware of

Evelyn's wan, strained face, she wouldn't have dreamt of saying so.

As soon as Evelyn left, the two of them looked at each other. It was still early and neither were due on shift until eight o'clock.

'Why don't we bag some tea and toast from Elsie and take it to the music room, if you don't mind me joining you?' suggested Betty when Judith looked at her watch for the fifth time in as many minutes.

'Not at all. I'm so nervous for Evelyn. It's like waiting to go to the dentist or something. To be honest, I'll be glad of the company.'

'Me too,' said Betty, linking her arm through Judith's. 'Let's go brave Elsie's den.'

Elsie was unable to mask her surprise at seeing them so early, as breakfast didn't officially start until seven forty-five.

'But it's the early bird that catches the worm,' she said. 'I've got a couple of eggs if you'd like them.'

Betty exchanged a quick look with Judith who shook her head. Toast was about all she could manage this morning. 'No thanks, Elsie. We'll stick to toast.'

'Fair enough. There's tea in the pot, I made it for me and the girls, so help yourself, and the toast'll be two ticks. Oh and Betty, did you hear about the hen house back home?'

'No.'

'Apparently something happened to it late last night. Vandals or something. Not sure what but the whole thing's collapsed.' Elsie gave her a kind smile. 'Your sister sat outside all night with the chickens because she was worried about the fox.'

'That sounds like Jane.' Betty winced and pursed her mouth. 'I haven't got time to do go down there now and sort things out. I don't suppose I could ask you to ask one of the girls, when they finish breakfast, to give a message to my ma? Tell her I'll be down later after my shift finishes at four.' She shook her head and scowled and Judith heard her curse under her breath. 'Bloody Bert.'

'Will do,' said Elsie, turning back to the big stove and efficiently moving the heavy pans around as she started to prepare the porridge for breakfast.

'Do you think Bert did it?' asked Judith in a low voice.

'A chicken coop doesn't fall down by itself,' Betty whispered back. 'And it's his style. Sneaky and mean. Those chickens are my ma's livelihood and bless her, my little sister, Jane, adores them. They're her pets and they all have names, named after characters in *The Beano* comic.'

'She likes chickens?' Judith couldn't imagine anything worse. Ugly things that pecked and scratched in the dirt.

'Here you go, ladies.' Elsie handed over faded linen napkins, that Betty remembered from working in the house, filled with slices of toast and jam, and they scurried back up the stairs from the old servants' quarters and along the corridor to the back of the house, where they slipped into the music room.

'I'd almost forgotten this room existed,' said Betty, going to sit on one of the deep window seats and unfolding the napkin on her lap. Judith sat opposite her in the bay window and took a loud crunching bite of her toast, savouring the thickly spread lovely raspberry jam, which still seemed a delicious luxury, although she suspected Elsie had given them preferential rations because she was so fond of Betty.

'The family hardly ever used it, apart from some mad uncle who played the piano, and they left him to his own devices. He had the room to himself.'

'I found it by accident; I don't think many people know it's here. I suppose if no one has reason to come this way, they wouldn't see the door. Although I don't know how the piano stays in tune. It has the most gorgeous tone.'

She glanced across at the beautiful instrument in the opposite corner, the crowning glory of the room. This morning sunlight slanted with golden beams in through the window, highlighting the gold and yellow floral designs on the Aubusson rug and turning the dust motes into tiny fluttering fireflies.

'Ah, that's easy. Elsie's brother, the Vicar. He's also a piano tuner and he used to come and play in return for tuning it. I bet he still pops in. When you're a Vicar nobody questions what you're doing somewhere, do they?'

'That's true. The dog collar gives them an open invitation.'

They lapsed into silence, sipping their tea, and giving the door an occasional look, both hoping that Evelyn might appear soon.

'It will be terrible if Evelyn has to leave,' said Judith, finishing her cup and putting it down on the window seat. She stood up and wiped the toast crumbs from her skirt.

'It won't come to that,' said Betty.

Judith stared out of the window looking at the muddy tracks across the grass where the lorry had driven to collect the defused bomb. The drama of that day seemed a lifetime ago.

'Don't worry. Don't borrow trouble until it gets here. That's something my dad always used to say.'

'I can't help it. I think I've always worried.' She turned and walked into the centre of the room, studying the intricate patterns of the Persian rug on the parquet floor. The thought of Evelyn leaving unsettled her. It reminded her of how she'd been when she'd first come to this country. That hollow, empty feeling. Until now, she hadn't appreciated how much she liked and admired the other girl or how deep those tentative roots of friendship had already sunk. It seemed impossible to imagine their little room without Evelyn or without Betty, for that matter.

For the first time in such a long time, she belonged. She enjoyed sharing a room with the two girls, liked their differences and relished their different outlooks on life. During these last few months, she'd learned so much from both of them and she couldn't remember a time when she'd been happier. Life had taken on meaning in this house; she'd found a purpose, friendships and the closest thing to a home she'd had since she'd left Germany.

Somehow without realising it, she'd drifted across the room and found herself in front of the piano and lifted the lid and idly stroked a couple of keys. She sat down on the piano stool. The sheet music she'd borrowed from Evelyn's brother was where she'd left it a few days ago. She'd played a few times before her evening shift but not as often as she'd thought she would because Walther had other ideas. She smiled. He'd filled their off-duty time with another lunch to the Kircheners, whom she adored, and he'd taken her to the local theatre one evening.

'What are you smiling about?' asked Betty, coming over to stand by the piano.

'Walther,' said Judith.

'That's getting serious,' said Betty.

Judith nodded and pressed her fingers to the keys, playing a couple of notes. 'I think so. It's nice having someone who cares for you, who makes you feel that you are important.' Walther had a way of making her feel that she was the centre of his world.

'That's how Major Wendermeyer makes me feel, but then I don't believe it will last. I think he'll find me out. But he also makes me feel as if I could fly, fizzy inside like champagne.'

'Do you think that's what being in love is like?' asked Judith, a little uncertain. Did she love Walther? Last night Betty had glowed when she talked about her Major, and her eyes had sparkled. Judith wasn't sure her eyes were capable of sparkling. Had her emotions been so numbed and inured to life that she couldn't feel like that, or was Walther not the man for her? He was safe and steady. Was that enough? Did she want romance and grand gestures? Did you get the love you deserved? With Walther, was she settling for something easy and comfortable?

'I think it might be,' said Betty, clutching her hands to her chest and doing a quick twirl on the spot. 'It ought to be. Does Walther make you feel like that?'

Judith paused, not wanting to be disloyal – he was a wonderful man – but she'd never had a girlfriend to talk with about this sort of thing before. 'I'm not sure. I enjoy being with him, but it's not exciting. It's safe, but I know he'll always catch me and he understands me better than myself sometimes – no, a lot of the time. It's almost as if he can see inside me, to all my fears and worries.'

'That sounds good, though. Compared to what it was like with Bert, I'd be happy with that, if I hadn't met Carl. Maybe love gives you what you want. Do you want excitement and gaiety? I don't think you do. I'm frivolous and silly. Maybe love is different for everyone and it gives you what you need. Look at Evelyn with her Peter, I think their love is a much deeper thing. More of a connection. She's not the trapeze artist flying through the air—'

'Or the elephant plodding through the sawdust,' mused Judith.

'Not that I think you're anything like an elephant, but it sounds as if you want something solid and reliable, and I think Evelyn is more like the Ringmaster, she wants a hand on the reins and to be a partner. In control and a master of lots of different things.'

'I don't mind being an elephant, you know. I've had too much excitement in my life and it wasn't good. I want a nice, quiet life, a space to grow and be left alone.'

Betty sat down next to her on the padded seat of the piano stool and put a hand over hers. 'Then that is good. I think I want to live a bit, get away from the village when the war is finished. Away from everyone who thinks they know you and your business.'

'And I've done that and now I want to settle. We're opposites in many ways, wanting what the other has.'

'Which makes us understand each other better, I think.' Betty shot her one of her optimistic, cheery smiles. There was something to be said for looking on the bright side of things and it made her think of the jaunty happy tune she'd played the other morning. Perfect for Betty.

She began to play and Betty bounced on the seat beside her.

'Oh, I love this song, "You Are My Sunshine".' She began to hum along to the music and then began to sing in her rich, sweet voice. It rang out beautifully within the proportions of the music room. Someone had known what they were doing and the acoustics were perfect. Judith couldn't help smiling at the little stab of joy that the lyrics, the music and Betty's singing brought. This was happiness, she thought as her fingers raced over the keys and Betty's voice dipped and soared in flawless synchronisation. She really was a beautiful singer.

When the song came to an end, Betty clapped. 'Oh, that was heavenly. Play another.'

So she played 'Don't Sit Under the Apple Tree' and again Betty sang along. Then Judith slowed the tempo, keen to see Betty's range in action, swapping to the more mellow 'The Starlit Hour', which Walther had told her was sung by the singer Ella Fitzgerald. Much as she'd loved her father, she realised that he had a very narrow definition of music, considering only classical music as music worth listening to and playing. These popular, jazzy compositions called to her in a completely different way. She'd always love Mozart, Bach and Liszt but there was something about the vibrancy and excitement of modern music that lit up her nerve endings. It made her want to move, to improvise, to make her piano sing in a way that she'd never experienced before.

'We should go on the stage,' said Betty, as Judith played the dying chords of the last song. 'Connors and Stern, musical double act.'

'I'd like that,' said Judith, suddenly a little shy at the idea. It wasn't like her to push herself forward but she did love to play and she loved to perform. Somehow when she was playing the piano in front of people, she became a different person.

'I think it's an excellent idea,' drawled a voice from the doorway. Neither of them had noticed it opening and someone slipping in through the heavy oak door.

'Evelyn!' screeched Betty, jumping up from her stool. Judith followed a bit more slowly but they both ran towards her because the slow, pleased smile on her face suggested that things had gone well.

'I still have a job.'

'I told you.'

'Thank goodness.'

Betty threw her arms around Evelyn in an ecstatic hug. Judith hung back a second until Evelyn held out her arm in invitation. Then the three of them were hugging and crying.

'What did he say?'

'God, it was awful. I told him everything and then he told me to wait and he left me in the office on my own for ages. I honestly thought he'd gone to get the MP to march me off to prison.'

'No!' murmured Betty, her big blue eyes wide with the drama of it all.

'Poor you,' said Judith, imagining how awful that must have been.

'When he came back, he told me to sit down. I got a bit of a ticking off because I should have told him, but then he said he admired my initiative and that I'd delivered some excellent intel. So now I have to talk to Peter about becoming a stool pigeon. That's the trade-off for my peace of mind.'

'It's a good one,' said Betty.

'Mmm,' said Evelyn, and Judith could see that she wasn't convinced.

'Well, at least you can rest easy now and not worry about being caught out,' said Judith. 'Do you know when you'll next see Peter?'

'All being well, this afternoon. In the meantime, I need to go and make some apologies. I was rather beastly to poor Freddie yesterday.'

'Just tell him it was your monthlies,' said Betty with a naughty grin. 'That always makes men uncomfortable. He'll be so embarrassed he'll forgive you anything.'

'You are awful,' said Evelyn with a laugh.

With her spirits lifted, Judith went into the M room for her shift and Walther gave her a quizzical smile when she took her seat and beamed back at him. It was obvious he'd been wondering where she was this morning. No doubt Betty would say something like it was good to keep him on his toes. The thought made her smile more and now Walther was definitely looking puzzled. He pulled off his headphones, grinned back at her. 'You look happy this morning.'

'I am. One of my room… my friends had some good news. In fact both of them did.'

'That's good. It reminds me of a quote. *Friendship improves happiness and abates grief by the doubling of our joy and the dividing of our grief.*'

'What a wonderful saying.'

'I can't take the credit. It was Cicero, a Roman scholar.'

'I must remember it. Can you write it down for me? I want to share it.' She pulled on her headphones as she decided that perhaps she could write it out on the postcards that she'd bought in Amersham last time she'd been out cycling with him, and give one each to Betty and Evelyn.

Then she flicked on the switch to open up the channel and all thought of friendship disappeared as she had to concentrate on listening to two prisoners who'd recently arrived. Both simmered with resentment and frustration at being captured and were full of scorn for their captors and their 'soft' treatment thus far. Judith had time to muse that killing with kindness had its merits as she scribbled down their comments and quickly assessed their attitude. They were unlikely at this stage, she knew from experience, to be co-operative but their derision made them unguarded in their comments about what they did know and planned to conceal from the enemy.

Their talk turned to their experiences on the front and she kept her pencil poised for any useful information. When one of them said that he'd been posted in occupied Poland and had spent some time in a town called Mizoch, her muscles tensed. It wasn't the first time she'd heard of the ghetto where many Jews had been sent under enforced segregation.

'What a hellhole. I was glad to leave that place.'

'I heard the Jews fought back.'

Judith heard the grunt of mirthless laughter. 'Much good it did them. They were all shot. Every one of them. Over a thousand. Women, children as well.'

Judith closed her eyes, bile rising up in her stomach. With a shaking hand she turned on the turntable and lifted the needle onto the acetate to record the conversation.

'Over a thousand. That's a lot of bullets. How long did it take?'

Judith pressed her lips together and under the desk clenched her hands into tight fists. She didn't want to hear this.

'They made the women and children take off their clothes and line up.'

'You saw it?'

'From a distance, yes.' The voices were flat, emotionless, as if they were describing a street full of people shopping. Where was their empathy? Their humanity?

Those poor, poor people. The terror and fear they must have experienced. Her fingers clenched tighter, so hard that the skin over her knuckles felt as if it might burst and the tendons in her hands hurt. Man's inhumanity to man. Cold rage rushed through her. How had these soldiers managed to dehumanise another race so much that they no longer saw them as real people? People who lived, loved, laughed, had families – living, breathing people? She couldn't understand how they could do it or how this man could be so dispassionate.

'There was one woman with a baby.' Judith's heart contracted with fear and dread, while revulsion crept through her veins at his mocking tone.

'Pissed herself. Begging them not to kill the baby. They pushed her to the front of the queue.'

The man laughed and Judith thought she would be sick.

He carried on talking, adding further detail, with malicious paintbrush strokes that made an already horrific picture even clearer.

She had to get out of there, she couldn't listen to another word. Her own imagination was a terrible thing, already the images were embroidered into the fabric of her brain. There wasn't enough air in the room. She wrenched off her earphones and pushed back her seat, the chair tumbling to the ground. The loud clatter and the vibration across the floor made everyone turn her way. Almost blind with panic to get out, she stumbled towards the door, desperate for fresh air, desperate to erase the toneless, heartless voices, even though she knew she'd never wipe away their words.

She reached the door, fumbled with the lock with clumsy hands. *Let me out! Let me out!* her brain screamed but her fingers wouldn't work, and the sensation of panic grew like a winged bird beating frantically in her chest. She couldn't breathe, it was as if the air was stuck and couldn't get past the bird's wings.

Then, a hand pushed hers aside and opened the door for her, another hand flat in the small of her back, as if trying to ground her. She burst through the door and out into the fresh air, doubling over as her stomach cramped and the bile thrust its way out, purging her of the evil she'd just heard as she was violently sick.

'How could they? How could they?' She gasped out mangled words mingled with involuntary sobs as she collapsed to her knees, wiping her mouth with her sleeve.

Walther's hand, solid and steady, rested on her shoulder, his strength an immediate anchor.

'Why?' she moaned. 'Why would… How could they?'

She wiped at her wet face but the tears kept coming. When Walther knelt down beside her and took her into his arms, she turned to him without thought and leaned into his granite strength, giving in to weakness and letting herself cry properly for the first time since she'd come to England. She wept out her grief, for her father, her life in Germany and all the families who had lost so much. She wept for the unknown men, women and children massacred in that faraway ravine in Mizoch and prayed for their souls. She'd never had much faith and now she doubted there could possibly be a God, but she prayed for those people anyway.

When she'd calmed down she found herself sitting on the grassy bank outside the M room with Walther's arm around her shoulders. 'I'm sorry.'

'You don't need to apologise. It's horrible to hear those things. And the worst thing is that they're not isolated incidents. The Nazis are exterminating our race.'

'I can see them,' she whispered, closing her eyes, wondering if she'd ever lose those images.

Walther's arm tightened around her. 'Try not to think about it.'

How could she do that? This had really happened. In some faraway part of Poland on the other side of Europe, people had lived and died and she bore witness to their death. It was her duty to remember, to see justice served.

'How do you bear it?' she asked.

'Knowing that we are recording the information. Those people will be punished one day.'

'How can you be so sure?'

'Because we are doing all we can to fight this evil, to win this war.'

'Is it enough?'

He laid a hand on hers. 'It has to be. We have to have faith that we are on the side of the angels.'

'I'm not sure I believe in angels.'

'I find I have to believe in something,' said Walther sadly.

They sat in the summer sunshine with the birds singing around them, the sun slanting on the rich red bricks of the house, and Judith wondered if her soul would ever be clean again.

Chapter Twenty-Nine

Betty

B etty stomped up the stairs to the office. Now that she could relax about Evelyn, she'd had time to reflect on her ma's problems. She had no doubt it was Bert's doing. What she wouldn't do to strangle him. Bloody oaf.

'You look fierce, this morning,' drawled a familiar voice as she rounded the top of the stairs.

'Huh! Bert's been in action again,' she blurted out indignantly before she had time to think. It seemed natural to confide in the Major, although surely, having kissed him, she should think of him as Carl, but when he was standing there in his uniform with those big broad shoulders, she felt all quivery and girlish inside.

'Has he?' The bright twinkle in his eyes died and immediately he changed, the switch from easy to alert and on edge.

'I don't know that it was him,' she said, 'but the hen house has been mysteriously vandalised in the middle of the night. It stinks of Bert.' She pulled a face, wrinkling her nose in disgust. 'The sort of vicious, calculating nastiness he's capable of. He knows how much those hens and the eggs mean to Ma and Jane. I'll have to go down there as soon as the shift is over to see what I can do to repair it. Jane's probably got the chickens in the kitchen, which will drive Ma mad, but they need to keep them safe.'

'Still got that toolbox of your dad's, then?' His lips twisted in a wry smile and she could see that he was amused.

'Yes, and I know how to use it. Just have to hope that it's salvageable. Heaven knows where I'll get any wood.'

'Would you like some help?'

Her mouth dropped open, which probably wasn't the least bit attractive, but *he* was offering to help her. 'No, you don't need to do that.'

'I'd like to. Besides, it's a while since I've done anything practical. I miss it. I used to help my grandpa on the farm, building and mending stuff. And I need you to point out where Bert lives. I might need to pay him a little call. But aside from that, I would really like to help.' His voice lowered and there was a husky timbre to his words that made her catch her breath, and how could she resist?

'That would be lovely,' she said with a dazzling smile, wondering what on earth her ma would make of him.

Eight hours later, give or take twenty minutes, they were walking down the drive, away from the house, with Carl carrying the toolbox, and Betty was starting to have second thoughts. What would he think of their tiny terraced house with its modest furnishing, most of which had come with

Granny when she moved in from her house at the other end of the village during the last war? As the house came into view, she surveyed its familiar outline with critical eyes. The red-tiled roof had a slight dip in it, the paint on the dormer window had peeled and cracked, and the diamond-leaded window-panes looked dull and dusty. The garden was a mass of blowsy flowers, a proper cottage garden that, left to its own devices, looked pretty by accident rather than design. In the winter, it would be a brown and grey wilderness. She led the way through the garden and round to the back of the house. As the end of terrace, they had a slightly bigger plot than their neighbours, and it was all given over to vegetable beds, which to Betty's surprise looked a lot tidier than of late. Ma was an indifferent gardener, never having had to do it before, and Jane had no interest at all, but they'd taken 'Dig for Victory' to heart and there were potatoes, carrots and beans growing in haphazard rows.

Carl stopped and looked up at the house. 'This is so quaint. It feels like proper history. How old is the house?'

Betty shrugged. 'I'm not sure. Latimer House is quite new, only a hundred years. The old mansion house burned down but that was built in Elizabethan times, so some of the houses in the village date back that far. Not this one, though. Probably only a couple of hundred years old.'

'Wow. A couple hundred years. That's ancient history where I come from.' He continued to stare up at the tall brick chimney at the end of the roofline, a look of wonder in his eyes. 'Makes you think about all those bombs in London. Real shame.'

'It is,' said Betty, suddenly struck by the fact that she'd enjoyed the peace and quiet of being back in Latimer and the clean air, free from dust and smoke. Funny how quickly you got used to things. She turned the corner and stopped dead. The chicken coop lay in a collapsed heap as if a cyclone had picked it up and dropped it. One wall had been pushed into the other three so that the whole thing listed drunkenly at almost forty-five degrees. 'Oh heck!'

'That's it?'

'Yes,' said Betty faintly. 'It's worse than I thought.' Now as they moved closer they could see that one of the wall panels was smashed in, as if someone had kicked it hard, the wood splintered and cracked beyond repair.

'Oh Betty, love.' Ma came running out of the house, her wispy blonde hair floating around her head, a sure sign of her distress, and her face crumpling. It was such a rare sight that Betty's heart contracted. Her mother always seemed so indomitable and this was the first time she'd seen her look so defeated.

'What happened?'

'I don't know. There was a great crash at ten o'clock last night and Jane came rushing out and the hen house was like this. She stayed out all night with them with Dad's old stick to beat off the fox if he came near. Course, with her out here, I couldn't leave her, so I stayed in the chair in the kitchen, so I could hear her. Didn't get a wink of sleep.'

Betty put her arms around her, shocked to hear the quaver in her voice. Her ma never cried. Only when Dad had died. She patted her back. 'It's all right, Ma. We're going to fix it for you.'

Ma clung to her and Betty felt as if she were the adult, as she rubbed her back, feeling the brief shudder that ran through her ma's sturdy body. 'I don't know what we'll do without the chickens.'

'Ma, it's all right,' she repeated.

Her ma lifted her head and weary eyes peered at Betty. 'You're a good girl. But it's a big job.'

'I've got some help.' Her ma blinked and then registered the tall man behind Betty that somehow she'd managed to miss.

'Who's this?' Ma's suspicion quickly turned to keen interest when the blond good looks of the Major registered.

Before Betty could introduce him, he stepped forward and took her ma's hand. 'Major Carl Wendermeyer at your service, ma'am.'

Betty almost giggled. She could see her mother waging war with herself as to whether to bob in a little curtsy, but then when she looked at the Major afresh, from her ma's viewpoint, she realised that he was quite an imposing figure and cut quite a dash. No wonder she was impressed. The 'ma'am' had certainly helped.

'How do you do,' she simpered, immediately brushing at her hair with her hands. 'Excuse me, I don't know whether I'm coming or going. Pleased to meet you, I'm sure.'

Betty smiled, seeing the flicker of interest spark in her mother's eye. It was no secret where Betty had got her looks from. In her youth Mrs Connors had been the village beauty.

'Pleasure, ma'am. Looks like we've got quite a job. We're going to need some lumber.'

Betty winced. He was right. They needed to rebuild one of the panels but she knew there was nothing in the shed that was anywhere near big enough.

'Howard next door has offered some wood,' said Ma.

'Howard!' Betty stared at her mother. 'Since when has he even been speaking to you?'

Her mother pursed her lips. 'Since Bert took up with that barmaid at the Red Lion. Bold as brass. I take it you knew.

Didn't so much as speak to me at Church last Sunday. Too embarrassed, I reckon. And she's as brassy as they come.'

Betty widened her eyes and nodded. She hadn't known but she was pleased to realise that she really didn't care; in fact it was a relief and clearly Bert had managed to save face by publicly replacing her. No, she really didn't care one jot but she was intrigued. 'Why would that affect Howard?'

'Turns out, he has a long-running feud with Bert. Says you're well shot of him. He reckons Bert did this.' She shot the Major a speculative gleam. 'So, Major, do you think you can help our Betty get the hen house fixed up?'

'We're going to do our best, ma'am.'

Betty groaned inwardly. Ma was so obvious and fickle. She'd been expecting a row for falling out with Bert, but clearly the Major trumped good old Bert Davenport.

As they were inspecting the hen house, Howard appeared with a large sheet of plyboard.

'Thought this might come in useful,' he said.

'That's great, Mr Bentham,' said Betty, still slightly amazed that he'd even ventured into the garden. For years he'd given the whole family a wide berth, barely speaking to them above a polite hello.

'Your ma about?'

'Yes, she's indoors.'

'Right,' and with that he disappeared into the next-door garden along the path that ran along the back of the terrace.

'Man of few words,' observed the Major.

'Yes. He hardly ever speaks to us and now he's bringing supplies.' She shook her head.

'Well, excellent supplies. This will do nicely. Right, let's set to work, if we want this baby finished before nightfall.'

The Major – would she ever get used to calling him Carl? –

was a neat, organised worker and Betty thoroughly approved, especially when he consulted her on how they should approach things. He had a way of making her feel like her opinion mattered. Together, and it was together, not him giving orders like other men would have done, they set up a work bench, getting out the tools they were going to need, along with a couple of boxes of nails and screws.

'Right. I think we should use the existing posts but dig them in at each corner to make it much sturdier, and then attach the wall panels to the posts with some struts on the back to reinforce them. What do you think?'

'Yes.'

'Then no big bad wolf can come and huff and puff it down next time.'

'Good thinking.'

'Not really. I'm going to have to dig those post holes nice and deep. Your pa have a sledgehammer?'

'I think in the shed, there are more tools and a spade.'

'A spade,' he teased, mimicking her English accent, following her into the shed. Rooting around in the corner, she found the heavy sledgehammer and a couple of shovels. She also dislodged quite a few cobwebs and when she stood up again, she swiped one from her face.

'Here, let me.' His hand smoothed across her cheek and there was a crooked smile on his face as he looked down at her.

'I think it's gone now,' she said, a touch breathlessly but she couldn't have moved if she'd wanted to. What she wanted was for him to kiss her and when she glanced up at him, he was smiling at her.

'Those dang cobwebs. They get everywhere,' he said, sliding a gentle hand around her neck, making her shiver with pleasure. With a sigh she lifted her face as his lips found hers and she relaxed into the soft, bone-melting kiss that left her knees like jelly.

'Betty Connors, you're somethin' else,' he said when he finally straightened up. 'But this isn't going to get that hen house built.'

'It isn't,' she said primly, grasping the sledgehammer and handing it to him.

'Perhaps we'll take a raincheck.'

She blushed as his hand caressed hers. 'Right. Let's dig.'

It was hard work digging into the sun-baked ground as they each took a corner after Carl had carefully measured out the dimensions. Her hands were sore already by the time she started on her second hole and she was relieved when Carl took over, but what a treat watching him bang those posts in. By this time he'd stripped off his shirt and was swinging the sledgehammer in a fierce, on-target arc. She gave herself up to the sheer pleasure of watching the muscles in his back and shoulders ripple with each movement, feeling herself getting hotter and hotter. At one point she had to wipe her forehead and it was nothing to do with physical labour. The man had a body, that was for sure.

'That's a sight for sore eyes,' muttered her ma, coming out to stand beside her. 'He's all man. You don't want to let this one get away. I got some clothing coupons you can have. I'm not going to use them and Jane's not that fussed. She's got your old clothes to be going on with.'

'Ma, he's my boss. I'm not trying to impress him.' Although it would be nice to have a new dress for the dance next week. She was on a late shift from tomorrow and could easily pop up to London to treat herself, and if Ma was offering clothing coupons, she wasn't going to turn them down.

'So.'

'He's used to better things.'

'Looks quite at home to me. I brought out some ale. Howard let me have it.'

'Howard seems to be full of neighbourliness, all of a sudden.'

'He's a nice man.' To her amazement, her mother blushed. 'He's put in a good word for us with old man Davenport about us staying here.'

'Really?' Betty raised an eyebrow.

'Don't go getting any ideas, girl. He's just being friendly now that Bert's not hanging round all the time. I owe you an apology. Howard told me he knocked you about. He saw it. You should have said.'

Betty wanted to say, 'Would you have believed me?' but there was no point. What was done was done. Instead she shrugged. 'He won't anymore.'

'He's a troublemaker, that one.' She cast a dour look at the hen house. 'He'll be back.'

'No, he won't,' said Betty, her mouth flattening and giving her mother a fierce glare. 'I can promise you that.'

Ma took a step back and then nodded. 'Do you think your GI might want a bit to eat? He's certainly expending plenty of energy. I got a nice bit of bacon and I could do some fried eggs and potatoes.'

Betty looked back at the strong, lithe body swinging the sledgehammer with athletic precision, her mouth just a little dry and a funny little flutter in the base of her belly. Like her ma had said, he was all man and a far cry from the dapper, uniformed Major she was used to. This man was someone like her and it was such a revelation, she almost sat down on the floor there and then. Before then, he'd seemed an unattainable movie-star dream that she didn't really believe would ever settle for her, but this earthy, practical man, Carl, was a different matter altogether and they had far more in common.

'Betty Connors, are you going to watch or are you going to do some work?'

She grinned. 'It's a rather fine sight. I think I might just watch a while.'

He grinned back and swung the hammer one final time before dropping it and coming over to her to give her a sweaty kiss that she didn't object to in the least.

Chapter Thirty

Evelyn

As soon as she uttered the words, Evelyn knew she'd played it wrong. Peter slammed his hand down on the table and gave her a look of such ferocity, her throat tightened.

'You want me to be a spy,' he spat. 'To spy on my fellow countrymen.'

Evelyn faltered and sat back in her seat as if trying to put distance between her and his palpable anger. He almost quivered with it, from the tip of his blond hair to the jitter of his left leg, jumping up and down beside the chair leg.

'It's ... it's not spying, per se, just encouraging other prisoners to talk. All you'd have to do is ask them questions.' Her heart thudded in her chest. 'You agreed before to help,' she added in quiet desperation. She wasn't going to plead with him. That wouldn't have been professional, even though her heart begged her to.

The walls of the interview room seemed to close in on them and she wished that she'd followed her original instinct and taken Peter for a walk, but somehow she'd persuaded herself that this would make it more legitimate. She ought to do things by the book this time, and even despite the tongue-lashing she'd received, she had to admit she felt so much better for making a clean breast of things.

'That was for us,' he snarled, his mouth twisting with apparent disgust. 'This is about honour. I gave that information of my free will. You're asking me to dupe my compatriots. Lie to them. Men I've fought alongside.' He fixed her with a disappointed glare. 'You ask too much.'

'I'm not asking for me.' She tried to keep her voice level; this was supposed to be a negotiation but it was so hard when your heart and hopes were involved.

'Aren't you?'

Maybe she was. The lines had blurred so much, she was no longer sure. What she did know was that if Peter said no to becoming a stool pigeon – the official term, which she hated – then he would move on to another prisoner-of-war camp and she wouldn't see him again before the end of the war, if then. Who knew what was going to happen in the coming months, years? They were already in the fourth year of the war and the tide had yet to turn their way. Hitler had overrun Europe.

'For us, Peter. But if you...' She couldn't baldly state the words, it sounded too much like emotional blackmail, but in black and white, that's what it was. 'If you co-operate like this, then you would be here longer.'

Her eyes met his in silent plea even though she hated herself for it.

His jaw hardened and he shook his head. 'No. I can't do it. You shouldn't have asked me.'

With that he folded his arms and stared out of the window.

She closed her eyes; they felt itchy and blurry but she wasn't going to cry. She had her pride too.

'Is that your last word?' she asked, because she had to.

The only response was a tightening of his lips and she knew she'd lost him.

'All right. I have to go now. The guards will escort you back.' She wanted to ask him to think about it but she knew he had a stubborn streak. He also had a strong sense of honour and that was one of the things she loved about him. She was asking him to betray his principles; could she do the same thing if the tables were turned? In her heart of hearts, she knew she couldn't. That country loyalty, the need to serve, to do one's duty, had been ingrained in her from birth. Their similar backgrounds were what had drawn them together and ironically their commonality would now divide them. The unwelcome clarity of thought cut through everything and left her with a sense of aching sadness.

She left the interview room with an inward sigh, walking down the corridor with its insipid institutional-grey walls. Each step seemed to take more energy than she could muster. Her brain kept going over and over the conversation, picking at every word and nuance. Could she have said things better? If she'd approached it differently, would there have been a better outcome? By the time she reached the house she was sick of second-guessing herself.

As she passed the entrance to the Officers' Mess, the noise spilling out jarred and chafed at her, so she skirted the doorway quickly, not wanting to see anyone, especially not Freddie, who since her recent apology for her bad-tempered lack of sportsmanship had bent over backwards to be amenable, with over-solicitous zeal, which she found horribly irritating.

Avoiding everyone, she trailed up the stairs. Whatever had happened to her? Once her life was simple; it moved along on a nice level line without drama or conflict and she'd always known what to do in every situation. It had been easy to follow the rules and do the right thing, but then it had been obvious what the right thing to do was. Now confusion clouded her mind along with an overriding sense of loss. With hindsight, it was so clear. She'd been insensitive and thoughtless. She knew Peter, inside and out – that was love for you. She should have known how he would feel. Tomorrow she would have to apologise.

At first she was disappointed that someone was in the room, but then she realised that Judith, lying face down on the bed with her shoulders heaving, was crying with proper heart-wrenching sobs. She darted forward and sat down on the edge of the bed, her hand immediately going to Judith's back.

'Judith, whatever's the matter?'

Judith hunched into the bed, almost tortoise-like, as if she didn't want to be found, and her sobs became more muffled but her body shook with the strength of them. For a moment, Evelyn wondered if she should leave her, but that would be cruel, like leaving an animal to suffer in pain. Rather than retreat, she rubbed the other woman's back, as if she were soothing a small child, feeling desperately ineffectual. Judith quietened but she didn't raise her head or turn. Evelyn sat quietly waiting and Judith's hand crept into hers. Weariness swamping her, she lay down on her side next to Judith and put her arm around her. It felt like the right thing to do. She closed her eyes and waited, thinking of Peter. Tomorrow, she'd go and see him first thing and tell him how sorry she was. In the meantime, she'd be here for Judith, offering her unconditional comfort.

The next thing she knew, she woke to find the room bathed in early evening sunlight. As she shifted, Judith, who was now facing her, blearily opened her eyes, blinking in confusion before she sighed and winced, moving slightly as if her whole body ached.

'Are you all right?' asked Evelyn, giving her a hug as she sat up and swung her legs off the bed.

Judith shrugged, her eyes bleak.

'Do you want to talk about it?'

'It won't help.' Judith's tone echoed with bitterness.

'A problem halved…'

'This is too big. Too awful.' She buried her face in her heads. 'Do the prisoners ever tell you what they've done?'

Evelyn closed her eyes. 'Sometimes. The atrocities.'

'Atrocities?' Judith reared up, her dark eyes flashing, fierce and furious. She had that edgy jitteriness as if she might explode at any second. 'Atrocities. That's too neat a word. It sounds like a parcel tied with string, packaged up to enclose the contents of something that should never be contained. When really it's something ugly that spills out and shouldn't ever be contained, neatly or otherwise. Mothers and their children murdered in the coldest of blood. Shot. They make them take their clothes off. Imagine standing naked, holding your child, waiting in line to be shot. Woman upon woman. In a line.' Judith's face crumpled as Evelyn's breath left her lungs in a gasp.

'Oh my God,' she whispered.

'Men with guns, mowing down innocent women and children.' Judith began to weep again. 'I can't bear it.'

'Oh, Judith.' Evelyn put her arm around her. She didn't know what to say. What was there to say?

'How can men do such things to their fellow men? Such wickedness.' She shook her head and stared at Evelyn with red-rimmed, swollen eyes.

'I don't know,' murmured Evelyn, her own stomach tightening at the images that Judith had drawn.

'I feel so helpless. There are thousands of Jewish people out there, suffering. The camps. The ghettos. Why? What have we done that makes them hate us so much? It's as if we're not even people anymore. They treat animals better than this. I don't understand.'

Evelyn shook her head, unable to answer. It made her wonder if she dared to ask Peter about such things. Were men that committed such acts monsters, or would they claim to be following orders?

'I don't understand either but it makes me realise that there is a point to this war and that we are on the right side.' She prayed that David was being well treated, but hearing things about such brutality made her feel sick. *Please let him be all right.*

'Do you know what is almost worse?' said Judith.

'No.' Evelyn turned to her, puzzled by the flatness in her tone.

'That we're happy. We're safe while these people are facing the most terrible situations.'

Evelyn had never thought about it like that.

'I feel so guilty. I escaped and ran away. One of the lucky ones. Those women... That could have been me.'

'You mustn't feel guilty. You're here, playing an important part in the war effort.'

'Am I? Really?' Judith's mouth turned downwards in a

half-sneer. 'It doesn't feel like it. Safe. Cocooned here. Well fed. Officers drinking gin every night. Going to lunch. To the cinema. The theatre.' She gave a bitter laugh. 'People are suffering and we're carrying on as normal. It's wrong. Look at your mother. In her grand house, still with her servants. What's she lost? Where's the sacrifice?'

Evelyn knew that Judith was upset but she'd made it too personal. Stung, she responded, 'This isn't her war. Or even our war. It was brought upon us by Germany. My brother is a prisoner of war but I haven't heard from him for months. There are different types of suffering and sacrifice.'

Judith snorted rather rudely and Evelyn gritted her teeth, reminding herself that it was unladylike to get into a slanging match, but she rather wanted to slap Judith and remind her that everyone had their own burdens to bear and that the war touched people in many, many different ways. She wasn't about to apologise for her upbringing or her privileged background.

'I think I'll go down for some supper.' Evelyn stood up and stretched, deliberately not looking at Judith. 'Do you want anything?'

'No, I'm not hungry.'

Evelyn left the room, her lips firmly pressed together, to stop herself saying anything she might regret. Falling out with people wasn't her style but sometimes one had to be positive and not dwell on the negatives. The war was bloody for everyone in different ways.

Of course, the first person she saw as she crossed the hall at the bottom of the steps was Freddie.

'Evelyn, how are you today?'

Oh God, she couldn't take her mood out on him again but the last thing she needed right now was his well-meaning concern. She paused. When had she turned into this horrible person who was short-tempered and irritable with other people?

'Hello, Freddie. What are you up to?'

'We're thinking about a bridge four. Do you fancy partnering up with me?'

'Are you sure?' she managed to give him a playful smile while her heart sank. 'After my performance on the tennis court.'

Freddie coloured and looked embarrassed. She shouldn't tease him like that.

'I'd love to,' she lied gracefully. Bridge was possibly the least appealing pastime right now but it would take her mind off both Peter and Judith and probably do her good. She needed to 'buck up', as David would have said.

'Jolly good.' Freddie brightened immediately. Bless him, like most of his generation, he really didn't do emotion and she normally had a much better handle on hers. Yes, she definitely needed to buck up.

'Ah, Evelyn. Could you attend a meeting with me and Lieutenant Colonel Weston, at oh-nine-hundred? My office.'

'Yes, Sir,' she said as she filed into the meeting room, her spirits immediately lifting. If she was meeting with the psychologist, that was good news. He would probably be outlining a strategy for negotiating with Peter to encourage him to rethink his position. Weston often gave valuable insight before they went into interrogations. She wished she'd thought to consult him before she'd gone in yesterday. With a touch of chagrin, she realised that she'd made a terrible assumption, that Peter loved her enough to betray his country.

During the meeting the assignments were allocated and she spent most of the meeting gritty-eyed, stifling yawns and doodling on her notepad, pretending to make notes so as to avoid Freddie's eye. He seemed to be determined to make sure she was all right and she didn't want or deserve his attention. To her disappointment, as they allocated today's interviews, she had an extremely tight schedule. How was she supposed to fit in seeing Peter today? But then every day was busy. The flow of prisoners coming into the camp had increased dramatically in recent weeks. Everyone worked flat out, every day. No wonder they were all tired.

At the end of the meeting, she followed Colonel Myers and Lieutenant Colonel Weston up to the offices on the first floor. She passed Betty, who gave her a quick wink as she dashed past with an armful of files, and she managed a smile. Betty was in fine form this morning, singing at the top of her beautiful voice in the bathroom, which had seemed to irritate Judith intensely. Personally, Evelyn was glad to see someone else was happy.

To her faint surprise, a couple of the other Naval Intelligence Officers had also been invited to the meeting, including Katherine, who sat down next to her. 'Wonder what this is about?' she whispered as everyone took their seats.

When everyone had settled Myers steepled his fingers. 'We have a number of new guests. They'll be here with us for a few weeks before they go on to Trent Park. We want to brief you in more detail on them. You will be their specific liaison officers for the duration of their stay. Weston here is going to give you a brief psychological profile of each general and we'll discuss the best approaches for each.'

Evelyn forced herself to concentrate but decided that she would ask Weston's advice about Peter at the end of the meeting. When it finally drew to an end, she waited until everyone else had gone and approached Myers.

She wiped her hands on her skirt as she stood up. 'Sir, I wonder if I could talk to you about Peter Van Hoensbroeck.'

'Certainly. I saw the notes from the meeting. In fact Weston and I discussed them.'

'Yes. I wanted some advice as to how I might approach him again.'

'I'm afraid that won't be necessary.'

'Have you assigned someone else?' There was a moment of panic.

'No. But it was quite clear from what he said that Van Hoensbroeck would not be turned.' He nodded to the psychologist.

'Oh, yes. A man of honour. A man like that views his honour as the only viable currency once he's a prisoner. He feels he's let down his country by being captured and the only way he can justify himself going forward is by clinging to that sense of honour. I know you knew him before the war.'

Evelyn flinched slightly. She hadn't actually told them that they'd had a relationship or that he was once her fiancé.

'But war changes men. I don't believe he's the man you knew.'

'But...' Evelyn started.

He shook his head. 'No, I could tell that man's views about "spying" were entrenched. It's a treasonable offence, you know, both in this country and in Germany. For some men it is a line they can't conscionably cross and he is one of those men. Shame – he seemed a decent sort. But then if you knew him and his family, he must have been.'

'Perhaps if I spoke to him again,' she said, hearing the strain in her voice and praying that her despair wasn't showing.

'Unfortunately, that can't happen.'

'Why not?' she asked, desperate now. She had to make them change their minds.

Myers narrowed his eyes. 'He was transferred to a permanent prisoner-of-war camp at oh-seven-hundred this morning.'

Chapter Thirty-One

AUGUST 1943

Judith

The following morning, feeling wrung out after a fitful night's sleep, Judith got up at the same time as Betty and Evelyn, ignoring their sleepy morning conversations to slink into the bathroom to dress without speaking to them, before leaving the house, desperate to escape. Quite what she was running from she couldn't have said but there was a driving need inside her to get away. If she could have ripped her own skin off, she probably would have done.

After walking through dew-laden grass, her shoes sopping wet, she found herself in the walled kitchen garden, which ironically reminded her of the Kircheners' garden, although this was arranged on a far bigger scale. Every row had been organised with ruthless precision and row upon row of greens marched in rank and file. The head gardener obviously ruled his troops with clear-sighted strategy. Every piece of the garden was being used: espaliered fruit trees lined the walls, mounded ridges of potato plants filled one area, trellises of climbing beans and peas took up another section – all of it immaculately tended. Judith turned, movement in her peripheral vision catching her attention. On the far side of the garden a couple of men worked, their khaki uniforms camouflaging them so that they almost blended into the shrubs beyond them. It took her a moment to identify the uniforms and realise that they were prisoners. It seemed odd actually seeing them in person. Listening in to their conversations on a daily basis, she found it hard to imagine them as real people. They were shadowy half-figures who existed only in words.

Uncharacteristically emboldened by the sudden flare of hatred, she walked forward, following the path that took her through the centre of the garden to where four men worked. For a moment she stood and stared at them, trying to see the monsters below the surface. Disappointingly, they looked like ordinary men and she scowled at them, watching them work. The man nearest, only a few rows away, looked up.

'*Guten Morgen*,' he said with a pleasant smile, standing up straight and leaning on his hoe. '*Schöner Tag*.' He pointed up at the sun in the bright-blue sky, indicating his words, 'Lovely day.' Anger and bitterness had a stranglehold on her vocal cords. She could barely bring herself to speak to him. Her hands flexed, claw-like, as if, given free rein, they might scratch his eyes out.

'*Entschuldigung*. No English.' He shook his head and smiled at her again, a handsome young man with the sun shining on his dirty-blond hair and bright-blue eyes. He could have been a poster boy for the Hitler Youth. Her lip curled in disgust and in her native language she spat, 'I speak German.'

His smile faded as he registered the contempt on her face and he actually took a step backwards.

Good, she thought viciously, *you deserve it*. She stared at him for a second longer, enjoying the sensation of intimidating him and making him feel uncomfortable. A surge of power ran through her and she lifted her chin and sneered at him.

With a toss of her head, she turned on her heel and marched out of the garden feeling a euphoric wave of vindictive satisfaction. See how they liked being treated like dirt! Filthy German soldiers! They were scum.

Her triumphant bile carried her as far as the grove of trees where she promptly burst into tears. But they deserved it. They fought for Hitler, they represented him. There was no reason for her to feel bad. Instead she resurrected the image of the women waiting to be shot. It firmed up her resolve. She had nothing to feel ashamed about. They had it too cushy here. She hoped the next prison camp would treat them more harshly and that they would suffer. That's what she wanted, for every last one of them to suffer in the way that her father had, her friends, relatives. Her fingers cramped into spiteful claws again, the tension rising up her arms into the tendons in her neck, and she gloried in the bilious hatred coursing through her veins.

'Judith, I've been looking for you.' Walther hurried over as she arrived at the entrance to the M room. 'You weren't at breakfast.'

'I wasn't hungry,' she said sullenly.

'You need to eat,' he said with a quick smile, tucking a strand of hair from her face behind her ear. She flinched and she saw the hurt in his eyes.

'I'll survive,' she said, thinking of those starving elsewhere.

She walked past him into the operations room and sat

down at her station, pulling on her headphones and deliberately avoiding looking at him. Why did he have to be so nice to her? So kind and considerate, thoughtful and insightful. It made that overarching sense of self-loathing feel even worse.

The morning passed painfully slowly as she flicked from channel to channel monitoring the conversations in the cells. All of the current batch of prisoners had been here a few days and had little to say. In their quiet exchanges, she sensed boredom and unease, especially among a few of them due to be transferred the following day. As they talked about what the next camp would be like, she enjoyed their faint apprehension at the thought of the unknown. Her lip curled when one of them said, 'Wherever we go, I can't imagine the food will be as good as it's been here.'

'Unless we've been misled and England isn't suffering from the blockade.'

'I think that's been largely abandoned now. We suffered such heavy losses in May. More than forty U-boats in that month alone.'

Judith took some desultory notes, her mouth twisting as she listened to them. They had it far too easy and as she was thinking it, she made the mistake of looking up and saw Walther's eyes on her, a worried expression dogging his face. The quick, brusque smile she sent him obviously did nothing to alleviate his concern, so she ducked her head and concentrated on the job in hand, as much as she was able to through the seething resentment and anger.

During the tea break she successfully managed to avoid him by joining a group of women translators who worked in the series of rooms next door. They were responsible for transcribing the notes the M room made into English, which were then passed on to the officers in the house. She knew this because occasionally they would send a transcription back because they couldn't read a word and they would tease the listeners about their appalling handwriting. As she sipped her tea, pretending to laugh along with the other women, she felt Walther's keen gaze upon her and knew that there would be a reckoning at some point, but she preferred to delay it for as long as possible.

'Who's going to the dance on Saturday?' asked one of the livelier women around the table.

'Not me. I'm on duty,' groaned another girl.

'I can't wait,' said another with genuine excitement. 'I hope I get myself a proper GI to dance with.'

'Gee whizz, I just hope I get a partner,' drawled another in a weary voice and the others all laughed. Judith tried to keep the smile pasted on her face to hide her growing sense of disapproval. Didn't they have anything better to think about? People were dying all over Europe, and all they could think about was a stupid dance. Betty had been beside herself with excitement this morning, talking about *Carl* and the dance even as she yawned in bed, and then started babbling about going to London to buy herself a new dress. Evelyn, admittedly, had been a little quieter, although she had mentioned that Freddie had asked her to go with him. She hadn't mentioned what had happened with Peter yesterday, but Judith assumed that perhaps she was being deliberately diplomatic after her outburst about German soldiers last night. That was the sort of thing Evelyn would do, she was so very British.

Judith's luck ran out when the afternoon shift finished and she wasn't able to get out of the door quickly enough. Walther was waiting for her, his brows drawn down in thought. Being a coward all day hadn't sat well; he was a good man and he deserved better. She didn't want to talk to anyone.

'Walther.' She nodded and he fell into step beside her.

'Shall we go for a walk?'

She let out a small mirthless laugh. 'You know I don't want to.'

'I do, but sometimes friends are there whether you want them to be or not.'

She remembered that very first walk she'd taken with him down towards the river when he'd managed to make her feel so much better about being here and the role she was doing. This time she didn't want to be soothed and have her emotions smoothed out; she wanted to smash and break things.

The word 'friends' halted her stride; it cut a little. They were more than friends, weren't they? But then, she hadn't exactly been treating him as such today.

'Walther, I'm really not in the mood.'

'No, I don't suppose you are,' he mused good-naturedly.

She glared at him for being so calm and reasonable.

He simply nodded with that faint smile touching his lips. 'You want to shout and scream and rage, don't you?'

Now she glowered at him, the ever-present anger starting to fizz up in her throat, almost a physical thing. She gritted her teeth and growled under her breath.

'Go on. Shout. Scream.'

She rounded on him, frustrated and cross. 'I can't do that.'

'Why not?' His gentle insistence irritated her.

'Because…'

'Because?'

The lift of his shoulders and the piercing gaze made her throw her head back and as she did it, in a single moment of clarity she knew exactly why not. Because if she started she might not stop. The anger, the anguish, the hideousness, it would all pour out. Her bitterness and spite would spill like bile, poisoning the air around them, and then she couldn't stop herself.

'I hate them. I hate them. I hate them. Every last German. I hate them and I hate myself for forgetting. For being drawn into this life and forgetting how much people have suffered, how people are suffering. I hate myself.' Angry tears rolled down her face as she strode furiously across the lawn away from the house. 'I forget my father. My aunt. My cousins. They're dead. And thousands of others suffer, and look...' She waved a hand at the beautiful brick house behind him. 'This. It's easy. We live in comfort. People have forgotten the real suffering. They laugh, joke, drink, eat. We don't deserve to be happy. I don't deserve to be happy. It's wrong.'

Walther didn't say anything; he let her rant on until she finally ran out of steam and couldn't contain the flood of tears that punctuated her outburst. He led her to a grassy bank and pulled her down to sit next to him, putting an arm round her as she cried into his chest, her body racked with sobs.

'All that bitterness will sour you if you let it,' he said.

'I don't care,' she said, sounding rather too much like a sulky child.

'Yes, you do. And it isn't you, I know it isn't.'

'How?'

'Because you have a gentleness of spirit. A kindness within. This isn't you.'

'I want it to be.'

'Do you? Really?'

'Yes. It's the only way I can cope with hearing those things.'

'You could ask for a transfer.'

Judith stared at him in surprise. Where would she go? Her instinct rejected the idea straight away. 'I couldn't.'

'Why not?'

'Because I won't let them win.'

A slow, knowing smile lit up his face.

She glared at him. 'I suppose you think you're clever.'

'Just a little.'

She punched him lightly on the arm, unused to this side of Walther.

He sighed. 'Judith, what we do is important but no one promised it would be easy. But think – if we don't record this, those people will die without proper notifications, without anyone knowing they are there. We are the record keepers. It is our job to make sure that they are remembered. In the future those sites will be checked, the perpetrators will be brought to book. Every recording we make of those atrocities is kept. They're sent away to somewhere safe, where they'll be kept for posterity. There will be a day of reckoning.' He said it with quiet ferocity and again she realised she'd underestimated that calm; underneath he kept his anger tightly in check but it bubbled there with righteous fury.

'I know you're right, but it seems wrong to be able to be happy when I know what is happening.'

'Would your father have wanted you to suffer? Do you think the suffering of others condemns us to suffer too? If that were the case, surely they are dying in vain. Don't we owe it to the memories of our lost ones to live our lives to the very fullest limit we can? To squeeze every drop of happiness from it, to share the joy as far as it will spread, to laugh, cry and celebrate. That is life. The highs and the lows. The good and the evil. If we let ourselves be tainted by that evil, let ourselves be consumed by that bitterness, aren't we wasting the life that has been blessed upon us?'

'I don't know,' she said dully. 'You sound like a priest or a rabbi.'

'No, I sound like a man who, like you, has lived through horrors and has chosen not to let the suffering dictate the path I choose.'

She stared at him, the cold burn of resentment still filling her chest. 'I'm not sure I'm able to do that.'

Chapter Thirty-Two

Betty

It was a morning filled with promise, thought Betty as she popped her lipstick into her handbag and for the fifth time checked that she had all her ration books and the extra clothing coupons from her ma in her purse. Strictly speaking, people weren't supposed to cut the coupons out of the books but most shops turned a blind eye, even though it was illegal to use someone else's coupons. Everyone did it.

'Have a good trip,' said Evelyn. 'You going in uniform?'

'Yes, so that I can go straight on shift when I get back this afternoon. Gives me plenty of time for shopping instead of worrying about getting back in time.'

Evelyn smiled. 'I hope you find the perfect dress.'

'So do I,' Betty replied. 'I'm so looking forward to a night out and some dancing.'

Although Evelyn tried to hide it, Betty saw her wince. She glanced at her face. 'Fancy a cigarette before I go.' She noticed the other woman had been smoking more of late.

'Why not?'

Loath to leave Judith out, Betty turned to her. 'Fancy coming onto the balcony for a chinwag?'

'No.'

'Right-ho,' said Betty, trying to stay cheerful and pretend that Judith was a bit down and not just plain rude. Evelyn had tipped her off as to what was bothering the other woman and she didn't know what to say. Of course she'd read the reports. She knew what was going on in Germany and Eastern Europe.

'Are you sure? It might...' What? Take her mind off things? Cheer her up? Betty bit her tongue, realising that she only had platitudes to offer. Sometimes she wished she were better educated, then she might know what to say, like Evelyn, who always had diplomatic words.

They climbed out onto the roof leaving Judith behind.

'Poor thing,' whispered Evelyn. 'She's not herself. I wish there were something I could do to help.'

'She's not helping herself though, is she?' Betty muttered, a little frustrated with the tense silence that had characterised the atmosphere in the attic room for the whole of the morning.

'I think it's brought a lot of things back that she'd put behind her,' said Evelyn in her usual even way, which made Betty a little ashamed of herself.

'You're probably right. I'm being a bit insensitive.' Betty's mouth turned town and Evelyn immediately nudged her. 'Don't put yourself down, and if I'm honest, I'm inclined to agree, but we're all different. Some of us are better at hiding our emotions and others wear everything on their sleeves.' She grinned at Betty who rolled her eyes, knowing the comment was directed at her. 'And some of us brood. And that's Judith.' There was a wistful twist to her mouth as she gazed out across the fields, her cigarette ·

held loosely between two fingers. As always, she appeared totally elegant but Betty could tell something wasn't quite right. Impulsively she asked, 'And what are you hiding at the moment?'

Evelyn's eyes narrowed and she took her time blowing a lazy plume of smoke from her mouth before she said with a wry smile, 'You don't miss much, do you, Betty?'

'Not just a pretty face.' Betty framed her chin in her hands and gave Evelyn a winsome smile which made her laugh.

'And you make me smile when I don't feel like smiling.'

'Peter?'

'Yes. No prizes for that guess.'

'I thought it was all sorted out with Myers.'

'It was.'

'But it's not now? Are you in trouble?'

Evelyn's mouth quivered and when she looked up at Betty, her eyes swam with tears. 'Don't be nice to me. I'll start to blub. He's gone.'

'Gone. You mean…' Betty's mouth opened but she couldn't think of the words. Instead she pulled Evelyn to her and hugged her. 'Sorry, I have to be nice to you. Oh, that is bad luck! Seriously rotten. I'm sorry.'

Evelyn sniffed and pulled out one of her monogrammed lawn handkerchiefs from the pocket of her silk dressing gown. 'It was inevitable but I … I hadn't prepared myself. I thought we had more time.'

'Do you know where he's gone?'

Evelyn shook her head. 'No idea. Myers couldn't or wouldn't, I'm not sure which, tell me. I've no way of finding out.' She swallowed and blinked furiously. 'We had a bit of a row the last time I saw him. I never got to apologise and now I feel beastly about it. At least if I knew where he'd gone I could write and say I'm sorry. That's the worst part, knowing we parted on bad terms.'

'Oh, Evelyn, I am sorry.'

'Don't be. I'm trying not to let it get me down, but if Freddie asks me one more time if I'm looking forward to the dance, I might just slap him.'

'Don't you want to go?'

Evelyn huffed out another sigh. 'I could take it or leave it. If I go, I'll have to put on a brave face which is the last thing I feel like doing, but as Judith's not going, I might stay and keep her company.'

'Judith's not going?'

'No. She says it's wrong to be enjoying herself when people elsewhere are suffering.'

Betty pulled a face. 'But what's that got to do with going to the dance?' She didn't understand someone martyring themselves for something that they couldn't change or help. Did that make her shallow or frivolous?

'You and I know that, but I think hearing what she did has crystallised everything that has happened to her. She's lost such a lot.'

'All the more reason to celebrate what she's gained. She was looking forward to going to the dance with Walther.'

'She's already told him she's not going with him. I think they've disagreed about it.'

'Lord. Talk about hair shirt. I don't understand that woman at all.'

'Yes, you do, you understand her a lot better than you think.'

'Why would you say that?'

'Because you both want the same things, ultimately. What we all want. Safety, love and security.'

'How did you get to be so wise?'

Evelyn laughed. 'I'm not sure I am.'

Betty did another twirl for the mirror and watched the skirt of the dress flare up to flash her legs. The periwinkle-blue crepe fabric made her eyes look almost violet and the sweetheart neckline, padded shoulders and fitted waist accentuated her figure. The dress was going to use up all eleven of her and her ma's combined clothing coupons but she knew that she wouldn't be leaving Selfridges without it. In her head she could picture herself spinning and dancing with Carl at the dance tomorrow night. It was a shame that Judith and Evelyn wouldn't be coming too; she'd been rather looking forward to having some fun with them, the way that they had done that magical day at Evelyn's house. She'd also hoped they might act as a buffer between herself and Carl in case he didn't ask her to dance. Which was silly, because he said he would.

With one last spin she stepped forward to the mirror and gave herself a stern look. 'Betty Connors, you've got it bad. You need to remember you're not Cinderella. For all you know, he might have a wife back in the US. He could be shooting you a line. Life isn't like the movies. Don't go getting carried away.' She wagged a finger at herself, that strong streak of practicality rising up. 'Don't go losing your heart.' But when a man came and helped you rebuild a hen house, how could you not lose just a little bit of your heart to him? He'd sat in Ma's kitchen in his shirt sleeves – and boy, was she glad he'd covered up, that handsome body of his had set her pulse rattling along – eating eggs and bacon as if it were the most normal thing in the world, chatting away to Ma and Jane about all the things he found funny in England compared to the way it was 'back home'. He made Jane laugh and teased her, he flattered Ma and complimented her on her cooking. The ruddy man had charmed the pants off both of them.

And as for her, she was a little bit addicted to those delicious kisses of his and when he smiled into her eyes as if she were the only woman in England, there was a pang in her heart as if an arrow had been shot right into her chest. She blew out a sharp breath. 'Yeah, Betty, you've got it bad.' She smiled at herself in the mirror. 'But maybe dreams do come true and handsome princes stick around.'

Reluctantly she undid the buttons and put her uniform back on and checked her watch. She had plenty of time to catch the train back to Latimer, which would get her there in time for a quick bite of tea before going on shift at four. Outside in the bright sunshine, she decided that as it was so lovely out, she'd walk back up to Baker Street, cutting up through Manchester Square to Marylebone rather than catch the underground.

With her new dress in its bag swinging in her hand, she turned left outside the front of the store, ready to turn left again. As she did there was a screech of brakes as one of the big red buses veered across the road, clipping an oncoming one. Almost immediately a crowd gathered and a heavily pregnant woman, who looked as if she were close to fainting, was brought to the pavement. From what Betty could see, she was the cause of the accident, having swooned on the edge of the road and fallen inwards. She was being well supported by a host of civic-minded shoppers and a couple of air-raid wardens, who'd darted down from the side road, were helping to direct the traffic and talking to the respective bus drivers.

Deciding there was nothing she could do, she wasn't about

to stand and watch like the other gormless idiots, she rounded the corner and set off up Duke Street, glad that no one had been hurt. The street was surprisingly quiet after the bustle on Oxford Street, in fact completely deserted, which was unusual. London in the sunshine always made her smile, although there was a puff of dust above coming from one of the buildings. Puzzled, she looked up and from behind her she heard a loud bellow.

'Oy, Miss!'

She turned and saw both of the air-raid wardens waving at her as if trying to flag her down.

'The road's closed. You're not supposed—' Their words were cut off by a thunderous rumble, vibrating up through her feet. The building in front of her shook, rocking side to side, teetering as if it couldn't decide which way to fall. She stood transfixed for a moment, as indecisive as a shocked rabbit. Even as the walls majestically started to sink into themselves, she was paralysed by a sense of unreality. The upper windows began to pop out, the noise like gun cracks as showers of glass exploded, raining out and down.

Unable to urge her legs into action, she stood and stared, dimly aware of the shouts of the two air-raid wardens. Then as two more windows cracked out, snapping out into the air, she gathered herself, clutched her precious bag to her chest and turned to run. With a horrifying groan, the building began to crumble and fall, and she was caught up in the hailstorm of bricks tumbling down onto the pavement. It was like being in the centre of a thunderstorm as the walls crashed down and a rising cloud of dust enveloped her.

With faltering footsteps, she tried to rein in the panic threatening to stall her, but then found the momentum to plough on, ignoring the sudden sharp sting that slashed across her face. Blinking as the dust scoured her eyes, she realised she'd lost the sight in one of them and everything had turned a vivid red. There was an unpleasant stickiness to her cheek. Just as she raised a hand to try and swipe it away, a heavy thud caught her on her back. It robbed her of her breath. A second thud on her shoulder made her knees buckle and then, terrified, she looked up and saw that there was no escaping the roaring monster bearing down on her. She dropped the precious dress in its bag and threw her hands up, trying to cover her head, and then as suffocating dust rasped at her throat, filling her nose, everything went black.

Chapter Thirty-Three

Evelyn

E velyn turned over again, the sheets rustling as she sighed to herself. Despite being exhausted, sleep seemed impossible. Her head was full of thoughts of that final interview with Peter. If only she could wind the clock back and approach it differently.

She turned again and squinted through the dim light at Betty's bed. She dug under her pillow and fished out her torch to check the time. It was nearly two o'clock in the morning. Where was Betty? Evelyn knew the offices on the first floor had closed down for the night because she'd dropped some paperwork in as that miserable Sergeant Major Baxter was locking up. Baxter had complained bitterly about having to unlock the filing cabinets to put away the folder. Evelyn frowned, an instinctive prickle of unease troubling her. Betty took her work seriously; it wasn't like her to stay up late, not when she was on shift the next morning. She sat up and shoved aside her bedding and padded across to Betty's bed.

Where could she be? Was she with the Major somewhere, having a secret tryst? The more Evelyn thought about it, the more she knew that wasn't likely. Major Wendermeyer was a gentleman and Betty, for all her confidence, wasn't the fast sort. What if Bert had attacked her again?

'Judith!' She shone the torch towards her bed.

'What?' came the bleary reply.

'Betty isn't here.'

'What do you mean?' Judith pushed her way up out of the shadows of the bedclothes.

'Betty. She's not here. I'm worried something has happened to her.'

'Bert?'

'Possibly. Did you see when she came back from London? Did she come into the Mess for tea before she went on duty?'

'No.' Judith pushed her hand through her hair, blinking in the torchlight. 'In fact, Elsie asked me where she was. I said she'd probably gone straight on duty because she was running late.'

'What if she didn't come back from London?'

'What?'

'I've got this feeling.' As she said the words out loud, she knew they sounded ridiculous. What had got into her? Naval Intelligence Officer Brooke-Edwards was the one whom people relied on for practicality and common sense.

'Let's go and ask someone, then. Sergeant Major Baxter.'

Evelyn stared at her, surprised by her quick acceptance. 'What, now? In the middle of the night?'

'Yes,' said Judith decisively, in her usual practical fashion, as if it were the most logical thing to do.

'Oh God, do we have to? She was in a foul mood when I saw her earlier.'

'She's billeted in the house. I had to deliver a message to her last week, I know where her room is. I'll go.' Typical Judith, once she'd decided on a course of action, she was like a train, determined to follow the track to the very end of the line.

'You will? But what if I'm just being…'

Judith huffed out a small laugh. 'Evelyn, you're never "just being", so if you're worried, I'm worried.'

She was already out of bed pulling on a cardigan and digging her uniform shoes out from under the bed.

The two of them crept down the servants' stairs, along the hall of the silent, dark house to the main staircase. Evelyn shivered, not from the cold but from the oppressive atmosphere. At night all the dark secrets of the house seemed to come together, whispering in shadowy corners. It creeped her out, making the hairs on the back of her neck stand to attention.

Crossing the head of the stairs, seemingly oblivious to her surroundings, Judith led them, marching down another long corridor, until they reached the last door on the left.

'It's this one.'

Evelyn swallowed, a rare moment of disquiet shaking her usual confidence. What if she were making a fuss about nothing? What if Betty had gone for a romantic walk? She put a hand on Judith's arm.

'Maybe—' But before she could say another word to halt her, Judith had rapped smartly on the door.

Evelyn's heart dropped to her boots. This had been a mistake. She was overreacting because her system was all in a spin over Peter. That was it. Worrying about him had made her anxious and neurotic. This was a terrible mistake. She wanted to turn tail and run. Baxter would tear them off a strip. She was a cantankerous old bat at the best of times and would not be impressed at being woken in the middle of the night, especially not by Evelyn, who'd already annoyed her once tonight.

The door jerked open.

'Yes,' snapped Baxter, her bearing as straight and uncompromising as ever. Even after being yanked from her bed by an unexpected summons, her robe was neatly belted as if she meant business.

'Sorry to disturb you, ma'am, but we're a little concerned about our friend, Sergeant Connors.'

'As well you might be,' came the furious reply. 'I'll be reporting her tomorrow.'

'R-reporting her?' Judith's voice quavered.

'Didn't turn up for her shift today! Going AWOL is a serious offence. She won't be batting those baby blues to get out of this one, no matter how good an analyst she is. Was there anything else?'

Judith clutched the Sergeant Major's sleeve and Evelyn had to bite back a smile at the affronted expression on Baxter's face as she shook Judith's hand off.

'Sergeant Major, we're worried. Betty went into London yesterday morning.'

'Well, that explains it. Silly girl has probably gone off with someone. Although…' Baxter paused, her eyes narrowing and she tilted her head. For a few seconds she seemed to be weighing things up. Then with a reluctant scrunch of her face she said, 'She might not be able to type for toffee but she's got a damn fine brain and she's not afraid of hard work. She's actually one of my more committed girls.'

'She takes her work very seriously,' said Judith with an encouraging 'you know this as well as I do' lilt to her voice. 'It really isn't like her.'

Baxter's mouth quirked. 'No, you're right. She deserves the

benefit of the doubt. However, there is nothing to be done at this time of the night. I suggest you get some sleep and I'll make some enquiries first thing in the morning.'

'Enquiries?' prompted Evelyn.

'I'll speak to her next of kin. If anything has happened they'll have been informed.'

'Y-yes, of course.' Evelyn's head really was all over the place. She should have known that.

'Thank you for bringing this to my attention. Goodnight.' And with that Baxter closed the door in their faces.

Evelyn released a heavy sigh. 'I'm never going to be able to sleep.'

'Well, we can't go marching down to Mrs Connors' place in the middle of the night,' said Judith. 'We don't even know which house it is. There's nothing we can do now. Baxter's right. We'll try and sleep and then see what Mrs Connors has to say in the morning.'

'I bet Baxter doesn't even know Betty's from the village. We could go down there.'

Judith grasped her arm. 'Not now. As soon as we wake up in the morning, we'll go. Like she said, there's nothing we can do now.'

'All right, but I bet we don't get a wink of sleep.'

They did sleep but it was the sort of fitful dozing that didn't provide any real sense of rest, and when Evelyn awoke with the dawn chorus, Judith was already awake.

'Let's go down to the Mess. Elsie might know something. She seems to know everything that goes on in the village and she can give us directions to Mrs Connors' house.'

They washed and dressed quickly and as soon as they were both ready, rushed down the grand staircase, their hands running lightly over the glossy banister.

Evelyn hadn't been to the Sergeants' Mess before and was surprised by the rabbit warren of stairs and corridors leading to the old servants' kitchen, reminiscent of Mrs Dawtry's domain at home. Down here, despite the spartan appearance in comparison with the Officers' Mess, there was a cosy, slightly fuggy atmosphere as large steaming pans boiled on the huge Aga. Judith made a beeline for a tall, slender woman pouring tea from a huge teapot into a row of solid-looking green china teacups, very different to the bone china cups used by the officers. Evelyn frowned at the sight; they were all here doing important work. Were these people less useful in any way just because of their rank? It seemed an absurdity to her.

'Elsie.'

'Hello, lovie. You're up early. Want a cuppa? I've just made this pot.'

'No, thank you. I don't suppose you've heard anything about Betty, have you?'

'Betty? No. Everything all right?'

'We're a bit worried about her. She went to London yesterday and she doesn't seem to have come back.'

'Have you checked with her mum?'

'No, we were just about to do that. Can you tell us where she lives?'

Elsie gave them extremely clear directions to the cottage at the end of the terrace opposite the green, next to the timber-framed cottages.

'How long will it take us? We're on shift in an hour,' said Evelyn. They didn't want all three of them on report for being AWOL.

'Tell you what, why don't you borrow my bicycle and young Connie's, the kitchen maid. She won't mind.'

Judith looked at Evelyn and without saying anything they both walked straight towards the back door of the kitchen and Elsie, following them, pointed out the two bicycles propped against the wall outside. 'I'll tell Connie, although you'll be back before she'll have had chance to draw breath. It'll be busy this morning. I do hope Betty's all right. I'm sure she will be, she's always had luck on her side.' But Elsie's words held a touch of doubt and she cast a glance heavenward, her lips moving as if she were uttering a quick prayer. 'I'll be watching for you coming back, girls.'

'Thanks, Elsie,' said Judith.

'She's a sweetheart,' observed Evelyn as they took the bicycles out of the kitchen courtyard, turning the corner onto the driveway.

'Yes, she is. We always get preferential treatment, or rather I do because I'm with Betty.'

'Everyone loves Betty,' said Evelyn.

'They do,' said Judith, her face suddenly thoughtful. 'God, I hope she's all right.'

They pedalled down to the village and found the cottage, thanks to Elsie's clear instructions.

'Do you think we should knock on the front door?' asked Evelyn.

Judith shrugged. 'I don't know. Why not?'

'Some people use the back door all the time. I'm not sure.'

'I don't think I'd feel comfortable walking through their garden. We don't know Mrs Connors.'

'True.' Evelyn raised a hand and rapped hard on the wooden front door, which had seen better days.

It took a while and they could hear bolts being dragged

back, the scrape of something being moved and finally the door opened with a creak and a groan. A woman peered out at them.

'Hello, Mrs Connors.'

'Yes.' Her voice resonated with suspicion. 'What do you want?'

'We're friends of Betty's. Have you heard from her?' Evelyn tried to sound bright and breezy in the face of the woman's clear misgivings about two young women standing on her doorstep.

'You'd best come in,' said Mrs Connors. 'I thought maybe she was in trouble for a minute. I forgot to phone and then, when I did remember, the post office was closed and I thought Betty wouldn't want me going up to the house, showing her up.' Without waiting she turned and disappeared through another doorway on the left.

Evelyn and Judith exchanged yet another glance; they seemed to have got non-verbal communication down to a fine art this morning. Evelyn, leading the way, followed Mrs Connors into a small kitchen with a wooden table at which sat a young girl who had to be Betty's younger sister, Jane. There was a strong resemblance but she was like a duller, less lustrous version of Betty and a stark reminder of Betty's vivacity.

'Do you want a cup of tea?' asked Mrs Connors. 'This is my other daughter, Jane. Jane, say hello to the ladies.'

Jane stared at them, her eyes wide with wonder, and tilted her head as if trying to weigh up whether they were worth speaking to.

'We haven't really got time,' apologised Evelyn. 'We've got to go on shift soon. But we're really worried about Betty. Have you heard from her?'

'I have. You'd best sit down.'

Judith sucked in a little gasp and Evelyn put out a hand to steady her.

'She's ... she's all right.' Mrs Connors' face was grave despite her words. 'Banged up. In hospital. I saw her last night.'

Evelyn stifled her impatience. *And you didn't think to let anyone at the house know?*

Judith had less tact. 'Why didn't you tell anyone? We've been worried sick.'

Mrs Connors looked genuinely surprised, as if this thought had never occurred to her.

'Where are you from?' She looked accusingly at Judith.

'Poland,' said Judith with a discreet eye roll at Evelyn. 'What happened to Betty?'

'Oh, it were terrible. It was an unstable building. Collapsed while she were walking by. She's a bit banged up.' She winced and sighed. 'Terrible, terrible shame. I don't know what'll happen to her.' Evelyn's heart did a funny leap of fear in her chest but before she could voice the question, Mrs Connors added, 'They said they might discharge her later today, after the doctor's rounds at six. Although they couldn't say for sure. If they do, she'll be getting the train. So I guess she'll be back at the house this evening.'

Evelyn frowned, puzzled. 'So she can walk.'

'Yes, she can walk just fine.' Mrs Connors pursed her mouth and shook her head. 'I don't know what'll become of her, though.'

'Is she badly hurt?' asked Judith, clearly as confused by her mixed messages as Evelyn. Surely if she was being discharged, she couldn't be.

'As I said, banged up.' She shook her head, her mouth twisting. 'Bad business, though.'

'Poor Betty,' said Evelyn. 'Which hospital is she in?'

'St Thomas's. Why they took her there, I don't know. It's miles from Baker Street and I can't spare the time to go chasing up to London again to get her, if they don't discharge her today. I've got work at the dairy. The cows come in at five. They got to be milked. I missed yesterday, I can't miss it again today.'

'Sorry to hear that,' said Evelyn politely. 'Do you know which ward she's in? Perhaps we could go and see her.'

Mrs Connors stopped and examined Evelyn carefully. 'I'm not sure that's a good idea. She might not want to see you. No disrespect, like. She definitely doesn't want to see that Major chappie. She was wailing and crying about that.'

'We're her friends,' said Judith, her forehead wrinkling. 'Why wouldn't she want to see us?'

'We're her roommates,' explained Evelyn, thinking that perhaps in their uniforms Mrs Connors saw them in an official capacity.

Mrs Connors took a minute to reply and then she said reluctantly, 'I guess you'll have to see her sometime. She's in Margaret Ward. It's on the second floor in the main building.'

They took their leave and walked back out to collect their bicycles. 'Stupid woman,' muttered Judith. 'I can't believe she forgot to phone. Doesn't she know how serious an AWOL charge is?'

'I can't believe she thinks that Betty wouldn't want to see us. We have to go.'

'We do.'

'We can go up straight after shift this afternoon. I'll try and ring the hospital and see if I can get any news. Pull rank.'

'That's a good idea.'

'In the meantime, we'd better speak to Baxter straight away. And the Major, although why doesn't Betty want him to know?'

'I don't know, but he cares about her. You only have to see the way he looks at her.'

Evelyn looked at Judith, surprise written all over her face. 'What?'

'Since when did you turn into a romantic?'

Judith lifted her shoulders in quick rebuff. 'I'm not, but a man who helps to rebuild a hen house is worth ten of those movie heroes that Betty is always so keen on.'

Evelyn laughed. 'So the way to your heart is purely practical?'

'A practical man is so much more useful.' She gave her a sudden mischievous grin. 'Don't you think?'

'I think you've changed.' Judith had loosened up a lot since she'd arrived and thankfully, in her concern for Betty, seemed to have thrown off her melancholy mood of the last few days. 'The Bentley has petrol in it. I reckon a mercy dash is within regulations.'

'I don't care if it is or isn't, we have to see Betty.'

As soon as they returned to the house they agreed that Judith would deliver the news to Baxter and Evelyn would seek out Major Wendermeyer in the Officers' Mess.

As soon as the big hand on the clock closed on the twelve and the small hand on four, Evelyn abandoned all pretence of finishing the paperwork she was supposed to be working on, packed up her desk in record time and raced to the front door of the big house where Judith, prompt as ever, waited for her.

'All set?'

'Yes.'

They were both still in uniform but they'd agreed they'd didn't want to waste any time and risk not getting to Betty before she was discharged, if she was discharged today.

'With a bit of luck, it should only take us an hour,' Evelyn said as she led the way to the Bentley.

'What did the Major say?'

'Poor man, still doesn't know. He was in meetings all day yesterday and luckily didn't know she'd been reported AWOL. There are visiting US dignitaries today, so I didn't get to speak to him. I suggest we wait until we know more and then can give him the full story. Especially if Betty doesn't want to see him.'

'Do you think that's true? Why would she say that?'

'Shock? She's probably terribly torn up by what happened. Or maybe Mrs Connors got it wrong. She must have been pretty shocked. Imagine getting a call saying your daughter is hurt and in hospital. She did seem to be a bit all over the place. Being unkind, I don't think Betty got her brains from that direction.'

Judith shook her head. 'No, you're right. Perhaps she got it wrong. She thought Betty wouldn't want to see us and I know that can't be the case. Why wouldn't Betty want to see us? We're her friends.'

Evelyn had been puzzling about this all day and still didn't have any answers, or rather the ones she did have, didn't bear thinking about.

Judith settled back in her seat.

'I could get used to this,' she said as they drove away from the village. 'It's so much nicer than taking the train.'

'It is,' said Evelyn. 'But I will have to give it back one day.'

'One day,' said Judith wistfully. 'That magical day in the future when all this is over.' She paused before saying in a small voice, 'I think sometimes I'm more afraid of the war finishing. What will happen to us all? Latimer House has become my home.'

Evelyn swallowed. She'd thought about that a lot as well. Would she still work? She enjoyed using her brain. The war had given her an opportunity that she'd wouldn't have missed. It was highly doubtful that she'd ever be content to be like her mother, with her charitable causes and positions on committees.

'I know what you mean. It seems unimaginable in some ways.'

'I didn't ask you about Peter. Sorry, I've... I'm really sorry, Evelyn. Betty having this accident has put things in perspective. I've been a horrible martyr. I don't know how you've put up with me. A real misery. And I pushed Walther away. I'm such a bad person.'

Evelyn glanced at her, taking her eyes from the road for a brief second. 'No, you're not. You just lost your way. We all do. I've been horrible to poor Freddie.'

'Is that the very loud, bouncy boy with the bushy eyebrows?'

Evelyn spat out a laugh. 'Oh dear. Yes. He's rather sweet, really.'

'But he's not Peter?' asked Judith with a quirk of an eyebrow.

She sighed. 'How did you guess?'

'Because you talk about them differently. Peter, it's with a touch of wistfulness and reverence; with Freddie, polite impatience.'

'That's very acute observation,' said Evelyn with a wry smile.

'I listen a lot.' She shrugged. 'You get into the habit of hearing what's not said.' She paused before adding, 'I'm a little worried about what Mrs Connors wasn't saying.'

The admission concurred with Evelyn's thoughts. 'Me too. Something is wrong. We'll find out soon enough.'

'We will. And you've still not told me what happened with Peter.'

'He's gone.' Evelyn couldn't help the bleakness in her words. 'Moved on to another POW camp.'

'Oh, Evelyn, I'm sorry. Do you know where? Will you be able to write to him?'

'I wish. I don't think that Naval Intelligence will be terribly pleased with one of its officers corresponding with a prisoner of war. Even if I knew where he was, I don't know if I'd be allowed to write to him. Anyway, it's immaterial because I don't know where he is.'

'We must be able to find out,' said Judith, sticking her jaw out with sudden obstinacy. 'And they can't stop you writing to him. Or through an intermediary. I'm sure the Red Cross would have something to say about that. Prisoners are entitled to letters, I'm certain.'

They drove in companionable silence as Evelyn concentrated on the traffic, leaving Judith to look at the residential streets. 'It's so different from Germany. I sometimes wonder if I'll ever go back.'

'Do you want to?'

'I don't think I do. It's not home anymore.'

They pulled up outside the hospital and Evelyn stiffened, seeing the damage the building had suffered. Jagged outlines framed spaces where blocks had once stood, the blackened timbers like eerie skeletons interspersed with forlorn piles of rubble. She remembered when she was still at Oxford in 1940, reading and shuddering at the news that the nursing home had been destroyed by a high-explosive bomb. Miraculously only five nurses were killed, although many had to be dug out of the ruins.

How did people stand it, she wondered? Being bombed day after day. How did they get the courage to pick up and carry on? There was a large sign on the corrugated-metal fencing designed to keep people away from the dangers of the bomb site. *St Thomas's down but not out.* She smiled. And there was the answer to her question. The resilience of people, that British spirit and the determination to not give up. It was what kept this country going and a pertinent reminder that she needed to be brave. She needed to find her own courage and bear with fortitude the knowledge that she might not see Peter again, but at least she knew he was safe. That had to be enough. But it didn't stop her heart aching or the dark despair that enveloped her waking moment in the mornings.

'Come on,' she said, her voice a little harsh as she shook the thoughts away. 'Let's find Betty.' In the main entrance they found the signs to Margaret Ward and went up a wide stone staircase, following the arrows which led them down a long corridor with lots of sets of doors leading to wards – Stephen, Florence, Edward and Nightingale – before they finally came to Margaret Ward. As they pushed through the double doors it was like stepping into another world where a sense of calm dominated, along with the overpowering smell of carbolic soap.

'Can I help you?' asked a nurse in a starched cap and clean white apron, looking up from a desk that was organised with neat precision. For all the chaos outside, Evelyn noted, thinking of the bombed-out blocks, inside they ran an extremely tight ship.

'Yes, we're looking for Betty Connors.'

She nurse smiled although there was a hint of sadness where the smile didn't quite reach her eyes. 'You chums of hers?'

'Yes,' said Judith, almost puffing her chest out. It was both amusing to see her so ready to claim friendship and heartwarming to see how much of that initial reserve and prickliness she'd lost over the last few months.

'She'll be glad to see you, I'm sure.' The nurse was suddenly brisk professionalism and a small shiver of foreboding ran up Evelyn's spine. 'Visiting times are over soon but you've got half an hour and she needs cheering up. Last bed on the right. And er … well, I'm sure she'll pleased to see you, although she might not show it.'

Evelyn's eyes sharpened but the nurse gave no other clue.

'Isn't she being discharged today? Her mother thought she might be,' asked Judith.

The nurse gave a non-committal shrug. 'That's the hope, but it will depend on the doctor's round, which is straight after visiting hours. It really depends on how she's feeling.'

They walked down the ward, both of them softening their steps in response to the subdued atmosphere. Iron bedsteads lined the ward on either side, each with a uniform locker and chair. Visitors were clustered around most but not all beds, talking in low, flat tones. The light was dull and Evelyn realised that the majority of the windows had been bricked up. At the far end of the ward were two sets of ominous-looking red screens clearly shielding the occupants of the beds within. In the time they walked the length of the ward, several nurses went in and out of the screens, walking with an efficient bustle of urgency that left no one in any doubt that they were attending seriously sick patients. Again Evelyn wondered how people bore it; none of the nurses looked very old.

'There she is,' whispered Judith, nodding to the bed on the end.

Betty was sitting up in bed and as they approached she turned her face towards them. They both faltered for a second before rallying and stepping forward.

'We've come to spring ya,' drawled Judith in a perfect Humphrey Bogart accent, which Evelyn thought was a stroke of genius, as it immediately dispelled any potential awkwardness, as there was no missing the big white dressing that covered the whole of the right-hand side of Betty's face.

'Evelyn. Judith. What are you doing here?' Alarm flared across her pale, drawn face and she slumped down against her pillows as if she wanted to back away from them.

'Aw shucks, I don't know. Maybe visiting our friend,' teased Evelyn with a quick forced grin that belied her sudden fear at the sight of the dressing and Betty's obvious dismay. Her mouth quivered and Evelyn paused, realising that she might not want to see them or anyone. Some of Mrs Connors' fears coalesced and made sense.

'We've been so worried about you,' said Judith, walking round to the other side of the bed and plonking herself into the chair there, seemingly completely unperturbed by the bandages on Betty's face. Evelyn almost smiled at her lack of awareness. It hadn't occurred to the German girl that there was a problem and it was probably the best approach. Judith continued, oblivious to Betty's wary gaze, 'We went to your mother's house. She told us what had happened. Are you all right?'

Betty nodded slowly, her left eye darting from each of them like a doe about to spring away to flee. There was an awkward silence and Evelyn could see that she was fighting back tears. A big fat tear spilled out of her eye and rolled down her cheek as her lips quivered.

'You sh-shouldn't have come,' she said with a heart-broken sniff.

'Yes, we should,' said Judith stoutly, like a fierce guard on the other side of the bed, ready to fight to the death. 'We're your friends.'

At that, Betty let out a hiccoughing sob. It was clear she was trying hard to hold back her emotions.

'D-don't. D-don't be nice to me, I don't d-deserve it. It's my own stupid fault.'

'Oh, sweetheart.' Evelyn enveloped her in a gentle hug, sitting on the edge of the bed, sliding her arm across her shoulders. 'How can you say that? You were in the wrong place at the wrong time. This isn't your fault.'

Betty clung to her. 'Yes it is. I'm such a fool. Being so vain. Wanting a new dress. For what?' What they could see of her face crumpled and she raised her hand protectively towards the dressing. 'I'm so stupid.'

'No, you're not.' Judith's voice was firm. 'Evelyn's right, it was an unfortunate accident. You have every right to be feeling sad. Your mother said a building fell on you. It must have been terrifying. Where are you hurt?'

Betty winced and shifted against her pillows. 'My back, my shoulder, my legs, but nothing's broken. Just badly bruised, but my…' Again the hand hovered by the dressing and the left side of her mouth twisted, fresh tears running down her cheeks. 'I know I'm lucky, but I want to die and that's an awful thing to say.' She began to cry quietly and both Judith and Evelyn shuffled closer and put their arms around her, offering the only comfort they could. Evelyn's heart ached with each of her quiet sobs. Poor, poor Betty. Her pretty face. No wonder she was distraught; in her mind it was her currency. She didn't see the bright, sparky woman that lit up a room with her gay, positive personality as soon as she walked in.

Eventually her sobs subsided and she clutched their arms. 'Sorry.'

'Don't apologise. We're so glad to see you alive. We were so worried when we realised you hadn't come home.'

'I'm sorry and I'm a wicked person. Worrying about my face when … when.' Her voice lowered to a whisper. 'There are women in here who have lost legs, been blinded and…' She nodded to the red screens. 'Worse. One of those girls has lost most of her face. A bomb blast the day before yesterday. She's only eighteen. We all know she's going to die but she doesn't know about her face. I know I shouldn't, my face is nothing compared to hers, but I'm…' Her mouth crumpled again.

'Betty, we love you as you are and no one is going to judge you,' said Judith fiercely, squeezing her hand. 'You're our friend.'

'We were so worried about you,' added Evelyn. 'It's such a relief you're all in one piece. It could have been so much worse. Honestly, we've been imagining all sorts of terrible things.'

'I'm sorry.' She sniffed again and Evelyn could see she was trying to put a brave face on. 'You shouldn't have worried. It was my own stupid fault for going into London. Like you said, it could have been far worse than a stupid building falling on me.'

'You could have been killed,' said Judith with a fearful shudder.

'I thought I was at first. There was so much dust, I couldn't see. I thought I'd gone to hell.' Betty half laughed and half cried, and both Evelyn and Judith leaned in to hug her again as she told them about the whole experience.

'Luckily they found my handbag and phoned Ma, but she was supposed to phone the switchboard at CSDIC. I had no idea who needed to be told.'

'I think she forgot,' said Evelyn kindly. 'She had other things on her mind.'

Betty groaned. 'Oh no. How much trouble am I in? She doesn't understand the Army. I told her they'd think I'd gone AWOL and I'd be court martialled if she didn't call. I was so worried.'

'You won't be in any trouble,' said Evelyn confidently, 'although once Carl knows, he's sure to make sure you're not in trouble.'

'Carl?' Alarm filled her eye and then she closed it, giving a little shiver.

'Yes. I'm sorry, he was with VIPs today so I didn't manage to tell him what's happened, but I'm sure as soon as he knows he'll be here.'

'Don't let him come,' said Betty with sudden urgency.

'Why ever not?' asked Judith.

'He won't want me now,' she said in a small voice.

'Why would you think that?' Evelyn hated the way that she suddenly seemed to shrink in the bed.

'My face. Not as bad as…' she nodded towards the screens again, 'but it's a mess.' She touched the dressing and her mouth turned down in a mournful crescent. 'No one will ever look at me again.'

'Rubbish,' said Judith with stalwart determined support.

Evelyn had to say more. 'Betty, if that's all he cares about, then he's not the man for you. But I think that he's more than the man for you. How many men go and build hen houses? Rescue you from dastardly villains? Punch your ex for you? I think it's going to take a lot more than that to put him off.'

'I wish I could believe you,' said Betty. 'But look at him. He could have any girl he wants. Why me?'

'Because you're smart as a whip, you've got brains and you know how to use them.

'And you have *das Leuchten*,' said Judith. 'When you walk into a room.'

'Das what?'

'*Leuchten*,' repeated Evelyn with a broad smile. Judith had summed it up perfectly. 'Luminosity. You light things up.'

'Pshaw,' said Betty with a wave of her hand, batting away the compliments.

'It's true,' said Judith earnestly. 'You have a special talent. It's not about your looks, it's the way you look at life. "You Are My Sunshine".' She began to hum the tune softly.

Betty shook her head.

'No, you have sunshine and you bring it to other people. Especially when you sing.'

'That's one of the nicest things anyone has ever said to me,' said Betty, her eye blinking. 'And you're going to make me cry again.'

'Sing instead,' said Judith, humming the refrain of the song again.

Betty took a deep breath and began to sing quietly along. Almost immediately, at the sound of her beautiful voice, the conversation at the neighbouring bed stopped and the elderly woman propped up against the pillows turned and gave Betty a rheumy-eyed smile, which lifted the whole of her thin, mournful face. 'Oh, darling,' she called over. 'That's something else. We all need some sunshine. Sing up, duck!'

In response Betty sang a little louder to include the woman and what looked like her daughters, who were crowded round the bed. There was a soft clap of delight from the woman in the bed on the other side, and Betty turned to give her a tentative smile. The woman, her leg swathed in bulky bandages, gave her a cheery thumbs-up.

'That's grand, love.'

Betty's voice gradually swelled, gaining volume as she sang the next few lines and her face, or rather what could be seen of it, brightened. The rest of the ward had grown silent, almost as if everyone were holding their breath and listening.

Evelyn clasped her hands over her heart, her eyes meeting Judith's in silent wonderment. It was such a special moment of magic and hope, and it seemed to infect Betty, who held out her hands to both of them, raising her voice and singing with a piercing sweetness, as if reaching out to the other injured patients. All three of them had tears pouring down their cheeks by the time Betty's song drew to a close. Complete silence held the ward in its grip for a few seconds, as if blanketed in heavy emotion. Then a round of spontaneous applause rang out, along with a few shouts.

'That was luverly, ducks.'

'Beautiful, lovie.'

'Gorgeous.'

Betty lifted her chin and waved to everyone, without a shred of shyness. 'Thank you.' She nodded her head regally at the other patients.

'I'm for it now,' she suddenly muttered as the three of them spotted a Staff Nurse coming across to them at a speedy pace. 'Probably disturbed those poor girls.' She caught her lip between her teeth.

'So—'

'Miss Connors.' She clutched her hands to her chest in front of her. 'That was … simply wonderful.' She stood at the end of the bed, beaming, her cheeks pink with pleasure. 'What a treat. I don't suppose you'd sing another song, would you? It would do wonders for the morale. Especially…' she tilted her head to the two beds at the far end of the ward, surrounded by screens. 'They're unconscious but they're aware. You'll be doing them the power of good. I promise it will help.'

From the nurse's expression, those poor souls behind the screens needed the help of angels and more.

'What shall I sing?'

'I know.' Judith began humming and Betty smiled and nodded.

'Perfect.' She started to sing the opening words of 'We'll Meet Again', the timbre of her voice low and sure, flooding the words with meaning. All around the ward heads lifted; some eyes shone with tears and several hummed along, gradually gaining in confidence until most of the ward was singing along to the famous refrain. Both Evelyn and Judith joined in, the three of them singing together, catching each other's eyes and smiling. Evelyn could feel a lump in her throat. The sound of all the women's voices was oddly moving and brought home a sense of unity and peace as she squeezed Betty's hand.

The human spirit was an amazing thing and they would triumph through adversity. She, Betty and Judith had had their share of trials in recent months, but life went on and the three of them had forged a bond of friendship which would help carry them through the coming months, whatever this blessed war threw at them.

After the impromptu singalong, a ward maid began bringing round cups of tea for everyone and a doctor appeared at the end of the bed, clapping as he approached her side. 'Thank you for that. Sometimes music and laughter are the best medicine. You've cheered up a lot of my patients and you are looking a lot brighter. How are you feeling? Want to go home?'

'Can I?' asked Betty, sitting up straighter. 'I could go with my friends. Then I wouldn't have to travel on my own on the train.'

'I have the Bentley,' said Evelyn.

'Travelling in style.' The doctor looked impressed and gave Evelyn a quick appraising glance. Used to this sort of attention, she gave him a cool smile in return, although he was rather good-looking. Once upon a time she might have flirted back but now her heart felt too sore and her head too full of thoughts of Peter and what a mess she'd made of their final meeting.

'I think that's probably an excellent idea then. Let me speak to Sister and we'll sort out the paperwork, if you ladies don't mind waiting about for a little while. I would like to examine Miss Connors. As well as the lacerations to her face, which will need further treatment over the coming months, she has some nasty bruises, so she will need to take it easy for a while. What is it you do?'

The three of them looked at each other, tiny smiles on their faces.

'I work in a distribution centre. Administration. That sort of thing,' said Betty.

'No heavy lifting or physical work?'

'No.'

'Well, I'd still like you to rest up for a few days. You had a very lucky escape. I'll write you a sick note for your commanding officer.'

Evelyn and Judith went out to a small waiting room while the doctor and nurses undertook whatever procedures they needed to complete to release Betty. While they were waiting a petite nurse, so tiny she didn't look as if she could lift a bedpan, let alone a patient, came into the room clutching a brown paper parcel.

'This is your friend's. She says she doesn't want it but … well, it's such a pretty dress, I'd hate her to change her mind. Will you take it for her?'

'Yes,' said Evelyn, taking the parcel and folding it over before putting it into her big handbag, remembering with sadness how excited Betty had been at the prospect of shopping for a new dress for the dance.

'She won't want to go now, will she?' said Judith astutely.

'I don't suppose she will.'

'Then it will be the three of us together, in our rooftop eyrie.'

'Looks like it will be,' said Evelyn sombrely.

Chapter Thirty-Four

Judith

U p on the roof, Judith listened to the excited voices filling the air from down below and then the slam of the coach door and the rumble of its engine as it drove away down the drive. It took a moment for the big green bus to come into view before it wove its way down the lane towards the village.

That was it, everyone had gone off to the dance at RAF Bovingdon. She grimaced. It was all anyone seemed to have talked about for the last week and today the whole house seemed to have hummed with preparations.

'They've left,' she announced, clambering through the window back into the stuffy room. It had been yet another beautiful day – whatever happened to the myth that it rained all the time in Britain? – and the heat had gathered under the roof, leaving them restless and scratchy. None of them seemed to have much energy today. Betty lay listlessly on her bed and Evelyn was propped up against her bedhead reading a copy of *Vogue* magazine. If anyone spoke it was in monosyllables.

Judith sat down on her bed and picked up her knitting, thinking about how much pleasure she'd had wearing the red jumper she'd made and the sense of hope she'd had while working on it. All that had gone but she was making a scarf for Betty with the remainder of the scarlet wool. Perhaps it might cheer her up, but she doubted it. She glanced across the room where Betty sighed and linked her hands behind her head, staring up at the ceiling.

Both Judith and Evelyn had seen the livid red gash stitched together with jagged teeth-like stitches that tracked an uneven curve from the top of her forehead across her cheekbone to her ear. It was a miracle that the ugly wound had left her eye intact, the gash stopping at her eyebrow and starting again at the top of her cheek. Now a smaller dressing covered her face beneath her eye, but the angry, puckered, swollen skin and black zig-zags on her forehead were clearly visible. As they'd driven home it was noticeable that Betty had become quieter and quieter on the journey, the bravado in the hospital wearing thin, and since they'd arrived back at the house she'd barely said a word apart from insisting that they used the servants' passage from the hallway up to their room, so that she wouldn't see anyone.

Somehow, as it always seemed to in a closed community, news of Betty's accident had spread and everyone in the house appeared to know what had happened to her, although not the full extent of her injuries. As a result, plenty of well-wishers sent their best, from little notes through to personal messages when Judith had ventured into the Mess for a cup of tea, which showed how popular Betty was among the other ATS women. Unfortunately, she didn't want to know and had stayed in bed all day today.

Carl had contrived to send up a note and a gift-wrapped

pair of nylons via Elsie, who'd brought up a food tray for Betty, but Betty had refused to read it and looked so woebegone at the sight of the nylons that Judith and Evelyn had exchanged a silent agreement that they wouldn't press her about it. Betty also turned down the plate of food that Elsie had so kindly put together, saying she wasn't hungry.

'The bus has gone,' announced Judith again as she'd got no reaction the first time. Evelyn looked up and gave her a steady stare. Betty didn't even move.

A horrible sense of inertia and fatalism pervaded the room as if all three of them had been drugged by gloom, and it wasn't right, not at all. She cast a worried look at Betty, her usual bright light extinguished. Where was Betty's golden optimism? What had happened to Evelyn's forthright positive outlook, with her gung-ho determination to get things done? This was all wrong. Judith was the one that normally looked on the bleaker side.

All week her thoughts had been dogged by those awful images of the slaughtered women and children in Mizoch on the other side of Europe. Now it was as if her mind suddenly cleared, clouds parting to reveal a stark truth. There was nothing she could do for those women and children. They would never dance again. Their time had gone but she, Betty and Evelyn, they had a life to live. They still had hope.

'We have to go,' she said, standing up with uncharacteristic resolution, her voice resonating with sudden conviction. Those women hadn't had the chance to fulfil their lives. She, they, owed it to the dead to live. To live life to the full, to celebrate being alive and do all the things that those women and thousands of others across Europe would never have the chance to do again. 'We have to celebrate our freedom. Celebrate what we have.'

'Pardon?' Evelyn enquired in her calm voice.

'We should be at the dance. All of us. Betty nearly died. All the women suffering across Europe. They won't dance again. We owe it to them to live. We still have so much.' She looked across at the other two women, remembering their words of a few months before. 'We have to think of tomorrow because today is done.'

Betty sat up, cocking her head thoughtfully for a second and then as Judith watched, the light trickled back into her eyes and she nodded. Uncurling from her bed, she stood up, her chin lifted and shoulders back, like Boudicca going into battle. 'For those women in the hospital. They'll never dance again, either. Judith's right.'

Evelyn sighed. 'You're both right. We should celebrate our freedom, for those that can't.' She didn't say his name but Judith could tell she meant Peter. She suddenly rose to her feet with a sudden grin. 'All right, then. Let's hope there's enough petrol in the car.'

'We're going?' Judith looked at both of them, a small smile touching her mouth as a thrill of delight fizzed through her that her words had meant something to both of them. It was unlike her to take the lead, she normally left that to others, but doing so this evening had energised her and she found herself standing straighter.

'Yes,' said Betty with a determined bite. 'Enough feeling sorry for myself. You're right. We do owe it to all the others who are less fortunate. I need to be brave and face everyone. Those poor damaged girls in the hospital,' she shook her head, 'they had it so much worse than me. I can't hide away from everyone. I'm still the same person I was last week.'

'That's the spirit,' said Evelyn. 'And I have lots to be

grateful for. Peter's not dead. I'm just going to have to be patient and wait until the end of the war.'

'And I owe Walther an apology for being so self-indulgent.' Judith winced. 'I hope he'll forgive me.'

'I rather think Walther will understand,' said Evelyn with a teasing smile.

'He will,' said Judith with a sudden surge of confidence, because he was a wonderful man and had wisdom enough for both of them.

'Let's get ready then,' said Betty, the light of battle glinting in her eye. 'It's just like Cinderella. We are going to the ball. Although what are we going to wear?'

Evelyn shot Judith a triumphant grin. 'I've got the very thing.' From under her bed, she pulled the paper bag that the nurse had handed them and shook out the dress.

'How did you get that?' Betty's mouth fell open in surprise.

'The nurse thought you might regret it. It is a lovely dress and you're going to look beautiful in it.'

'I'm not sure I'll ever look beautiful again,' said Betty, her mouth turning down a little as she held her hand up when the other two began to protest. 'But I'm alive and that's what I'm going to think about when I walk into the room.'

'You can do it, Betty,' said Evelyn. 'I know you'll feel self-conscious at first, but after that first step it will get easier. Always remember people love us for who we are.'

'You're going to have to keep reminding me of that. My knees are shaking at the thought of facing everyone.'

'Yes,' said Judith, going to link her arm through Betty's, 'but you're not going to be on your own. We'll be with you.'

'Promise?'

'Absolutely,' said Evelyn, moving forward to link with Betty's other arm, so that they both flanked her.

'Always,' said Judith. 'I promise we won't leave you.'

'Oh God, I'm going to cry again. I've turned into a terrible watering pot. Why are you two so nice? What did I do to deserve friends like you?'

'I told you before, you have *das Leuchten*.'

Betty gave a soft laugh. 'You talk rubbish but I'm going to believe you, otherwise I'll never get out of here. And thank you for rescuing my dress; I will wear it. In the hospital I never wanted to see it again, but life goes on. And I spent eleven flipping clothing coupons on it.'

They all laughed.

'What about you, Judith? What will you wear?' Betty began to look her up and down and Judith cringed at the business-like assessment. She could tell Betty was going to attempt to make her over again. 'I never thought about it. I don't have a dress.'

'I have just the thing,' said Evelyn with sudden enthusiasm, and she ran to the trunk nestled in the corner of the room and began to rummage, before pulling out a black polka dot-dress in a shiny fabric with a full skirt. She thrust it at Judith before she could say no.

As soon as her fingers closed over the soft, rich material, any thought of saying no went up in smoke. She'd never worn anything as beautiful or stylish like it in her life.

'Are you sure? It's very glamorous.' Judith stroked the dress, unable to help herself. Her clothes had always been serviceable and practical. This was like something out of a fashion magazine. She was almost too scared to say yes.

'Try it on,' urged Evelyn.

'Oh yes, that neckline will be perfect on you,' said Betty with sudden animation. 'And if we put your hair up in a roll, it will show off your neck and shoulders beautifully, and a bit of lipstick.'

Judith gave Betty a rueful smile, rolling her eyes. 'I knew you were going to start.'

'You love it really. I bet Walther liked it when I did it for you last time.'

'I liked it and that's what counts.' She blushed because Walther had liked it and she'd enjoyed his quick appreciation.

'What are you going to wear, Evelyn?' asked Betty.

'I thought this.' With a flourish, she pulled out a glorious, almost floor-length, bias-cut, shot-silk dress in a deep shade of pink with tiny cap sleeves. The delicate fabric swished through the air, as light as gossamer, and Judith could imagine it flaring out on the dance floor. 'If we're going to be late, we might as well make an entrance. We'll be the belles of the ball.'

Judith gulped. She'd never been the belle of anything but she was willing to give it a try.

'Let's do it.'

'Half an hour, ladies,' declared Evelyn and the three of them began to scramble out of their clothes to get ready.

'Are you sure this is the right place?' asked Betty as they drove up to where they had been directed by the guard on the gate. He'd said that the block at the far side of the car park was the entertainment hall and they couldn't miss it, and have a dance for him as he wasn't off duty for another couple of hours.

'It must be,' said Evelyn, killing the engine.

Even Judith frowned; there was no sign of life anywhere apart from a few military jeeps in the car park.

'It's always difficult to tell with black-out blinds in place.' Evelyn had already stepped out of the car.

'But I can't hear any music,' said Betty, leaning out of the passenger door. 'Not that I'm supposed to be dancing.'

Judith got out and tilted her head, straining to hear and then, there, on the edge of the breeze, a very faint beat. 'I can hear something.'

'Gosh, I hope it was worth coming,' said Betty, shaking out her skirt as she stood up. 'After all the effort I went to, to get this dress.' She grinned at the other two. 'Doesn't sound much of a party.'

'Well, we'll liven it up,' said Evelyn. 'Come on.'

The three of them carefully picked their way across the car park to the long, low building. Across the field they could see the dark-green hangars, sheltering the planes from overhead observation, and the white control tower.

As they drew closer the sound of the music rose but even so, Judith frowned. It didn't sound like a live band to her.

When they opened the door to a small lobby area, an American soldier jumped to his feet from a wooden chair just inside, and it was almost comical the way that the hope on his face faded away as if the sight of the three of them was a huge disappointment.

'Hello,' said Betty with her usual bright smile, ignoring his change of expression. 'We're here for the dance.'

'Gee, sorry, ladies, welcome to USAF Bovingdon. I'd really like to have given you a warmer welcome. I was kinda hoping you were the rest of the band arriving. We're missing a piano player and one of the singers. They ain't arrived yet.' He pulled a ghoulish face, 'We're relying on the Squadron Commander's gramophone at the moment.' Then he brightened as took in the sight of all three of them in their finery. 'But you're most welcome, ladies, and don't worry, folks are still having a good time. Come join the party.'

He led them across the lobby to a set of double doors. 'The party's through here. Have a good time, ladies.' The three of them hovered by the door for a second and Judith noticed that despite her earlier bravery, Betty hung back, ducking her head a little. It had to be so hard facing the world for the first time. Judith reached out and gave her arm a squeeze. 'You can do this. We're with you. Remember, you have *das Leuchten*.'

Betty let out a nervous laugh. 'I think you made that word up to make me feel better.'

'Tell her, Evelyn.' Judith nudged her.

'It's a real word. And we're here with you. We're not going anywhere.'

'I know, I'm a bit... It's like all the butterflies in my stomach have gone into battle and my knees have forgotten what they're supposed to do.'

'We're the belles of the ball, remember,' said Evelyn, linking arms with her as Judith did the same on the other side.

The three of them walked into the room, which had been dressed up with cheerful bunting and flags hanging everywhere, along with a glitter ball hanging from the ceiling, bouncing tiny glittering flashes all around the walls. Despite the rather magical effect of the flickering light, the mood inside was a little sombre and Judith sighed and lifted her chin. They'd made all this effort to get here, and she was determined they were going to have fun. The three of them had made a pact – to enjoy themselves for all the women that couldn't.

'It's a bit sad,' volunteered Betty as she looked around the room, pleased to see that without exception, all of the women were dressed to the nines, their hair immaculately arranged, wearing slim-fitting dresses with sharp shoulder pads and short sleeves in bright, solid colours. Most people were standing around the edge of the dance floor and while a few brave souls were making an effort to dance to the tune that was playing on the gramophone, far more were grouped in round-shouldered huddles. Freddie, who'd obviously been looking out for Evelyn, immediately crossed the dance floor, not even bothering to heed the sparse dancers as he barged his way through.

'Bit of a washout,' he muttered as he came to stand in front of them, his gaze zeroing in on Evelyn, not even acknowledging the other two. With a twinge of sympathy Judith eyed him; he clearly adored Evelyn and had no idea that her heart was already taken.

'Freddie, nice to see you. These are my friends, Judith and Betty.'

Freddie, realising that he'd been gently reminded of his manners, immediately turned and included both of them in his wide smile. 'I do apologise, ladies. Very nice to meet you.' Judith gave him credit for gamely ignoring the train track of stitches cutting into Betty's forehead and the white dressing covering her cheek, as he averted his eyes almost immediately. Although that might have been because he had eyes for no one but Evelyn. 'It's a shame that the band haven't turned up. They've played all three dance records three times. It's wearing a bit thin.'

'Oh dear,' said Evelyn, glancing around the room. 'People do seem a bit cheesed off.'

'Everyone's been looking forward to it for so long.' Betty peeped around the room, still keeping her head down, which Judith didn't really blame her for. 'What a shame.'

It was a shame, for everyone, not just the three of them who had screwed up their courage to come. Everyone at CSDIC worked so hard, the workload had been relentless for the last three months. Judith caught sight of some of the ATS girls from her section. She remembered their excited chatter over tea a few days before. No wonder they looked so disappointed. Judith would never forget how wonderful it had been to dance with Betty and Evelyn at Evelyn's home. If she were completely honest with herself, she'd been looking forward to having another go, looking forward to enjoying that rush of happiness.

Judith glanced across the floor and could see the band clustered together in a group by the makeshift stage like lost souls. Walther was standing with them, holding, of all things, a saxophone.

That was his surprise. Of course. He was so musical, why hadn't she ever asked him if he played an instrument? Guilt pricked at her when she thought of all the questions he'd asked about her, and her own reticence. Had she shown so little interest in his life? She really didn't deserve him. It was time she took charge of her life, stopped hiding and started living.

With sudden decision, she grabbed Betty's arm. 'Come on.'

'What are you doing?'

'Taking charge. And starting the dancing.'

'But I'm not supposed to dance unless it's very gentle.'

'We're not dancing. We're going to play and sing. Come on.' Judith caught the eye of Evelyn, who gave her a slow nod and a big smile before mouthing, 'Perfect.'

'But I can't.' Betty's hand went protectively to her face. 'I can't sing in front of all these people.'

'Yes, you can,' said Evelyn, flanking Betty's other side.

'It'll get it out of the way,' said Judith a touch ruthlessly. 'It's for your own good.'

Even Evelyn looked at her with surprise while Betty stared

at her, pursed her mouth and then rolled her eyes, her mouth touched by the faintest of smiles. 'Who knew you'd turn into such a bossy boots? What the heck. Why not? In for a penny. Everyone's dying for a gander. You're right, this will get it over with. They can all have a good gawp. I've got nothing to hide.'

'Atta girl,' said Evelyn. 'And they're going to be so bowled over by your voice, they probably won't even notice.'

'I think that's doing it a bit too brown, Evelyn darling,' said Betty, rolling her eyes again. 'But I appreciate that both of you are trying to help. But you're right. I'm going to have face them all at some point. At least, if I make a complete fool of myself, they'll feel sorry for me rather than booing me off the stage.'

'Exactly.' Judith grinned at her, unexpected confidence blooming inside her. 'Come on.' She grabbed Betty's arm and towed her with mulish strides across the dance floor, as if daring anyone to get in her way. When she came face to face with the group of musicians milling around the front of the stage, looking to all the world like lost sheep, she pushed her way through to the middle, pulling Betty with her and Evelyn following. Walther, standing with his back to her, turned and his eyebrows rose in surprise. 'Judith.'

'Walther.'

She stared at the instrument. 'You didn't tell me you played.'

'I ... I wanted to surprise you. But I didn't think you were coming.'

'I'm sorry.' She held out a hand and touched his fingers resting on the keys of the saxophone. 'It took me a while to come to my senses. Can you forgive me?'

'Always,' he said and she knew that he meant it and no further apology was necessary, because he was that sort of man.

'Thank you.'

'Well, now you're here, perhaps you could make yourself useful.'

She grinned at him and just like that, no further conversation was needed. He turned to the other band members.

'Everyone, this is Judith, she's one heck of a pianist.'

'You are?' asked one of the men. 'Hallelujah!'

With a modest smile, Judith shrugged. 'I can play a few things and Betty here can sing one,' she paused at the unfamiliar word, 'heck of a tune. Our repertoire is limited and we're not particularly polished but,' she paused and then said with no small amount of pride, 'I think we can liven things up.'

Walther gave her a second look, his eyes twinkling. Taking charge of things was ... actually it was rather wonderful.

He winked at her. 'I don't know. I've heard you play. I think you've got a few tunes up your sleeve.'

'Do you need to warm up or anything?' asked one of the band, looking very relieved. 'Because if we don't get started soon, we might get lynched.'

Betty lifted her shoulders, an alarmed question in her eyes as she sought Judith's. 'Are you sure? This is a big crowd.'

'And you have a big voice. Remember the hospital. They loved it. This is going to be a breeze and we've got a band to hide behind.' Several of the musicians nodded and Betty shot Judith a swift, resigned smile.

'Right-ho. In for a penny, in for a pound.'

'Right.' Judith quickly gave the band a rundown of what she and Betty could play and they quickly agreed which songs they would play and in what order.

'We're really doing this?' asked Betty, looking around the room. So far no one had noticed them or the little buzz around the musicians, all of whom had straightened up from their drooping postures as if they'd been switched back on.

'Yes.' Judith put her shoulders back. 'Let's play some music.' The musicians began to file up the steps on the left of the stage and she followed them, waiting halfway up the stairs for Betty to follow.

Betty hovered on the bottom step, her teeth catching her bottom lip. Evelyn was standing beside her.

'We can do this,' urged Judith. 'But you don't have to if you really don't want to.'

With a small huffed-out laugh, Betty shook her head. 'I don't want to, but I have to.'

She and Evelyn followed Judith up onto the stage where the piano sat beside the microphone on the stand. There was a growing hush among the crowd as they realised that there was movement on the stage.

'I'll be right beside you,' promised Judith.

'And I'll be in the wings,' said Evelyn. 'Look at me if you need to.'

'I know, but I'm scared.'

'Of course you are.' Evelyn took both of her hands and squeezed them. 'But I promise you, every single person in this room will be on your side. You can do this.'

Betty narrowed one visible eye to give Evelyn a rueful look as Judith sat down at the piano. 'If I bomb, I'm blaming you and you have to lend me that dress.'

Evelyn laughed. 'Atta girl. I'll give you this dress.'

'Seriously?'

Evelyn nodded. 'Why not?'

Betty looked over at Judith. 'What are you waiting for?'

With a laugh and a roll of her eyes, Judith sat down at the piano stool.

'Hey, I'm still as frivolous and shallow as I ever was. This doesn't change it.' Betty tapped her face.

'You're not any of those things,' said Judith softly. 'You're a part of the Stern and Connors duo and we're about to bring the house down.'

'Connors and Stern, I think you'll find,' teased Betty, lifting her nose and sniffing.

'Whatever, girls, but the band is ready.' Evelyn nodded towards the other musicians who'd all climbed back on stage. Judith realised that the brass players and the drummer were waiting for her signal.

'Right-ho. Let's do this.' Feeling nerves and excitement thrumming through her, she gave a brief nod and the drummer counted three on his sticks and, as if they'd been practising together for months, they launched with gusto into 'Boogie Woogie Bugle Boy'. As one the whole crowd straightened, as if an electric current had raced around the room, and in seconds the dance floor began to fill. Judith's fingers danced across the keys, her heart in her throat as she watched Betty waiting for the intro to finish. She needn't have worried, Betty launched into song exactly on cue and the electricity in the room spiked even higher. Suddenly the entire atmosphere transformed, the lethargy replaced with burning-bright energy as uniformed men grabbed partners to spin and twirl. The room came alive, the mirror ball spinning, refracting a kaleidoscope of light over the dancers' brightly coloured dresses, as limbs and bodies whirled and twirled, brilliant smiles and joyful laughter lighting up the place instantly.

Judith beamed, happy to see the sheer delight on the dancers' faces. She glanced over at Betty and almost stopped playing. It was as if the other woman had blossomed right in front of her. Gone was the shy, diffident, ducked head; now she stood bold and strong, singing out at the audience, her voice soaring clear and bright. The *Leuchten* was back. Betty's confidence burgeoned before her eyes. By the second verse, Betty faced the crowd and was flirtatiously hamming it up, playing up to the audience as if she were one of the Andrews Sisters herself.

Judith thought she might burst with pride and happiness. How had she forgotten the pleasure of playing to an audience? It gave her so much joy. It was as if she'd been lit from the inside. She'd missed this. When she surreptitiously glanced over at Walther, who was playing the saxophone, his eyes met hers and she couldn't help beaming at him. There was something about playing in harmony with other people that couldn't be matched. With a burst of euphoria, she realised this was genuine happiness and it felt wonderful.

Somehow, despite all that had gone before, she'd made a new life here. She'd made some good friends, she had her music and if she let him in, she had Walther too. Poor man, she'd been keeping him at arm's length for too long and he'd been endlessly patient with her, biding his time and waiting for her to recognise the love that was shining in his eyes right this very moment. As soon as they finished playing she was going to do something about that. She almost laughed to herself. Where had this super-bold, confident Judith come from?

With a grin she nodded at Betty as they segued into 'Chattanooga Choo Choo', to the delighted claps and shouts of the crowd. It was quickly followed by 'We Three (My Echo, My Shadow and Me)'. Betty looked in her element; Judith needn't have worried about expecting too much from her. She might have only come out of the hospital the day before, with the doctor saying she ought to rest and recuperate, but she was smashing it, although this probably was not what the doctor had had in mind. Thankfully, in her order of songs, she'd suggested the instrumental 'In the Mood', which would give Betty a break. The favourite Glenn Miller tune was an instant hit and Betty moved into the wings.

It warmed Judith's heart to see the golden light back in Betty's eyes, and as Judith watched her friend, she saw Major Wendermeyer leap up onto the side of the stage, every inch the movie hero, and cross to her side. With one fluid move he swept Betty into his arms, and even Judith melted ever so slightly inside.

She smiled as Carl swooped down to give Betty a very passionate kiss. At first she saw Betty demur a little, putting a hand up to her face and trying to wriggle out of his arms. The Major was having none of it and Judith's smile turned up a few notches more when she saw the Major shaking his head and taking Betty in his arms and kissing her rather thoroughly. Judith grinned. It looked like that argument was over, not that she'd ever had any doubts. Feeling as if she were party to an epic romantic film scene, still playing the piano, Judith's gaze followed them as the Major led Betty down the stage steps to the edge of the dance floor. He stood there holding her hand, talking earnestly to her while she nodded shyly and looked longingly at the dancers on the floor.

Betty needed to believe in herself. Just like she needed to. Turning towards Walther, she found he was watching her. She smiled back, hoping that he could see how happy she was. He began to walk forward, still playing his saxophone, and came to stand by the piano as if he were serenading her. Lifting her head, she played back to him and as their notes blended together, there might have been no one else in the room but the two of them playing music together. When the final notes died away, she and Walther held each other's gaze. A moment of epiphany unfurled in her heart. They didn't need the words, they'd said everything with their music.

It had been agreed that after this number the band would take a break and as Judith was about to rise from the piano stool, she caught sight of Betty's wistful face. She sat down heavily and began to play a new song, her fingers stroking the keys with sure confidence born of years of practice. The music flowed from her and most of the room turned to face the stage. As she played Strauss's 'Blue Danube Waltz', Evelyn waved to her over the crowd and put both her thumbs up. The Major (a smart boy, decided Judith) immediately took Betty into his arms and with the most perfect footwork, began to dance gently with her round the room, holding her with tender care as if she were a delicate princess. At first they were the only couple on the floor but then Evelyn dragged Freddie up too and before long the dance floor was filled with waltzing couples. Perhaps the only time the staid ballroom dance had been performed at a forces dance like this, but everyone appeared to be having a good time.

Betty's face lit up and shone with luminous happiness as she gazed up at her prince. Judith remembered the conversation in the music room and Betty's words, *Maybe love gives you what you need.* That girl was so much smarter than she gave herself credit for.

When the last notes of the waltz drifted into the air, everyone on the dance floor turned to the stage and began to clap. Judith blushed and for a moment was glued to her seat until Walther came over, gallantly took her hand and led her to the front of the stage, presenting her with a flourish to take a bow, standing to one side and clapping along with the enthusiastic applause. Betty raised her hands and blew kisses, as did Evelyn. Judith was wondering when she could make a grateful exit when there was a loud crash at the back of the hall and the door flew open.

'They're here. The rest of the band is here,' called the American sergeant who'd welcomed them on their arrival. Everyone burst out laughing and Walther took Judith's hand and led her off the stage. She reached up, put her arms around his neck and kissed him.

'I ought to ask what that was for,' teased Walther.

'Because you're a wonderful, wise man and I should have listened to you earlier. You were right – the dead won't thank the living for not living. I'm sorry I...'

'You don't need to apologise. We're living through difficult and dangerous times. The rules haven't always been written for how we should respond to things, but when we make a mistake, admitting it is better than not.'

'I made a mistake.' Judith lifted her chin and looked into his eyes. 'I should have told you I loved you.'

Walther smiled. 'I think I already knew that. I was waiting for you to realise it. What are your thoughts on a winter wedding?'

Her heart bounced in her chest and she stared at him, too flustered and surprised to speak.

He simply raised an eyebrow and looked over her shoulder with an enigmatic smile. 'I think your friends would like to talk to you. You can give me your answer when you dance with me.' With that he sauntered away, leaving her heart in her mouth, fluttering like a light-dazed moth.

'You were brilliant, Judith,' said Evelyn.

'Fantastic,' agreed Betty.

Judith still stared after Walther.

'What's the matter?' asked Evelyn, glancing back to catch Walther giving Judith an airy wave.

'He … he asked me to marry him, I think.'

'Woohoo!' cried Betty, immediately launching herself at Judith.

'That's wonderful,' said Evelyn.

'I still don't know how it happened.' Judith rubbed at her lips, still feeling dazed.

'Because you let it,' observed Evelyn with her usual quiet authority. 'Today we all realised what's really important in life. We have to do the living for those that can't, even if it's tough going. I have to get on with my life while I wait for Peter, but that doesn't mean I can't enjoy myself and make the most of the opportunities that come my way.'

'I have to believe in myself,' said Betty, 'and that the Major loves me for who I am and not what I look, or rather looked, like.'

'You're right, and I have to believe that there is a future, after all that has happened.'

'So I'm assuming we'll be your bridesmaids,' said Betty, linking her arm through Judith's. 'After all, we are your best friends.'

'Too right,' agreed Evelyn.

Judith beamed at both of them. 'I wouldn't have it any other way.'

Epilogue

Distribution Camp No. 1
Latimer House
Latimer
Buckinghamshire

January 15th 1944

Dear Peter,

*You have no idea what a relief it was to receive your letter.
Please let me be the one to apologise for how badly I handled
our last meeting. You had no need to apologise to me. It
should have been within me to display more sensitivity and I
truly regret that we parted in anger and moreover that I
didn't have the chance to see you again to apologise properly
for the terrible lack of judgement. I hope you can forgive me.*

*Receiving your letter has been the highlight of my week. There
was no way of finding out where you had gone and I have*

regretted a thousand times over, that we were parted before we could even say goodbye. Until that morning I didn't even know that you were to be transferred.

I'm hoping and praying the conditions at Boughton Park are not too bad. Are you being treated well? I won't hesitate to help if you need it, although it's good to hear that the food rations are sufficient even if they're not as generous as here. We're very lucky with our gardener helpers, as you probably know.

I can't say too much about life here, for obvious reasons, but I can tell you a little about the friends that I've made. One of my roommates, Judith, got married last week. A bittersweet occasion for me as you might imagine, but one day, my darling. One day, I would still like to be your wife. If you will still have me.

It was a beautiful winter's day and the marriage took place near here. They're both Jewish and have found a community in a nearby town. It was a wonderful occasion and my other roommate, Betty, and I were her attendants. Neither the groom nor the bride had any family to stand for them, although a lovely local family, the Kircheners, stood for Walther. I've not been to a Jewish ceremony before but the rabbi was so warm and welcoming, it didn't matter. It made me realise that we have more in common than our differences and I fervently hope in the future that people will remember that.

After the wedding, our commanding officer allowed a small gathering in the music room for the wedding party. It became quite rowdy as the happy couple are both musical. She played the piano and Betty, who has the most beautiful voice, sang. The party carried on until the wee small hours. It was a splendid occasion and Betty's mother, along with the cook here, who is the Vicar's sister, managed to rustle up a wedding cake, which as you can imagine was quite a treat. (Sorry, I know your conditions won't include cake but it was such a joyous occasion, I had to share.) Walther and Judith have gone away for a few days to the Lake District. They're both keen on the outdoors, so I'm sure they'll have a wonderful time.

I wonder if one day we might go there or perhaps back to Switzerland or even start afresh somewhere new. How will the world find itself when this war is finally over? Will enemies ever become friends again? Who knows? So many questions.

But one thing I have learned is that life is for living and we must make the best of it. I learned that from Betty. She had a terrible accident in the summer which has left her with a disfiguring scar across her face. She bears it well, saying that there are others far worse. If anything it has made her even more positive and determined to make the most of her life. She's quite an inspiration. She hasn't had the benefit of an education but she's very bright and has been promoted again, not that I can tell you what she does.

It's made me realise how privileged I am and how wrong it is that some of us have so much and others so little. But I'm excited for her as she's engaged to an American Air Force officer and they plan to return to the USA after the war, which is amazing given that she grew up in this village. I think life in America is much more egalitarian and will suit her. Luckily her widowed mother has taken up with her neighbour in an unexpected romance which Betty is thrilled about. Her previous boyfriend was an unpleasant sort who caused all sorts of problems but Betty can rest easy now that her mother and sister have their own protector. Although apparently her fiancé, Carl, is rather handy with his fists.

This week I had some excellent news. David finally wrote to us. We'd not heard from him for over six months. He escaped from his camp and had been on the run but unfortunately has been recaptured and is now in a place called Colditz. But it's such a relief to hear that he's still alive because we hadn't heard from him for such a long time. I take comfort in knowing he is safe for the time being.

I continue to play a lot of tennis with the other officers here but it is rather quiet with just Betty and I up in our attic bedroom. Did I ever tell you we were billeted in the servants' quarters, no less? We miss Judith in our little rooftop eyrie. The three of us have become like the Three Musketeers. It's been a real comfort having the friendship of other women. Judith gave me a postcard with a wonderful quote. Do you know it? From Cicero.

'Friendship improves happiness and abates grief by the doubling of our joy and the dividing of our grief.'

Being able to talk to them has made things easier to bear. I do hope that you have some good comrades among the other men to provide you with the same sort of support and friendship.

On that positive note, I will finish, dear Peter, but before I go I must say again that despite you offering to release me, my feelings have not changed in these past four and a half years. If you will have me, I will wait for you and wear your ring, no matter how long this horrid war lasts.

Please write again soon, with all my love,
Evelyn x

Acknowledgments

Latimer House in Buckinghamshire was indeed a top secret location during WW2 and the activities I describe are based on true events, however, all the events and characters I describe are fictitious. The story was a complete joy to write and the result of one of those wonderful, serendipitous occasions that writers dream of – I woke up with the whole story in my head one morning.

I'd attended a book launch with my dad the previous evening about the secret military intelligence activities that took place in Latimer Hall, Buckinghamshire, which I used to drive past every day on my way to work. The talk presented by Dr Helen Fry, who is the expert in this field, fascinated me, revealing not only a world of secret intelligence and secret listeners but just as interesting to me, a world in which women thrived. A world where they were promoted on merit and did the sort of interesting jobs that prior to the war they'd been barred from.

The following morning, the characters of Evelyn, Judith

and Betty marched into my head, fully formed with their own distinct voices and stories. I couldn't not write their story, they wouldn't let me! Thanks therefore go to my super agent, Broo Doherty, and fabulous editor, the wonderful Charlotte Ledger, who both trusted me enough and gave me the chance to write a completely different genre to my usual one. Thanks are also due to my invaluable research assistant, Dad, aka Guy Caplin, who supplied help and support with the sort of contemporary day-to-day details that you would never find in a book, from Germans living in England sometimes having to pretend to be Polish, about record players, radio batteries, broadcasting and the mindset of people at the time.

Obviously writing a historical novel requires plenty of research but because it was written during a period of lockdown, a lot of my works had to be done as desk research. I'm therefore particularly grateful to author Derek Nudd and his book *Castaways of the Kriegsmarine*, which gave valuable insight into life at Latimer House and the type of information gleaned from prisoners, Dr Helen Fry's *The Walls Have Ears*, which revealed what went on at Latimer House and also to Deborah and Vivienne Samson who wrote *The Rabbi in the Green Jacket*. This gorgeous book gave me a really detailed view of the lives of Jews living in and around the Latimer area in Buckinghamshire during World War 2 and inspired the Kitchener family.

As always huge thanks to my readers, those who have taken a chance on a new author and readers of my contemporary books who have followed me here. I hope I've done justice to this period of history and that you'll forgive any mistakes I've made.

Also huge thanks to my fellow author, the lovely Pernille

Hughes, who provided me with lots of local historical knowledge including the very useful fact that General Von Ribbentrop was a regular at the Green Dragon pub just outside Latimer. Hopefully one day we'll get that drink there. I owe her.

YOUR NUMBER ONE STOP

ONE MORE CHAPTER

FOR PAGETURNING BOOKS

One More Chapter is an
award-winning global
division of HarperCollins.

Sign up to our newsletter to get our
latest eBook deals and stay up to date
with our weekly Book Club!
<u>Subscribe here.</u>

Meet the team at
<u>www.onemorechapter.com</u>

Follow us!
@OneMoreChapter_
@OneMoreChapter
@onemorechapterhc

Do you write unputdownable fiction?
We love to hear from new voices.
Find out how to submit your novel at
<u>www.onemorechapter.com/submissions</u>